UNWELCOME PROPHECY...

The old seeress rolled her eyes but then met Kazakov's gaze. "You ask a lot, Detektiv. Perhaps that is why your wife left you."

The unexpected comment set Kazakov back in his chair and the old woman chuckled. "Now you are flustered that I could know something like that about you. You forget: I am gifted with the sight. Remember?"

Gritting his teeth, he slid the paper back to her. "Then please use your precious sight to provide me with dates. Any you can recall would be helpful."

Instead her twisted fingers clasped his hand and an electric charge shocked through him.

He jerked back, glaring, but Madam Sobol's gaze was far away.

Get up and leave the old woman to his partner, or stay? He gritted his teeth. He was not letting some old charlatan scare him away even if he'd be very happy to leave her, this room, this house behind. It couldn't happen soon enough.

Madam Sobol nodded as if listening to a silent voice. Kazakov glanced up at Chelomeyev, whose eyes had widened.

"You are troubled by this country. There are dark clouds ahead that swirl around a dark figure, for the future is set. All is preordained. A man will die at your hand. Do not fight it, for you cannot stop what is to come."

IVAN'S WOLF

DETECTIV KAZAKOV MYSTERIES BOOK 4

K.L. ABRAHAMSON

COPYRIGHT

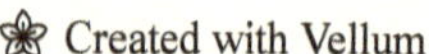 Created with Vellum

IVAN'S WOLF

DETEKTIV KAZAKOV MYSTERIES BOOK 4

K.L. Abrahamson

1

———

In the first tremulous April brilliance of sun and warmth green stained the cottonwoods along the Syr Darya River and the patches of dead grass showing through the snow on the hills. Of course, it was most likely a false promise, because the cold white claws of the mountains still encircled the valley on three sides like a fist threatening to close.

Closer in, the backwater, capital city, New Moscow, suffered through the slush and grey streets that were the omnipresent experience of spring in the small country of Fergana. People, and the crag that edged the city and was known to the mostly Russian population as Yekaterina Mountain, all seemed to hunker down awaiting the next spring storm. The storms always came. The trees' promising green was only a portent viewed with suspicion, not a hopeful foretelling of milder weather to come.

In the center of the city, next to the business district with its ten-story-tall buildings, sat Yekaterina Square, which celebrated the last tsarina of long-lost Holy Mother Russia. Once, it had sported a tall statue of Yekaterina the Great, but someone had toppled it—and quite possibly the Ferganese psyche. At least it felt like that to Detektiv Alexander Kazakov, who worked out of the grey stone New Moscow *politseyshiyuchastok*—the police station that sat on the edge of the square. The explosion that had toppled the statue had blown out many of the police station windows and injured those inside. Of course, those windows were primarily in offices occupied by *politseyshiy* bigwigs, so perhaps the explosion had been targeted. So far no one had been charged for the crime, though a large part of the city's tribal population—those who called New Moscow's five-peaked Yekaterina Mountain by the far more venerable name of Sulieman's Mountain—still languished in detention.

Many of the city residents, including police, were certain that the Kyrgyz, Uzbek, and Tajik tribals were to blame for the recent attacks on the city. Detektiv Kazakov was one of the few who felt otherwise.

"It reminds me a lot of the tale of Ivan Tsarevich, the grey wolf, and the firebird," said Detektiv Chelomeyev as he looked up from the documents Kazakov had set before him. The squad room was empty except for the two of them, which was why Kazakov had chosen to produce the documents. The cinder block–walled room was small, with barely room for the nine desks, a data machine console in the corner, and an alcove for making tea and storing lunches. The other desks were cluttered with papers, typewriters, and half-empty, scum-topped cups of tea, their owners presumably out on enquiries. The explosions still preoccupied the squad because their failure to capture and convict a subject was looking bad to the public, and Detektiv Chief Inspektor Rostoff was feeling the heat of public opinion. The walls of the room were mostly covered with memos except on one side, where clear glass panels separated the detective squad room from the elevator and the hallway that led to officer country.

Chelomeyev was young and was the youngest detective on the New Moscow police force. He also bore the haunted look of his recent hospitalization—too hollow-eyed, pale, and thin after three months of unconsciousness after being beaten and left for dead and then being injected with a drug to induce memory loss.

"Tell me the story." Kazakov hooked his leg over a corner of Chelomeyev's desk. The young detective might not be Kazakov's partner, for he preferred working alone, but the blond youngster was a good detective. He had also completed his degree in Russian folk tales—an interest Kazakov shared. More importantly, Kazakov could trust this youngster, along with his partner on his previous case, Detektiv Elena Egorova, to keep their mouths shut and their eyes open. He couldn't say the same of most of the detectives he worked with.

Chelomeyev eyed the papers again. There were eight pages, each in their own separate, plastic, evidence-document holder. They had been found in an installation high in the mountains southeast of New Moscow. Each of the documents was evidence of surgical alterations of people to look like someone they were not. They documented limb lengthening, removal of epicanthic eye folds, and other cosmetic procedures.

"Well, the folk tale tells about the youngest son of a tsar, who goes on an adventure after his two oldest brothers failed to find the firebird who was stealing the golden apples from the tsar's garden. The youngest son's stallion is killed by a great grey wolf, and in repayment, the wolf becomes the son's steed and helps him to perform numerous deeds so that he returns to his father's kingdom with a beautiful princess, the firebird, and a great horse with a golden mane, all of which he stole from other kingdoms with the wolf's aid. But before he arrives at his father's palace, he is come upon by his two brothers, who kill him and claim the princess, the firebird, and the horse as their own. The oldest son is to marry the princess, but the grey wolf appears once more and revives Ivan Tsarevich so that he can return home and claim his bride. His brothers are exiled and Ivan and the princess live happy and long lives together. So the wolf is the agent who allows the tsarevich to return home." He grinned wanly up at Kazakov. "Sorry. I know too many fairy tales. My father reminds me of it every time I see him."

Kazakov shook his head, but the story jarred an old memory loose. His mother's face swam before him, telling him a bedtime story about a young tsarevich. It was a long time ago, but perhaps she'd once told him such a tale.

He shook his head again. "There's wisdom in the old tales, that's for sure, even if the magic is unreal. Interesting that the evil wolf helps the hero, but if my suspicions are true, I don't think that the real Boris Bure is about to return to the land of the living." He sighed and gathered up the documents and slid them into an envelope that went into the inside breast pocket of his jacket. The envelope was bulky and barely fit.

"It would be a nice bit of police work if the real Bure could testify for us, but I'm afraid we're going to have to do this the hard way." He patted his pocket. There was nowhere else he trusted the documents to be safe—not in a country that looked to elect a president who was probably a Chinese spy who had replaced the real Boris Bure and killed the rest of his family when Bure was a young man.

Detektiv Chief Inspector Rostoff strode the hallway beyond the squad room and Kazakov tensed. *Please let him be heading to the elevator.* But the door to the squad room thunked open and Rostoff stepped into the small room. He had always been a large man, but over the years the muscles of youth had softened to more lard and stubbornness. His enduring quality was his ability to supply favors to higher-ups that had led to early promotions to his current exalted position, though he had never been particularly gifted at police work. Rostoff was all about case closure rates, not about the conviction of the real suspect for the crime.

"I knew you'd be here, Kazakov." The big man stepped into the room, his ruddy cheeks the sign that he might often be drinking something other than tea in the china cups he sipped in his office. His thick black hair was worn brushed back from his face as if to advertise a clear conscience.

Still perched on Chelomeyev's desk, Kazakov cocked a brow at him. "And yet you tell me I spend too much time out of the office."

Rostoff stepped farther into the squad room—something he rarely did. "I heard that you might be mentoring Chelomeyev. I could split the two youngsters up if you'd prefer a partner?"

Kazakov glanced at Chelomeyev and shook his head. "I work alone."

"I know. I know." Rostoff held up his hands in mock defeat. "With that in mind, then, I am assigning you a case. There is a dead girl, but I understand that there are sensitive parties..."

Kazakov stood. Dead girls were all too familiar to him these past six months. His first meeting with Boris Bure had been over the death of Bure's stepdaughter—a stepdaughter that Bure had apparently gotten pregnant, according to DNA tests. His heart thumped a little harder in his chest.

"What girl?" he asked.

Rostoff shrugged and Kazakov winced inside. In his experience, a shrug was often a sign of an untidy mind that did not have its thoughts in order. With Rostoff, experience had shown that was definitely the case.

"Some girl—a performer of some kind." Rostoff pulled a folded piece of paper from his pants pocket and coins jingled faintly. "Here's the address. Uniforms are there now and the M.E."

Kazakov nodded and accepted the address, wondering why Rostoff was assigning him a sensitive case, when Kazakov would never overlook evidence in favor of a prominent suspect. Over the years Rostoff had dealt with numerous complaints regarding Kazakov's honesty and clearance rate. It had been a point of ongoing friction between them until the last few months when evidence from Kazakov's cases had led to Rostoff being at least willing to consider Kazakov's wild theories about the terrorist attacks occurring in Fergana. But then Rostoff could simply be trying to sidetrack Kazakov's attention away from the more contentious investigation.

When he met Rostoff's murky brown gaze, surprisingly the Detektiv Chief Inspektor nodded minutely. So, Rostoff thought this new case might be of interest to Kazakov's quiet enquiries.

Kazakov nodded. "I'll get out there." He glanced down at Chelomeyev. "You want to come along?" Chelomeyev had returned to work on light duties since his horrible head injuries, but riding a desk wasn't the young detective's idea of police work any more than it was Kazakov's.

Chelomeyev was up and slipping into his coat before Kazakov could retrieve his black winter coat from where he'd tossed it over his desk chair.

"Good. Good." Rostoff said as he watched them out the door.

Kazakov wondered just what the detektiv chief inspector was sending them into.

———

The address on Rostoff's paper turned out to be a fine old house on Volga Lane, a small, dead-end street that gave onto the curved road that edged Yekaterina Park. The park was a combination of muddy gray snow, barren trees, and patches of matted brown grass that revealed where the sun shone the warmest. On the opposite side of the street sat stately townhomes modeled after English noble's homes, complete with cornices, columns, and filigree. Their white paint hid a darker core as some housed brothels and others Ottoman businessmen who sought to undermine the Ferganese government. But turning the corner onto Volga Lane was like leaving Fergana's trying elections and social problems behind. The houses were tidy replicas of Russian dachas as they truly had been a few generations ago. Small, cozy, and built stoutly to withstand Russian cold —unlike the new dacha-style that was more window and less wall.

The street was plowed, the sidewalk shoveled. Old gaslight-style, iron streetlights alternated on either side of the street. The houses stood back in their yards, but covered porches suggested that these people still might take the evening air outside and speak to their neighbors. Dark winter coats pulled around shoulders, but without the usual winter fur hats, those neighbors now milled around the front of Kazakov and Chelomeyev's destination. He found a place at the curb, parked the unmarked police sedan, and climbed out. Chelomeyev unfolded his height to stand on the other side.

The air was almost balmy after the long dark days of winter. Kazakov inhaled. It was almost possible to smell the warming soil, the stirring blood. And there was an election only one week ahead to further stir that blood.

Enough for bloodshed.

Kazakov shook himself from the morbid thought, patted the pack of papers in his pocket, and worked his shoulders to settle his heavy coat. More days like this and he'd pack this coat away and go in his suit jacket. Of course, that was when the spring storms would pass through, so he'd keep wearing his coat to keep more snow at bay. Magical thinking, but in a country like Fergana that still lived in a fairy-tale fog of Russia's long-past greatness, a little magical thinking was nothing.

He studied the house with the M.E.'s van out front. Small. Tidy. Painted in the last few years, judging by the richness of the dark brown paint. A wicker rocking chair sat on the front porch, a brightly colored blanket tossed on its back as if someone actually had sat there during the winter months. Along the front edge of the porch, where some people might hang a small string of lights, the owner of this house had strung bits of glass small enough to swing on the wind and glitter in the sunlight. Odd.

The house's small windows had what looked like white lace curtains pulled back so that the place exuded an open, friendly air. As if the place would welcome you in.

Except that you might die there.

With a sigh, he led the way through the crowd to the house's hip-high iron gate. A uniformed officer stood there at attention. He was an older officer with little chance of promotion—the kind of officer often referred to as lifers—with fading brown hair gone gray at the temples and watery blue eyes that were also faded. He met Kazakov's gaze and nodded. They'd seen each other a time or two under similar circumstances.

"You first on the scene?" Kazakov asked.

The officer—Kazakov dug through his memory; Vitsin was his name —nodded. "My partner and I were on patrol. We got waved down by the owner of the house. She'd been away, and when she got back, she found her assistant dead."

Kazakov nodded his thanks and he and Chelomeyev headed across the yard. Unlike many homes in New Moscow whose owners simply compacted the snow and ice on the path to the door, here the owner had made sure that a wide path was clear up to the porch. The three front stairs were even salted, resulting in coarse grains of salt being tracked across the wood porch floor. At the front door he stomped his feet to clean his boots and pushed inside. Chelomeyev followed.

Inside, a broad hallway split just in front of them to lead toward the kitchen in the rear of the house or up a set of stairs. The house was busy with forensic staff collecting evidence in each of the two rooms that opened to either side of the front door. One was a dining room. The other was—something else.

Bright tapestries covered the walls with unsettling images of broadly spreading trees; of figures that were half men, half women; of snakes devouring their tails. Old-fashioned lamps sat on tables with sheer red cloths dangling tassels over their lampshades. Overhead, the ceiling was a field of stars, while underfoot, the hardwood floor was painted in what Kazakov could only assume were occult symbols. A round table sat surrounded by eight high-backed chairs, with one chair back spreading wide, gilt wings as if it was a throne. A forensic technician was taking fingerprints around the room, leaving behind a trail of gray-white powder. The room was atavistic, evoking thoughts of nighttime campfires and ancient seers spinning tales into the starlight.

"I know what this is," Chelomeyev breathed. "I've heard them described."

"Spiritualist," Kazakov said.

"I thought they'd died out years ago," Chelomeyev said.

"Apparently someone didn't get the message." Kazakov turned back to the hallway.

Through an open door at the end of the hall, Kazakov caught a glimpse of the M.E.'s blue paper coveralls. With a last grimace at the spiritualist room and the knowledge that Rostoff was probably laughing at assigning the murder to Kazakov—he headed down the hallway.

It was the sweet, musky scent that confirmed the kitchen was the death scene. He pushed inside into a white modern kitchen far removed from the draperied chicanery of the spiritualist's parlor. White cupboards and counters filled the walls on three sides, the fourth holding a door and a bank of windows over a sink. A white enamel refrigerator and stove and a new stand mixer seemed to confirm that this was the workplace of someone who liked order and everything in its place.

The body on the floor undid that impression. So did the pale, tearful, gray-haired woman seated with a police constable at a small table in an atrium space at the far end of the room. A single glass of water stood on the table between them that the tearful woman turned around and around in her fingers. The table was surrounded by windows that gave onto a small, snowy back yard, the sunlight bathing the woman only bleaching her further. But then, so did the long, multi-colored scarves looped around her neck and the long flowing dress and purple shawl that overwhelmed her thin body.

The body was not so encumbered. Young, naked, possibly midtwenties or even younger by her smooth skin. Blonde, just like Yekaterina Weber had been. Kazakov rubbed his side. It still pained him where he'd been shot during the Weber-Manas investigation. This girl's eyes were closed, her face calm; and somehow that made her naked body more exposed. She was slim, though slightly pear-figured, with long, smooth legs and arms and smallish breasts. There were no knife wounds, no pools of blood, simply the deep purple bruising to the back of the body caused by the blood pooling, and the graying flesh tone that came with the early stages of decomposition. A flash and whir and the M.E.'s photographer had captured another image of the girl.

The M.E. looked up from beside the body. He was a cadaverous Russian fellow with thinning blond hair who rarely smiled and was still more rarely completely accurate in his findings. Not for the first time Kazakov felt the pangs of loss and anger over the disappearance of Khalil Khan, the country's only Kyrgyz doctor, who was now wanted for murder and attempted murder.

"Gordiev," Kazakov said and nodded as the M.E. stood up from examining the body. "What have we got?"

Gordiev shrugged. "Female victim, say around twenty years old. No sign of major trauma to the torso or limbs. Skull intact. I'd say by the discoloration of the skin that she's been dead a few days."

"Strangled?" Chelomeyev asked from his spot at Kazakov's shoulder.

"No sign of bruising, so I'd say no," Kazakov said.

"It appears her neck is broken." Gordiev stripped off the gloves he'd been wearing. "Very neatly done."

"Where're her clothes?" Kazakov asked, scanning the room.

"Not here, as far as I know." Another shrug from Gordiev that set Kazakov's teeth grinding. "Maybe she undressed for our killer elsewhere and came in here where he killed her. Or maybe he killed her elsewhere and brought her in here where she was certainly going to be found."

"Did anyone search the room?" Kazakov asked.

"Not yet. They'll get to it after we remove the body."

"Is there anything to indicate where she was killed or why?" Kazakov asked fighting his frustration. Clearly, he'd become too dependent upon Khan's keen intelligence and dedication to excellence.

Gordiev gave another shrug. "You figure that out and you'll have your killer. That's your job, not mine." The M.E. nodded at his team. "You got your shots?"

His photographer nodded.

"Then we'll be moving the body to the morgue." He nodded to a pair of male coroner's attendants who'd been waiting. They preceded Gordiev down the hallway, presumably to retrieve their gurney.

"Anyone know who she is?" Kazakov asked the room.

"Anna. Anna Konstantinova," the tearful woman choked out. She bowed her head and began to sob in earnest.

"Perhaps you can sit with our witness while I examine the body," Kazakov said to Chelomeyev.

The young detective eased past the body and went to the table to slide in beside the constable. He nodded to the sobbing woman and introduced himself. The woman straightened and nodded and they began to talk.

Good. Chelomeyev even showed the compassion of not immediately bringing out his notebook.

Kazakov turned back to the body, not that there was much to see.

"Who did this to you, little one?" he murmured and walked around her, trying to get a feel for the scene.

The calm, almost serenity on the girl's face suggested that she hadn't been coerced into the room. No, she'd come here willingly and met her death as a result. But what would bring her into the kitchen disrobed? The need for a drink after sex? Or perhaps she'd assumed she was alone and come down naked to the kitchen for a drink. Neither option sat completely right with him, which suggested that there was something here.

There was nothing on the pristine white counters other than the mixing machine. Nothing sullied the sink other than a few drops that suggested someone had run the water today. Probably to get the older woman her glass of water.

The attendants returned with the gurney and the old woman looked away. They quickly lifted the body and strapped and covered it on the stretcher and then left down the hallway. A gurney wheel squealed as they left and closed the house's front door behind them. The sound of voices and a vehicle engine came from the street.

Kazakov pulled open the fridge door and checked inside. Not much there. A bag of spinach slowly transforming to mush. A jug of milk on the door and a half-drunk bottle of excellent vodka lying on the top shelf. Interesting. He couldn't afford that brand of vodka.

He closed the fridge door and went to the kitchen cupboards until he found the one that held glasses. All the space in the cupboard was full, but he held the cupboard door open.

"Excuse me, madam. Do you know if this is all the glassware or if anything is missing?"

The woman turned haunted brown eyes to him and rose almost bonelessly from the table. She came to inspect the cupboard contents and sighed. "That is all that I remember."

"Thank you, madam." He eased her back to her seat again and returned to the cupboard. He leaned in to study the contents and had a sense of déjà vu of his time with Annuschka, his ex-wife. She had been vehement that all glasses must only be put away after receiving a final wipe from a lint-free cloth. Most of these glasses had the same pristine gleam, but two of the glasses on one side had slight streaks on their sides. He made a note to collect them and turned back to the room.

Under the sink was a garbage bin. Inside were moldy tealeaf remains and a half-eaten sandwich, nothing more. He tugged the garbage bin out. Behind it, something was stuffed into the corner. He pulled it out and stood to examine it. A robe hung from his fingers, silken to the touch, but not fine enough for silk. A cheaper copy. He glanced at the woman.

"Do you know this garment?"

She shook her head, her lips pressed into a line. "No one in this house would wear something like that. I would not allow it."

Carefully, he folded the robe and placed it in an evidence bag for collection. Then he went to the table and the constable stood up and left the room. Kazakov slid into the vacated seat.

"I am Detektiv Alexander Kazakov," he said. "You have met my comrade, Detektiv Chelomeyev. May I have your name, please?"

"Magda—Magdalena Sobol—Madam Sobol," she said and laced her ring-laden fingers on the table. Not the usual gawdy rings Kazakov would expect, either. The gold of these rings gleamed ruddy, and the flash of green, blue, and red suggested real emerald, sapphire, and ruby. The largest ring was a clear-cut square stone that, if a diamond, would be fabulously expensive. It begged the question of how such a woman, livng in such a house, could afford such riches.

Kazakov nodded at Chelomeyev to take notes and then met Madam Sobol's watery gaze. "How many people live in this house, madam?"

Her watery gaze met his. "Two. There are two: myself and Anna."

Kazakov nodded. So the robe could be a secret possession of the dead girl—or something brought by the killer. "And who is Anna?"

Her gaze flicked away. "I told you her name."

"Yes. But a name tells me very little. Who was she to you? How did she come to be here?" he urged gently.

Madam Sobol shook her head, her long grey hair shifting around her shoulders. "A silly girl from some village who I was foolish enough to hire. She came to me six months ago with huge claims that she had the gift. She wished to learn from the best, she said. More like pick my bones. I've been doing this for forty years. Did she think I would not see through her?"

"See through her, madam?" Chelomeyev asked softly, looking up from his note-taking.

"Of course, I saw through her! She was an ignorant farm girl, while I come from a long line of women with the sight. She thought that she could come work for me for a time and then go out on her own. Claim that she had learned everything Madam Sobol knows and—look, I am more pleasant to look on than Madam Sobol, too." She shook her head, the sunlight through the windows catching on the lines deepening the displeasure on her face. Deep lines beneath the corners of her mouth seemed to pull her lips into a perpetual frown.

"You did not like her much, then," Kazakov said softly, though she had cried as though she truly mourned. For show? Did she not realize the contradiction?

Those watery eyes turned in his direction and for a moment they seemed to clear and look deep into him with Baba Yaga venom.

"Like? I am a realist, Detektiv. I am getting old. I needed help. The girl's determination to eventually undermine me did not stop her from being a good worker. For that I could appreciate her. So I kept her around and dealt with her prying into my secrets—not that she found any. I am far too good for that. Besides, I knew what her fate would be. It was written in her hands."

"Her hands." Kazakov awaited clarification.

"I read her palm when she first came to me. Fleshy mount of Venus. Truncated lifeline. Clear evidence of what was to come." Her thin shoulders lifted her scarves in a shrug.

"Did you perhaps get the name of the village that she was from?" Kazakov asked.

"Of course not. Why should I care? One village or another in the west somewhere, I think. It made no difference to me. She was just a girl, as long as she worked." She waved her hand at them.

"And yet you cry for her." He nodded down at the wadded tissue in her hand.

"Death is always a hard thing. We spend our days running from our own death and yet we begin our death walk from the moment we are born. We avoid thinking about our own mortality, but the death of someone we know reminds us of it. So we cry. Not for the dead—they are already gone—but for ourselves and the days and weeks that are chipped away from us every moment that we live. It begins slowly enough, but as we age, we see more days behind us than in front and still the days fall around us like leaves that we cannot return to the trees."

Her words seemed to press him into his chair. He knew those days, had seen the piles of golden leaves—treasures lost and blown away just as Ivan Tsarevich had lost everything he worked for until the gray wolf worked his final magic and brought the young prince back to life. Madam Sobol's gaze had grown knowing as she looked at him, as if she knew exactly how her words touched him. A cagey old woman, this one. But then a woman who made her living by telling fortunes surely lived by her wits and her ability to read the people around her.

He glanced at Chelomeyev and nodded. "A reasonable assessment of the human condition. So what were Anna's duties?"

"She cleaned and cooked for me. She would make sure that my cards and equipment were where they should be."

Kazakov cocked a brow at her. "Equipment?"

"There were—trappings. Things that customers expected though they did not impact the tellings. I am not a charlatan, Detektiv. I am a consultant. I do not knock on tables or have winds blow through my readings to impress the gullible. In fact, I abhor such things. Anna and I argued over just such matters. She felt that I could gain more fame by using such devices and I told her that she could leave and find another teacher if that was what she was interested in." Madam Sobol cast a sad glance at the now-empty kitchen floor. She swallowed. "She chose not to leave." Her eyes closed as if the sight pained her.

"Do you have any idea who she might have invited into your home?" Kazakov asked.

"Invited? Surely she was attacked and killed."

Kazakov shook his head. "You have an open bottle of vodka in your fridge and two newly washed glasses in your cupboard. Then there is the garment that you claim to have never seen before. It is a young woman's garment, madam. It seems more likely that she had a visitor."

A small twitch found the corner of Madam Sobol's left eye. She looked away, out the window to the small snow-bound yard where neat garden beds were just showing their raised edges.

"She said her family were dead. She had few friends—at least that I saw. A few afternoons a week she'd run errands, but she spent most evenings here with me."

"Think, madam. Any friends come calling? Any phone calls?"

She shook her head, but her face was troubled.

"And your clients, madam. Did Anna have contact with them?"

She turned a devastated gaze on him. She shook her head. "No. It could not be. She would answer the door for me to allow me to get ready for a reading. She would take coats and usher the client into my office. Then she would leave us and go to the observation room where she could watch how I conducted my sessions. I hoped she would learn from that that tricks are not what is needed to provide a reputable service. I do not see how such meager contact could suggest that any of my clients could be a suspect."

Kazakov straightened in his chair. "Then it is a good thing that you are not investigating this case if we want to find Anna's killer, madam. At this moment everyone is suspect, even you. I would say even myself and my partner could be suspects except that we did not know you and Anna Konstantinova existed." He stood up. "I will need to see her rooms and we will need a list of all the places Anna went on her errands and a list of all clients who may have met Anna over the past six months. Please prepare them for us while we inspect Anna's rooms."

"I will do as best I can to recall Anna's errands but I will not provide a list of client names." She scrambled up to face him, a light scent of ashes of roses coming off her heated skin. "My clients are corporate leaders and business people. They are private citizens and appreciate my guarantee of utmost discretion. Providing their names so that you can come clumping up onto their doorsteps—that simply cannot be done!"

He tipped his head down to her to peer at her from the tops of his eyes. "I appreciate your concern for your clients and how it may impact your business, but it must be done. A young woman has been killed. Surely you can appreciate that we must find her killer. If we do not, we leave him or her free to kill again. I promise that we will start with contacts she made on her errands, but you must provide us with a client list. There is no way around it."

Her gaze was stubborn as old locks, but gave way before him. She nodded. "I will try to compose the errand list while you are upstairs. The clients—well, it will take a few days to go through my records to find who visited while Anna was here. Anna's room is upstairs to the right."

Leaving Madam Sobol in the kitchen with pencil and paper and her tissues, Kazakov and Chelomeyev returned to the front hall. The forensic technicians had finished in the two front rooms. Kazakov and Chelomeyev climbed up to the second floor.

From the landing above the stairs, a dimly lit, narrow hall led left and right. To the left, two facing closed doors left the hall in darkness. To the right, one of the doors was open, spilling light into the hall.

Kazakov set off toward the open door, wondering who had left the door open. Judging by the other doors, the preference in this household was for the upstairs doors to be kept closed. The dead girl downstairs? One of the attending police? Or the girl's killer, perhaps.

He reached the door and stopped, motioning Chelomeyev up beside him as he studied the room. "What do you see?"

"Bedroom," Chelomeyev began. His gaze roamed over the room. "Woman's." He frowned. "The bed isn't slept in, but the covers are disheveled as if she had been lying there—or someone had."

"Or, perhaps, both," Kazakov said. It was a bedroom like many others he'd seen in his career. Single bed pressed against the wall with pillows against the wall as if the bed was also to function as a seating area for visitors. According to Madam Sobol, in Anna Konstantinova's case it was for no one at all.

And yet someone had obviously been here. He stepped into the room. In the days since the girl's death, any telling scent had dissipated; but there was the possibility that she had had a sexual tryst. He would have to make certain that Gordiev checked for that and collected semen and DNA evidence. He pulled on a pair of latex gloves and began a search for evidence.

A tall, battered armoire filled one wall. A small desk-cum-dressing-table, also showing years of wear, filled another. The desktop was filled with an orderly array of lotions and unguents that apparently a young woman would make use of. He didn't know what they were. A mirror hazed with age held only a photo of the dead girl smiling in front of a brocade curtain. He went to the armoire first and swung open the doors. Women's clothing hung there, mostly sensible dresses of thin floral cloth. Two cardigan sweaters—one white, one black—both, he supposed, suitable to wear with any of the dresses. A single pair of low-heeled black shoes sat neatly facing the wall beneath the dress hems. Beyond the dresses, which were certainly not unexpected, was the interesting way the clothing hung in the cupboard with each item evenly spaced across the length of the rack. That showed a different, methodical and orderly side to the victim.

He glanced at Chelomeyev.

"How many young women do you know who have closets like this?" he asked.

Chelomeyev colored slightly as if he didn't care for a reminder of his exploits with females. "Not many. The girls I know are messier than I am —mostly."

Not that Chelomeyev was particularly messy from what Kazakov had seen of the younger man's apartment.

Kazakov went to the desk-dressing table and began opening drawers. A box of tissue and tubes of lipstick filled the top drawer. A side drawer released a pungent puff of lavender from a froth of silk and lace underwear. For a girl with such sensible dresses and shoes, this was unexpected. He lifted the stack of underwear and ran his hand underneath, for often women hid surprising pieces of their lives amongst their unmentionables. Nothing. He slid the drawer in and pulled the lowest drawer open. An old blue metal box filled the drawer, the kind in which people traditionally kept mementos.

He pulled the box out and tried to open it, but the box was locked.

Frowning, he set the box down on the desktop and settled onto the hard-backed, wooden desk chair. The metal was scratched and dented from years of use, but the lock looked sturdy. The top, however, looked frayed around the edges as if someone had tried to pry it open.

Succeeded?

Probably, or else it was unlikely that the box would still be here.

He pulled a pocket knife from his coat and began to pry above the lock. After a moment, the top popped up.

"Glad to see I haven't lost my touch." He grinned up at Chelomeyev.

"You are supposed to use your powers for good," the young detective said.

"This isn't good?" Kazakov motioned around the room.

"And just where did you learn your lock-breaking skills?" Chelomeyev asked.

"A long time ago, when I was in prison." His smile broadened up at Chelomeyev as he saw the young man pause as if he considered whether such an unlikelihood could possibly be true.

Chelomeyev finally shook his head. "No wonder others don't want to partner with you. They don't know when you tell the truth."

"But I always tell the truth," Kazakov deadpanned and for a moment felt an unusual affection for the young detective. It was years since he'd had a partner, except for his recent partnering with Elena Egorova. Perhaps he had missed the camaraderie more than he knew. But he still preferred to work alone and it was better that he continue that way. He eyed Chelomeyev and hoped the young man wasn't going to expect to do this again.

But then Egorova would be here soon. The first female detective in Fergana was currently moving her household from the small mountain town of Biysk to New Moscow. She had been Kazakov's partner in a murder investigation in the mountains that had blossomed into something much more. Having her in New Moscow meant that she and Chelomeyev as well as Kazakov could continue to quietly look into the larger investigation around Boris Bure.

Kazakov flipped open the metal box and found a stack of old letters tied with a ribbon and a series of children's drawings. He unfolded one of the drawings to reveal a typical childish image of a square-block house with a triangular roof and a series of large stick figures standing off to one side. The image was signed Vasili in childish crayon.

A nephew? A son?

Kazakov went through the other drawings and all were similarly signed. He set them aside and carefully untied the ribbon binding the letters. Even through his latex gloves, the paper on top had the thin weight and feel of the cheapest quality note paper. He carefully opened the folded page to reveal the writing.

Dear Anna,

I hope this letter finds you well. Vasili has been asking after you. He sends this picture to his beautiful mother. He wants to know when you might come home for a visit. He is becoming more and more insistent that he does not like it here and wants to be with you. What should I tell him?

When might you get over this foolishness and come home for a visit? How long is this to go on? A child needs his mother."

The letter was signed by someone named Lidiya. There was no envelope and no return address.

So not Anna's mother, because a mother would surely sign as such. A friend? A relative? Someone that Anna paid to care for her son?

He set the letters aside to read more fully and hopefully learn where this Lidiya resided. The tone of the letter suggested reproach as if Anna was involved in something that Lidiya did not agree with. Something to do with a lover, or was it only to do with Anna's apparent choice of profession?

He peered into the metal box. The letters and pictures had not filled the box. There could have been more inside. Something taken, perhaps?

At the bottom of the box was a business card. He flipped it over with his finger.

"Pamir Communications: Taking you to the highest level" read the logo on the card. Beneath was only a phone number.

He had never heard of Pamir Communications.

Finished, he replaced the letters and the pictures into the box and clicked the lock closed before standing up.

"Find anything?" he asked.

Chelomeyev looked up from running his hands between the mattress and the bed frame. He looked about to say something, but then stopped and pulled out a narrow piece of colored paper. He held it up.

"This?" He studied what he held and Kazakov came up to him.

It was a royal purple, three-fold flyer, like a brochure for an event. Dates were written on the back.

Chelomeyev flipped the flyer over.

On the front, Boris Bure's face peered out at them.

2

———————

In the silence of the dead girl's bedroom, Chelomeyev's and Kazakov's gazes met. Sunlight gleamed through the bedroom window but inside it felt like gloom rose from the flyer in Chelomeyev's latex-clad fingers. It left Kazakov feeling breathless and exhausted.

"Why would this young woman have this and why hide it under her mattress?" he voiced his thoughts.

"Perhaps Madam Sobol does not approve of political activism?" Chelomeyev suggested. "Or perhaps it's simply she had nowhere else to put it or put it there out of habit?"

Kazakov shook his head. A naked young blonde girl found dead was too reminiscent of Yekaterina Bure. His skin crawled and a too-hot anger filled his throat.

"Young girls—for that matter, all youngsters—look for a place that they can hide something from their parents. Often it is exactly where you found that flyer. Some place close enough that they can retrieve their treasure to admire when they are alone in bed. Don't tell me you didn't do something similar as a boy?" He accepted the flyer from Chelomeyev and pulled the three folds open.

It was a political tract outlining Bure's platform of reforms and making scathing comparisons to Fergana's incumbent president, Leonid Nikolaev. It contained images of Bure shaking hands and holding babies, of him ministering to the injured at the scene of the explosion that destroyed the famous statue of Tsarina Yekaterina in the city square.

Kazakov blinked. He had been at the scene right after the explosion and Bure had been nowhere to be seen. He looked more closely at the image. He recalled the bedlam of that morning, had seen the injured being ministered to and being aided to ambulances. If he recalled rightly, there was a woman aided from the street exactly where Bure was allegedly picking up an injured and bloodied child. But the explosion had taken place in the early morning when there were mainly office workers about.

A doctored photo? But why do so when it was possible to check what had happened? Detektivs Pogolin and Razin had been in charge of recording what occurred in the crime scene.

He checked himself, for Bure always made him feel like a hound seeking scent; and this was a murder he was dealing with, not his own personal crusade against Bure.

"We need to get crime scene up here to photograph the room. Once they get the shot of the brochure, bag it and we'll take it back to the station."

Chelomeyev did as suggested and Kazakov took custody of the battered metal box and the photo of the dead girl. Together, they left Anna Konstantinova's room and returned downstairs. Madam Sobol was no longer at the kitchen table. Instead, she had found a seat in the throne-like chair in her fortune-telling room. She had also traded her water glass for something more potent in a livid red teacup, for the half-consumed vodka bottle from the kitchen was on the table.

"I'm sorry. I should not have left the bottle for you to use," Kazakov said. "It is evidence in this case." He confiscated it and reminded himself to collect the two glasses he had spotted from the kitchen cupboard. Then he settled himself across the gaudily covered table from Madam Sobol with Chelomeyev standing unobtrusively to one side with his notebook ready. "Tell me more about Anna. About her habits. For example, was she an orderly person or one prone to disorganization?"

Madam Sobol sipped her vodka and color seeped into her lined skin. Golden tassels hung from burgundy curtains and from the high corners of her chair, like lanterns, to illuminate her face. "What do you think?" She shook her head and the tassels shivered beside her head as if something invisible moved around her. "She was a young girl always fluttering about. I had no use for that sort of behavior, so she soon changed her ways. Still, every now and again I would catch her leaving messes about my kitchen or my parlor."

Kazakov nodded. And if the girl was naturally disorganized, then it was highly unlikely that her personal space would be as immaculately tidy as the room upstairs unless Madam Sobol had had a more significant impact.

"Tell me, was Anna interested in politics? In the upcoming election? Perhaps she volunteered some of her time to assist a party?"

Madam Sobol actually threw back her head and laughed. "She was a child: charming, but certainly with no head for politics. If you asked her, I'm sure she wouldn't know one party from the other."

"And have you been able to list Anna's recent excursions?"

Nodding, Madam Sobol slid a folded piece of paper from the pocket of her sweater and across the table to him. He accepted it and flipped it open. Ten different locations were listed.

He lifted his gaze to her. "Thank you. I know it is difficult, but can you perhaps recall the dates she attended these locations?"

She rolled her eyes but then met his gaze. "You ask a lot, Detektiv. Perhaps that is why your wife left you."

The comment set him back in his chair and the old woman chuckled. "Now you are flustered that I could know something like that about you. You forget: I am gifted with the sight. Remember?"

Gritting his teeth, he slid the paper back to her. "Then please use your precious sight to provide me with dates. Any you can recall would be helpful."

Instead she clasped his hand and an electric charge shocked through him.

He jerked back, glaring, but Madam Sobol's gaze was far away.

Get up and leave the old woman to Chelomeyev, or stay? He gritted his teeth. He was not letting some old charlatan scare him away even if he'd be very happy to leave her, this room, this house behind. It couldn't happen soon enough.

Madam Sobol nodded as if listening to a silent voice. Kazakov glanced up at Chelomeyev, whose eyes had widened.

"You are troubled by this country. There are dark clouds ahead that swirl around a dark figure, for the future is set. All is preordained. A man will die at your hand. Do not fight it, for you cannot stop what is to come."

A cold shiver ran up Kazakov's back, but he shook it off as a shudder wracked through Madam Sobol and set the chair tassels shaking. She fell back, eyes closed, into her chair and heaved in a huge breath. Then her eyes flashed open and the woman he had been talking to was there. She blinked and then leaned forward for her glass of vodka, knocked back the remains, and regarded Kazakov.

"I'm sorry. I did not intend for that to happen. Sometimes the spirits visit unintended with an important message. What was said?" She picked up her now-empty teacup and glanced longingly at the vodka bottle.

Kazakov shook his head. "Nothing of consequence." With his index finger he pushed the list back to her again.

She reclaimed the paper and tugged a pair of pince-nez glasses out of her bodice to scan the locations. Quickly, she wrote down three or four dates. "These are guesses as close as I and the spirits can remember."

She grinned at him, exposing yellowed teeth, almost as if she knew that she'd affected him with her little act. Kazakov gritted his teeth.

"So tell us where you were this weekend?"

For an instant uncertainty swam in her gaze. Then it was gone. "As I told the constable, I was in my village near Asaka visiting family and providing readings to those in my hometown. They have been my clients for many years if you would like to speak with them." She serenely slid the paper with the errands and dates back to him. "I will try to recall the other dates for you."

But her smile was close to predatory, as if she thought she had him on the run.

Thanking her, he and Chelomeyev took their leave, asking her not to touch anything in Anna Konstantinova's room.

Kazakov barely remembered to collect the glasses from the kitchen.

I n their police sedan, inhaling the scent of too-warm wool on a too-warm day, Kazakov leaned back in his seat behind the wheel.

"So. What do you think?"

Chelomeyev shook his head. "It was downright spooky if you ask me. I swear I felt a draft when she suddenly fell back in her chair. It was like something invisible moved past me out of the room. What was she saying? What did it mean that you would kill a man?"

"It meant nothing. I'm a police officer. I've killed before. Circumstances could force me to kill again. But that's not what I was asking." He turned a measured look on the younger detective and Chelomeyev colored slightly.

"Something doesn't quite fit. I'm not sure what it is," Chelomeyev said.

"My sense exactly." Kazakov started the vehicle. "Let's head back to the station. Egorova should be here soon and we can get her to help with checking out these locations." He handed Chelomeyev Madam Sobol's list. "And you were standing near the front door. You could have felt a draft from there." He turned out into traffic aware that Chelomeyev tilted a brow at him.

The New Moscow streets were awash in slush and snowmelt, leaving pedestrians on the narrow sidewalks risking complete inundation in waves of filthy saltwater. The only thing that saved them were the high berms of swiftly melting snow. When the next freeze came, the streets would be almost impassable.

They crossed the river that the Russians called Potemkin on the old stone bridge at the end of Yekaterina Park and drove through some of the older brick and stone apartment buildings that gradually were being torn down and replaced with businesses. The center of New Moscow was glass and steel by Fergana standards, and touted as a world-class city by city fathers, though from the images of Constantinople, London, and Berlin Kazakov had seen, New Moscow was nothing more than a second- or third-rate backwater town. At the moment, though, all of Fergana was getting too much attention from the various world powers as they jockeyed for the best outcome of the upcoming Ferganese election.

Fergana sat like a plug in a bottle between the two superpowers of the Ottoman and Chinese empires. Yes, there were other areas where the superpowers' borders met, but Fergana was the heart of the ancient crossroads linking east and west. Ancient Sogdian traders had brought silk, tea, porcelain, and spice across the continent. The trade routes through Fergana had been the melting pot of religion and culture over the millennia. And as a result of the riches that had accumulated in the trade cities, they had been the victims of wave upon wave of despotic conquerors, from the great Khans to the Persians and Tamerlane. Even Alexander the Great had swept through.

It had led to the local tribal peoples having a strong sense of who they were and of their connection to the land they lived upon. It had also probably contributed to their long-suffering attempt to accommodate the Russian refugees, who had turned out to be invaders and who had taken over their country. But now Fergana stood every chance of once more being invaded. A strict attitude of political neutrality had kept Fergana free so far because neither the Ottomans nor the Chinese wished to be viewed as the initial aggressors in what would certainly grow into a world war. Whichever empire won such a conflict would no doubt turn their ever hungry eye to the Anglo-Germans and then to the small independent countries that filled much of the non-Anglo-German Americas. So as the tensions mounted over the Ferganese election and the clearly Chinese leanings of the front-running candidate, Fergana seemed to be awash in spies.

At least Kazakov had continued to run into such people as he investigated his last three cases.

In the squad room they found a strained silence. At their desks, Detektivs Pogolin and Kuznetzov pretended to be deep in paperwork, but they were giving Detektiv Elena Egorova the evil eye. Both men were in their fifties with almost-black hair going silver, but where Pogolin's silver-shot hair was slicked back with some kind of pomade and his cheeks were newly shaven, Kuznetzov's hair was a rough tangle that hung over his ears, and his day's growth of beard gave him a bleary, bear-newly-wakened look.

At five feet six, Egorova was certainly the shortest detective New Moscow had seen. Though her bright, honey-blonde hair worn pulled back in a loose ponytail made her look far younger than the thirty-odd years Kazakov estimated her to be, she wasn't the youngest detective ever to work from this squad.

And now the two youngsters would be working together and they would be assisting Kazakov in a larger investigation that was looking for evidence that would support or disprove their suspicions of Boris Bure's background and intentions.

Egorova, dressed in a plain navy pantsuit and crisp, light blue shirt, was busily unpacking a cardboard box into her desk drawers.

"You got back," Chelomeyev said as he slung his coat over the back of his chair and sat down. "How was the trip?"

"From Biysk?" Egorova shook her head. She had plain, pale features, but in sunlight her face seemed to catch the light and show a beautiful side of her. "Awful. Ice and more ice. There were so many accidents I thought I might be delayed a day, but the highway patrol dealt with things. Nice to know you were thinking of me."

She grinned and a dimple flashed that Kazakov hadn't noticed before. But then, he didn't recall her smiling so deeply during their investigation in Biysk. She pulled a Ferganese Criminal Code from the box and set it upright on the corner of her desk with an elephant-shaped bookend to either side. Next, she carefully unwrapped a tissue-covered piece that turned out to be her crystal slipper ornament that she used to hold paper clips. A few files went into a lower desk drawer. A box of tissues and a bottle of headache medicine followed. Lined paper. Pens and pencils. A dozen or more old black-bound police notebooks. She lifted the cardboard box off her desk and deposited it on the floor, then sank into her chair with a sigh.

"Done. It feels good to be here." She swung her grin between Chelomeyev and Kazakov.

To one side, Pogolin gave a disgusted grunt.

"I don't think they appreciated Dabria helping me bring my stuff in and showing me around." She said with mock sternness and deepened voice that was surprisingly Pogolin-like, "An affront to the squad to have a constable wandering in."

Pogolin's neck reddened.

"You're going to have to get used to Egorova," Kazakov said. "She can be a pain in the ass, but she's a good detective."

Kuznetzov looked up at him. "And we should believe everything that comes out of your mouth?"

Kazakov smiled. "Haven't I always been the charmer of the office?"

A double harrumph from the two older male detectives. They, and the other detectives in the squad, minus Chelomeyev and Egorova, had no love lost for Kazakov. The years had rounded down the hard edges of justice for the others so that they, like Rostoff, were likely to look the other way for incidents involving the well-heeled and influential of New Moscow. Kazakov liked to think that the years had only made his rough edges rougher. Justice was never an easy thing, but someone had to speak for the victims. Someone had to make sure that justice was truly done, no matter how difficult.

"We've got a murder to investigate," Kazakov said, pulling his chair up to Chelomeyev's and Egorova's desks. He let Chelomeyev fill Egorova in on what they knew—not much—and what they had found, while he went to the data machine in the corner to query Anna Konstantinova's name.

The data machine was an unwieldy metal console set into the wall with a small screen, a low stool, and a tray with a keyboard for typing his query. Kazakov settled uncomfortably on the stool and typed in Anna's name to the criminal records data base. The machine's lights blinked as it considered the request and then it dinged. The screen filled with a list of possible subjects. Kazakov scrolled down. None of the images were of the dead girl. So no criminal record, then. He did a query of the driver's license registry, but nothing came up. So not a driver, either. This was going to take more research unless they could find someone who knew her. Pondering this, he returned to Chelomeyev and Egorova.

"Nothing in the system," he said. "We'll have to make enquiries of the Health Department and Vital Statistics." He sighed. "Let's take a look at Madam Sobol's list of errands."

Chelomeyev produced the list and they read it over. A greengrocer. A pharmacy. A bakery. A butcher. Small shops Kazakov had never heard of. One name leapt out at him. Kasimir Krupin.

Frowning, he sat back in his chair.

"Is that the same Kasimir…?" Egorova asked.

"Yes." Kazakov cut her off because he didn't want to spread the old man's name around. What the hell was a fraudulent old fortune-teller doing sending an errand girl to the aging newspaperman? Krupin had once been Chief Financial Officer for a major international trucking company. He'd supposedly been fired for misappropriation of funds. Since then he had become a newspaper columnist and had been a source of information in two of Kazakov's investigations. The man was caring for his terminally ill socialite wife, Margarete, while still writing his business editorials for New Moscow's most prestigious newspaper. The man was intelligent, committed to truth, and honorable, so mixing with Madam Sobol seemed even more unusual.

"I need to talk to him," Kazakov said and stood.

"We'll start visiting the others," Egorova said, standing to join him. "I'll drive. It will be a good way for me to relearn the streets of New Moscow. It's been years since I've lived here."

She actually grinned at Chelomeyev.

"I think I may actually miss the bad old days of partnering with Sherepov." Chelomeyev said with a roll of his eyes. His unpleasant previous partner had, unfortunately, recently died of cancer.

Kazakov left them verbally sparring and, instead of taking a police sedan, went out to his well-used and dependable Perseus. The boxy old vehicle was built higher off the ground so it was good in the heavy snow found higher up in the foothills where he lived. It would also be less conspicuous when he parked in front of Krupin's home.

It was a short drive to an older section of the city where small neat homes were set back into small yards with snowbound gardens. A few of the yards had barren trees that held skeletal branches up to the sky. The yard of Krupin's bungalow held no tree, and the two-story house seemed to have sagged into itself even further than Kazakov remembered. The paint had peeled further from the plaster exterior, leaving the place looking decrepit and uncared for—which was likely the truth given Krupin's energies were turned inward to his wife, who still lingered in the throes of terminal cancer. What had once been a well-cleared walkway to the front door now carried a burden of ice.

He climbed out of the Perseus, bearing the bouquet he had purchased on the way to the house, and pushed through the squeaking iron gate in the concrete block fence. A thin trickle of smoke rose from the chimney as he picked his way up to the chipped blue door and knocked once before stomping the snow off his feet. Once Krupin and his wife had lived in a grand house and Margarete had been the doyenne of New Moscow society, but their station had been reduced when Krupin was quietly fired and forced to become a newspaperman.

A whisper of sound finally came from beyond the door—the sound of soft-soled slippers sliding on well-worn wood. A curtain stirred in the glass panel beside the door and Krupin's wizened old blue eye peered out for a second. Then the curtain fell back into place and the lock turned. The door pulled open.

Kazakov had never known Krupin in his heyday, but even in the few months that Kazakov had known him, the man was clearly failing. His always-wild grey hair had grown into a leonine tangle that now fell over his ears and his collar. His always-wan cheeks were sunken and his eyes overbright. His usual worn cardigan fell from his shoulders in folds that shifted around him like curtains around a bony corpse.

"Kazakov. Come in." The old man stepped aside and let Kazakov step into the cloying sweetness of the house—the scent of slow death, Kazakov had learned. The old man's trousers were stained and shiny. "Did you come to see Margarete?"

"How is she?" Kazakov and Margarete had developed a certain affection for each other over the few months since they had met. Kazakov tried to visit the lovely old woman as often as he could, but it wasn't often enough.

Krupin shook his head. "Not good. She wanders in delirium most days. I try to guide her back to me with my voice, but even that is failing." The old man's voice caught and he looked away, but not before Kazakov saw the tears.

His chest tightened. There was so much death in the world. Some had been at his hands. He had seen so much of it at times he almost felt too tired to get up in the morning. Working with Chelomeyev and Egorova had helped allay that feeling, but seeing Krupin's pain made Madam Sobol's pronouncement swoop in again like a carrion bird. He had caused too much death and would kill again—if he believed.

He sighed.

"Then perhaps I may just pop my head in to say hello. It is actually you that I've come to see. At least I think so." Perhaps the girl's visits had been with Margarete?

The place was as disheveled as last time. Dust pillowed in the corners and edges of the hall floor, the pictures hanging on the wood paneled walls hung at odd angles. The stairwell straight ahead showed a narrow path upward where the dust had been disturbed. The stacks of crumpled clothing and books on each riser of the stairs had grown and a pile of mail sat unopened on a small table by the door. Some of the envelopes had spilled onto the floor.

In the parlor to the left, the two chairs looked unused, the pile of Margarete's blankets neatly folded as if for the last time beside a fireplace that was filled with ash. Even the dining room that Krupin had converted to his office so that his office could serve as his wife's sickroom looked disheveled and forgotten, with dust on the books stacked on the floor and the table and only a narrow path leading to a single empty chair at the table.

"This way, but please keep your visit brief." Krupin led Kazakov back past the stairwell to a wood paneled room filled with shelves. Once they had held Krupin's library, but now they held brave mementos of Margarete's life set up like talismans to ward off death. There were bouquets of silk flowers, photos of Margarete as a beautiful young woman in evening gowns. Others of her dressed in cocktail dresses and surrounded by other women like a princess with her handmaidens. Awards and acknowledgment plaques for her service to the community abounded. But the room was dominated by the beep-beep-beep of a heart monitor and the presence of the narrow hospital bed in the center of the room.

Margarete Krupin lay swathed in blankets, her body shrunken, the spirit he had always seen burning in her diminished by her closed eyes. Her almost translucent eyelids twitched with her dreams. Her mouth worked as if she was chewing on a word and her fingers clasped and released the yellowed bedcovers as if she could not decide whether to cling to her life or not.

Kazakov crossed to her side, glanced at Krupin who nodded, and then clasped Margarete's hand. It was hot, her skin paper thin.

"Margarete, it's me, Kazakov. I came to see how you are. I brought you these. You always seem to love flowers." Indeed, the bouquet of lilies and daisies vanquished the scent of death and filled the room with the scent of spring and living.

Margarete said nothing, though her chest rose and fell and her hand might have twitched in his clasp. Then her lips slowly curved in a gracious smile.

That was Margarete.

"I'll let you rest," he whispered and lay the bouquet on her bedside table so that the perfume could continue to please her. He set her hand back on her chest with a pat and stepped away to Krupin. "How long has she been like this?"

Krupin shook his head. "Three days, but it feels like years."

Together they left Margarete's sickroom and returned to Krupin's workroom. Following the trail between the books was like burrowing into the newspaperman's world. Krupin slumped wearily in his chair and looked up at Kazakov.

"Sorry. There is no other chair. Now what can I do for you?"

Kazakov thought of the parlor that held two chairs, but the old man was so weary he didn't suggest it. Instead, Kazakov leaned his hip against the table.

"I am involved in another investigation. What can you tell me about a woman named Madam Sobol?"

Krupin's watery gaze wavered and dropped to his hands, folded on the tabletop. He didn't speak, but raised his face to Kazakov almost in defiance.

"She is an expert in human behavior and a counselor to many influential people."

His words were surprising and so was his tone, but Kazakov nodded at Krupin to continue. There was clearly something the newspaperman did not want to say.

"She offers guidance to those in need." Krupin's words were choked.

And who was more in need than a dying woman and the husband who loved her dearly?

"How long has she been counseling you and Margarete?"

Krupin slumped back in his chair, his face collapsing and tears starting to fall. "Since Margarete received her diagnosis. We hoped—at first we hoped for advice that would save her. Now it is more how to carry on without her." His hands closed into fists, whitening as he appeared to fight for composure. His eyes squeezed shut, but when he opened them again, he presented the calm reporter Kazakov had always known.

"She comes from a family of well-documented psychics who lived in a small village near the ruins of ancient Asaka. There are rumors that her people were once priests and seers of ancient temples before the word of the Prophet spread. So she has a pedigree. Her mother was known to advise the president—quietly, of course. Magdalena has followed in her footsteps. Corporate leaders and politicians seek her out."

"You know there's no such thing as prophecy," Kazakov said.

Krupin smiled wearily up at him. "So *you* might say, but to desperate people, prophecy is all we have. How can you rob us of our hope?"

It was Kazakov's turn to uneasily look away. It was true. He did not want to rob this man of hope, though hope lay dying with his wife. "May I ask what she advised you on?"

Krupin's deep sigh filled the room. "How to carry on, mostly. How I could live after Margarete is gone. Madam Sobol said that another cause would come along. Something to fight for." He shook his head. "I know it's a generalization that could apply to anything, but I choose to believe."

"And how much does she charge for these words of wisdom?"

Krupin met his gaze. "Margarete and Madam Sobol and I have known each other a long time. Margarete once did her a favor when she was a young woman. In honor of that, she charges us half the price. A hundred rubles a month and she will do readings for us and send us updates."

A hundred rubles was still not cheap. A hundred rubles would feed Kazakov's aging Kyrgyz neighbor for many months.

"How do you know what she charges others? Have you met them? Discussed her rates?"

Confusion laced Krupin's features for a moment. "She said…"

Then he shook his head. "I'm a fool, aren't I?"

"No. A worried man and devoted husband, more like. So tell me how it works. How did you begin to get these updates?"

"It was simple, really: I was doing a story about a corporate leader's climb to prominence and Sobol's name came up in one of my research interviews. I recalled Margarete's story about how she had helped a young woman of that name when the girl got in trouble—in the family way, they called it back then. Margarete helped the girl deal with her situation. Years later, Margarete received her diagnosis. I was angry, appalled, and determined that together we could beat her cancer even though every doctor said there was nothing we could do—not even in great Constantinople or Nanjing. Believe me, I asked." He shook his head. "How naive I was. Anyway, I had by then changed careers and I had come across Madam Sobol again. I did some checking to confirm it was the same woman and then checked her clients. They had amazing stories of what she had done for them. So I mentioned her to Margarete. At first she hesitated, but then she agreed. Thinking back, I think she did it more for me."

He pressed his lips together and composed himself again. "In any event, I bundled Margarete up and off we went to meet Madam Sobol in that horrid little office of hers. I felt like I was at a circus sideshow, but Margarete and Magdalena embraced like old friends, so I held my tongue. Magdalena clucked over Margarete as she lay down on a couch and then proceeded to do a reading. She said there was hope as long as Margarete changed her eating style: fresh vegetables and halal meat."

Another shake of his head. "As Margarete became weaker, Magdalena no longer asked her to come to her office. Instead she did readings on her own and sent them to us."

Kazakov nodded. "These messages—tell me about them."

"Not helpful. Not helpful at all. They were platitudes, except now and then something made sense. Margarete would seem to improve for a day or so and I would have hope again."

And for that hope, he likely stripped away what savings he had.

"How did the updates come to you?" Kazakov asked softly, for Krupin's gaze seemed far away.

"By messenger, of course. There is privacy in that, and a sense of importance. More so than something simply coming in an envelope in the mail. Whenever there was an update—almost weekly to start, but less frequent now—a messenger would bring the advice of Madam Sobol to our door."

He met Kazakov's gaze and must have seen the questions. "At first it was an older woman who I think was Madam Sobol's neighbor. Over the past while it has been a girl. Young, in her early twenties I would say. Blonde and pretty as young girls are. She would arrive or be waiting on the porch when I got home, all bundled up in her dark coat, scarf, and boots. Anna, her name is. A pleasant enough girl that I often asked her in for tea. She always asked after Margarete's and my health and I would tell her about what I was working on for the newspaper. But then perhaps I was simply flattered that a pretty girl was interested in what I did."

Kazakov made a mental note of this fact. It was possible that Anna was simply being kind, but he thought it more likely that she mined Krupin for information on other Sobol clients. Information that Madam Sobol could use in her "counseling."

"Tell me more about this Anna."

Krupin's weary gaze sharpened. "She's who this is about, isn't it? Not Sobol. Anna."

For a man dealing with so much, he was amazingly astute.

"Anna Konstantinova was found dead in Madam Sobol's kitchen this morning," Kazakov said. "I am trying to learn as much about her, her movements, and the arrangements with Madam Sobol as I can."

Frowning, Krupin seemed to study the tabletop. "I never saw her arrive so I really can't say how she got here. Perhaps she walked, or at least walked in from a main road, because I never heard a car. There would simply be a knock at the door and there she would be with Madam Sobol's envelope and a few kind words of advice. It was like a breath of fresh air when she came. Do you understand?"

Kazakov could. Maria, now months dead, had been like that to him if only he'd appreciated it at the time.

"How about when she left. Did you see where she went? Did she ever talk about anyone important to her?"

Krupin's frown deepened. "Nooo. No, she never talked about anyone in particular that I can recall. She'd let me go on and on about my research. But there was something about her, I do remember, because Margarete commented on it. The last few times we saw her there was a gaiety about her as if she was about to burst with news, emotions, who knew what; but Margarete described it as if she was in love."

He met Kazakov's gaze. "Could that mean something? Perhaps the reason she arrived here on foot was that she was meeting someone else nearby?"

The thought had crossed Kazakov's mind.

"When she came to you, did she carry anything with her?"

Pursing his lips, Krupin closed his eyes. "Yes. She often carried a shopping bag. If I think back, I can recall seeing a pharmacy bag and smelling fresh cabbage and onion when she stepped into the house."

So Madam Sobol's story of trips to the greengrocer were likely true.

"When was the last time Anna Konstantinova visited?"

"It was last Monday." Krupin nodded.

A week ago today. Kazakov needed the time of death from M.E. Gordiev, but it would likely be over the weekend.

Kazakov eased his hip off the table and worked his side and shoulders.

"Once more thing: Did Anna ever discuss politics with you? Did she ever mention her leanings?"

The room ticked around them and Krupin's sweater rustled as he shifted in his chair. "I don't believe we ever got into a deep political discussion, but a few times she mentioned how horrible it was what was happening in Fergana. When I asked what she meant, she said the explosions and that everyone was so scared, so that we needed strong leadership."

Their gazes met, and Krupin nodded. "Bure?"

Kazakov had an urge to shrug. Instead he nodded.

"What could he have to do with Anna's death?"

"That," Kazakov said as he pocketed his notebooks and settled his coat around his shoulders, "is a very good question and one that I have no answers for. As always, thank you for your time."

Krupin stood and escorted Kazakov to the front entry. A stream of false-spring air stirred the hallway when they opened the door. Kazakov turned back to face the older man.

"I will keep checking back, but please keep me posted about Margarete. She is—a remarkable woman."

Krupin only nodded as Kazakov set off down the treacherous sidewalk. New Moscow might be his city, but he felt like the young tsarevich must have felt in Chelomeyev's fairy tale. Everything was changing, and who knew where the enemies were?

At the Perseus he climbed in and glanced back at Krupin's house. The old man still stood there. By his expression, he felt the same.

3

It was after lunch when Kazakov left Krupin's house, the sun blindingly bright off the melting snow and the water on the road. The traffic on Suvarov Way sent up huge fantails of spray that threatened to blind the next vehicle. Kazakov kept the Perseus well back before finally pulling into the snow- and ice-covered curb in front of a small hole-in-the-wall café for a meal. He realized his mistake when he opened the driver's side door and was immediately drenched by a passing car. Brushing slush off his coat, he stood and slammed the door shut before wading through ankle-deep slush to the sidewalk and the café's front door.

Inside, the glass door clicked shut behind him and locked out the cool air and the hiss and roar of traffic. After being outside, the café was hot as a bathhouse, the broad front window covered in condensation that blurred the street. One side wall was covered in a mural of a too-white beach and impossibly blue-green water framed in palm trees. A low counter spanned the rear of the room and a flock of eight small, square tables sat between Kazakov and the rotund woman in the faded floral dress who wiped halfheartedly at the counter. There were no other patrons in the café, which was unusual given the hour. Unless the patrons of this café ate early or late —or knew something about the food that he didn't.

The woman waddled up to him. She had tightly curled yellow-blonde hair and the lines on her face said she'd seen a thing or two. There was no nonsense in her gaze. "Pick your pleasure. Where would you like to sit?"

Kazakov, sensing her sizing him up, chose a table next to the mural wall and a chair that allowed him a view of the door. The woman gave a small nod as if he'd confirmed something for her and then plunked down a menu.

"We don't do breakfast at this hour."

"Do you do milk tea?"

Her lip curled in what might be a poor semblance of a smile. "Funny man."

She waddled off and Kazakov slid off his coat. Even in his shirt and jacket, the place was overhot and he felt sweat bead on his skull. He flipped open the menu and chose a mutton stew that was standard Russian fare.

The woman returned and plunked a cup and saucer on the table. She took his order and then walked away to turn on a television on a shelf on the otherwise barren wall across from Kazakov. At first the television screen was a hail of snow, but then the screen gradually coalesced into figures seated around a coffee table. A well-known lunchtime talk show host sat with his midnight black hair gleaming, across from a big man with white-blond hair and a shark's grin with too-large teeth. A studio audience were seated around them on stadium-style seating that had led to the program being called the Gladiator's Meeting.

Kazakov stiffened at the image of Boris Bure and his white-blond hair. He was everywhere these days and it felt like everyone was trying to curry favor with the man they expected was going to be the next Ferganese President. Kazakov wanted to ask the woman to change the channel or to turn it off. Instead, he forced himself to watch the screen. The woman turned the volume up.

"You've made a lot of points with some of the population by talking about something you call 'the tribal problem'." The host hooked his fingers in quotations. "These people, these tribals as you call them, were here before us. They took our people in and helped us. How can you call them a problem?"

Kazakov sat up. It was a question he'd wanted to pose to Bure.

"I'm truly glad you asked that, Alex," Bure said.

Kazakov's skin crawled at Bure's smooth voice.

"There is a great deal of misunderstanding about the relationship between our people and the tribals on the great diaspora. If one looks back into the true history, there were many tribals who attacked our people on our long journey, and those who helped us brought disease to our people; so you see, the weakened state of the people and the loss of our tsarina to disease was actually the fault of the tribals. When we arrived in Fergana, it wasn't these people—the tribals we see today—who helped us. It was nomadic people who have long since moved on from Fergana."

Kazakov tensed. His hands curled into fists at the revisionist lies that were being told.

"Those are history books I'm not familiar with," the commentator, Alex, said.

"They are old. Some are diaries that should be taught in schools," Bure said.

Kazakov clenched his teeth. The waitress startled him when she slapped a steaming bowl on the table in front of him. Oily broth slopped onto the table and almost into his lap. The woman pulled a spoon and napkin out of a suspect dress pocket and dropped them on the table, then retreated to the counter before he could ask her for salt and pepper.

He decided not to push his luck. At least the oiliness suggested that mutton had actually been used in the broth. He stirred the soup, dislodging small chunks of meat and thick noodles from the bottom of the bowl. He slurped up his first mouthful and it was surprisingly good.

"There are people who say that you are betraying the very people who saved your life. Wasn't it tribal people who found you when you were lost as a boy in the mountains?"

Bure took a moment to drink from a ready glass of water on the interview coffee table as if he needed to compose his answer. He swallowed and wiped his face with his hands. Then he smiled, exposing those overbroad teeth of his.

"I'm sorry," he said. "This is difficult. It was a tragic part of my life, losing my family. It is hard to discuss. In honesty, I cannot say much about my rescue because I barely recall it. I suppose I was too far gone. But if they say that tribals were involved in my rescue, how can I deny it?" He hung his head as if fighting emotions. "I will tell you this, though," he choked out. "Over the years I have had these recurring nightmares of waking, tied up, and people standing around me. People in tribal clothing."

The studio audience gasped and so did the usually taciturn host.

"Are you saying that tribal people may have kidnapped you? That they may have had a hand in the death of your family?"

Bure shook his head. "I'm not saying anything like that. I'm only telling you what I remember. As far as I know, there was no evidence of foul play at the time."

"Derr'mo!" Kazakov swore and shoved the barely-touched bowl of meat and noodles away.

"Can you believe that they did that to him! That poor man! His poor family! He was no more than a boy!" The waitress was suddenly beside his table, her gaze glued on the television. She looked down at his bowl. "You don't like it? I made it fresh this morning." As if he would be reprimanded if he didn't eat it.

He shook his head and stood. "I'm sorry. It was excellent, but there are places I must be."

"So you truly believe that the tribal population are a cause for worry for Russian people of Fergana?" Alex asked.

Kazakov stopped slipping on his coat to see what Bure would say.

"There have been bombings. There have been demonstrations. Can anyone deny that those are dangerous? These people—they are primitives. They have been thieves and murderers for generations, only most of their crime has been focused on their own people. Suddenly they have decided that we are their enemy even though we tried to integrate them into our society. No, it is time that Fergana must protect its Russian people. These tribals must be dealt with in a way they can understand. In a way that leaves Fergana for those of us who have built a life here."

Barely able to breathe around the furious lump in his chest, Kazakov threw money on the table and headed for the café door. Behind him Alex thanked his guest and turned to the audience.

"So you heard it here. It is time for Fergana to be taken back for Russians."

Deafening applause followed Kazakov out the door before he ducked his head and emptied his stomach contents into the melting morass by the road.

Feeling shaky once in his Perseus, Kazakov leaned his head back against his seat, still not believing what he'd seen on the café television. Or perhaps it was that he didn't want to believe it. Bure and his cronies had basically undermined any of the arguments that might have stood against his despicable plan to rid the country of the people whose land this had always been. Something had to be done.

His phone shrilled in his pocket and he fished it out.

"Did you hear what he said?" Egorova's voice was brittle with tension.

"Saw it on the TV where I had lunch."

"We just heard it rebroadcast on the radio. I'm surprised you could keep anything down."

"Let's just say I didn't. Where are you two?"

"We just finished checking the fifth place on the list. You get anything from your guy? How's the magnificent Margarete?"

Kazakov sighed.

"Oh no," she said softly.

"She's still with us. But it's bad." He gripped the steering wheel and pulled himself straighter. "How about I meet you at the office in half an hour?"

"We'll just hit the number six and meet you there."

"You getting anything?" he asked.

"I guess we'll see." She rang off and Kazakov inhaled deeply and started the Perseus. He felt hollow and he wasn't quite sure what to do about it.

Waiting for space in the traffic, he pulled out into the street and drove what he thought was aimlessly through the city. He realized it was anything but aimless when he found himself pulling in to the curb at the gate of the graveyard.

It was one of the oldest graveyards in the city and certainly the one with the oldest Russian graves. The oldest graveyards were all tribal burial sites. This one sat on a small knoll outside the ancient terra-cotta walls of the old tribal city that had stood here since time immemorial. The city then had been host to conquerors and kings. It had welcomed silk road caravans and been sacked by Genghis Khan. Its citizens had been traders and warriors and victims of despots. Now it looked like they would be victims again.

He climbed out of the Perseus and headed through the old wrought iron gate, then struck out uphill, following a narrow path through the snow. The footing was treacherous with snowmelt flowing over snow and his boots slipped and slid until he was forced to step away from the path and plow a new route up the hill.

Maria di Maria's grave sat just under the crest of the hill. It held a low headstone with the simple inscription of her name and "Daughter of Italia" carved beneath. He hadn't known anything more about her other than she was lovely and brave and honest and she had made him feel alive again even though he hadn't wanted to. And she had died because of him.

And Bure.

He had buried her here because there was a view. On a day such as this, the old city gleamed in the sunshine, and so did the crag of Yekaterina Mountain. Beyond the sprawl of New Moscow that now threatened to erase the grace of the old city, the plains of Fergana rolled down into the eastern breadbasket of the Ottoman Empire. In the sunlight, the hazy distance hid the far mountains and what must be the blue oceans that surrounded the Anglo-German province of far Italia. It sounded like a hazy place out of fantasy, just as his memories of Maria were. Just as the fantastic tales of Ivan Tsarevich were.

He sighed and looked down at the grave. After her death, he had come here often until his friend Khalil Khan had warned him away with the admonishment that he needed to look to the living, not the dead. But now Khan was dead, too, having been shot and fallen from the lookout high up on Yekaterina Mountain. His body had never been recovered.

"What would you counsel, old friend?" Kazakov asked of the wind that blew his coat around him. The air was pure as the mountain snow it had passed over and carried a heart of cold under the sun's warmth. Yes, the day might be warm and promise spring, but a cold time was coming, or perhaps that was just the chill he felt deep in his soul.

He couldn't imagine living in a country that would do what Bure was proposing.

Derr'mo! Why did everything keep coming back to the man?

Hands fisted, he closed his eyes, imagining Khan at his side. The diminutive medical examiner had been a brilliant man and dedicated to the truth. Yet he had made the damning choice to break the law in defense of his people. He had killed the man, Zholdosh, who was using his people, and had made an attempt on Chelomeyev's life. When Kazakov thought back, it shouldn't have surprised him. Khan had expressed his frustrations with the Russian establishment often enough.

But the loss of his friend, of his belief in the man, still saddened him.

But as Khan had said many times, standing here among the dead was no way to help the living. It was no way to solve a crime, either.

"I hear you, my old friend." He glanced over his shoulder, almost expecting the dark-haired Khan to be there. There was only the sunlight on melting snow and the dark silhouettes of headstones. He stroked the top of Maria's headstone and removed old leaves snagged at its base, then began to pick his way back down the hillside, to the sound of the wind and the tinkle of running water. The sun laid deep shadows in his footprints.

Across the road from the graveyard's gate, the old wooden doors were open to a mechanic's shop. A dark van stood before the shop and two men

—the slim, Kyrgyz owner and a larger man whose bulk suggested Uzbek heritage, unloaded crates.

Kazakov raised a hand to the owner who had helped him in a prior case, but the man simply looked away. He said something to his partner and they hurriedly moved their crate inside. Kazakov climbed into the Perseus and checked his watch. Just enough time to get back to the office. As he pulled away, he checked his rearview mirror and saw the mechanic and his compatriot step out of the shop. Both stood in the street and watched him leave.

Egorova and Chelomeyev were waiting in the squad room when he arrived. There were no other detectives in the room. Kazakov came in, doffed his coat, and slumped in his desk chair feeling wrung out and tired before he'd even begun.

From the entrance to the break room, Egorova eyed him as she stirred a mug of tea. She looked bright and ready, like a hound on scent. Chelomeyev sat at his desk, busily writing notes as he listened to the phone balanced between shoulder and ear. He nodded at Kazakov.

"You look like you've been through a war," Egorova said.

Kazakov shook his head and worked his neck to get the kinks out. "Sorry. That interview with Bure…" He shook his head. "Did you see it?"

"Heard it at least three times. They were replaying it continuously all over the radio," Egorova said. "You actually saw it?"

He nodded and wished he had the energy to make himself a cup of tea.

She held out her cup. "You look like you could use this more than me."

Grateful, he accepted it from her and sipped. He came up sputtering. "Let me guess: only one sugar."

She tipped a brow at him. "Beggars shouldn't be choosy."

He lumbered up and went into the break area to add more sugar and put the kettle on for another cup of tea to replace Egorova's. "So what have we got?"

"Not a lot." Chelomeyev joined the conversation. "Anna Konstantinova visited the shops from time to time, usually after Madam Sobol phoned in a list. Most of the places she simply arrived, picked up the package, and left. A few, she came to know the shopkeeper and might stop for a tea with the proprietor. None admitted to knowledge of anything more."

Kazakov looked from one young detective to the other. He nodded. "Okay. Not much there. Did you happen to ask if they ever knew where Anna was going when she left their establishment? Did they get any sense of whether she might be meeting someone?"

Another cock of Egorova's brow. Her suit was more modern, cut closer to the body than she had worn when she was in Biysk, and the coat folded on the side of her desk also looked new. Clearly, she was making good use of the shopping available in New Moscow. Though her hair was still pulled back in its loose ponytail, its luster seemed to have improved as if she'd had some sort of expensive treatment. A changeling?

Egorova shook her head and glanced away. "We didn't ask."

He sighed. "I had an interesting visit with Krupin."

He told them of Krupin's long association with Madam Sobol and the hint that Anna might support Bure's most controversial political platform.

"Krupin wasn't sure, but he indicated that Anna might be meeting someone when she left his home. She always seemed to arrive at his home on foot and he assumed that she left the same way." He finished and leaned back in his chair.

"So where does that leave us?" Chelomeyev asked. The young blond detective tiredly ran his fingers through his hair. Shadows had deepened under his eyes. He'd probably done more police work today than he should have, given he was supposed to be on light duties. Still, his eyes gleamed as if he'd enjoyed the exertion.

"We need to check those questions with the businesses we spoke to and there's still five other businesses to canvass," Egorova said.

Kazakov nodded and considered Chelomeyev. "I suggest that you follow up with the businesses you've already interviewed and I'll start on the others," he said to Egorova. "Chelomeyev, I think you should call it a day. Head home and get some rest. We'll have a busy day tomorrow."

"No. I'm fine," Chelomeyev protested and went to stand, then swayed, sank back into his chair. He rubbed his head, then met Kazakov's gaze. "Sorry. Dizzy for a moment. But I can do this. Really."

Kazakov hid a smile behind his teacup. Chelomeyev's determination reminded him of his own. Kazakov shook his head.

"Listen, unless something comes up today, this is likely going to be a long and difficult investigation just like anything else that touches on Bure. I need you rested and ready. You did well today, so let's make sure that you can do more tomorrow."

Chelomeyev looked about to argue, but then his shoulders slumped. He nodded. "You better not solve this today."

Kazakov raised a brow. "So hold off on justice to meet your schedule?"

"No! Yes! No!" Chelomeyev spluttered. "Damn you, Kazakov. Don't go putting words in my mouth." But he grinned and grabbed his coat before shaking a finger at them and vacating. The elevator dinged behind him.

"So how was he?" he asked Egorova.

"You're asking me?" she seemed surprised.

"You're his partner."

"He was—good. He tired easily, but he's getting stronger, I think," Egorova said, sinking into her chair. "I like him. I think I'm going to like working with him."

All good to hear.

From the kitchen came the sound of the kettle boiling and then clicking off, but Kazakov drained his teacup and stood. "Thanks for the tea. Sorry you won't get yours." He nodded at the break area. "We should get going if we want these interviews done."

With a sigh, Egorova stood and pulled her coat on. It skimmed her length, making her look taller and more elegant than he'd ever thought her to be.

He held the squad door open for her and was surprised that he had.

4

───────────

It was a long afternoon. Kazakov made it back to the squad room well after his usual quitting time and was surprised to find Egorova at her desk while the silver-haired Pogolin and Kuznetzov conferred quietly over Pogolin's desk. Both detectives nodded in Kazakov's direction and he returned the favor as he headed for Egorova. The room smelled mustily of tea and unwashed clothing, and the fluorescent lights placed a yellow cast over everything as if the squad room was an image on old newsprint.

"I didn't expect you to wait for me," he said softly.

She shrugged. "I needed to type up my notes for the file. How did your interviews go?"

He shook his head. "There wasn't much there, other than Anna Konstantinova regularly dropped in to pick up supplies. Most of the time it was regular necessities, but some of the time it was small luxuries: a lipstick, a special cheese, a particular cut of meat. I suppose she must have cooked meals for some of Madam Sobol's clients."

Egorova looked back at her notes and flipped through her notebook. She shook her head. "That's different than most of these places. They were all about commonplace needs for the home."

"Except for my friend," Kazakov said and glanced over his shoulder at the two other detectives. He rarely shared his investigations with anyone on the team because he feared that someone might undermine the evidence. That is, until circumstances forced him to work with Egorova and he'd come to appreciate her brain and her commitment. Like him, she sought the truth, though the administration might be stacked against her.

She nodded. "Your friend, yes." In thought, she tapped a well-trimmed nail against the side of her typewriter. "Did you notice that all the other contacts Anna had involved collecting things for her employer?"

"Madam Sobol, yes." Kazakov nodded and then stopped. He looked at Egorova. "Derr'mo! You're right! And I was an idiot to miss it!"

"What's that? Kazakov finally admits he's a fool? We've known it for years!" Pogolin's voice boomed through the room. So he'd been listening in on the discussion with Egorova.

Kazakov was on his feet and pulling his coat back on. He hooked his head toward the door at Egorova. She scrambled up, questions on her face.

Kazakov led the way out of the office. "I'm always a fool, Pogolin. The difference is, I know it and attempt to rise above my deficits. It's why I keep bright lights like Egorova around."

Pogolin's brows almost touched above his nose and were lost in the folds of his forehead.

Chuckling at Pogolin's apparent confusion, Kazakov led Egorova into the elevator and stabbed the button down. He leaned his head back against the metal wall and let his smile broaden. No wonder Pogolin was confused. Even though Egorova was technically Chelomeyev's partner, Kazakov had to admit he liked working with the woman.

"What's going on? Where are we going?" Egorova demanded after the elevator was moving downward.

"I thought we'd go see your partner and perhaps stop in at Krupin's place on the way. The old bugger was holding out on me and I was too trusting or stupid to notice!" He shook his head and scrubbed at the stubble on his chin. This late in the day he could use a shave, but this late in the day such niceties could wait.

They reached the parking garage and, still kicking himself for not asking the right question of Krupin, he climbed behind the wheel of the Perseus. Egorova climbed in the other side.

"It's getting late. Should we really bother him now? Margarete…"

"Is barely conscious from what I saw, and Krupin is likely up. He strikes me as a night owl. At the least he stays up to care for Margarete."

He accelerated up out of the police underground parking and down the street. At this hour much of the evening traffic had dispersed to homes in the suburbs and the streets were relatively quiet. A good thing as the rear end of the Perseus slipped wide in a corner. With the setting of the sun, the cold had descended again and the ice was forming. Greater New Moscow was going to be a skating rink as the night progressed. He took his foot off the gas to slow the vehicle and made the few turns to reach the neighborhood that held Krupin's small home.

"Did any of your interviewees have a sense of where Anna was going when she left their businesses?" he asked as he drove.

"Not much of consequence." Egorova said as they pulled to the curb in front of Krupin's house.

"How do you want to play this?" Egorova asked.

"Man-to-man. Straight up. I neglected to ask and he didn't volunteer the information. Now we'll see whether he does."

He clicked the door open and climbed out into shivering cold that rolled down off the mountains. To the west, the sky still held a faint tinge of orange; but to the north, south, and east, there was only darkness looming. Overhead, the stars pinpricked the cold night sky. He shivered in his great coat and headed for the door. A curtain twitched in what he knew was the parlor window. Krupin was waiting for them.

The door opened as they climbed the three stairs to the porch and the rumpled reporter was silhouetted by the warm light gleaming weakly behind him.

"I knew you'd be back." Krupin nodded them inside, his hair wild about his head.

Kazakov and Egorova stepped past him.

"It's a pleasure to see you again, sir," Egorova said.

"And a pleasure to see you, as well, young tsarina," Krupin said with a slight bow.

What the hell? Kazakov looked from Krupin to Egorova. The last time they had visited the Krupins together, Margarete had said Egorova was the direct descendent of the great Tsarina Catherine. At the time, Kazakov had discounted the story as some wild fabrication. There were too many pretenders to such bloodlines, not the least of whom was Boris Bure. He looked at Egorova speculatively, but there was nothing royal about her.

"We're not here about Egorova's supposed heritage. We're here because this morning you left out a great deal of information, didn't you, Kasimir?"

The old man's sigh seemed to echo in the quiet of the house. Too quiet. Kazakov caught himself. "Margarete…?"

"Is sleeping, for the moment. And it's true that I didn't tell you everything because you didn't ask." A wry smile curved his lips. "We might as well speak in the parlor."

Shaking his head, he led them away from his dining room-cum-office and into the parlor. Pressed back against the wall was a low, blue couch Kazakov hadn't noticed in his perfunctory glance through the open doorway. Krupin nodded them to the couch and then tugged a footstool over to sit before them like a shoe salesman. The two chairs in front of the fireplace he left as they were: a shrine, with one still swaddled in blankets, the other with arms stacked with reading material. The gleam of the room's old hardwood floors was faded by a layer of dust now marred by their footprints. A worn carpet sat on the floor in front of the couch. The footstool sat on it.

Kazakov sat down and nodded at Egorova. She pulled out her notebook and pen.

"When I was here earlier today, you left me with the impression that the purpose of Anna Konstantinova's visit was because Madam Sobol sent you an updated report."

Krupin nodded. "What I told you was correct."

"But you left out that Madam Sobol expected something in return."

Krupin's straight gaze fell away to his knobby knees and his hands fluttered over the pleat in his pants. Kazakov read the nervousness and knew that he was right. "I did pay her," he mumbled.

"So you said," Kazakov agreed. "But what else was going on, Krupin?"

"She paid me for information on her clients. I know it isn't ethical or right, but Margarete's medical costs were more than my salary could afford. The money had to come from somewhere..." He looked beseechingly up at Kazakov. "It was so simple, really. At first she was a friend visiting Margarete and we would sit and talk and I would share insights with her. Then, one day she told us that she could no longer visit because it was too far, too difficult, and too expensive. We got into a discussion about the increasing costs of living and I shared the challenge of making ends meet."

He shook his head and sighed again. "Thinking back on it now, I have to wonder whether it was all simply a set-up to get me to help her. You see, she offered to help me—us—by buying research from me—if I would care to do it. Well, I accepted the offer given we needed the money."

He looked small and old as he perched there before them. The room held the remaining scent of old fire and ashes though nothing was laid in the fireplace. Egorova's pen scratched the silence as Kazakov just waited for Krupin to carry on.

He studied his long, boney hands as if wondering at what they had done. "At first it seemed so simple. Anna and her predecessor would arrive with names and I would learn all I could about the person and their family and prepare a report for Madam Sobol. Anna would collect the report and leave more names for the next week. Sometimes she would leave a reading for Margarete. Life went on—at least for me and Margarete, though she was slowly failing."

"What sort of things did you report on?" Kazakov asked.

"Financial situations. Issues within the family. Friends. Lost loved ones. I think back on it and from the information I gave her, she could likely do amazing readings for the involved parties. At least they'd think they were readings. In fact they were based on my research. I am good at what I do."

He lifted his head, his gaze almost defiant.

Kazakov nodded and let his hands droop between his knees. "Tell me again about Anna's last visit, and this time leave nothing out." He was not going to allow Krupin an out this time.

Krupin inhaled. "Keep in mind that everything I do, I do for Margarete. She is my life."

Kazakov understood that it was true, but it was also an excuse for whatever it was Krupin had done. He waited and Egorova sat with pen poised over notebook.

"It *was* like I told you. She came and provided us with Madam Sobol's latest advice. But Anna also came to receive from us. When Margarete was well enough, Madam Sobol would send questions that I was to pose to her about people she had known in her youth. It was easy enough to do—I would get her talking. Remembering the old days was one of Margarete's pleasures. But it didn't feel right. It felt like I was stealing from her and pawning off her memories. When I couldn't do it anymore, I told Madam Sobol the deal was off. I would manage Margarete's medical costs without her, somehow." Krupin looked up from his hands as if seeking exoneration.

Kazakov nodded at him to continue. Egorova's pen scritched across the notebook paper.

"But I couldn't do it. The costs—of the bed, the monitors, the nurses— were too high. I tried writing freelance articles to make up the monetary shortfall but there are only a few magazines in Fergana. Finally, I phoned

Magdalene Sobol and offered my services—as researcher. Much of what you see in there is as a result of that agreement." Krupin waved vaguely at the dining room-cum-office across the hall.

"Tell me about the research?" Kazakov asked.

Krupin shrugged and Kazakov prepared himself for a vague response.

"It was generally background material on the subject. Sometimes it was looking for information from the past, sometimes focusing on recent indiscretions. Most recently it was whatever I could find." Krupin's embarrassed gaze came up to meet Kazakov's. "Not good enough for you?" Krupin shook his head. "I suppose not. You'll want specifics."

Another sigh, a sad smile. "I guess I'm not very good at this. A reporter doesn't reveal his sources and we protect our stories until they're in print. The last six months I've been doing research on politicians and their connections. The politicians you see in the media are not the private men and women. It was the truth of the men and women that Magdalena Sobol wanted. For example, did you know that our illustrious leader Nikolaev has an illegitimate daughter whom he fathered in high school? The secret is well-guarded, especially with the tough election race he's facing. You can imagine what Bure's crew would do if it were found out. Nikolaev's donors have been quietly paying child support by employing the mother and paying her far higher wages than she deserves for the entire time he's been in politics. I wonder if he would have ever gotten sponsors for his original run for president if he hadn't already won the mayorship of New Moscow as an independent." He shook his head.

Kazakov held back any reaction and Egorova maintained an impassive expression—something Kazakov wasn't sure he'd have done when he was her age.

"And what were your more recent subjects of research?"

Krupin shook his head again. "Not Bure, if you're wondering. There's been nothing even close to him. Two months ago it was a fellow named Kirill Chaykovsky. He's a longtime truck and trailer manufacturer here in New Moscow. Ethical fellow. He runs a top business and his wife is a longtime friend of Margarete's from the society circuit. She came by regularly until Margarete's condition deteriorated. But looking into Chaykovsky's background, the firm wasn't always on such steady ground. Chaykovsky's father had almost bankrupted the firm, so when Chaykovsky-the-younger took over, he took some risky moves to keep the firm afloat."

"Like what?" Kazakov asked.

"Like took on a silent partner—someone with less than savory connections. Does the name Andrei Borisov mean anything to you?"

Kazakov straightened. Egorova's pen stopped scratching. Andrei Borisov was a top gangland figure with fingers in numerous pies like drugs, weapons, and prostitution. Having a partnership in a trucking firm was news to Kazakov, but made plenty of sense given the man's illicit business would need trucks. But then so would plenty of other businesses.

Kazakov caught himself from going after more information on Borisov. That wasn't his task today, though Pogolin might be interested. Gathering information on Borisov had become something of a crusade for the silver-haired detective.

"That was two months ago," Kazakov prompted.

"Yes. It was. A month ago Sobol's interest shifted from Chaykovsky to a woman named Charlotte Newcomb, the wife of a British diplomat. She manages a polo team here in Fergana. She has been transporting more than her team's polo ponies across the border. In fact, she had a small side arrangement with Borisov's competitor. She's been very discreet in greasing the right palms to get back and forth across the border, but apparently she stopped sleeping with the right Ottoman official and her truck and ponies were confiscated at the border just a week ago. Only back-channel diplomacy kept her out of jail. She and her husband are returning to England."

Kazakov glanced at Egorova in hopes that Krupin wouldn't see that Kazakov knew the woman. He had probably even searched the trailer in question and was well-aware of its secret compartments.

"Most recently I've been looking into someone you might know. Ottoman gentleman who makes his home here a good percentage of the time and coincidentally also owns a trucking firm. Enver Pasha."

Kazakov sat back, momentarily stunned. The darkness beyond the lace-covered windows seemed to seep into the room. Pasha was an honorific given to Enver for his battle service to the Ottoman Empire. He had been instrumental in the Ottoman victory over an Egyptian rebellion when he was only a young man. Now he ran a conglomerate in New Moscow, though his wife, a daughter of the Ottoman royal family, remained in Constantinople. Enver had also been a primary actor in two of Kazakov's last cases. If Bure was the suspected nemesis from the Chinese Empire, Enver Pasha was his analogue from the Ottomans, save, perhaps that Enver wasn't poised to become Fergana's new president.

"Enver. Enver is one of Madam Sobol's clients? What did you find?"

"Nothing that would surprise you, I think. His spying. Infidelity. Beyond his wife and three children in Constantinople, he has another wife in India."

"What?!" Kazakov exclaimed.

Krupin sat back with a satisfied expression. "Apparently there are things that you don't know. Did you know that Enver studied in China in his youth?"

Kazakov shook his head, uncertain what it all meant except that he had missed information on the man; but then, Enver had never been a chief suspect to require a complete background check. And a second family in the Ottoman's Indian provinces and training in China didn't exactly give reason to kill Anna Konstantinova.

"I had prepared a complete dossier on Enver and passed it to Anna when she came,"Krupin said.

"Did you get any sense whether this was Madam Sobol's request or Anna's?" Kazakov asked, leaning forward.

Krupin frowned. "I cannot say. All of the requests were made the same way, but whether it was hers or Madam Sobol's, who can say?" He sighed. "That visit she did not stay as long as she usually did and she acted distracted. Perhaps she was thinking of her next appointment. That had not happened before. Usually she took the time to have tea and conversation. She was a gifted girl." He paused.

"Gifted?" Egorova asked softly.

Krupin nodded. "From time to time she would drop hints of the future. At first I took them with a grain of salt, but then they came true. Rather extraordinary, don't you think? It is a shame she is gone."

"What type of predictions?" Kazakov asked and felt stupid asking. Why ask when he didn't believe in these charlatans?

"Well, she predicted that I would aid the police, for one. It was why I was so shocked when you walked through the door of my office that first time. And the explosions in New Moscow. She predicted that Great Yekaterina would be toppled." He shook his head and looked at his hands. "And she predicted that I would soon be alone." He swallowed back the pain that had entered his voice.

Kazakov pondered this new information. There was no way that Anna Konstantinova could predict the future. Nobody could. Knowledge of Margarete's loss was nothing surprising, and even the prediction that Krupin would help the police could be predicted with some certainty. He was a reporter, after all. But the explosions—that was less explainable…

"When did she predict the explosions?" What would bring her into contact with such information? Had she some prior knowledge through Madam Sobol or some other area of her life? A relationship with Bure, perhaps? Or was she simply aware enough to read the social situation in Fergana?

"About six months ago—not too long after she started acting as Madam Sobol's messenger. When they occurred, I was horrified, but amazed at the same time."

Kazakov thought a moment, his thoughts whirling. "Were there any other predictions?"

Krupin smiled and for a moment Kazakov could see through the years, the loss, and the sorrow to the hopeful man who had once been. "Only that the world is changing and that I will have a key role in it."

Hope. The panacea of the masses. Telling them what they wanted to hear. In Krupin's case it gave him a reason for living after Margarete was gone. The damned girl had played on Krupin's situation like a vulture.

Kazakov's fists tightened and he inhaled. "Thank you for the complete story." He turned to Egorova. "Anything else?"

"Mr. Krupin, I'm going to ask you a question and I want you to answer without thinking. Okay?"

Krupin nodded.

"When Anna was last here, you said she seemed distracted and in a rush to get somewhere."

Krupin nodded.

"Here's the question. Just say what immediately comes to mind. When Anna left your house, where did she go?"

"To her lover."

Kazakov held his tongue and left Egorova to follow up.

"Can you tell me anything about why you say that?" she asked.

Krupin shook his head. "I—I don't know. Except—she seemed almost unbearably happy. She left my yard and turned left with a jaunty little wave and headed off toward the main street. I thought she must not have to go far—perhaps she was catching a taxi, because she didn't have heavy boots on. Instead, they were stylish—something with a heel that flattered the leg." He glanced at Egorova. "Like yours."

Egorova colored slightly and skimmed over her notes. "I think I'm done. Thank you, Mr. Krupin."

Kazakov stood and felt ponderous and old. Egorova's question had been brilliant and brought an insight they hadn't had. He shook Krupin's hand as they left. After the unhealthy sweetness of the house, the night air was bitingly fresh and cold off the mountains. A full moon lit the half-circle of mountains north, east, and south of them. Above, the stars were faded by moonlight and streetlights.

Enver Pasha, like Ivan Tsarevich and the wolf, had been reborn in Kazakov's mind.

———

On the way to Chelomeyev's, both Kazakov and Egorova remained silent as if contemplating Krupin's information. The Perseus' heater chugged out warmth against the clear cold air streaming into Fergana from the north. Spring's warm ascendance would soon be over, usurped by spring storms, the fierce cousin of the winter.

"What does it all mean?" Egorova asked, her question barely audible above the rumble of the tires on the frost-heaved road.

"Good question. I don't really know, other than Enver Pasha has a past and we need to understand more—about him and his trucking firm." He glanced over at her, her pale skin lit only by green dials of the dash and the staccato flash of amber streetlights as they passed beneath them through the center of town. Then they turned off toward the old city, into an area that had once been all warehouses but was now experiencing gentrification. Along the main street, three- and four-story apartment buildings were replacing the dilapidated concrete and steel warehouses. Chelomeyev lived in one of these.

Kazakov pulled into the lone guest parking stall at the side of the building and climbed out to stand in the cold air and silence. There was very little traffic on Chelomeyev's street, though there was more on the side streets where prostitutes worked the darkness. To the west, Yekaterina Mountain's five peaks hulked out of the darkness, a light glowing almost at the summit illuminated the great tsarina's statue. At the base of the mountain, the walls of the old city seemed swaddled in slumbering darkness, but Kazakov knew better. There was an anger brewing there—at the age-old exclusion of the tribal people from the greater Russian economy, and more recently, over the death of their favored son, Doctor and Medical Examiner Khalil Khan.

The memory still hurt.

Egorova's footsteps crunched in the freezing slush. The cold air burned down his throat as he turned to the building to follow her. At the door they buzzed Chelomeyev's apartment and were buzzed through the glass doors to the wide lobby. Kazakov led the way to the stairs and they climbed to the third floor.

Chelomeyev's apartment door was open, the young detective waiting for them. He wore soft denims and a stretched-out woolen sweater that hung loosely around his slim body. His feet were bare, exposing long, elegant toes that matched his elongated fingers. Unfortunately, dark circles still underlay his eyes. He clearly had not been resting since he came home.

"You've got to rest when you get the chance, detective," Kazakov muttered as he passed Chelomeyev into the apartment.

Egorova nodded up at her partner as Chelomeyev closed the door behind them.

They stood at the edge of a great room. The room had brick walls, almost two-story-high ceilings and a small main floor with spaces defined by a couch and two unlikely chairs shaped of curved plastic, a dining room table and a rudimentary kitchen tucked into the corner beneath a set of iron stairs that, Kazakov knew from a previous visit, led up to a loft bedroom. At this hour the expansive windows on the outer wall bore traceries of frost, but no curtains; for there was no nearby building high enough to allow people to peer in. Cold radiated off the expanse of glass, which explained Chelomeyev's sweater but not his bare feet.

Not the kind of place Kazakov could ever imagine living in, but Egorova examined the place with interest. Something about the place must be attractive to the young.

"Not bad," Egorova said. "I wouldn't mind a place like this. Maybe I'll think about buying when I'm sure they're not going to bump me back to Biysk."

"Tea? A drink?" Chelomeyev asked, offering to take their coats. Egorova gave him hers, but Kazakov waved him off. The cold off those windows was going to have Egorova shivering soon enough.

Egorova had a vodka but Kazakov asked for tea. They settled in the living room area, Kazakov on one of the surprisingly comfortable chairs that seemed to conform to his backside and Egorova on the couch. Chelomeyev shifted around the miniscule kitchen and then brought their refreshments back to them with a vodka bottle and three glasses in case Kazakov changed his mind.

"What's that?" Egorova tipped her head to where a map had been taped over a picture hung on one of the room's brick walls.

Chelomeyev knocked back his vodka and licked his lips. "I couldn't very well just sit here at home, could I? I decided to map out the places Anna Konstantinova visited." He poured himself another drink and went to the map. Egorova stood and followed him. Kazakov heaved himself up out of the chair and realized that he was getting overly warm in his coat. He left his tea and went to the map of New Moscow. Chelomeyev had placed black dots to mark Anna's errands.

The trouble was, Madam Sobol hadn't necessarily provided the locations visited on a specific day. Instead she'd simply provided a list of Anna's frequent errands except for the few when she could recall the date. He studied the map.

"What's it telling us?" he asked. The black dots looked like a scattershot across the shopping areas of the city, with the one anomaly being the dot of Kasimir Krupin's home, which sat a good distance inside a residential area.

"Most of her errands are not too far from Madam Sobol's home," Chelomeyev said, tapping his finger on a red dot placed over the address of the woman's home/office.

"Looked at like this, Anna really went a long way away from her usual areas in order to visit the Krupins," Egorova said.

"Krupin was likely very important to Sobol. Where else would she get such good information without the greater world knowing? Frankly, I'm surprised that she told us." Kazakov said. Were there other sources that were more important? He glanced at Chelomeyev and Egorova. "Thoughts?"

"Places people congregate and are off their guard," Chelomeyev said.

"And where would that be?" Kazakov asked.

"Beauty parlors," Egorova said.

"Barber shops?" Chelomeyev echoed. "What about bathhouses?"

Kazakov nodded and stepped in closer to the map. "Have you got a phone book, Chelomeyev?"

The young detective retrieved one from a low bookshelf along the wall by the stairs. Kazakov flipped to the listings for barber shops and started checking the addresses. "There are a couple here near some of the stops on Sobol's list."

He flipped to the beauty parlor listings and ran his fingers down those. "A few more here, too."

He closed the phone book and turned to Chelomeyev. "Good work with the mapping. I'd like you to carry on with this, noting barber shops, beauty parlors, bathhouses, and anything else that might gather information near Anna's other stops. I wouldn't be surprised if Madam Sobol has a whole string of informants around the city. A 'counselor' such as she must keep up to date on the rumors of the city."

"But how does this get us any closer to Anna's killer?" Egorova asked.

He frowned. "Honestly? A feeling? Something was going on here and something brought Anna into the sights of her killer. We need a better sense of what she was doing, what her regular process was, and where she was going. I'd bet my badge that Madam Sobol isn't going to tell us the full story.

"Chelomeyev, I want you do the mapping here. Start with the establishments that are more likely to serve New Moscow's well-heeled residents. As you identify places, Egorova and I are going to visit those establishments and see whether they are familiar with Anna Konstantinova. The other thing I would like you to do, Chelomeyev, is to look at the businesses, etc., around the Krupin residence. Apparently Anna left the place heading west from the house toward town. What's nearby? I'll take a cruise around, but we need to get a list of addresses and occupants for the area."

"Okay…" Chelomeyev said. He looked from Egorova to Kazakov. "What am I missing? What happened this afternoon?"

"Of course!" Kazakov said, shaking his head. "We've neglected to fill you in."

He returned to his chair and finally removed his coat and loosened his tie for relief from the heat. "I don't understand how it gets so warm in here, with the windows radiating cold."

"Simple," Chelomeyev said. "In-floor heating."

The most modern of conveniences. Thus the bare feet.

Feeling chastened, Kazakov nodded to Egorova to tell the story of their little discovery and return to Kasimir Krupin's home. Unlike many people, she glossed over her part in the discovery that Krupin was only telling part of the story and focused on their follow-up interview. She pulled out her notebook and made her report quick, complete, and professional. She also filled both Chelomeyev and Kazakov in on the results of her check-backs with the businesses Anna had visited. With officers like Egorova and Chelomeyev, perhaps there was hope for the New Moscow police force.

"Wow." Chelomeyev shook his head. "Madam Sobol is a cagy woman,

I'll give you that. No wonder she can convince people that she knows things."

Something rose like a fish out of the depths of Kazakov's brain. Something was there, but then sank and was gone again. Derr'mo! These youngsters were running circles around him and suddenly he felt old and tired and probably like the older brothers of Ivan Tsarevich had felt when they discovered him sleeping with all manner of good things that they hadn't been able to achieve themselves.

He shook himself. He could understand their desperation, but he would never be desperate enough to plot to kill another human being.

He stood up, to remove himself from the thought. "We should go. We have a great deal of work to do tomorrow. Egorova, I'll give you a lift home or back to the office."

They left Chelomeyev eyeing the map and the phone book. Kazakov would put money on the youngster being up late into the night to get a head start.

Youth was like that.

5

———

Kazakov's dacha was a small, wood, one-room cabin built amid the trees in the foothills of the mountains. It had a small water closet built off the side. His bed sat against the wall across from the door, with a small couch to one side. A desk sat against another wall and a table and two chairs held prominence in the center of the room next to a wood-burning iron heater. A small kitchen of sink, cupboards, and an icebox filled one corner.

It was a cold, dark place when he woke the next morning. He disturbed Koshka, his small female black cat, from her place next to his legs on the bed. Koshka complained as he swung out of the bed, planting his feet on the cold wood plank floors. Apparently he'd banked his wood heater too far last night and the fire was almost out.

Padding the two paces from his bed to the heater, he stirred the coals, added kindling and another log, and the fire sputtered to life. When he opened the flue, the air started roaring through the chimney and warmth started radiating from the iron heater. He fed the piteously mewing Koshka a bowl of kibble from the bin he kept under the sink and set the kettle on the wood heater to boil, but couldn't bring himself to look through the cupboards for something to eat. Instead he pulled open the old floral curtains over the windows that flanked the doorway and allowed in a thin stream of pale, early morning sunlight. A pall of clouds veiled the lightening sky and muted the eastern glow of the sun on the treetops. Winter wasn't done with Fergana yet.

Sighing, he turned back to the room that was filled with the slurps and lip smacks of Koshka happily eating.

It had been a bad night. An empty vodka bottle and a single glass sat on the table. After two months of being sober, he had no idea what had set him off. Well, perhaps he did.

He felt like he was missing something, as if he was a spider with too many threads floating on the air. There were too many areas to focus on: Ascertaining Anna Konstantinova's full movements, exploring the alibis of people Madam Sobol had been gathering information on, and on Madam Sobol herself. Had Anna stumbled upon something so sensitive that she was killed before she could share the knowledge? Why was Enver Pasha once more on his radar? And what was happening with the shipping companies? Three of his last cases had involved someone transporting goods across Fergana's borders to and from China and the Ottoman Empire, and once to the small country of America. Was that relevant to this case?

And then there were the results of the search of Anna's room and the small brochure of Boris Bure's political views and events.

The water boiled and he made himself a cup of milk tea, adding his three sugars to the cup, but didn't wait for them to melt before he took a sip. If only the vodka bottle wasn't empty, he could have a pick-me-up...

Derr'mo, he was going to have to be very careful or he was going to slide into the Kazakov he'd been fighting off ever since he was shot last fall.

He slouched at the table and shoved the bottle and glass away to nurse his tea. Had the girl been politically active? He'd have to check again with Madam Sobol. Perhaps there was more that she knew. She wasn't exactly a forthcoming witness.

It was difficult with only the single source of information about the girl and, frankly, it was difficult to imagine that a pretty girl like Anna had no one in her life other than Madam Sobol. It went against everything Kazakov knew of human nature. Even he, loner that he was, had Koshka and his aging Kyrgyz neighbor, Agafya Ryabkov. And there had been Khalil Khan.

He winced at the memory of gunshots and Khan falling into darkness. His friend gone, apparently without a trace.

Three friends over a lifetime, and one of them was a cat and another was probably dead. Perhaps Anna's reported lack of friendships wasn't as unnatural as he thought—but then everyone seemed to think that *he* was unnatural.

He slurped the last of his tea and stood because this was not the time or place to become maudlin, not least because he had nothing to numb the feelings with. He washed his face and did his teeth in the sink, checked his armpits and realized that he was going to have to either visit a bathhouse or haul out his tub and heat water for a bath in the next day or two.

He pulled on clean underwear and a shirt and then retrieved his suit from where he'd left it draped over the couch. His shoulder holster went under his jacket. Then he hauled on his coat still with the bulge of the sensitive papers he dared not leave elsewhere, pulled on his boots against snow that the pall over the sun foretold, tamped back the heater vents, and gave Koshka a pat. The little cat meowed and head-butted his hand.

"I will be back late again. Perhaps I'll bring you something special." He could do some shopping and bring Agafya some supplies, too. It had been a week since he last checked on his elderly neighbor.

Then he stepped out into the cold and inhaled ice down his throat before stepping down the four stairs to his sloping front yard.

The dacha sat surrounded by a front space that in summer was his garden, and by walnut trees and white spruce that spread down from the mountains to surround Kazakov's dacha. It was one of only two residences on this road that had fulltime residents, Agafya Ryabkov being the other. Other, more expansive and more expensive dachas had been built farther up the mountain road, but they were mainly used during the summer or perhaps on holidays.

Kazakov followed the well-worn path through the aging snow around the dacha to where the Perseus was parked in the meager shelter the dacha provided. He climbed in and inhaled the cold as he turned the key. The engine groaned, but then turned over and sparked to life. Kazakov sat there with the cold air blowing from the heater until he began to feel heat. Then he backed out and rolled down the driveway under the shelter of the spruce, aspens, and walnut trees that spread silhouetted branches over the lowering sky.

The main road was plowed and he'd dug out the entrance to his driveway and Agafya's days ago when the weather cleared. Most of the time he left the huge snowplowed banks un-shoveled to discourage visitors. Sometimes it even worked, though the people he *really* didn't want to visit still seemed to find their way.

Down the hill, the Perseus left the trees behind and crossed a steppe of open grasslands. Some spots actually showed bare brown patches through the snow. Farther down, the creep of New Moscow housing spread its fingers onto the steppe with unnaturally neat subdivisions of identical houses. Election signs were posted on too many front yards, Boris Bure's overlarge smile staring out at Kazakov. He averted his gaze and focused on the road as he wound down into the city to Suvarov Way.

The broad boulevard led directly into the heart of the city, but Kazakov turned away toward Our Lady Yekaterina hospital and the M.E.'s offices. It would be the first time he'd been back since Khan was gone.

The forefathers who had built the hospital had graced the building with a small park, separated from the building by the parking lot. At this hour of the morning, the lot was a sheet of corrugated ice. The park was a lovely copse of barren trees that languished around a huge pile of salt- and debris-filled snow pushed up by the plow. In the summer a small fountain played in the trees, but at this time of year, everything was still frozen.

The hospital building was a utilitarian cement block, a four-story building with wide front stairs leading to broad glass doors. Kazakov parked the Perseus but turned away from the main entrance, heading for a set of stairs halfway down the side of the building. The concrete stairs led down one flight to a narrow door that opened under Kazakov's push. It gave into a small, institutional green waiting area with worn plastic chairs that Kazakov had never seen used, and a high counter that separated the waiting area from the unpleasant woman they had on reception. She was young, brown-haired, and wore blouses buttoned up to her chin and under cardigan sweaters. Khan had been certain she had been placed in the position to spy on him. But why spy on a lowly M.E.?

She looked up brightly as he stepped through the door, but her mouth turned down in a moue.

He went up to the counter. "Detektiv Kazakov for M.E. Gordiev."

"He may not be available," the receptionist said. "He is a busy man." Said as if she was enjoying a potential triumph.

"Please tell M.E. Gordiev that I am here for his insights about the body recovered yesterday."

The woman nodded but didn't pick up the phone.

"Now, please." Kazakov worked to remain pleasant.

The woman made the call, uh-huhed, hung up abruptly, and smiled up at him. "He says he is very busy. Perhaps you can come back this afternoon. He may be able to fit you in then."

Kazakov felt the frustration and loss of Khan and an empty stomach. He placed his hands flat on the counter and leaned toward her. "How about you call M.E. Gordiev back and I will talk to him."

"Are you threatening me?" she asked, wide-eyed.

Perhaps he was. He pulled back a little. "Please. Make the call?"

She picked up the phone and dialed the number, then stabbed the handpiece at Kazakov.

He accepted it and heard the ring at the other end of the line.

"What is it now?" Gordiev's rough voice came over the phone. "Tell that damned detective that hell will freeze over before I'll get that report done if he doesn't come back later."

"Tell him yourself," Kazakov said.

There was silence on the phone for a moment. "Kazakov?"

"The same damned detective."

"You heard that, then."

"Hard to miss."

Gordiev's sigh came across the phone. "Come through. I can give you two minutes."

Kazakov handed the woman back her phone and headed through the door beside the counter that led back to the M.E. offices and the autopsy rooms. It felt strange to walk past Khan's office. From what he saw through the office's open door, Khan's massive collection of medical literature was gone.

Gordiev's office was farther down the hall, where he was less likely to be disturbed by anything happening in the front office. The door was closed, but through the frosted half-glass there was movement.

Kazakov knocked once.

"Come."

Kazakov stepped inside and closed the door behind him.

It was a very different office than Khan's. The expansive bookshelves behind the desk had a bare two feet of medical tomes. The rest was taken up with photographs of family members, various children's athletic trophies and framed children's artwork, and something that looked like it might be a firebird and might have been painted by an adult of marginal talent. Then again, it could have been a rooster.

"You really are a pain in the ass, you know," Gordiev set down his pen and pushed his chair back from a black desk with a pristine, clean top and a single file spread open.

"Khan had come to realize it was part of my charm," Kazakov said and slid into the chair in front of Gordiev's desk. "Don't let me take up more of your time than I should. I just want to know what you found with the girl, Anna Konstantinova."

Gordiev shook his head. "I just had her on the table this morning. Tests aren't complete yet. It appears to be a simple case of a broken neck. Her killer likely took her by surprise."

Kazakov thought about it. "So, there would have been a fair bit of violence unless the killer was a professional. Such a killing is about the farthest thing from something gentle. Was there bruising? Any skin or hair under her nails?"

"I know my business, detective." Gordiev's expression narrowed on Kazakov. "No there was not anything unusual about bruising. Of course, bruising could be somewhat hidden by the livor mortis. The girl had been dead for a while."

"How long?" Kazakov asked.

"Two days. Three tops, as I told you." Gordiev looked at the documents on his desk. "I really do have a lot to do…"

"You were going to get me a more accurate time of death," Kazakov reminded the M.E. "And was there anything under her nails?"

"Nothing. Nothing at all. As if she had just washed her hands."

"Or had them washed for her? Could she have been moved?"

Gordiev rolled his eyes. "Of course, she could have been moved! But I'm no clairvoyant. For all I know, she could have lain still and let them kill her. Now can I please get back to this report?" He nodded down at his desk.

Kazakov sighed and stood up. "Thank you for your time. I would appreciate receiving your report with a detailed time of death, an assessment of her injuries, information on what she'd eaten or drunk, and toxicology screen results by end of business tomorrow at the latest." He turned toward the door.

"A tox screen! Why the hell waste the resources?"

At the door, Kazakov turned back to the seated M.E. "Because you're telling me that this girl was killed in a violent manner and yet she has none of the bruising that someone fighting for their life should have. Either she had given up and decided to die, or it seems possible she was drugged. I want to know which. As for the other details, Khalil Khan showed me many times that rigor in assessing the evidence is an asset to solving the case. In this case—a case linked to many powerful people—the only confirmed physical evidence we have is Anna Konstantinova's body." He nodded, almost embarrassed at his fabrication of the powerful people, but given Rostoff's concern about the case, it was a reasonable deduction. "Thank you very much for your time, Dr. Gordiev."

He stepped out to the hall and pulled the door shut, hearing the low oath of displeasure behind him. He headed out of the M.E.'s offices smiling. He had been polite. Now he had to hope that a polite Kazakov could get the information he needed. He could picture Khalil Khan laughing at Kazakov's transformation.

At the office he found Egorova waiting. Today she wore a long camel-colored coat and tall brown boots that made her legs seem longer in her slim-legged trousers.

"You have a good night?" Kazakov asked as he took off his coat and draped it over the side of his desk.

She nodded. "Dabria and her friends and I went out to a club. I shouldn't have stayed out as late as I did, but I'll make an early night of it tonight."

Kazakov cocked a brow at her. "In this job, it's hard to make plans like that. Let's hope we finish early." He glanced as his phone. "Any word from Chelomeyev?"

Egorova smiled and lay a quarter-inch thick sheaf of paper on the desk. "He came over with this but looked gray as old laundry. I sent him home. I hope that's okay. I think he was up all night."

"Could be." He pulled the papers closer, pulled on his reading glasses, and nodded to Egorova to pull up a chair. Together they started flipping through the document.

Chelomeyev, bless him, had definitely been up all night. He had not only done the research into the more expensive barber shops, beauty parlors, and bath houses, he had organized the information by errand location with estimations of the distance from the errand location.

"I guess we'd better split up to take these on," Egorova said.

Kazakov flipped through the list. The trouble was, following up on all these places of business felt like busy work. There was something he wasn't seeing. Finally, he shoved Chelomeyev's work away.

"I think… I think that before we use our time this way, perhaps we should interview the people that Madam Sobol was apparently researching. Find out whether they were clients and whether they knew Anna. We can ask what they knew of her."

Egorova nodded slowly. "Maybe Chelomeyev can get started with checking the premises when he's had a few hours of sleep."

"Good idea. We can phone him in a few hours. In the meantime," he checked his watch. "In the meantime, I know an Ottoman spy we want to talk to."

They both grabbed their coats and Kazakov took the sheaf of names with them. Down in the parking garage, Egorova signed out a police sedan and Kazakov let her drive as they left the station. He gave her a few directions, but she clearly had already studied the city's layout. They cruised over the old stone bridge at one end of Yekaterina Park and entered the expensive enclave of houses beyond.

Yekaterina Park was a broad swath of grass and trees that had a winding concrete path that was used in the summer. In the winter and early spring, the park was mostly abandoned, first to the snow and wind and then to the mud and struggling grass. On the outside of the park ran a crescent street, with the park on one side and on the other, huge three- and four-story mansions that housed a number of New Moscow's wealthy along with the city's highest-end brothel. That establishment had also been a front for a Chinese spy ring and was situated next door to the columned house that was the New Moscow home of Enver Pasha.

Egorova pulled into the curb and scanned the house. "Nice place."

"It is indeed, and he has all the creature comforts including an Amazon warrior as his security guard." Kazakov shook his head recalling the blonde-haired woman he had first met at the house. She had appeared demure, but had been anything but.

"You mean Marta?" Egorova asked. "You think she made it out of the mountains with Enver? What makes you think he'll even see us?"

"I meant his first housekeeper, Olga," he said putting air-quotes around housekeeper. "I was doing some figuring: if he was thirty-something when he quelled the Egyptian rebellion, he's in his late sixties now. Hard to believe, given how he looks and acts. I think he'll see us because he deserted us in the mountains. He's a soldier, or he used to be. And given he saw action as a young man he understands about owing someone. Besides, he's a spy. He'll want to know what we're up to."

Egorova looked dubious, but she opened her door and climbed out. Kazakov did the same, and even with the pall of clouds, inhaled air warmed by unseasonable spring sunshine; but beyond the turreted and laced roofline in the distance, thicker clouds smothered the peaks of the

Pamir Alay Mountains. Another storm was coming. He felt the promising electricity in the air. This would be a big one.

Together, they climbed the long flight of stairs to the front door. To either side stood whitewashed pillars. A lace curtain stirred in the parlor to the right of the stairs, but he couldn't see who it was. Then the rattle of a door chain preceded the door being pulled open.

Marta, Enver Pasha's latest housekeeper and security chief, faced them. She was a tall woman with olive skin and black hair pulled back in an attractive bun at the nape of her neck. She wore a slim-fitting, navy-blue dress that showed off her athleticism with each inhale and exhale, each slight adjustment of position. Her dark gaze flicked over Kazakov and Egorova and her shoulders sank slightly into preparedness. Her lips curved in what passed for a smile as she inclined her head to them.

"Detektivs. It is good to see you again." Even in her throaty voice, her chill tone was anything but welcoming. Beyond her were the gleaming wood walls of the foyer and the curving rise of stairs that led to the broad balcony of the second floor.

"I'm glad to see you made it out alive," Kazakov said. Egorova said nothing. "I trust that your employer survived as well?"

A slight nod was all his question received.

"We are involved in an investigation, and for some reason, your employer's name has come up again. Is he here?"

Kazakov was pretty sure that he was. Enver might put in long hours working at his office, but he also enjoyed his creature comforts, and a leisurely start to the day had replaced the rigors of soldiering—or spying.

Marta's expression gave every sign that she was going to deny that Enver was at home, but a soft pad of feet came from beyond her. Enver Pasha appeared on the second-floor balcony clad in camel-colored trousers and a red polo shirt.

"Kazakov! Egorova! How good of you to come!" As if he had invited them. Enver started down the curving stairs, his footfall swallowed by the soft black moccasins on his feet. He crossed the foyer and caught Kazakov's hand and shook, then repeated the gesture with an impassive Egorova.

"I wondered when I would see you again. I was worried that something ill had befallen you in the mountains, but then I heard about that doctor of yours. A shame. A real shame." He shook his head. "To think I liked him."

For all that his military history indicated Enver Pasha was well in the latter years of his sixth decade, he appeared in the blossom of his virile life. Thick dark hair covered his head. A full moustache separated his hawk nose from a sensuous mouth, both of which bespoke the man's character. He loved women and promoted Ottoman interests by any means possible—or at least that was what Kazakov suspected, regardless of Enver's protests that he was nothing but a businessman.

His subversive but unproveable actions in Fergana had tried to incite a Tribal rebellion and had helped bring about the downfall of Khalil Khan. Kazakov wasn't afraid of assigning blame, but he inhaled and tried to put aside his anger. Khan had made his own choices. This was business. This was an investigation. If Enver was implicated, Kazakov would arrest and charge him with pleasure.

"Khan's loss was a loss for all the people of Fergana. They just don't realize it yet."

A puzzled light filled Enver's gaze.

"He did a lot to keep cooler heads prevailing," Kazakov said. "Not exactly a lot of that going on these days."

"As I said. A loss." Enver rubbed his long-fingered hands together. "Now what can I do for you? The two of you on my doorstep suggests this is a business meeting."

"Police business," Egorova allowed.

"I see. Very important, then." Enver sent a mocking smile in her direction as he turned to Marta. "Tea, please, Marta. We'll take it in the parlor."

The parlor Kazakov had last sat in for another murder investigation.

Enver motioned Kazakov and Egorova to follow, but neither he nor Marta offered to take their coats. This was hospitality for show, and probably because Enver wished to know what they were up to. The man might own a transport company and other subsidiaries, but really his stock-in-trade was information.

He settled himself in a large wingback chair that reminded Kazakov of Madam Sobol's throne. It sat next to a huge marble fireplace that burned without apparently giving off any heat. Kazakov settled on a brocade couch, Egorova beside him, and he thought of the firebird in Chelomeyev's fairy tale. He thought of familial love that was so cold it allowed fratricide. That was Enver Pasha and this room of cream wallpaper and brocade furniture.

"Now what can I do for you?" Enver leaned back in his chair, one leg crossed across the other knee.

"As my partner said, we are here on an investigation. A young woman named Anna Konstantinova was found murdered in the home of a woman named Magdalena Sobol."

Enver's face remained impassive. Then he lifted a brow. "And you come to me why?"

"Tell me what you know of these women," Kazakov asked.

"Am I a suspect?" Enver asked. "Why is it, every time someone dies in New Moscow, you come to question me?"

Kazakov had to smile. "Perhaps it has something to do with your sideshow of spying for your government."

Enver shrugged. "There is that."

"Do you know, or have you had any association with, either of these women?" Kazakov asked.

"My, you do have to cut to the chase, Detektiv. Not even pleasantries while we have our tea?"

As if on cue, Marta arrived with a brass tray laden with a green celadon tea set. She set it down on the coffee table between them and poured, holding the tall teapot high above the cups so that the tea would aerate as it was poured. Then she carefully passed cups to Enver, Egorova, and Kazakov.

"Thank you, Marta. That will be all." Enver sipped his tea and eyed them over the rim of his pale green cup. He set the cup down with a sigh. "I see by your evil eye that you are not about to enjoy your tea without me being forthcoming with information." He shook his head.

"I know of Madam Sobol. Her reputation is large, both here in New Moscow and abroad. My wife asked me to consult her on a family matter and so I did so. That house of hers…" He shuddered lightly—probably for show.

"Tell me about that," Kazakov asked. Egorova had already set down her cup—untouched—and pulled out her notebook and pen.

Enver glanced at her. "It was about two months ago—about the time we met in Biysk. I tried to send someone else with the request for information, but Madam Sobol refused to do business that way. I was forced to attend her residence." A shake of his head. "We set an appointment and I went. She sat me in that horrid room of hers and proceeded to give me a reading—all fabrications, you understand. I told my wife not to bother, but she insisted; and so Madam Sobol was to send her readings to me for forwarding on."

Which meant that Anna Konstantinova had likely come to this house.

"And the reading? What did it say that were fabrications?"

Enver shifted in his seat. "You're asking me to remember made-up lies? I am a busy man. I put them out of my mind immediately."

Kazakov just studied Enver and waited. The Ottoman flushed slightly. He knew what Kazakov was doing, because he did the same from his office "throne room," waiting for the other person's will to crumble.

Enver finally shook his head. "Fine. It doesn't matter. There were silly things about aspirations of grandeur. Great works that were even now coming to fruition—and would fail. I mean, what is that? I run a trucking firm. I am happy, wealthy, well married, and connected. Why would I need more?"

A good question, but Enver was not a man who ever seemed content with the status quo. It raised the question of exactly why Enver was here when his wife and family were elsewhere in the Ottoman Empire.

"You tell me," Kazakov said. He was not about to get into answering Enver's questions.

"The short answer is that I do not, though liars might tell tales that I aspire to something greater in the Empire." He grabbed his teacup so abruptly that liquid slopped over the top and he stared at the result as if fascinated. Then he inhaled a great breath and suddenly appeared calm again. Kazakov had lost his chance to get further candid answers.

"Tell me more about the visit," Kazakov asked.

Enver rolled his eyes. "What is there to say? I arrived by car. I pulled up out front and went inside. They took my coat and ushered me into that room where Madam Sobol proceeded to give me her reading. She asked for an item that my wife had also handled. I provided a scarf that she had worn on our wedding day. She held it in the palm of her hand, closed her eyes, and her voice changed as if there was someone else speaking through her—she says it is her spirit guide—someone named Ibrahim. It was this Ibrahim who spoke the lies."

Kazakov thought a moment.

"What did she tell your wife?" Egorova asked softly.

Enver's gaze flickered between them. Then he licked his lips. "Another lie. That we would never be reunited."

Strain lines had formed around the outer edges of Enver's eyes as if the man was not the master, but the slave trying valiantly to save himself.

An odd thought and one Kazakov filed away for further consideration even though it made no sense.

"How did that make you feel?" Egorova asked.

"Feel?" Enver spat out a laugh. "I felt like hell. Is that what you wanted to hear? I was furious. I left the place as swiftly as I could and have not been back!"

"Anna Konstantinova." Kazakov took back the interview. "Was she the one who took your coat for you?"

"Young, blonde, pretty?" Enver asked.

Kazakov nodded.

"Then, yes. It was her. And before you ask, yes, it was her who brought more lies to my door for me to send to poison my wife." He slumped back in his chair as if spent.

Kazakov sipped his cup of tea—bitter and fragrant with tannins and flowers. He hadn't tasted its like before. "I am surprised you would send them on," he said.

Enver's slow smile spread across his face. "We are so alike, Detektiv. In better times I think we could be friends. But you are right. I did not send them as they were. I read and edited them. It is better not to pollute the waters that you drink from."

"Rumi?" Kazakov asked if the saying was from the great Sufi poet.

"Enver Pasha," the Ottoman smiled and checked his watch. Then he stretched and stood. "I am afraid that is all the time I have, Detektiv. Anything else must wait another day."

"One more question, please." Kazakov stood with him. "When was the last time you saw Anna Konstantinova?"

Enver thought a moment. "See her? I perhaps caught a glimpse of her a month ago. The last time she came to the house, she left her sealed envelope with Marta. That would have been… last week, I believe. Marta can give you more details."

At the mention of her name, Marta appeared by the door as if waiting for Kazakov and Egorova to join her. Enver half-bowed and abandoned them for the foyer, leaving them under Marta's inscrutable gaze.

"What is it that you need?" Her voice was deep and throaty as she eyed them.

"We are investigating the death of a young woman who apparently visited your home. Her name was Anna Konstantinova. She worked for Madam Sobol. Apparently she came to deliver something to Enver a number of times."

Small lines appeared above Marta's lips as they tightened. She was not as young as she normally appeared.

"Do you recall the dates that she came by?"

Marta's dark gaze met his. Finally, she nodded. "A moment, please."

She retreated down the hall that ran beyond the stairwell toward Enver's office and presumably to a kitchen. She returned a short time later carrying a small, leather-bound black notebook. Diary?

She flipped the pages and came to an entry. "Here."

She turned the book to him and pointed to an entry dated two days before Anna was found dead. "She was here then."

"And before?"

Marta flipped the pages back in time. Many pages. She must record every interaction of the household members. An interesting book to get his hands on.

Marta showed him the pages twice more. "This one was another delivery, as was the last." The date was one month ago. She flipped the pages again to another entry. "This was when Madam Sobol first sent an invitation to Enver Pasha."

The date was almost a year ago.

Kazakov frowned. "Your employer made no mention…"

"He likely did not know. There are some marginal visitors that I do not brief him on."

"I see," Kazakov said, but he distinctly did not see, for Enver Pasha was not the sort of man who let any small detail go unnoticed.

"Did Anna say anything about her actions or people she knew when she was here?"

Marta thought a moment. "I don't believe so. She explained who she was and what she wanted each time she arrived. Then she handed me an envelope and left again. She never truly stepped inside the house."

Kazakov thought about it and nodded. "When she left here, can you recall where she was going? Did she mention anything?"

"Nothing." She glanced over her shoulder as if there were places she wished to go.

"When she left the last time she was here, did you see what direction she took?"

Marta frowned. "I closed the door, but I glanced out the window. I believe I saw her heading toward the old bridge along Yekaterina Park, but she could also have visited any of the neighbors." She shrugged, but the gesture was uncharacteristic of the militaristic woman. What was she not saying? He decided to try out Egorova's question of Kasimir Krupin.

"I am going to ask you a question that may seem foolish, but I want you to answer without thinking."

She nodded.

"Where was Anna Konstantinova going?"

"To see someone she knew," she said and stopped, apparently surprised.

"Now think about what made you give that answer. What was it?"

She looked thoughtful. "It was the half-smile of her lips and the sparkle in her eyes. Anticipation, I would call it." She nodded. "A very clever questioning technique, Detektiv." But she edged them toward the door. "I believe that is all the information I have for you."

Kazakov and Egorova went out to the police sedan. He looked at her and grinned. "A very clever questioning technique, indeed."

6

———————

From the exclusive enclave of the crescent around Yekaterina Park, Kazakov had Egorova head westward out of the city. Gradually, the city center and the sprawl of warehouses and light industry fell away and they were surrounded by the rolling fields and pastures that once stretched all the way from the Kara Kum desert to the steppes of the Pamir Alay and Tian Shan mountains. The pasturelands were still covered in a layer of snow that glittered in the sunlight glare. A gray pall of cloud was spreading out from the mountains like smoke, dulling the warmth and the pleasure of the spring day.

"Where on earth are we going?" Egorova asked.

"Would you believe a local stable?"

"What?" Egorova took her eyes off the road to glance at him.

"Think about what Krupin told us. I've met the woman he was talking about on an earlier case. Hopefully she and her husband haven't already returned home to the Anglo-German Empire. Her husband's an attaché to the ambassador—or was. She's the manager of the AngloTec polo club and responsible for trucking the club's horses God-knows-where for competitions. I won't say anything more and let you judge for yourself."

Egorova looked like she chewed on his information as she guided the sedan along the highway. When Kazakov pointed out the turn, she turned off onto a long country lane that led through open countryside and they pulled into the stable's mostly empty parking lot just before 11:00 a.m. A battered small truck and an expensive-looking German sedan sat by the barn. The large horse shipping trailer Kazakov had previously searched wasn't there.

"Not much activity," Egorova said, taking in their surroundings.

"I'm betting the expensive car is Charlotte Newcomb's."

The barns of the stable were metal sided and arranged as rows along the long sides of a huge covered riding arena. He climbed out of the sedan and hooked his head toward the building. He and Egorova set out across the parking lot. The footing was treacherous. Ruts and furrows made by vehicle tires had hardened and frozen. Then the sun and warmth had slicked the ice with water. In an open paddock, a couple of blanketed polo ponies loafed in the sun.

They reached the sliding barn door and Kazakov used the smaller, human-sized door set into the middle and stepped through into warmth and the scent of horses. Manure, clean hay, the mélange of the warm-sweet scent of horse sweat and clean leather.

The polo players who had been brushing off their horses when Kazakov was last here were nowhere to be seen. From far down the row of stalls came the sound of shoveling from an open stall doorway. Cleaning the stall, most likely, but that didn't strike him as Charlotte Newcomb's job.

The door to the arena wasn't quite pulled closed and strains of a marshal German tune came through the opening. He stepped up the slope to the door and peered inside. What felt like acres of tanbark covered the floor of the indoor arena. Across the arena under the overhead lights, Charlotte Newcomb sat astride a huge, gleaming black horse that looked like it was dancing to the music even though its rider appeared to do nothing. He watched for a moment as she came around a corner and then sent the horse floating across the diagonal.

Kazakov slid the door further open and stepped inside, Egorova following behind him. His shoes sank into the tanbark. He just stood there as the black horse turned down the centerline of the arena, skipping like a happy child, and then suddenly turned to the side, pirouetting in place. Kazakov couldn't help himself. He clapped.

The black horse suddenly leapt out of the pirouette, thundering across the arena toward him. The damned horse was going to run him down if Charlotte Newcomb didn't regain control. He was about to duck back through the door when the horse came to a dead stop, four feet planted and square like a statue a bare five feet from where he stood. Charlotte Newcomb grinned down at him.

Her chestnut hair, pulled back in a ponytail, had charming flyaway strands around her lean, freckled face. Her gray-green eyes sparkled and her face was flushed. She let the reins of the black horse go loose and the animal stretched its long neck down and then out to snort at Kazakov's chest. He didn't move, for fear the animal might try to bite.

"Detektiv," Charlotte Newcomb said and slung her leg over her saddle and lightly leapt to earth. She landed in the tanbark and patted the horse's neck. "Walk with me. He needs to be cooled down a bit."

The black horse's coat was slick with sweat.

He nodded and he and Egorova walked along beside her as she led her horse.

"What can I do for you, Detektiv? Surely the case of Collin Archer's death has been solved and I had no part in it."

"Correct," he said. "But there has been another murder and your name came up."

She peered up at him, her gray-green gaze wide. "I hope I am not a suspect."

Kazakov inclined his head. "That is our challenge: we have no suspects. We are trying to establish a picture of our victim and we were hoping you might help us."

"Ye-es." But Charlotte Newcomb's voice was guarded. So was her gaze before she turned back to the horse and stroked his neck. "Who has died?" She glanced back at him.

"A young woman named Anna Konstantinova. Does the name mean anything to you?"

Charlotte blinked, frowned, and looked down at the dusty toes of her tall, lace-up boots. "I don't believe so."

"If I told you that she was an associate of Madam Magdalena Sobol, would that make a difference?" He watched her closely and saw her expression spasm briefly, but then smooth. A diplomat's wife, she clearly was.

Finally, she nodded. "That witch. I know her." Her tone was bitter.

"Tell me about it," he asked.

She glanced at him, then quickened her pace as if she did not want him seeing her face. Then she sighed and slowed for him to catch up. "I had not met her until recently. I was in town at a function with my husband when this woman suddenly appeared, clad in a plain black dress and too many scarves. She wore too much makeup and too many rings, like some kind of carnival worker, and yet there she was at a function sponsored by the Boris Bure campaign—horrible man, by the way. Fish eyes, cold hands." She shook her head.

"Anyway, this woman appears and won't leave my elbow. She introduces herself as Madam Sobol and tells me that I have serious troubles and that perhaps she can help me. At that moment I was in a bit of a pickle and that got me to listen to her. She offered to help me, but her 'help'..." she placed quotation marks around the word with her fingers, "but her help was to offer me counsel. She gave me her card and offered me a free reading. I said I wasn't interested and gave her back her card."

Another shake of her head as they rounded the arena for the second time. Egorova was madly writing.

"She remained quite insistent, saying that I could avert tragedy if I would only listen, but I was of no mind to be taken in by some counselor-charlatan. That is all I know." She looked up at him again, her gaze clear of all guile.

And he was pretty sure she was lying.

"So how did you rid yourself of her?" he asked.

She shook her head. "I inserted myself into another conversation and turned my back on her—quite rudely if the truth be told—but I wasn't going to have my evening ruined by someone like that. I saw her later hanging on the Ambassador's wife like a leach, but the old lady didn't seem to mind."

"You mentioned that she warned you of a tragedy. Do you have any idea what tragedy she was referring to?" he asked.

Her clear gaze suddenly turned hazy and she looked away. "If you must know, I was pregnant at the time and not long afterward I had a fall off my horse. This horse. I miscarried. That is all that I can think of it being."

Without warning she turned the horse across the arena and headed for the door. Kazakov stopped and Egorova came up beside him.

"That touched a nerve," Egorova said softly as Charlotte Newcomb rolled the arena door open and led the massive black horse out to the stable.

"And she didn't even mention that trouble at the border that Krupin told us about," Kazakov said. He sighed and set off after Charlotte Newcomb. There were still things to talk about.

In the breezeway between the two rows of stalls, Charlotte Newcomb had unbridled and haltered the horse's head to ties from each wall as she unsaddled the animal and brushed his back. Kazakov and Egorova stood back and let Charlotte center herself. When she had brushed the animal down, she turned him into a stall and turned back to them. "Carl!" she called. "Can you clean off my tack for me, please. I'm tied up with the detectives."

"Carl" was apparently a gray-haired fellow who stuck his head out of a stall farther down the row. He nodded and she closed and latched the black horse's stall and then turned to Kazakov. "I could use a drink. Come on."

She led them up the hollow stairs that led to the viewing lounge at one end of the indoor arena. The lounge had one glass wall that looked out onto the now-empty arena, and was filled with lounge chairs and tables. Along one wall was a gleaming wood bar that Charlotte Newcomb slipped behind. She pulled out a bottle of vodka and poured herself two fingers and offered a drink to Egorova and Kazakov. Both declined.

Charlotte drank her drink in one gulp and poured again. Then she screwed the top back on and took her drink to one of the chairs where she sat, booted legs outstretched, and sipped. "Sorry. Hair of the dog and all that. Discussing my recent misfortune kind of ruins me for the day." Her voice was throaty with emotion.

Kazakov sat down in one of the low chairs to face her. "Then I'm sorry to have to discuss this. It's come to our attention that you may have been involved in some difficulties at the border. Can you tell me anything about this?"

Her body went rigid. Her face went white. She abruptly stood up and went to the broad window. Beyond, someone turned out the indoor arena lights and she was left, her slim form in boots and breeches, reflected back by the darkness. She downed her second vodka.

"Jeezus. Jeezus, jeezus, jeezus." She turned back to them, white-faced. "I thought that was dealt with. If this gets out any further, my husband will be finished. He's already being recalled to London."

Kazakov and Egorova glanced at each other.

"So the rumor is true?" Kazakov asked.

"Rumor? There is a rumor?" Panic flooded across Charlotte Newcomb's features.

Taking pity on her, Kazakov shook his head. "Perhaps rumor is a poor choice of words. A reputable source had been asked to do research on you and had found the information. Tell me, Mrs. Newcomb, what made you think the matter was dealt with?"

Wringing her hands, she paced the breadth of the broad window onto the arena. "My husband… he used his connections to smooth the whole thing over and keep it quiet. He was furious. He threatened to leave me in custody and let me rot. Then he threatened to send me home alone. We settled on me limiting my travels with the horses during the remaining time we are here. For the time being we will rent transport." She scrubbed at her face and returned to her chair. "Who was doing this 'research'? Who would bring this up again?"

"I am not at liberty to say, other than it is a reputable source." He thought a moment. "Has Madam Sobol ever contacted you again since your meeting at the event?"

Charlotte Newcomb's gaze steadied on him. "It's her. It's her, isn't it? She's spreading rumors."

"Please answer the question."

Her gaze steadied. "Yes. If you must know, yes. About a month ago she sent hand-delivered correspondence to my residence inviting me to her house for a complimentary reading. I was still dealing with the aftermath of my miscarriage and all the guilt that came with that. I did not bother replying."

Egorova's pen scratched softly on her notepad.

"Did you receive her messenger personally?" Kazakov asked.

Sighing, she shook her head, her wringing hands between her knees, no longer the mistress of all she surveyed. Now she was simply a worried woman. "In fact, I did. I don't usually, but there was something about my housekeeper when she brought the message that there was someone at the door. I decided to see who it was for myself. A young blonde woman. Pretty in a rather dowdy way. She handed me the envelope and said that Madam Sobol sent her greetings and would like to meet with me. I didn't bother opening the invitation—simply handed it back to the blonde and sent her on her way."

"What did she say or do when you returned the envelope unopened?"

Two deep lines formed between Charlotte Newcomb's shaped brows. "She said, 'Be it on your head, then.'" Her eyes widened. "She was threatening! Oh dear, and here I thought it was simply that Madam Sobol would wash her hands of me. She's been spreading rumors about me, hasn't she? I'll sue. I will."

The worry had been buried in Charlotte Newcomb's outrage. She stood. She paced again. Then she whirled to face him. "Well? What are you going to do about it?" She stood, hands on hips, feet shoulder-wide apart.

"I suppose I could consider how angry you are as a motive for murder. You could have thought that you were going to find Madam Sobol alone and ended up killing Anna Konstantinova by mistake." He studied her face, saw the horror and then the defeat setting in. "But that is only a theory based on your reaction."

He hauled out a photo of Anna to be certain. "This is the girl you had at your door delivering Madam Sobol's message?"

Charlotte Newcombe nodded.

"Think carefully. Did you ever see Anna Konstantinova again?"

She shook her head. "No. Never."

Then she paused and a faraway look crossed her gaze. "No. Wait. Maybe it's something, or maybe it's not, but once I thought I saw her when I was in town. When I did, I crossed the street rather than run into her. But I only saw her from the back. Maybe it wasn't even her."

"And where was this?" Kazakov asked. Egorova's writing had paused.

"Outside the New Moscow library. She was just coming out with an envelope in her hand. Then she crossed the street and ducked into the Royal Caravanserai. You can imagine my horror. I thought she might come and speak to me again."

The Royal Caravanserai was the premier New Moscow hotel, named after the lodgings found along the silk road but with all the opulence that money could buy—unlike its utilitarian namesake. The information set off a chord in his brain. Something was shaking loose. Something was coming.

He met Egorova's patient gaze. "Anything else?"

She nodded. "When was it that you thought you saw Anna?" Egorova asked.

Charlotte Newcomb shook her head. "Perhaps a week after she came to my house? Yes, I think that is right. So about two weeks ago." She glanced at her watch. "Is there anything else? I really need to be going. My husband has a reception to attend, and since the border fiasco, I have to attend—all of them." Her lips curled in distaste.

Kazakov rose and nodded down at Charlotte Newcomb. She looked smaller than he'd remembered, her sexual magnetism all but eroded by tension and fatigue. "Thank you for your time. We may need to ask you some follow-up questions. Please don't leave New Moscow without contacting me."

He nodded at Egorova, who had packed her notes away, and they clumped down the wooden stairway to the stable. The sound of shoveling had ceased. Through the quiet of horses contentedly munching grain came the soft sound of weeping through the floorboards above them.

Kazakov stepped out of the narrow, human-sized door with the realization that people like Charlotte Newcomb would be hard-pressed to fit through the large sliding stable door behind him. Their problems were just too large.

T he afternoon was well advanced as they climbed back into their vehicle. Clouds off the mountains were erasing the blue sky and the sun had turned sullen. The wind carried a chill that had caused Egorova to button up her coat. The bite of cold had put rosettes in her cheeks as she started the vehicle.

"Thoughts?" he asked as she backed the sedan up and then started out, crunching across the uneven parking lot toward the lane. The snow-covered fields spread away from them in all directions.

"Not a very happy woman," Egorova said thoughtfully. "She's lost a lot. A child. Her freedom. Perhaps the love of her husband—if she ever had it. You know what we forgot to ask her? What she was doing in town the day she thought she saw Anna."

"A good point," Kazakov agreed.

"Her emotional responses show capacity for great passion. Anna could have crossed her somehow…"

Kazakov nodded. "A possibility, but I think something else came out of today's interviews. Both Enver and Charlotte Newcomb had motive that could have led them to kill, but I have to ask myself, why kill Anna? It does not make sense. Madam Sobol dead would make sense."

Egorova pursed her lips. "Mistaken identity?"

"Another possibility."

She looked heavenward as she sped up down the long laneway back to the highway. "Another possibility—just what we need. So we make enquiries at the Royal Caravanserai?"

"And the library."

Egorova glanced at him. "Your old friend, Dedushka?"

Kazakov smiled. "Who else? We start with him first."

The old man everyone called Dedushka was named Artyom Shepovalov. He was an ancient periodicals librarian, apparently with a close to eidetic memory, though he made those who came to him do their own research. He had played a role in a number of Kazakov's other investigations and claimed that he had known Kazakov's mother, though Kazakov could not recall the man from when he was a small boy.

The New Moscow central library sat in an old brick edifice downtown. By the time they reached it, it was nearing four thirty and Kazakov feared that they might miss the old man. The period of warm weather had worked wonders on the massive snowdrifts left along the curb over the winter, so it was easier to find a parking spot close to their destination, but the cold snap had crusted the remaining snow with a half-inch rind. The sidewalks were slick with frozen runoff. They slip-slid their way to the library main doors and inside into the scent of dust and age. The place was hushed as usual. The high, cream-colored ceilings were lit by lights strategically hidden in carved cherubim. Shelves of books divided the front desk area from student desks and tables that filled the rear of the main hall. Two fresh-faced librarians at the front desk gave them the evil eye and one of them pointedly checked her watch as Kazakov led Egorova toward the periodicals section housed in an adjoining hall.

The door to the room was blocked by a black wire gate. A closed sign hung askew on the wire.

Kazakov turned back for the front desk and the two young women, one blonde, one brunette. Both looked to be in their midtwenties with blunt-cut, shoulder-length hair and bangs. They wore sweater sets that could have been worn by women twice their age—a uniform requirement, perhaps, but their skirts had inched their way well up past their knees in the latest, controversial, style.

"Excuse me. Dedushka—Artyom Shepovalov—when will he be back?"

"He won't be," the blonde said as she sorted through a pile of books. "He retired." And by her tone it was no loss that he was gone.

That he was gone was a surprise. That he had retired, more so. "I thought he'd have to be carried out of here," he said.

"Well, that was the problem, wasn't it," the brunette said as she stamped books as returned and readied them for reshelving. "He just couldn't change with the times. They're going to digitize the periodicals and he didn't even know how to turn on a data machine."

"So he decided to retire?" Kazakov asked.

The blonde shrugged as she studied a book cover and decided where to stack it. "Not exactly. There's so few people coming into the periodical section these days that management decided they could close it as a cost saving measure. They'll reopen when it's digitized." She smiled as if she enjoyed the taste of the word.

"Better that old man retire than have one of us let go. At least he gets a pension," the brunette said.

A pension and empty hours to fill. The newspapers had been Artyom's life—his children.

Kazakov pulled out the photo of Anna Konstantinova and showed it to the librarians. "Have you ever seen this woman? She was known to come into the library."

Both of the women left their books and studied the photo. The brunette shook her head, no. The blonde, however, leaned in closer and frowned.

"I think… maybe. A lot of people come in here, you know, and we certainly can't remember everyone, but she was in a few times and I always thought it was such a shame. She was so pretty, but she always dressed so dowdy. You know what I mean? Those awful, knee-length floral dresses like my grandmother always wears. I tell you, no one is going to notice you if you look like that. Remember, Nadia? I pointed her out."

The brunette took a second look. "Maybe. I can't be sure."

"Well, I think it's her. She'd come in and head—hey—to the periodical section. Maybe you should speak to Dedushka."

He glimpsed Egorova roll her eyes, but Kazakov held his peace. "Can you tell me where I might get in touch with him?"

"Nadia?" The blonde said. "Don't you have the information on employees?"

The brunette went to a battered wood desk behind the counter and pulled out the tall bottom drawer. She rummaged through files and finally came up, triumphant, with a fat file. This she laid on her desk and rifled through, eventually coming up with a single sheet of paper.

"Here it is. I guess I need to send it upstairs to the office so he gets his pension." She lay the sheet on the counter for Kazakov to read. It was a payment form that held basic information about the old man. Name, date of birth, address, phone number, and year of employment. An empty space remained for the date he left library service.

Kazakov noted down Artyom Shepovalov's address and phone number. "When was the decision made about Dedushka's section?" he asked.

"Last week. It was pretty sudden in library terms. They must have been thinking about it for a while," the brunette said.

Since Anna was seen here and just before she died.

"And what does this mean?" He tapped the paper where a bright red Asterix sat beside Artyom's name.

"That? Oh that's just a mark they put on files where the person worked elsewhere in government before coming to the library. You know—like maybe they were disabled in one job but could work here…"

"Any idea when the periodicals will be digitized and available?" he asked.

The blonde shrugged again. "From what I've heard, it's not a priority. Definitely not until after the election."

And if Boris Bure won, as it appeared he would do, Kazakov could imagine that the historic records of the library might be closed forever.

He thanked the two women and exited with Egorova at his heels.

Outside in the cool moist air, he looked down at the address he held and then at Egorova. Getting to Artyom felt even more important now that his periodicals were locked away from them.

"I'm thinking we split up. You check out the Royal Caravanserai and then head back to the office. Check in with Chelomeyev and see how he's coming with charting Anna's movements. We also need to get in touch with the author of the letters in the metal box we found in Anna's room. I'll go visit Artyom and meet up with you both back there."

"Sounds good," she said and handed him the car keys. Then she crunched over the snowbank and darted through traffic to the side of the street that held the great hotel with its faux stucco and clay exterior and its great iron-bound wood door. He watched her inside, the door pulled open by a burly doorman. Then he climbed in and started the sedan.

Artyom Shepovalov's address was a small apartment in an old part of New Moscow. The area was near the river, but farther west and close to the factories that belched out the smoke that often hazed New Moscow's skies. As a result, the area was home to many factory workers, canning summer produce from Fergana's fields or produce shipped across the border for the cheaper wages still to be had in Fergana. Most of the workers were the Russian lower classes, though a few tribals had braved the prejudice for better wages than could be paid anywhere in the old Kyrgyz city. The streets were lined with brick and concrete block buildings, most with small street-level shops and restaurants advertising Russian delicacies and vodka at cheaper prices than elsewhere in the city.

Men in dun-colored trousers and shirts with the sleeves rolled up, regardless of the change in the weather, loitered outside local pubs and bars, enjoying their drink and conversation in the waning sunlight. A greengrocer had plain wood crates of sorry-looking vegetables set outside his store, as he kept guard from the door against the flock of children racing down the street after a terrified cat. Who knew what they would do if they caught it.

Above the street-level bustle, most of the buildings were three or four stories with their age-hazed windows spiked with lines and braced broom handles from which hung drying laundry so the buildings' upper stories seemed to ripple with a ragged rainbow pelt.

There was very little vehicle traffic—a few delivery trucks, even fewer old rusted hulks that the owners obviously babied along. The police sedan was conspicuous enough that the drinkers outside the bars turned to follow the sedan down the street. The children stopped stalking the cat to watch him pass by.

At Artyom's address he pulled into the curb and climbed out to stare up at the building. The bricks and concrete were crumbling and the windows looked small. Only a few of the windows were cluttered with laundry, but that suggested that the other residents cared less about the cleanliness of what they wore. This was where a respected civil servant was expected to live out his life?

Not for the first time, Kazakov was glad he owned the dacha. This street—this neighborhood—with its gray buildings and gray people and dearth of trees—if he was forced to live here, he would not want to live.

A child—for a moment he couldn't tell if it was a boy or girl because of the dirty curls cut close to the head—parked its body in front of him, hands on hips. "Who are you here for?"

The piping voice had to be a girl, didn't it?

"I am here to see Artyom Shepovalov. Do you know him?"

"Maybe." Blue eyes turned cagey. "Give me a ruble and I might show you where he lives."

Kazakov leaned down to the child's height, hands on his knees. "A ruble and you *might* help me? That sounds like a very bad deal for me."

The child glanced nervously aside and Kazakov glimpsed the other children huddled together, watching.

"How about you take me to Artyom Shepovalov's apartment and I give you a ruble then?" He straightened up to await her answer.

Her thin throat worked. Her trousers were cinched in around her narrow waist with a rope and her shirt hung too large on her. A waif, an urchin, but the luminosity of her skin and her large eyes said she would grow into a beauty. He wondered what she would become and knew the chances of a positive outcome were depressingly slim.

Finally, she nodded and started toward Artyom's building. That, at least, boded well for her truthfulness. The other children had vanished. She pushed open a narrow door between a butcher shop with fly-speckled carcasses hung in the window and a hardware store that sold plastic buckets and traditional straw brooms amongst the piles of other odds and ends he could see through the filthy front window.

Inside, the thick stench of urine said how the foyer was often used. A steep set of stairs led up two flights before doubling back to continue up. A narrow hallway led to the rear of the building.

The girl scurried up the stairs and Kazakov followed more slowly, but when he reached the first landing, the girl was nowhere to be seen. Instead, three of the larger children faced him, obviously having gotten into the building to wait for him. The tallest boy, with floppy brown hair, looked him up and down, a sneer on his dirty face. His dun shirt was faded and holed at the elbows, his trousers had been patched so many times Kazakov wondered whether any original material was left.

His two compatriots stood behind him, one armed with a three-foot-long piece of two-by-four lumber that he patted in his palm.

"You looking for someone?" the spokesman asked. He was maybe fourteen, his voice newly broken.

"Artyom Shepovalov. I believe your young friend was going to show me for a ruble."

"No one gets to anyone in this building without going through me." The kid drew himself straighter and tried to look menacing.

Kazakov eyed him. "So I pay you the ruble." He shrugged.

"Price has gone up. Give me your wallet."

Chuckling, Kazakov shook his head. "Now that's not going to happen, is it? Looks like we're at an impasse."

The kid stepped up to him. "Give me your wallet or I can't vouch for what might happen."

"Son," Kazakov said with a shake of his head. "It seems to me that anything that happens, I can lay it on you. Now do you want the ruble or nothing?"

Kazakov stepped forward and something hard grazed the side of his head and slammed into his right shoulder. His arm went numb. He stumbled forward. The kid with the two-by-four swung and Kazakov lunged for him. Better to get inside the swing. He did and the swing lost its power against his shoulder. The spokesman was on his back, his arm around Kazakov's neck. The two-by-four hit the back of his knees.

He stumbled, slamming the kid on his back into the wall. The kid fell off and Kazakov faced them, breathing hard. "What do you want? Me to use my gun?"

The kids looked at each other, shock on their faces. Their leader brushed dirty fingers back through his hair. "You a cop or something?"

"Yes, I'm a cop or something. Detektiv Alexander Kazakov."

Somewhere upstairs a door squeaked opened. "What's going on? What's all this noise?" demanded a querulous old voice. Artyom.

"Artyom. It's me, Kazakov. It seems your neighbors want to charge a toll for me to use the stairway."

The old man's thin figure appeared at the stairwell rail the next landing up. "Hey, you, Leyv. I see you down there and don't think I won't tell your old man what you're trying to pull, or Boris that you're working his turf. Now let the man up here or I will."

Leyv, who must be the leader, looked from Artyom to Kazakov.

"Let's get out of here. A cop probably hasn't got much anyway." Scowling, Leyv passed Kazakov for the stairs, his henchmen behind him.

Kazakov started up the stairs and found Artyom with the girl held by the arm. If anything, the old man was more wizened than the last time Kazakov had seen him only a few months ago. His face was creased with too many lines, while his almost naked pate was smooth with only a small ring of gossamer a fallen halo around his ears. He wore overlarge black trousers shiny with age and a white shirt that looked like it had been ironed within an inch of its life. A pair of thick glasses hung by a string around his neck.

He looked down at his prisoner. "This is my neighbor's daughter. What did she do?"

Kazakov used his left hand to touch his still-numb shoulder. "Lured me in. Hit me with something."

Artyom motioned at a piece of two-by-four that matched the one the boy had held below.

"That'd do it."

Artyom dragged the girl toward a door. "That's it. Get inside. You're not to go out again until your mother says you may. Understand?" The old man loomed over her and the girl nodded meekly, then ducked through the door to her mother's apartment and closed it behind her.

Kazakov dug in his pocket and pulled out a ruble. "Give it to her as a reward if she does as she's told. Remind her not to tell the others because they'll have it from her as soon as they know."

"But she hit you," Artyom protested.

"But not that hard." If she'd truly hit him hard, he was pretty certain that he'd have been on the floor and left for dead.

The old man relented and led Kazakov to his apartment.

It was a surprise after the dingy, urine-scented hallway. The halls were covered in faded floral wallpaper, but someone had clearly scrubbed it clean, though yellow patches showed in the corners and up close along the tobacco-stained ceiling. An old, pale-blue sofa filled the center of the room, its brocade upholstery worn shiny in places just like Artyom's trousers. A simple, square, wood coffee table stood in front of the sofa and to one side waited a chair of faded purple, but the wooden legs and chair arms were carved beautifully into flowers and the wood itself carried a luster that spoke of quality and age. The same quality came off the ranks of leather-bound books filling the bookshelves on both sides of the room.

A small kitchen table sat under the lone window in the room and the imperfections in the glass set rainbows across the wall by the door. Two other doors—both open—gave onto a bedroom with neatly made bed and a bathroom that looked newly scrubbed. In the corner of the main room, a small kitchenette about the size of Kazakov's dacha kitchen held a sink, a small icebox, and a single-burner electric hotplate.

Kazakov hesitated before stepping inside.

"Don't worry about your boots," Artyom said. "Cleaning this place gives me something to do. Tea?" he asked, still not asking why Kazakov was here, nor even showing surprise that he was.

Kazakov nodded and scanned the book titles. A few classic fiction titles, but most were books Kazakov had never heard of. He glanced at Artyom as the elderly man shuffled around his kitchen making tea. In this room, the man's movements whispered like moth wings. His breathing placed a low hum in the air.

"I went into the library to talk to you today. They told me you retired," Kazakov said.

Artyom stopped spooning tea into a metal tea infuser and he turned to the window. A spasm of regret crossed his features and his gaze was faraway. Then he looked at Kazakov and gave a sad smile.

"They may call it that, but really it is about getting me out of the way."

Kazakov frowned, trying to decide what Artyom meant. Getting him out of the way for younger employees to come in? Getting him out of the way because he was old? Or getting him out of the way because his care of the old periodicals coupled with his eidetic memory meant that he knew too much?

"All right," Kazakov said. "I'll ask the question: What do you mean by that?"

Artyom filled his kettle and placed it on the burner. "I mean that those documents tell too many stories that people don't want told. Those documents are our memories when we can no longer remember, or choose to believe something other than the truth. Those documents confront us with a version of reality that we aren't always willing to grasp. And now they are gone."

"Gone? What are you talking about?"

Artyom shook his head and leaned his hands on the counter as if he did not trust his legs to hold him up. "I mean that there have been trucks leaving the library. They are boxing up the periodicals and taking them elsewhere." He turned a desperate face to Kazakov. "I don't know where."

"Could they be taking them for digitizing?" Kazakov asked.

Artyom shook his head. "Impossible. The digitization process had not been finalized. We did not even have the equipment installed. I suspect we'll never see the equipment now. They've taken the papers all away. I have to believe they plan to destroy them."

The kettle boiled and Kazakov sank down onto the couch. Old springs groaned under his bulk as Artyom poured the hot water over the infuser he'd placed in a battered copper teapot. He brought the pot around to the coffee table along with a pot of honey. "Sorry. I have no milk to offer."

He settled into the purple chair and Kazakov got the sense that Artyom spent a lot of time there. That was the old man's chair. It fit his thin body, and where his hands stroked the wood, the luster had faded as if from years of such caresses. Old, yes, and part of Artyom's history. Part of who he was.

Artyom poured the tea from a height into fine china cups and then offered a translucent white cup to Kazakov. Then the two men sat back to sip in silence, Kazakov still in his coat.

It was good tea. Fragrant and rich in tannins and the sunshine of the tea plantations in the mountains of the Indian subcontinent.

Artyom set his cup back on the table and seemed to assess Kazakov.

"So, Detektiv Kazakov. By the fact that you still have your coat on, you have not come for tea, though it might be pleasant. Nor have you come to hear an old man's complaints about his previous employer or the destruction of our history. There is something else."

Kazakov set his cup down as well, the fine china cup rattling in the saucer. "I am investigating the death of a young woman named Anna Konstantinova. I thought you might know her." He produced the photo of Anna from his pocket and handed it to Artyom, who perched his glasses on his nose and considered the image. He nodded and handed the photo back.

"I know her. At least I have spoken to her and helped her in her research. How did you know?"

"She was seen entering the library. Given what I know of her activities, I thought it was possible that she'd talked to you. Can you tell me what she came to you about?"

Artyom's gaze narrowed slightly. "She came on behalf of another."

"Madam Sobol. We thought so."

Artyom's gaze steadied on him and Kazakov paused. The old man was setting another test just as he had all the times he had placed entire newspapers before Kazakov to see what he would gain from them.

"If not Madam Sobol, who? She worked for Madam Sobol and collected information for her."

Artyom reclaimed his teacup and drank. He sat back in his chair like a throne. "It is possible to serve more than one master."

"So the person we suspect she was meeting…" Kazakov said.

Artyom sipped and tipped his head.

"She was gathering damaging information on others. At least she was from other sources."

"Such information could be useful to many people, presumably."

Kazakov nodded. "What I don't understand is how anyone could think that someone communes with the dead. How can people believe such a thing?"

"People believe many things if it pleases them, or if it agrees with thoughts that they wish were true."

"Or if it agrees with what they already believe," Kazakov said.

"True." Artyom inclined his head. "The Ottomans and Chinese have their court seers. Spiritualists have long been in favor amongst our people. At heart, Russians are a superstitious lot. Perhaps more so than their counterparts in the empires. We are not long raised from traders in fur and humans or from the farmers who carried the weight of our Great Yekaterina. There are still religious zealots who wander the countryside preaching different forms of faith and making prophecies. Our farmers and workmen feed and clothe them. Someone with the ability to put on a show and share knowledge that no one else should know is likely to be sought after even in the city."

"And likely to have enemies," Kazakov said. "But that would be Madam Sobol, not Anna Konstantinova." Kazakov looked at his hands, then studied Artyom from the tops of his eyes. "You've avoided my question, old friend. What information was Anna seeking?"

"The young woman pursued questions similar to you, Detektiv. She came in asking about Enver Pasha a few months ago, as well as about a number of New Moscow diplomats. I pulled recent newspapers for her as I did for you, but her attention soon waned. She wanted me to dig farther back into history. I brought her more papers. Then she asked for information on the political parties and the election. It was almost as if there were two lines of enquiry and she was using each one to partially obscure the other so that I could not quite see what she was doing or where she was going—like a magician's sleight of hand."

He dipped his head and took another sip of tea. The sound of the street seeped through the warbled-glass window. A shout. Running footfall. A scream. Kazakov stood and went to the window. The youngsters were racing down the street. A woman stood shouting after them, a string bag of apples spilled around her feet. One of the boys looked like he carried something. A purse? No sleight of hand here. Here it was overt theft instead of trickery. "I am surprised you live here, Artyom."

"It was not always like this. Once it was a pleasant enough street with working-class people, but the factories are mechanizing and people are out of work. The vodka comes out and the children see their hopeless fathers and give up on their studies. It is all someone's fault, but they cannot aim the blame—until now."

Kazakov turned back from the window. His shadow loomed across the room, but Artyom was caught in the murky sunlight like an insect in amber. His flesh glowed golden and his hair was a halo as he nodded and put his cup down on the coffee table. The wood of his venerable chair glowed like honey.

"Bure," Kazakov said.

Artyom nodded. "He aims their anger like a dagger. Did you hear the news this morning?"

Kazakov shook his head.

"There was an incident at the old market."

The old market, located near the train station, was one of the few places in the city where Kyrgyz, Uzbek, and other tribals mixed fully with their Russian counterparts. Vendors from all over New Moscow brought their wares—fur hats from the mountains; coats bartered and shipped from the Ottomans; the last of the previous year's fruit and vegetables; goat and chicken carcasses; small appliances that had been broken, thrown out, found, and repaired. There were lengths of cloth and tea shops and barbers and knife sharpeners all in their traditional spaces in a sprawl that echoed some of the greatest markets across Central Asia.

"What happened?" Kazakov asked.

"There was an altercation. According to the news, a Russian vendor recognized a toaster being sold by a Kyrgyz. The Russian claimed it had been stolen from him. The Kyrgyz said it had been found broken in the garbage and that he had fixed it and so it was his to sell. A fight broke out that was quickly joined along racial lines. Fifteen tribals were arrested. Bure has made a statement that supports the Russian's viewpoint: the tribals are troublemakers, murderers, and thieves."

"And of course, no Russians were arrested."

Artyom shook his head. "Actually, there were five arrested, but they have since been released—according to the news."

"Derr'mo," Kazakov swore under his breath. He returned to the couch and sat. "It's getting worse. What's going to happen after Bure's elected? He'll be in control. He'll be beyond control…"

"Perhaps someone wants to control *him*." The old man nodded. "Bure was Anna Konstantinova's last query. I showed her the same newspapers that I showed you. She seemed excited."

Kazakov thought back to the first investigation that brought Boris Bure to his notice. The periodicals had shown links between Bure, a Chinese-Ottoman spy, and Enver Pasha. It had given hints of Bure's background and possible involvement in assaults on young girls, but nothing had been said outright. Instead the matter simply evaporated. More articles trumpeted Bure's miraculous rescue as a teenager after two weeks of being lost in Fergana's rugged mountains. It had been what first brought Bure into the public eye. Reading those articles seemed like a lifetime ago.

Since then Kazakov had been shot, had lost a woman he thought he could have loved, had nearly been lost in an avalanche, and suddenly found himself working not with one partner but two. The world felt different—and unsettling for a man who always worked alone.

"The information in your newspapers was sketchy at best. Surely that would not be enough to hold a man hostage. There's no evidence to prove anything."

"And there you show your detective training, always thinking in terms of what you can prove. A seer proves nothing, Detektiv. They make a prophecy and by a miracle such a thing comes to pass and they are a miracle worker. If it does not come to pass—well, the time is not yet ripe, or human hands undid the future. And what you fail to understand is that these seers seek to curry favor with leaders. Once leaders have befriended such a one, they are influenced in their decisions. Who knows what could happen. Do you recall the purge in the Royal Chinese family a generation ago?"

Kazakov recalled reading something about it in school. He nodded.

"The Chinese court seer prophesied that the king's brother would ascend the throne. The king had his brother and all his brother's family murdered, including his own mother, for he would not take the chance that there might be another brother. The prophecy did not come true. On the other hand, in the fifteenth century, the court astrologer for King Duarte of Portugal predicted greatness and secrecy at the birth of the King's son, Henri. And so was born Henry the Navigator, who was responsible for sending the first explorers farther than anyone European had gone before along the coast of Africa. It led to the Age of Exploration and the discovery of the Americas. So the prophecy can be seen to have come true."

"So whoever owns the seer could own the politician, too?"

Artyom inclined his head. From the hallway came the slam of a door. Footsteps pounding down the stairs. He shook his head. "Ignore it. It is only young Grigori heading off to work. He is late leaving every day."

"You know all your neighbors, don't you?"

"And they mostly know me. I knew all their grandparents and some of their great-grandparents. They are, by nature, good people. Three of the women even come in to help me clean this place and the children help me carry my groceries up the stairs. They have simply lost their way. Poverty can do that."

Poverty could breed all kinds of ills, it was true, but Kazakov thought of the story of the tsarevich, the firebird, and the wolf. It had not been poverty that led to the elder brothers killing the younger. It had been pure greed and evil.

He looked to the window again, out into the haze of afternoon and the tarnished sun as it fell westward toward the Ottoman Empire. Greed and evil. When hadn't those motives been present in one of his cases?

No, what was happening in Fergana, and what had happened to Anna Konstantinova, was nothing new.

7

———————

It was late afternoon by the time Kazakov left Artyom Shepovalov's apartment. The sky had grayed, the sun had fallen far to the west so that a sullen red glow caught the underside of the clouds over new Moscow as if the city was burning. Perhaps it was true, for the faces of the people in Artyom's neighborhood all seemed overlain on a cauldron of anger. What would happen if such people confronted the anger of the tribals?

More of the fighting that had torn apart New Moscow's old market?

Outside Artyom's apartment, the air was laden with factory cinders and the awful stench of a rendering plant. He climbed in the sedan, relieved that the vehicle had not been damaged by the gang of youngsters, but the rendering plant stench followed him, like the queasy feelings arising out of his and Artyom's discussion.

With further questioning, Artyom had indicated that Anna had said nothing about where she was going, but there had been an eagerness to her that, now that he recognized it, got Artyom thinking. The girl had visited at much the same time for each of three visits. Each time she had, to Artyom's recollection, left precisely at ten minutes to noon. Perhaps she had a lunch date with someone?

Some kind of appointment. Artyom had used his amazing memory to identify the last time Anna Konstantinova visited. It had been a Friday one week before she died.

Kazakov started the sedan and turned back toward the city. The information gave them a specific date to check at the hotel. It was also interesting that the New Moscow library periodicals section was suddenly closed between her last visit and the time she died. It could be that a long-awaited decision was finally made, but it was odd that such an important source of information was suddenly locked away from the public just as a woman who had gleaned information from that source was murdered.

The burning clouds had turned to embers when he reached the police station and parked the sedan in the underground parking before riding the elevator up to the third floor. The hallway glass windows showed a squad room that was amazingly full for the hour. Kazakov pushed inside and was struck by a reek of ashes as he waded through the desks until he reached Chelomeyev and Egorova, who were both busy typing reports. Chelomeyev was pale. A dark bruise colored the side of Egorova's face. He sank down into his chair and sighed.

"What's happened?" he asked quietly.

"Did you hear about the market?" Egorova asked.

He nodded.

"Well, the trouble that started there expanded," Chelomeyev said. "Everyone was called out to help stop a confrontation between the tribals and a group of armed citizens at the entrance to the old city. There were citizens there with torches."

"Where the hell were you, Kazakov? Or were you too important to respond?" Pogolin said. His five o'clock shadow was emphasized by a dark slash of soot down one cheek and bloody knuckles.

Kazakov scanned the room and the unfriendly faces. Even Egorova and Chelomeyev looked at him expectantly. "Conducting an interview. I had my phone off." It was something he always did to guard against unnecessary interruptions.

There were headshakes and grumbles, but the others went back to their reports—except for Chelomeyev and Egorova.

"Dedushka?" she asked.

"The same." Kazakov nodded.

"What did he have to say?" Chelomeyev asked.

There were too many detectives in the room. Too many whom he did not trust to talk in great detail.

"He confirmed Anna had been there. How did the hotel visit go?" he asked Egorova.

She shook her head. "Not well. The receptionist claimed not to remember Anna, but the look she exchanged with the bellhop suggested otherwise."

"Would it help if I could provide a specific date that she visited?" He told them what Artyom had told him about the date of the visit and then lowered his voice. "I find it interesting that since that date, Anna has died and Artyom finds himself retired and the entire periodicals section closed and transported to an unknown location."

Egorova nodded.

"And how did your enquires go?" Kazakov asked Chelomeyev.

The young detective glanced at the other detectives and shook his head. "The follow-up enquiries didn't provide much more information. Most did not recall anything, but three did. I've mapped them." He nodded to his desk drawer. "Perhaps we can meet at my place later to review the results?"

Kazakov glanced beyond the glass partition to the hallway. Beyond, three small windows gave onto Yekaterina Square and the amber light that preceded nightfall.

"How long?" Kazakov asked.

"Say twenty minutes," Chelomeyev said.

Egorova nodded.

"Then I will pay penance for not being at the riot and pick up food for dinner." Kazakov shoved to his feet and headed through the desks to the door. He hadn't made any friends by being unavailable to help in the riot. He wasn't making any more by leaving early, even though he was often the last to leave the office.

He headed down to the Perseus and left the station behind, cruising the streets until he reached a small hole-in-the-wall Chinese restaurant that he had discovered a year ago. He parked in a lane that reeked of garbage and wet cardboard beside the building, stumbled through sloppy snow that almost topped his boots, and went inside.

The place was dimly lit by candles and red paper lanterns. The air was heavy with hot oil, fried garlic, and fiery peppers that almost made his eyes water. At the counter, the fine-boned hostess turned from speaking to the kitchen through a pass-through. Her face lit up. Ping was a middle-aged woman with thick dark hair swept back off her face and coiled and held in place by two chopsticks. High cheekbones gave her black eyes a lovely tilt and she wore a simple pair of tan trousers topped with a satin brocade top of deep blue with yellow sleeves.

"Detektiv!" her smile was welcome after the office. "It is a long time since we see you here. I thought you forgotten us."

"The best Szechuan food in New Moscow could never be forgotten. I've just been pulled in other directions. How are you and your family?"

Ping owned the restaurant with her husband, who did much of the cooking. Their son and daughters all worked as servers when they weren't away at school back in China.

"The girls are fine—doing well in university. The youngest got a scholarship to continue her advanced studies. Lee, here, still cooks as well as ever." She hooked a finger toward the kitchen.

"And your son?"

A shadow passed over her face for a moment. "He has joined the military. They were recruiting at the university and were interested in him for his knowledge of Fergana. Perhaps they will raise him to diplomat or translator." She shook her head. "I kid myself. Between you and me, he was never an academic. He should be a cook like his father. Now what can I do for you? You are well?"

Kazakov smiled. "As well as the job allows. I need a feast for three very hungry detectives. I will let you choose."

She tipped a brow at him and thought a moment and then turned to the kitchen and her husband, spouting off a rapid-fire order. Then she turned back to Kazakov.

"You will like the food. You will have Szechuan noodle and vegetable, smoked tofu and broccoli in black bean sauce, crispy fish, and tomato-beef chow mein. Rice will come with it. Should I pack you tea as well?"

Kazakov turned the tea down and took a seat against the wall to wait. There were three tables taken in the small restaurant and all were taken by ethnic Chinese. That boded well for the Chinese, but he wondered if that was what Fergana was to become after the election if Bure won—Russians and Tribals gradually sinking into second class citizenry while Fergana's Chinese allies gradually took the country over. In some ways it would serve Fergana right for spending all its energies on lost glories instead of moving forward. Russia was lost in yesterday. Fergana was not Russia and never would be. What would tomorrow bring? Chinese masters? Ottoman? While the Ferganese public was lost in its dreams of past glories, they were losing what future they might have had. And the allies that might have supported them.

The Americans were one such ally. The strip of American states that ran along the east coast of North America and inland not quite to the

Mississippi River had gained their independence from the Anglos before the Anglos and Germans joined to form the Anglo-German Empire that was ranged first against the upstart Napoleon and then against the land-hungry Ottomans. The Americans had courted Fergana as a potential member of an alliance of independent states, meaning those countries who were not part of the Ottoman, Chinese, or Anglo-German empires, or satellites of those empires like Anglo-German North America and central and southern Africa. The Americans and their allies feared that if Fergana fell and war arose between the Ottomans and Chinese, whoever was the victor would not stop there. The Anglo-Germans would fall and the smaller independent countries would be absorbed not long after.

At least that was what the American spy, Eric Clinton, had espoused. As far as Kazakov could see, the theory made too much sense and left him with a growing knot of dread in his stomach.

The rustle of brown paper and the redolence of spice filled Kazakov's senses as Ping set two large brown bags on the counter. He stood and paid her, even though she at first refused his money, and left with the bags and growing disquiet. Something was brewing in Fergana, and after the riots today, it could not be good.

At Chelomeyev's apartment building, the night had fallen and the streetlights were too far apart to fully light the parking lot. The temperature had dropped significantly so his breath steamed around him and he slipped and slid on the half-frozen ice coating the pavement. He carried the bags to the front door, noting that Chelomeyev's vehicle—an inexpensive but somewhat stylish two-door First Auto—was in its stall.

He called up to the detective's apartment and was buzzed inside to ride the elevator up to Chelomeyev's doorway. It swung open and he entered, toed off his boots, and carried his bags to the kitchen counter. His coat he removed and lay across a chairback. Egorova had pulled out plates and cutlery while Chelomeyev busily hung a paper map on his living room wall. The food containers were opened on the counter and the room filled with the delicious scents.

"I hope you both like Chinese food," Kazakov said. If they didn't, too bad for them. He suspected they'd be eating a lot more of it after Bure was elected. If he was elected. No, the way things were going it was, unfortunately, "when."

"So what happened with Dedushka?" Egorova asked as they all sat down on Chelomeyev's low-slung couch and chairs.

The couch felt awkward and too low, leaving Kazakov's knees up to his chin so he had to balance the plate in one hand and eat with the other.

He told them about the neighborhood and the challenge just getting into the apartment building. He didn't bother with the potential beating, but focused on Artyom's information and the fact that Anna Konstantinova had been researching Enver Pasha, Boris Bure, and other diplomats, and how a "seer" could hold a lot of power by providing advice and counsel to believers in that power.

Chelomeyev nodded, but Egorova looked thoughtful. "It sounds like a seer and a spy could be one and the same thing. They both gather information and use it for power. The difference is the seer uses the power for themselves while the spy uses it for their country."

That sounded about right, but Chelomeyev shook his head. "There's a third option. There are…let us just say, Societies. These organizations may gather information and use it to gain power and influence over government decisions."

Kazakov regarded the young man. Chelomeyev almost appeared to be daring Kazakov to ask questions.

"Can you give us an example?" Egorova asked.

Chelomeyev set his half-finished plate on the floor. "Historically there were religious orders like the Templars and Hospitalers. The Khlysty are a more recent example. They used their alleged spiritual powers to gain tsars' favor in old Russia and advised on matters they knew nothing about other than through their alleged spiritual connections. You still see the odd one around preaching their oddball beliefs and making prophecies."

"Are you suggesting Madam Sobol is a member of such a group? That they still exist?" Egorova asked. She forked another mouthful of tomato-beef chow mein into her mouth and chewed thoughtfully.

Chelomeyev was silent as Kazakov watched him.

"What is it that you're not telling us?" Kazakov asked. His question fell into the void of quiet in the room.

Chelomeyev sighed and met his gaze. "A while back I was approached about joining such a group. Its membership includes many senior police and senior bureaucrats."

"Like your father," Kazakov said.

Shadows seemed to flood Chelomeyev's face as he nodded.

"Did you turn them down?" Kazakov asked.

Swallowing, Chelomeyev shook his head. "I didn't get the impression that that was an option. They call themselves the *Ordo Tempi Orientis*, the OTO, or the Order of the Eastern Temple. I've attended a number of their sessions. Their prophets speak of the ascendancy of Russia and the purity of our blood, distilled through the great diaspora." He shook his head. "They have been dropping hints that I could advance far by using my connections to police work to advance their cause."

"And what is their cause?" Kazakov asked.

Chelomeyev hung his head as if he wasn't proud. "Bure," he said.

Egorova leaned back on the couch, her gaze narrowed as she faced Chelomeyev. "So why are you telling us this if you're on the fast track to success?" Her voice was a chill hiss.

"Because I don't believe in such stuff," Chelomeyev said. "Or Bure. Frankly, I was a new member and not party to its inner workings, but I got the sense that there were differences of opinion about the man. For the moment, though, the Bure fans were ascendant."

"You could be telling us this to gain our trust and our information," Egorova said with a shake of her head.

"Thank you for telling us," Kazakov said, considering what the existence of such a society meant. Nothing good, certainly. The entire Ferganese society seemed mired in secrets and history. But more and more of Fergana's establishment was throwing its weight behind Bure. "So we need to look for possible connections between Madam Sobol and Anna Konstantinova and either Bure directly, and/or with this society. Perhaps one or both of them was a member."

Chelomeyev shook his head. "The OTO—it allows only male members, though it may take heed of female seers."

"Had Madam Sobol come to the OTO's notice?" Kazakov asked.

Another shake of his blond head. "I don't know. As I said, I'm new to the organization."

"I need you to keep your ears open at these meetings," Kazakov said. "Perhaps ask around. Keep us informed."

Chelomeyev chuckled. "That's what they said of your investigation."

Kazakov felt as if he'd been punched. "They asked you to keep them informed of my investigation?"

"Correct. They seemed concerned that you are a wild card. That is their word."

"Well…" Kazakov said. "Let us find a way to increase their worry. What has your mapping shown us?"

Going to his map, Chelomeyev once more pointed out all the businesses and individuals openly visited by Anna Konstantinova. The dots on the map were a scattershot of points across the city.

"After our earlier discussion, I began to chart the direction and route that Anna was seen taking after she left each spot, where we could get the information. I also located beauty shops, barber shops, and bath houses near each one and contacted a number of the most promising."

He indicated blue lines that strayed across the map like frayed scarf endings. At first glance they looked like nothing at all, but Kazakov was still sure that something was there. As he stared at the array he became more certain of it. Many of the times Anna walked away, she went toward Suvarov Way; that would place her on a major thoroughfare that arrowed in to the center of the city. There was good transit on Suvarov Way. Anna could go anywhere.

But he didn't think so. Suvarov Way also led toward the New Moscow library and the Royal Caravanserai Hotel. He said as much.

"We need to go back there," Egorova said.

"We will, but I suspect that management will not be helpful. Any chance you can check whether the manager is a member of the OTO?" Kazakov asked Chelomeyev.

"Not easily, but I'll see what I can find out."

"You be careful. You've barely recovered from the last attack on your life," Egorova said.

"And if that isn't the pot calling the kettle black," Chelomeyev said. Egorova still favored the shoulder where she'd been shot.

"Yes. Yes. Yes. We've all been injured and must all be careful. That goes without saying. When you contacted the bathhouses and so on, what did you learn?" Kazakov paused in eating the last of his food.

Chelomeyev nodded. "As I mentioned, three of them knew her." He pointed out the locations on the map. All were in affluent areas and would serve a higher class of customer. "When I pushed, they admitted that they collected rumors for her. Mostly it was things like who is sleeping with whom and which husband has a business scandal brewing. That sort of thing."

Kazakov shook his head. "Madam Sobol had a busy little pipeline of potential customers." He finished his plate of food and leaned back on the couch. "Now. You will tell me what happened today with this riot."

Chelomeyev met Egorova's gaze, then checked his watch and nodded. "The news report is a place to start."

He fished a television remote out of the corner of his chair and clicked it at the machine. The screen stayed black and then flickered on. A news announcer made a pronouncement about the flagging Leonid Nikolaev reelection campaign and how the polls were predicting a huge Bure majority. Pundits on the television were speculating about what a Bure government would mean for Fergana and whether Bure would be able to keep his election promises.

A shiver ran through Kazakov as Chelomeyev changed news channels seeking the riot story. On the third channel, there was coverage. The voice-over announcer reported that at three this afternoon there had been a dangerous riot at the edge of the old city as a mass of armed men threatened to attack New Moscow. Thankfully, they were met with fierce resistance by local citizens protecting their property and the uprising was quelled.

Aerial images showed Russians armed with pistols, clubs, and tire irons streaming through the streets between warehouses toward the old city. A shift of view showed tribal men identifiable by their small *ak kalpak* caps and darker clothing carrying antique rifles and similar clubs running out of the old city to face what was coming. Not exactly as the announcer had proclaimed. This looked more like the men of the old city mounting a defense.

Kazakov sat forward as the two forces met. The tribals didn't fold, though they were met with a much larger force. Then police officers entered the scene clubbing anyone around them. They were followed by more officers, some in vests with police emblazoned across chest and back. He spotted Egorova amongst the flood of men, saw her punched in the face by a Russian and almost go down, but something else in the on-screen melee caught his attention just as the video zoomed in on the fighting. A point of quiet. A point of order in the bedlam.

Kazakov stood up and went to the television for a closer look, just as the scene changed again. He stopped. The coverage of the riot ended and the newscast turned to happier matters of recent centenarian birthdays that received an in-person visit from President Nikolaev. The screen shifted to an elder-village meeting room with a large flaming cake and the president making presentations to the latest citizens to reach one hundred years.

The announcer's voice was a drone in Kazakov's ears as he turned numbly back to Egorova and Chelomeyev.

"Kazakov? Are you all right?" Egorova's voice seemed to come from down a long tunnel.

He shook his head and glanced back at the television, wishing he could see the riot footage again. Half of him wishing what could surely only be a case of mistaken identity might actually be true. The other half praying he was wrong.

"Didn't you see?" he asked as his legs gave and he thumped down on the too low couch again.

By their expressions Egorova and Chelomeyev hadn't seen anything.

Though he felt like he couldn't breathe, from somewhere the breath found his lungs. He swallowed and glanced up at the television. "I think I just saw Khalil Khan."

8

———

After a brief stop at a market that was open late into the evening, it was a long drive home through driving wind and wet snow that had found its way down out of the mountains. The Perseus' headlights tried valiantly to cut through the wet mess of swirling flakes, but the flakes actually accumulated on the headlights themselves. Crawling up through the suburbs out of the city and then across the rising steppes toward the trees in the mountain foothills, Kazakov was twice forced out of the vehicle into the cold night to clear the packed snow off the headlights. He stopped, briefly, to deliver supplies to Agafya, his elderly neighbor, but the old woman would not allow him into her house. Instead she demanded he leave her porch. He had—but he'd left the supplies on her doorstep and hoped she collected them before wild animals got them. The old woman was getting more and more reclusive and it was becoming harder to check on her wellbeing.

By the time he finally swung up the gravel lane to his dacha and pulled in behind the dwelling, he was bone weary and ready for bed. When he turned off the headlights, the world was reduced to utter darkness and the wheeze of his own breathing, but his thoughts were spinning so fast that he knew he wouldn't sleep.

He climbed out of the vehicle and stumbled around the dacha and up the stairs and inside. When he lit his lantern, the soft light revealed the four solid walls of the single room. They provided a relief from the wind, and Koshka's mew and her rub along his leg were a comfort. He didn't relish being alone at the moment. With his coat still on, he got the fire going. His coat and gun holster he hung on a peg by the door and then he fed the very insistent Koshka. With kibbles in her bowl, she abandoned her urgent affections and busily crunched at her dinner. Her purr was loud in the silence. At least someone was happy.

Kazakov stroked her soft fur and dug a newly purchased bottle of vodka from the market bag, along with a loaf of black bread and a brown-paper wrapped sausage. Ignoring the bread and sausage, he rinsed a glass in the sink and slumped down at the wooden table in the center of the room to eye the bottle. Not too long ago he'd lost himself in vodka to dull the pain of his bullet wound and the loss of Maria. He'd cleaned the bottles out of his home after Khan had pointed out to him just how far down he'd skidded.

Just one drink wouldn't hurt anything. He'd had a drink the other night and had still functioned well today.

But one drink often led to the bottom of the bottle. He'd excused his descent into the bottle on Maria's death. What was he going to blame it on this time? Khan?

It dishonored the memory of everything good about the man.

But then, maybe all those good things had been Kazakov's imagination. He had never really known Khan, even though over the years he'd come to believe him to be something of a brother in combating the corruption of New Moscow's justice system. Just as Chelomeyev's young tsarevich had thought his brothers loved him.

Had it really been Khan he'd seen in the riot video? He'd seen the man die, or so he'd thought. No body had been found, but his family had conducted a funeral.

In the heat from the woodstove, the cool vodka bottle began to bead sweat. The tempting droplets caught the lantern light and slid slowly down the bottle.

He had to have been wrong—and if he wasn't, it only meant that he had another murderer to apprehend. For all the man named Zholdosh had been an Ottoman agent, he still shouldn't have been murdered. Khan meant nothing to him except that. A good man gone wrong, even if it might have been for the right reasons. What reasons had driven the tsarevich's older brothers to kill him?

The fairy tale spoke of greed and laziness, but really, had the tsarevich been any better? It had been greed that had gotten him into trouble on every step of his epic journey, and only the help of the wolf had saved him again and again. Funny that a dangerous wolf was really the hero of the story. It could be said that the tsarevich didn't really deserve any of the riches that had come to him. He'd stolen them or obtained them under fraudulent terms. A con man: that was what the young tsarevich had been.

Perhaps the brothers *had* done the right thing and been heroes when they killed him. The story never said what came after and the kind of kingdom the tsarevich created.

Kazakov shook himself and found the bottle still in his hand. The screw top turned easily in his hand, but shook as he poured himself a glass. He left the glass on the table.

Had Khan been right to do as he had?

Damn it, no! He'd broken the law—both God's and Fergana's!

Kazakov jerked back from the table and stood to pace the small space in the dacha. Koshka had finished her kibbles and had returned to sprawl on his bed, her small pink tongue busily giving her black pelt a bath.

It didn't matter. Khan was dead. That argument was over.

But he might be alive.

Kazakov went to his coat and pulled out his phone. He dialed Khan's mobile number and waited a moment before pushing send. Instead of the "not in service" recording he expected, the number rang and rang. Not surprising given bureaucracy was never efficient in doing things like canceling numbers.

Fifteen rings drilled into his ear. He could have listened longer, but the phone clicked in his hands as if someone picked up.

And just as quickly hung up again.

His phone felt like an enemy as it lay in his hands. He set it on the table. It shouldn't have rung so many times. It shouldn't have clicked as if someone answered.

It shouldn't make him doubt all his decisions and place all of his beliefs in question. Chelomeyev's story was a simple tale about a heroic prince who triumphed over his lazy and evil brothers. That was all.

Then why did he suddenly feel so ill?

All these stories about seers who impossibly spoke with the dead and suddenly he was seeing ghosts. At least that's what Egorova had suggested.

Egorova might often be right, but she wasn't this time.

Khan was out there. What was he plotting?

Kazakov picked up the glass of vodka and knocked it back, relishing the burn into his throat and belly.

————

The next morning found Kazakov and Egorova in the police sedan heading back to the Royal Caravanserai Hotel. Egorova drove while Kazakov nursed a thundering headache that he could only surmise was the result of his lone glass of vodka. Whether it was because of the vodka he drank or the fact that he hadn't drunk more was a question he dared not ponder. He sat in the seat, his head back and eyes closed as Egorova navigated the streets like she'd done it for years.

"What the hell happened to you last night?" she asked. "You look like hell."

Kazakov let out a sigh, but the motion hurt his head. "Let us just leave that topic closed."

He didn't need any reminders—the screwdriver stabbed in his brain was enough.

She was silent a moment, the sedan moving smoothly around a corner.

"You still think you saw Khan in that video?" Her voice was colder and it had every reason to be, given Khan's role in her recent injury.

"I don't know what I saw. It looked like him. Maybe his ghost." He forced his lips into a smile. "All this talk of communication with the great beyond. Maybe it got to me."

She said nothing and pulled the sedan into the curb of new snow that covered the decaying ice from the day before. "Chelomeyev is going to ask for a copy of the tape for us to go through."

His first instinct was to tell her no, but he nodded instead. Better to know.

"It was probably only a trick of the light," he said and hoped he was right. "Someone who looked like him. Khan would never allow himself to be filmed." But in riot conditions, would he even have noticed that a camera crew was filming from the top of a building?

The sidewalk in front of the Royal Caravanserai had been shoveled down to the concrete and salted and swept so that the sidewalk was cleaner than most New Moscow sidewalks in the dead of summer. The heavy, iron-bound wood door gleamed in the weak sunlight that filtered through a light fall of tiny icy flakes. They dusted Egorova's hair and Kazakov's shoulders as they pushed inside.

The warmth of the interior struck Kazakov like a heated blanket. Somehow the hotel managed to create the dry heat and slightly smoky scent of his dacha fireplace, while at the same time perfuming the air with heavy incense. The walls were painted white, terracotta, and deep sky-blue, but the terracotta was brought forward through deep carpets that picked up the color and seating alcoves filled with pillows.

The ceiling was higher than a caravanserai would have had, but huge, rough-hewn beams crisscrossed the expanse, their color as dark as if they'd spent centuries stained by open fires below.

Egorova led across the foyer to the reception counter and rested her hands on the smooth wood surface. Kazakov came up beside her, his identification in his hand.

"Detektivs Egorova and Kazakov to see the manager," Kazakov said. At least that way they could get a read on the person.

The receptionist, a fine-boned young man who moved like a dancer, stopped his mail sorting and turned to regard them. On his dark blue vest he wore a name tag: Ivan.

"Police?" His voice was soothing and soft—a good foil for angry customers. Or detectives.

"What do you think?" Kazakov said and reopened his identification.

"You wish to see the manager?" Could this youth only ask questions?

"That's what I said."

"May I ask what this is about?"

Kazakov and Egorova glanced at each other. Kazakov sighed.

"No. You may not. Unless you were on shift on Friday two weeks ago."

The young man pursed his lips. Then he nodded. "Actually, I believe I was."

Finally, not a question.

"What time were you on shift?" Egorova asked.

"Two thirty to ten thirty. Why?"

Aah. The question.

Egorova pulled out the photograph of Anna Konstantinova and held it out to him. "Did you see this young woman?"

"Anna? Why?"

"How do you know her?" Kazakov asked.

"Is she a suspect or something? Has she done something?" The young man asked.

"Answer the question." Kazakov said fighting to hide his frustration.

"Anna—Anna is a friend of mine. I know her from back home in Basil. She's the smartest, nicest person. We went to school together until she got pregnant and had her little boy. Then she came into the city to earn money to support him."

"And how was she supporting herself?" Egorova asked.

Ivan looked from Kazakov to Egorova and back again and suddenly the annoying attitude lessened. "Was? Something's happened. Is Anna all right?"

Even though they were questions, they were appropriate.

"I regret to inform you that Anna Konstantinova's body was found two days ago. She was murdered," Egorova said, giving nothing else away.

Young Ivan seemed to stagger behind the counter, but he caught himself and steadied.

"Oh my God. Oh my God." Then his eyes widened as if he'd thought of something. "Oh my God!"

"Anna was seen coming into the Royal Caravanserai last Friday. Did you speak to her?" Kazakov asked.

"Last Friday—yes. She always made a point of coming over to say hello," Ivan said.

"Why was she here?" Egorova asked.

Ivan blinked at her as if he was still in shock. Better to keep him a little off-kilter to get honest answers.

Ivan's throat worked. "She—I believe she might have had an appointment."

"Tell me about that," Egorova asked and stood waiting.

Ivan licked his lips and looked desperate to escape. Instead, his gaze dropped to the counter. "She came in every Friday at about the same time…"

His voice faded, but Egorova and Kazakov let the silence lengthen.

Pale-faced, Ivan swallowed again and again. Finally, he gave a little nod. "You see, I made the first appointment for her. There was a man. He was looking for a spiritualist—a seer. The man—he was important and needed the utmost confidentiality. He said he'd lost a family member and wanted someone who would come to him and keep their mouth shut. Back at home in Basil, Anna had always had the sight, just like her grandmother. I thought this might help her with her money problems so I called her and asked her if she was interested. She was, so she came." He looked from one to the other of them as if hoping that was enough.

"Go on," Kazakov said.

"I—I guess the first time went well because Anna came again and again. There—were other calls for her as well, but those meetings didn't happen here. Anna was afraid of word getting out of what she was doing. She needed the steady pay to send home. The money from these sessions was a bonus."

Kazakov nodded. It made sense, given what they knew of Anna.

"What did Anna tell you about the sessions?"

Ivan shook his head. "Anna was professional. She didn't talk to me about what she did—just thanked me for the referral."

"And paid you a little for it," Egorova said.

Blushing slightly, Ivan looked away. "That was the arrangement."

"How much?" Egorova asked.

"She charged a thousand rubles. They were rich clients. She shared two hundred with me. It was fair because I made the referrals. I found her the clients and I made the appointments."

"It seems you are going to have to make do with significantly less now, Ivan." Kazakov sighed. "We are going to need a list of her clients."

The young man shook his head. "But confidentiality…"

"There is no confidentiality in a murder investigation. Now answer the question," Kazakov snapped. "Who were her clients?"

"All of them?"

Egorova held up a hand to stop Kazakov's eruption and nodded at Ivan. She gave Kazakov a look that made him swallow back his frustration with this effete little man. Ivan fished in his vest and pulled out a folded paper. When he unfolded it, it revealed ten names and phone numbers along with a series of ticks beside each name, each tick crossed except for one.

At best, Kazakov dimly recognized the names of Anna's clients from the local newspaper society sections. Businessmen and women, all of them, except for one. Leonid Nikolaev: Fergana's current president. The name glared out at Kazakov, the last check mark unticked beside his name.

Kazakov tapped the check mark. "What does this mean?"

"It is an appointment that is scheduled this week, but not yet held."

Kazakov tipped a brow in question and Ivan bowed his head and once more swallowed.

"It is for this afternoon, two o'clock here at the hotel. I should cancel it."

"You will not," Kazakov said, confiscating the list of names. "We will keep Anna's appointment."

They left the Royal Caravanserai after getting Ivan's details and obtaining information on how to contact Anna's son's caregiver in the small town of Basil. Ivan was clearly shaken, but promised to come into the station to give a formal statement. Kazakov believed him.

Outside, wet spring snow swirled amid the vehicle exhaust in the air and made a mess of the roads and sidewalks except for the stretch of concrete in front of the hotel. It was as if they stood in a bubble and all the world was his imagination reflected back off the bubble's skin. Nothing was real. Kazakov swayed and inhaled the cold air and pollution. It was a relief after the perfumed hotel air that had threatened to make his headache worse. Or else this dull thud in the back of his brain was the result of the frustrating verbal style of Ivan. Maybe Kazakov was simply getting too old and jaded for his job.

He scrubbed at his face.

"You sure you're okay? You haven't looked good since you came in this morning," Egorova said. The cold air placed attractive red points high on her cheeks. Her gaze was bright as a hound on a scent.

He nodded. "I never was an attractive man."

He avoided further questions by heading back to the sedan. Inside in the passenger seat, he lay his head back again and closed his eyes. "Before you ask, I'm thinking."

"Where are we headed?" Egorova asked.

Where, indeed. Off into the wilds of the young tsarevich's adventure to lie and cheat and steal their way to answers? That seemed to be the way tsareviches came to power. Politicians, too. Had Leonid Nikolaev crawled to the top the same way? Had he killed along the way?

He shook himself and looked into Egorova's concerned gaze. "Back to the office, I think. We have nine phone calls to make to the names on this list—ten if you count contacting Anna's next of kin. And we need to interview Madam Sobol again. See whether her client list includes any of Anna's and find out if she knew what Anna was doing."

He closed his eyes again, feeling caught in the bubble of light through his eyelids. Egorova started the sedan and headed into traffic. Truly, with his eyes closed, he was floating. Nothing was real. None of this. Not prophets and seers, not politicians and elections, and certainly not Khan risen from the dead.

He must have dozed for he woke with a start when the sedan's tires squealed on the concrete ramp to the police station underground parking. His head felt muggy and filled with fog as he climbed out and followed

Egorova inside and waited for the elevator. She kept sending glances his way.

"I'm fine, okay! Totally fine. I've just got a lot on my mind," he said as they rode the elevator up.

"It's this Khan thing, isn't it?" Egorova asked. "I understand, if it is. He was your friend."

And betrayer. "He shot you. If he is alive, he'll rally his people. He's a danger to Fergana."

Or the ultimate loyalist. That was the confusing part because a part of Kazakov believed in what Khan believed. That was the trouble—where Kazakov had previously thought that everyone wore layers of masks, it was more like each person had their own reality. When you stripped away what you thought was a mask, you weren't confronted by something the person had been hiding; no, you were confronted by a different truth about the world—one you might not want to believe in.

It left his stomach queasy and his palms sweating.

Chelomeyev was alone in the detective office when they got back, though Kazakov had told the young detective to stay home and rest. His face was pale gray, his cheekbones seemingly the only thing his skin had to hang on. But he was on the phone as they arrived. He thanked whoever he was talking to and hung up.

"I was just going to phone you. I've been wracking my brain trying to remember anyone I know for sure is a member of the OTO. It seems there's more people joining right now, so I'm certain I won't have them all. The two new detectives belong. Probably why they got their promotions so young." He had the grace to blush slightly because Pavel Chelomeyev was the youngest detective in the history of the New Moscow police. "Most of upstairs are members, of course."

"What about Rostoff?" Kazakov asked, doffing his coat and tossing it across his chair. The room was cool and he missed the warm weight of the wool.

Chelomeyev shook his head. "Surprisingly, no. I would have thought..."

"Probably no one asked him," Kazakov said. And he was already in the powerbrokers' pockets. "Who else?"

Chelomeyev held up a list. "It's a who's who of New Moscow business: corporate CEOs, newspaper publishers, high government officials—even the head of the New Moscow library."

Kazakov picked up the list and flipped through it, noting names that had come up on recent cases, including the library head and the government's appointed chief communications officer. Both of them had oddly received tobacco import licenses when neither had any experience in the import business. Kazakov had suspected that they were linked to either Boris Bure or Enver Pasha.

Another name caught his eye: Nicolay Yevseyev. A highly placed government official and the second husband of Kazakov's ex-wife Annuschka.

"Any way we can check whether Boris Bure is a member?" Kazakov asked.

Chelomeyev blew out a sigh. "I've just about exhausted my contacts. I've been contacting them saying that I wanted to explore career options and wanted to talk to some OTO members in other areas to explore other possibilities. I can't very well phone them back again. They were asking questions. As it is, I am probably going to get a visit from my dad." He shuddered.

Chelomeyev might be the only son, but he and his father were barely speaking, regardless of Chelomeyev's recent bout in the hospital. The older Chelomeyev had rarely visited, even when his son was awake—at least according to Chelomeyev.

"I wonder if there's any commonality between OTO membership and Anna's clients," Egorova said, producing the hotel clerk's list. Together the three of them poured over the lists. Three of the names were in common, none were known to Kazakov.

"We need to interview these people about Anna and what she was telling them, as well as where they were the day she was killed. I need to talk to her family now that we know where she's from and follow up with Gordiev regarding what the autopsy found. Egorova, you and Chelomeyev take on the interviews. I'll contact Gordiev and also follow up with Madam Sobol. We'll get as far as we can before our interview at the Royal Caravanserai this afternoon. Okay?"

There were nods from Chelomeyev and Egorova.

Kazakov turned to Egorova. "When you're coming to the hotel, drop Chelomeyev at home. You," he said turning to Chelomeyev, "you look like hell. I want you to get some rest. Understand?"

The young detective gave him a sullen glare.

"You get some rest, or you're off this case. I will not be responsible for you killing yourself or getting ill. You'll never fully recover your memories or your strength if you don't give yourself the time." He held up his hand when Chelomeyev looked about to argue. "That is all that will be said about it."

For a moment, Kazakov felt like Rostoff must from time to time. He watched the two young detectives out the door and into the elevator, then picked up his coat. He'd been harder than he intended on Chelomeyev, but the youngster needed to learn to take care of himself. No one would do it for him.

Feeling old and ornery, Kazakov headed for the door. Gordiev should have had his report on Kazakov's desk already. What the heck was the holdup?

At the elevator, Kazakov stabbed the call button, but footfall down the hall turned him around.

"Aah, Kazakov. Just the man I was looking for," Detektiv Chief Inspektor Rostoff came down the hall. "This thing yesterday. I understand you were not at the riot."

Riot. So they were calling the attempted attack on the old city a riot.

"No, I was not. I can explain. I was conducting an interview."

Rostoff waved his protests away. "It is all done. In fact, it is a good thing that you were not there. It retains your neutrality with those people, correct?"

Kazakov nodded slowly, wondering where this was going.

"I need to speak with you in my office," Rostoff continued and turned back down the hall just as the elevator dinged open.

Kazakov glanced at it and sighed but followed Rostoff instead. Next of kin and M.E. Gordiev weren't going away and who knew where this was going.

Rostoff's office sat along the hallway that housed senior police officers and their assistants. Rostoff's assistant was the inimitably capable Constable Dabria Smirnova, a blonde beauty who was frustrated that her looks seemed to keep her trapped in Rostoff's reception area rather than out doing police work. She looked up from her desk when Rostoff led Kazakov in. He shrugged a question at her, but she only shook her head. She had no more information than he did and that was unusual, for Dabria Smirnova had always struck Kazakov as the brains in the office.

Rostoff's wood paneled office enjoyed a window over Yekaterina Square and the man railed at the destruction of the statue of the great tsarina by parties unknown—though the media laid the blame at the tribals —and at the fact that the statue had not been replaced. Nor had any plans to do so been announced. Rostoff crossed the room and settled at his desk so that he was backed by his collection of photographs of him glad-handing with New Moscow's rich and powerful. That was what Rostoff did best.

Rostoff fidgeted his pens into a perfect line at the side of a perfectly stacked sheaf of paper. Then he looked up at Kazakov.

"I was called into the chief constable's office this morning. There are… concerns about the upcoming election."

Kazakov stayed where he stood, but the news surprised him. That someone else was concerned boded well.

"There are fears that the tribals will disrupt the election. There are rumors of threats on candidates' lives."

Not the same concerns that Kazakov had. He swallowed. "What has happened?"

"Apparently, under interrogation, a tribal suspect from the riot gave up the information that there are assassination plans against Boris Bure."

Kazakov felt his strength drain out of him. He took a step forward and grasped the back of the lone visitor chair facing Rostoff. "Why tell me? You know I have no love for the man."

"Aah, but I know you are an honest man—painfully so. A man so righteous he ruins his career to live up to his standards." Rostoff steepled his fingers before him. "Am I right? Are you not the man who refused orders because he would not sully himself with our arrangements with certain businesses?"

Kazakov just stared at his inspector. Rostoff had tried to undo Kazakov's ethical standards by ordering him to accept the protection payments made by the city brothels to the police department.

Rostoff put on a set of glasses, pulled a paper off the stack on his desk, and began to read. "I want you to investigate this rumor amongst your tribal friends and I want you to devise a plan to ensure Boris Bure is protected."

Kazakov felt his jaw drop open. "Protect him? I'd be more likely to shoot him myself!"

Rostoff glanced up from reading, his gaze gone hard. "You will never say something like that again in my presence or I will be forced to have you arrested for uttering threats. Do you understand? Now you will conduct enquiries and you will devise a plan. The election is in a week. I want an outline of your plan tonight."

"But the Anna Konstantinova investigation. It continues to grow…"

"Leave it. That Egorova is showing herself to have a good head on her shoulders. A good addition to the squad, regardless of her past supervisor's assessment. She can shepherd Chelomeyev through the Konstantinova investigation."

"But…"

Rostoff took off his glasses. "Can't you tell that I do not wish to discuss this? You will keep this to yourself and you will report to me daily with your findings. Now get out." He tipped his head to the door.

Kazakov retreated across the office and closed the door behind him. He leaned back against the wood and tried to catch his breath against the swelling anger in his chest.

"You all right?" Dabria Smirnova asked.

"No," Kazakov growled and shoved himself away from the wall and out of the reception area. The Konstantinova murder investigation was too high profile and too connected to the election to leave it alone. Regardless of Rostoff's instructions, he wasn't leaving the case to a newcomer to New Moscow and a young detective who was still convalescing.

He'd find a way to take care of both.

Damn Rostoff.

Damn Boris Bure.

9

According to Ivan, the Royal Caravanserai receptionist, Anna Konstantinova came from the western border town of Basil, named after the same Basil as the replica cathedral that graced New Moscow's downtown and attempted to capture the grandeur of the original, though the original edifice was long ago burned down to the ground by Ottoman conquerors. The town was a two-hour drive from New Moscow, but Kazakov nevertheless set out across the undulating snow-covered fields and between the ugly warehouses that had begun to spring, mushroom-like, up across the countryside. At this rate, there'd be no farmland left and Fergana would be even more beholden to its monolithic neighbors. As he headed west, the mountains closed in like threatening pincers to north and south. Basil sat in the gap between the mountains and had sprung up as a border town set along the frozen banks of the storied Syr Darya River that had its headwaters in the Tian Shan mountains to the east. Once the river had marked the northernmost border of Alexander the Great's conquests from Greece.

The area around the town was laced with low furrows, canals that robbed the river of its water to irrigate the fields of cotton and rice that grew here during the summer. Small farmhouses dotted the sullen landscape under heavy clouds. The town itself was a dark smear on the white.

Like New Moscow, the outskirts of Basil were pocked with

warehouses, probably to support the transborder shipping. He spotted a complex of buildings and trucks, almost as large as the town, that sported the emblem of Transcontinental Shipping, Enver Pasha's company. Then the warehouses fell away and he found himself in the town of Basil.

It was built around two main roads that both ran east-west, terminating or beginning in the armed outpost that formed the border with the Ottoman Empire. The town's buildings were one- or two-story concrete. Most had small windows to keep out the summer heat and the winter cold. Shops had bright signs beside their doorways that listed their wares, probably because they couldn't display much in their truncated windows. Broad sidewalks along the road were clean of the latest snowfall suggesting that the people of Basil valued the ability to walk instead of driving wherever they wished to go. Indeed, at 10:00 a.m., the streets were crowded.

He pulled into a petrol station to refill the Perseus and got directions to Anna Konstantinova's family home, then left and turned north out and away from the bright signs of the center of town into an area of drab concrete buildings. Many were old warehouses, still in use. A few rows of run-down houses showed where this had once been family neighborhoods. The address he had for Anna Konstantinova was in a straggling line of unpainted, single-story houses with no yards but large, sagging porches. He parked at the curb and climbed out of the Perseus as a huge shipping truck rumbled by. The ground seemed to shake; so did the houses. The house he wanted appeared to have less of a sag than the others and the curtains behind the small windows weren't quite as yellow as its neighbors.

He climbed the stairs and knocked on the door, fighting the sense that someone was watching. When he turned back to the street for a moment, he caught a slight movement in the window of the next house down. It was the same, the world over: people watching their neighbors. He wondered whether, in this drab town, it was a kindness or mean-spirited.

A click behind him turned him back to the door. It opened four inches and a single blue eye peered out at him.

"Ye-es?" the voice quavered out at him, young and afraid.

He held out his badge. "I am Detektiv Alexander Kazakov. Is this the home of Anna Konstantinova?"

The door opened slightly so he could see a young woman, blonde as Anna had been. In fact, the family resemblance was unmistakable; and yet this girl also reminded him of another dead girl—Bure's stepdaughter Yekaterina. But the girl before him was finer boned and thin, as if she had not had a good meal for a long time. She was swathed in a long, blue woolen skirt and turtleneck, overlaid with an oversized gray sweater rolled up at the wrists as if she was trying to disguise her emaciated state.

"Yes," the woman said, swallowing. Then her eyes widened. "What's wrong? What's happened?"

"May I come in, please?" Kazakov said.

The woman's hands fluttered to her throat. "Oh God save us, no. No. No."

Her voice rose in a moan, but she stepped aside and Kazakov took that as the invitation to come in. The house was old, the linoleum floor worn and scrubbed to within an inch of its life. Even the floral wallpaper looked scrubbed and the place smelled like disinfectant. He faced a tiny parlor, in which a threadbare couch and chair had place of honor in front of an empty hearth. On the mantle stood only a candle and plaque containing the Lord's prayer. A light was on over the chair and a book lay open on the chair arm. A cold draft ran across the room, which explained the girl's sweaters.

"You are Anna Konstantinova's relative? A sister, perhaps?" Kazakov said, turning to her and starting to toe off his boots until she waved at him to leave them on.

Pale faced, she nodded. "Please. Have a seat." She motioned to the couch.

Kazakov waited until the girl sagged into her chair. Then he perched on the edge of the couch, his coat draped around him.

"May I have your name?" he asked gently.

"Lidiya Konstantinova."

Fear radiated off of her like hot iron. What could have the girl so scared?

"You are Anna's sister?"

Lidiya shook her head, but she huddled into her sweaters and pulled her feet up under her, too. "Her aunt. Her mother was my much-older sister, but my parents had me in their old age and Anna's mother had her in her youth. Anna and I were only two years apart. We grew up more like sisters."

"Are you her closest relative?"

She shook her head. "There is Vasili, her son."

"No one else?"

She shook her head again.

"Then I regret to inform you that Anna was found dead two days ago. I would have come sooner, but we did not have your contact information and did not know where Anna was from."

Lidiya appeared to crumple in on herself. She sagged back in her chair, her sweater and skirt making a formless heap as if all flesh and bone had evaporated.

"Dead," she whispered. Her eyes closed, the lids translucent so that it looked like she read secrets on the insides of her eyes. Then she looked at him again.

"I told her. I told her it was not safe to go to New Moscow. I knew something would happen to her. I sent her letters, hoping Vasili could lure her home again. That she would miss him and not stay." Her clear gaze filled with tears and she looked away. "She rarely came. Those damned dreams of hers. They were more important than her only son."

He stayed silent and let Lidiya gather her thoughts. She sprang up, hugging herself to pace the floor. "How could she do this to us? What am I to do?"

"Tell me about Anna," he asked gently.

She whirled back to him. "She was a selfish, selfish girl. So full of herself. She was always good at school—far better than me. She must have taken after her father, whoever he was. But not smart enough not to get pregnant. By then she was running with an older crowd—older than me, anyway. People she met at her job. When the father left, she decided to seek her fortune in New Moscow, or perhaps she went after him. She left me with Vasili. She said she'd earn enough to provide for us." She gave a bitter laugh. "She lied about that, too. At first, she sent money every week, but gradually the amount decreased and so did her letters to Vasili. It was as if she was slowly weaning us out of her life."

She sat down in her chair again, her expression gone hard as stone. "How did she die, Detektiv? I am thinking it was not natural, for then they would only send a policeman."

He looked away from the bitter gleam in her eye. "She was found murdered in the home of the woman she worked for. What can you tell me about Anna's time in New Moscow?"

She snorted. "Not much. She went with such hopes. She had always sworn she had the second sight. Her mother and mine had told fortunes, you see. From somewhere she got the idea that people in New Moscow would be hungry for what she could do for them. No, not from somewhere —it was a man. The same man who was likely Vasili's father."

"Tell me about him," Kazakov asked.

"What is there to tell?" She pulled her sweater closer around her neck. "She met him at work—some man. She never brought him home because I would have known. We shared my mother's house. The way she scurried after him, did his bidding, he must have been important—or at least important to her. I'll give Anna that: she must have loved him because she threw herself into making him happy. The rest of us no longer mattered. Not me in the beginning and not Vasili once the baby came. She went to New Moscow, I think, because he asked her to. Go to the city and become a prophet, she said. Instead she became not much more than a housekeeper, for all the money she sent. And yet here she was forever going on about the way she could see the future. Hers and mine were apparently intertwined. At least that was how she convinced me to quit my job to care for Vasili. I swear the boy is more my child than hers."

"Tell me about her prophecies. I know nothing about such things. What did she speak of?"

Lidiya's full lips downturned, imprinting frown lines on her young face. They were deep from too-frequent use.

"I swear she had no more special powers than me, but she needed to feel special. As a child, there were a few times when she actually did make a prophecy that came true. She was small and would scream and scream and scream every time her mother took a certain street. When she was older, she fought her mother and refused to go there. Her mother stopped taking that route when she had Anna with her. On a day when Anna was not with her, her mother was struck by blocks falling from new construction. It killed her." She shook her head. "It could have been a lucky guess, but such a fuss was made about her. There was another time that she told a pregnant neighbor that she should go to the hospital about her belly. The woman miscarried that afternoon. Rumors spread. People began to seek her out."

Kazakov studied her. There was wistful sadness in Lidiya Konstantinova's gaze, almost as if she wished it had been her who had such skills—if they truly existed. What she described could be coincidence or the result of a hyper-observant individual who picked up cues. He waited for Lidiya to continue.

"As she got older, she didn't make prophecies so much. I think the people coming to her had scared her, so there were no more episodes of screaming and no more warnings. She grew up, a smart, quiet girl, but after my mother died we needed income. We both got jobs. I was housekeeping for a few local officials. I helped her get an accounting job with a transborder shipping firm." Lidiya sighed as if the memories weren't pleasant.

"Suddenly she didn't keep the same hours. She was out with her friends, she said. At first, I think she was. I heard reports—not good ones —of her at local bars. Not that she was ill-behaved, but she was there. Not a proper thing for a lady to do—and then she was telling fortunes. The way she told it, one night there was a conversation. One of the men had just lost his wife, and on the spur of the moment, Anna apparently offered to contact her for him. They had a séance in a bar, can you imagine? Apparently, they crowded into the manager's office and she held a séance. The people attending were convinced Anna contacted the dead wife."

She looked at her hands. "Then the whispers changed, of course. And then she wasn't in the bars anymore and people left notes for her at the house, but she was never here. She'd met this man and spent too much time with him. He filled her head with nonsense and her belly with Vasili and then he left her."

"How did Anna react to that?" he asked, thinking about a girl who had more or less transformed herself into another person before being killed. By her lover?

"That was the thing." Lidiya shook her head. "On the one hand, she was upset that she was pregnant, but on the other, she was pleased. Perhaps she thought it would give her power over the father. Who knows? She wouldn't talk about it. But she was determined to seek her fortune in New Moscow. She said that she'd seen that her future lay there. That big things were coming and things were going to change."

"And did things change? You said she kept in touch after she left. What happened to Anna when she went to New Moscow?"

"We received letters, Vasili and I. At first they were love letters of a mother missing her son, but gradually they changed. She spoke about meeting important people. People who would help her. She thought that she might have a role as a private advisor, like the seers of the tsars all those years ago. Her mind seemed filled with these flights of fancy and little on her aunt and son who were waiting for her. At the same time, the money decreased…"

"Did she ever indicate anything in her letters that suggested something wasn't right? That she might be in danger?"

Lidiya met his gaze. "Nothing was right, Detektiv. Nothing is, when a mother abandons her baby. But no, there was nothing in her letters that suggested danger. Only excitement that her ridiculous dreams might come to fruition."

From elsewhere in the house came the sound of a baby's wail. Lidiya stood and smoothed her skirt.

"What were her dreams?"

She shook her head. "That a ridiculous girl from Basil could become a great lady, an advisor to tsars like the old days. Now, you'll have to excuse me for a moment. Vasili doesn't sleep as long anymore, now that he's older." She looked down at Kazakov, her blue gaze intense. "Tell me, Detektiv, how should one tell an infant that his mother is dead?"

Not waiting for an answer, she left the room and returned a few minutes later with a little dark-haired boy wearing a bright red, handknit sweater and worn dungaree trousers. His small feet were protected by thick adult socks rolled into thick cuffs at his ankles. Lidiya reseated herself in her chair and bounced the little boy on her knee. He had olive skin, thick black curls, and blacker eyes that gazed at Kazakov so intently for a moment he was taken aback.

He swallowed and looked up at Lidiya. "A good-looking child," he said.

She nodded and smoothed her fingers through his gleaming hair.

"Tell me," Kazakov said, barely able to look away from the child. "What company did Anna work for?"

Lidiya set the squirming little boy on the threadbare carpet and from somewhere produced wooden blocks for him to play with.

"Transcontinental, of course. It is the largest shipping company in Basil. My mother once worked there. That was how Anna was able to get her foot in the door."

Kazakov thought about it, checked his watch, and shoved up to his feet. "Thank you for your time, Ms. Konstantinova. I am truly sorry for your loss."

Transcontinental. Enver Pasha's damned company. Had the man told the truth when he'd said that he'd only seen Anna at Madam Sobol's house?

His gaze strayed to the boy now playing quietly with the blocks. Given Anna's fairness, the child must look like his father.

Lidiya saw him out to the door. As he stepped outside, from the parlor came little Vasili's gurgle and laugh as if he was party to a secret.

———

I t could not be. It simply could not.

Kazakov drove the highway back to New Moscow, fighting far too many big Transcontinental trucks amid the traffic, as if Enver Pasha somehow knew where he had been. Snow from a passing truck swirled up into the Perseus' windshield, momentarily blinding him. He slammed on the brakes and the flakes cleared, a shaft of sunlight through the heavy clouds glaring off the snowy fields.

It simply wasn't possible. Enver Pasha was not such a bald-faced liar. He could not afford to be. The man was far too careful about such things. A spy and infiltrator for the Ottoman government had to be. And yet he'd sat there facing Kazakov and Egorova and clearly stated that he did not know Anna. This from a man who made it his business to know *everything* —about Fergana. Could he possibly not know as much about his business? The impression Kazakov had of Enver's headquarters in New Moscow was that Enver took care of the slightest detail—right down to the clothing his clerical staff wore. Could a man like that not know Anna worked for him—even if it was at an outlying border town?

It was possible, but given the sensitivities at the Ferganese-Ottoman border and the fact that Transcontinental was all about shipping, he couldn't believe Enver didn't keep close tabs on what was happening out there. He should know Anna at least enough to recognize her.

So why lie, unless Anna Konstantinova was something much more than she seemed?

The question was, what was she?

He checked his watch. There was little time to contemplate it now. The meeting with Leonid Nikolaev was scheduled for two o'clock and it was already one thirty when he was barely into the warehouses encircling New Moscow. At this rate, he was going to be late. He pulled out his phone and dialed Egorova.

"Egorova." She picked up on the second ring, her voice cool and professional.

"How's it going?" he asked.

"We got three interviews done. I'm at the hotel now. The subjects weren't happy to see us. In each case they have a solid alibi for the day Anna was killed. As for what she was telling them, well, it was the usual claptrap prophecy stuff, but there was an edge to it. In each case it sounded like there were some seeds planted."

"Seeds?"

"Let's call them suggestions. As if Bure's election was certain and what were they going to do to prove loyalty and to get ahead under a new government. What that could mean. When I pursued it with the subject, each said that they'd been considering voting for Nikolaev and continuity. The known devil versus an unknown quantity. Now they were rethinking their direction."

She let that hang in the air as Kazakov considered.

"But that doesn't make sense. Or maybe I'm seeing ghosts." He told her what he'd learned from Lidiya Konstantinova and his suspicions about the father of Anna's son.

"Holy," she swore. "But how can we be sure? If it's true, what does it mean?"

"I've no idea. Listen, I'm on my way, but I might be late. Go on up and hold Nikolaev there. He came to meet Anna, so he has time scheduled. He'll just have to deal with us instead. I shouldn't be long."

He signed off and dialed again, this time the M.E.'s office. The officious young receptionist answered.

"Dr. Gordiev, please," he said.

"May I tell him who's calling?"

"It's Detektiv Kazakov. It's urgent that I speak to him."

He found himself on hold, ancient balalaika music squealing through the phone. Then there was a click.

"Gordiev." The M.E.'s voice sounded tired and Kazakov was reminded of his earlier revelation that each person inhabited their own reality. He wondered what in Gordiev's world exhaust him so.

"You all right?" he asked. "Sorry to bother you, but I've been trying to contact you for the autopsy results."

"I'm as well as this job allows. After a time, it begins to wear you down. I thought examining the dead would be less stressful than dealing with the living. It doesn't feel like it today."

"What happened?" Kazakov asked, viewing this conversation as something of a breakthrough with the M.E.

"Nothing unusual. Just reviewing your girl's labs. Another couple of dead women, both domestic disputes. My wife's been suggesting that I open a family practice to get some perspective."

"It doesn't always help. Khan had one, you know."

"Did he? We could still use him around here. Regardless of the rumors, he was a good man with a scalpel."

Kazakov wanted to ask what the rumors were, but he was entering

New Moscow and wanted the autopsy results more. "So what did the lab tests say?"

"She was drugged. A sedative. It would have made it easy to undress and kill her. It might have looked like she was killed by strangulation, but actually, her neck was broken, the nerves severed. It was either an accident or a professional job and my money's on the professional."

"So a professional hit done clean and clinical."

"That about sums it up," Gordiev said. "But there's one other thing. Your victim was pregnant. Only about six weeks along, but it wasn't her first child."

Kazakov's hands fisted on the steering wheel. Yekaterina had been pregnant, too. Pregnant by her stepfather, Boris Bure. There were too many similarities here.

He brought himself back to the thickening city traffic and Gordiev on the phone. "Can you do a DNA test on the fetus and send me a copy of the autopsy report?"

"Already winging its way to you, Detektiv."

"Thank you. Thank you very much."

Kazakov signed off as he swung in in front of the Royal Caravanserai hotel. By his watch, he was five minutes late. Five minutes late and another girl dead. But then being too late seemed to be his modus operandi.

H e found Egorova waiting in the lobby. She looked disheveled and pale. A muddy smear marred the side of her coat.

"What happened to you?" Kazakov asked, scanning the damage to her clothing. Her trouser legs were also filthy, but someone, Egorova probably, had already tried unsuccessfully to brush them clean.

"When I spoke to you I was just parking outside. I climbed out of my car and closed the door and a truck almost hit me. It caught me on the hip just as I leapt out of the way. Thus the smear. The pantlegs were done when I landed in a puddle of melted snow." She shrugged, but her palms were scraped and bloody and now that he knew what had happened, he saw she was shaken.

"What is it?" he asked. "There's more to this."

"I—I think I might have seen the truck earlier today following me and Chelomeyev. But then it could have been any truck. I don't know. I was so shocked when it happened that I didn't even get the license." She was clearly disgusted with herself. "I think the reason I'm so upset is that my mom died in a hit and run." She held up her hands and clenched them against the tremble.

She looked up at him with a serious gaze. "I was also thinking of what you said after the Biysk investigation. You said that pulling Bure's file could have alerted someone that we are looking and that it could bring repercussions. It made me think back since I got into the city. There have been other times that I thought someone was following me, but I always disregarded the feeling as a too vivid imagination."

Kazakov nodded. "We need to document everything. Have you got your camera on you?"

"It's in the car."

"Then when we finish with Nikolaev…"

She nodded and led him to the elevator. "The appointment is in a luxury suite on the top floor. Apparently it's a complimentary perk of being the president of the country. According to our friend at reception, it's often used for sensitive meetings with foreign dignitaries."

The suite sat at the end of a broad hall carpeted in thick Bukhara runners of muted blues and browns. The double doors of the suite were gleaming walnut, decoratively studded with black iron nails that outlined the golden Russian eagle. Kazakov knocked once and the double doors almost immediately swung open to reveal a narrow-chested young man with a high domed forehead pushing through thinning hair. He wore an immaculate gray three-piece suit.

"You're late! The president is almost ready to cancel the appointment…" His gaze widened as he registered the unexpected presence of Egorova and Kazakov and no Anna Konstantinova. His face quickly smoothed as he looked them up and down, his gaze sticking momentarily on Egorova's dirty coat. "I'm afraid you must have the wrong room…," he said.

"Anna Konstantinova won't be coming. I am Detektiv Alexander Kazakov and this is Detektiv Elena Egorova of New Moscow police. We are here to speak to Leonid Nikolaev."

The young man silently mouthed Kazakov's words like a fish. Then he shook his head. "I'm sorry, there is no one here by that name."

Kazakov sighed away the need to grab the youngster by his collar. "You just said the president is here. Which president were you referring to?"

"I—I—I don't know. I was confused."

Egorova had pulled out her notebook. "Your name, please."

" Albert. Albert Nikolaev."

"Keeping it in the family. Is the president your father, perhaps?" Egorova said and looked at Albert with interest. "Is this what you do? Answer the door for him? I hope you are well paid because the position is going to be short-lived once the election happens. It won't look good for our current president when it comes out in the news that there is a connection between him and a murdered girl and that he refused to be interviewed. The optics are all wrong." She shook her head.

"He's not my father, he's a distant cousin and I'm his communications advisor, if you must know. Are you saying Anna Konstantinova was murdered?"

"Exactly," Kazakov growled. "She was murdered last weekend. We're tracing her movements and her contacts."

Albert shook his head. "The president hardly knew her. He only met her a few times."

"How about you let the president tell me that," Kazakov said. He overpowered the young man's gaze and Albert stepped aside to allow them to pass. Kazakov stepped from the plush hallway carpet to even softer footing. Thick carpets that might be antique tribals by their muted colors filled a foyer with dark wood walls. A broad, arched doorway let them into a sitting room with a sunken floor and expansive windows that looked across the city toward Yekaterina Mountain. Leonid Nikolaev sat tensely on the sofa. When he saw them, he stood.

Kazakov stepped down the single step to the carpeted floor. The room was furnished in dove gray shades on an off-white carpet. The non-glass walls were decorated with photo enlargements of architectural details that might have been taken within the old city. It made for an odd juxtaposition of old caravanserai and nuevo riche.

Kazakov crossed the carpet to the president and nodded in greeting.

Nikolaev was a smaller man than Kazakov had expected—barely five foot eight—but his suit was so superbly cut that he appeared larger. But that might have been the force of the man's personality that shone from his clear brown gaze. Brown hair was cut with precision to present youthfulness and yet maturity. His square-jawed face carried an artificial tan. Kazakov hoped that was the man's only artifice, but then who could say. Nikolaev was a politician and all politicians lied.

"You are not who I was expecting," Nikolaev said. His voice carried the cultured clarity of the natural orator.

"You were expecting the seeress, Anna Konstantinova," Kazakov said.

Nikolaev's gaze widened.

"I regret to inform you that Miss Konstantinova is dead. We're seeking your help to understand her movements in the days before she died."

Nikolaev's tanned flesh paled slightly.

Kazakov introduced himself and Egorova, who made no apologies for her appearance.

"We have information that you were one of Anna Konstantinova's clients."

Licking his lips, Nikolaev hesitated but then nodded.

"Can you please tell me about your arrangements."

"When did she die?" Nikolaev asked, nodding them to chairs while he reseated himself on the low, dove-gray couch. Albert remained on guard in the doorway.

"She was found on Monday. The autopsy says she died over the weekend, probably Saturday evening."

"Then it can't have been me. I was at a rally in Kokand, not even in New Moscow."

Egorova took note of it.

"Where was this rally?" Kazakov asked, for they would have to confirm Nikolaev's appearance. It *was* possible to travel to Kokand and back in only a few hours.

"At the arena. Albert arranged everything. He can give you the information."

Kazakov nodded. "Then let me bring you back to my original question. Tell me about your arrangement with Anna Konstantinova."

Nikolaev's gaze shifted to Albert as if checking whether he had to answer. Then the president sighed and Albert stepped back and disappeared out of the room. "It began about six months ago. I had heard through friends about this wonderful psychic. She was a relative unknown —from a small town, you see. But everyone said she was genuine. Meetings with her were arranged through this hotel, so I had Albert make the arrangements." He looked at Kazakov as if seeking understanding. "It was not the sort of thing I had ever done before. But there was the upcoming election and things—well, there were rumors afoot that the other party had an outstanding candidate to replace old Andreev."

Andreev had been the opposition party head, but a stroke had incapacitated him last fall. Bure had stepped in.

Albert appeared with a tea tray as Kazakov waited for Nikolaev to resume his story. The young man poured the tea and offered a cup to Egorova. She declined, but Kazakov accepted his and waited.

The president seemed to have pulled into himself. The force of his gaze, perhaps, turned inward.

He turned a troubled gazed on Kazakov. "She came here. There was no special room or paraphernalia. She simply came in and we talked a little. You know, pleasantries. How did she like New Moscow. The city versus a small town. That sort of thing, while we drank a cup of tea. Then she caught my hands tightly and looked into my eyes. It was—disturbing, actually. It felt like she looked far deeper than most people did. Then she closed her eyes and sat there breathing softly so that for a moment I thought she had fallen asleep. I was about to say forget the whole thing when suddenly she started to speak. But it wasn't her voice. It was deeper —like a man's. The voice said it was her spiritual guide—General Alexander Vasilyevich Suvarov. I was about to call her fake and leave, for how could it possibly be Suvarov? That good general is long dead. His ravages in Crimea brought doom upon the Russian people. But then he said I was facing a great ordeal—a great battle—the final battle for the Russian soul. He said that I must question my motivations and what is best for Fergana. Then the girl jerked and her eyes flashed open. She pulled her hands away as if I burned her. She asked what she had said, but I would not tell her. To tell the truth, I was shaken by the whole experience. I wanted her to leave. But then she said and did the most amazing thing. She caught my hands again and said that my wife and I had been considering adopting a child. She said that we should look in Kokand and that there would be a boy for us. I was taken aback, for just before I came to the meeting, my wife had phoned with news that an adoption agency that we had contacted in Kokand had called. They had a baby boy for us."

He shook his head in apparent amazement. "I mean, how could she have known? When she left I had a long discussion with Albert about what she had said. I wanted to see her again, to see what else I could learn. And so I have been meeting with her every two weeks to get her advice."

"Tell me about that—her advice?" Kazakov asked.

Sipping his tea, Nikolaev eyed Kazakov. Then he set his china cup down in the saucer and shook his head. "I'm afraid that simply isn't possible. You're asking me to discuss my campaign strategies."

"So she gave you campaign advice? Anna Konstantinova did?" Kazakov thought of the slip of a girl and where she had come from. It was doubtful she had any more political acumen than Kazakov did, and that wasn't much.

Nikolaev shook his head. "You misunderstand. It wasn't Anna counseling me. It was the great General Suvarov—Yekaterina's chief general before we lost Moscow."

"Before *Suvarov* lost Moscow. He was not that great a general, one could think," Egorova said softly.

"No! The advice I received was well reasoned and sound. It gave my campaign direction."

Kazakov sat back.

"All right. Did you receive any other insights like the one about your adoptive son?"

"A few. One about the best date for a rally—it was a great success. And another about the importance of my wife having a medical checkup. It was found that she had a lump in her breast. You see? She was always helpful, unlike some other advisors who I have had to let go."

So Nikolaev had become one of the people who truly believed.

"Seeing her every two weeks, you must have had other conversations beyond her fortunes. What can you tell me about them?"

"Simple pleasantries, as I mentioned. We did not run in the same circles, Detektiv."

"Did she ever speak of other clients or associates? People she knew?"

"Never. She was very discreet. That was what I liked about her."

Kazakov looked at Egorova, who shook her head.

"Did you ever see where she went when she left you?" Kazakov asked.

Nikolaev tipped his head back as he thought. "On one occasion we left together. I had a car waiting and offered to drive her. She declined and said she had only a short distance to go for her next appointment. She turned right when she left the hotel. That is all I can tell you." Nikolaev stood up. The interview was over.

Standing with Egorova, Kazakov thanked Nikolaev for his time. Albert stood waiting to see them out. Kazakov took the one stair to the foyer and turned back, looking over Egorova's head. "Once more thing. Did Anna Konstantinova ever mention your opponent?"

Color drained from Nikolaev's face.

"This interview is over," Nikolaev said. "Get them out of here. I have better things to do with my day."

He stormed out of the room as Kazakov turned back to Albert. "A sensitive issue."

Albert nodded. "She warned him. Told him that Bure is an unstoppable force unless he did certain things. He is an honorable man and has not been able to bring himself to those kinds of decisions."

Kazakov looked back at the now empty room. He now recognized the look he'd seen in Nikolaev's gaze. Fear.

"What had she suggested that he do?"

Kirill shook his head. "Desperate times require desperate measures."

For some reason Kazakov thought of the death of the young tsarevich. He wondered whether the tsarevich's older brothers had had a similar look to their eyes.

10

The sun had sunk farther to the west when they stepped out of the Royal Caravanserai and into the street. The street was in shadows, a cold, damp, wind off the mountains gusting through and blowing soot into Kazakov's eyes. Egorova stood beside him on the sidewalk, her cheeks bright, but her gaze troubled as they took photos of Egorova's filthy clothing. The mud on her coat and trousers had dried and it flaked off when she brushed at it. The afternoon traffic was increasing, the vehicles sending up a steady spray of filthy water that cascaded over the sidewalks. Not a safe day to be walking.

"So, what do you think?" Kazakov asked. Overhead the afternoon sky was bright blue, with streaming strings of clouds carrying moisture westward over the Ottoman deserts.

"I think that we are in serious trouble as a country, no matter who is elected." Egorova shook her head. "Bure, or a man who takes campaign advice from not much more than a schoolgirl."

"He's desperate. You can see it in his eyes. And afraid."

She nodded. "I wonder what Anna counseled him to do?"

"He didn't like it, whatever it was." But Kazakov couldn't get the image of the dead tsarevich from the old folk tale out of his head. Was that the only way to stop Bure? Kill him?

Shaken at the thought, he led Egorova to the sedan. "You okay if we head over to Madam Sobol's?"

Nodding, Egorova climbed into her police sedan. "How about if we drop your vehicle at the station and ride together."

They did, and Kazakov climbed into the sedan, thunking the door shut behind him. Egorova was already accelerating out of the underground garage as he settled himself.

"So what did you learn from Anna's family?" she asked.

He told her.

"So are you thinking she followed her lover into the city?" she asked as she steered expertly through the growing traffic. The sun breaking through the streaming clouds reflected a brilliant glare off the windows of shops and houses as they left the center of the city behind.

"I am. Given Anna's similarity to Yekaterina Weber, Bure's stepdaughter, my inclination is to think Bure may be the father of her unborn child, but if Bure is Chinese under all that cosmetic surgery, his DNA would come through and Vasili clearly isn't Chinese. Given Vasili had a dark-haired, dark-skinned father, and Lidiya suggested that Anna followed her lover, her unborn child may not have been Bure's at all. If the father of her unborn child is Enver Pasha, I think it's more likely that he asked her to come to New Moscow. The fact that she was working as an errand girl for Madam Sobol is what puzzles me. And that she was working as a medium on the side. That doesn't strike me as something Enver would sanction. He's more the type to set a mistress up in a household. And why have Anna when he has Marta? Anna isn't his type from what I've seen." Kazakov shook his head. "This whole damn case is a puzzle and I'm afraid I'm going to have to abandon it to you and Chelomeyev."

"What are you talking about?" Egorova swerved to miss a pothole in the road. All around New Moscow the unseasonably cold winter had caused pavement to buckle and crumble.

"Rostoff caught up to me. He says a suspect gave up that there is a credible threat of an attempt on Bure's life. He wants me to use my connections—such as they are—to investigate." He sighed. "If that was really Khan that I saw in that newscast, there's no way anyone will talk to me."

"Did you tell him that?"

"Hell, no. I said I was more likely to do the shooting myself."

Egorova whipped a glance at him. "Don't even joke about something like that."

"That's what Rostoff said. I have to admit, it's crossed my mind that the country would be better off without him. Wouldn't it be better if someone like me killed him than one of the tribals? If they did it, it would cause a bloodbath."

Egorova turned a horrified gaze on him. "Are you listening to yourself? You shouldn't say anything like that out loud. Think it, maybe. Say it, never!"

He slumped back in his seat, wondering at how the words had actually slipped from his mouth. Speaking something had a bad habit of making things come true. He shuddered and felt the weight of his weapon in its holster. "Sorry. But the bottom line is this case is supposed to be yours and Chelomeyev's. You'll have to take the lead, but I'm not dumping it on you. I can manage both."

"All right." She nodded and refocused on the road.

Kazakov's phone shrilled in his pocket. He fished it out.

"Kazakov."

"Detektiv." Kasimir Krupin's voice seemed strangled through the phone.

"Kasimir? What is it? What's happened?" And then he knew. "Margarete?"

"Is gone," was all the old man could manage.

"We'll be right over."

"No! No. I don't want to interrupt your investigations, but I had promised to let you know."

Egorova glanced at him and nodded. She pulled a U-turn and sped away from Madam Sobol's neighborhood toward the aging area where the Krupin house stood.

"We'll be there in ten minutes." He hung up and held on as Egorova accelerated through the streets.

"That gracious woman…" Egorova said.

Kazakov nodded around the stone lodged in his throat. He might not have known her well, or known her in her heyday as a doyenne of charity events and galas, but the grace and loveliness of Margarete Krupin was definitely a loss to Fergana. So was the vast array of knowledge stored in her memory. He regretted that he hadn't seen her more often and that when he had, it had been about a case, but that was his life—a sea of regrets.

They pulled in at the curb in front of the house behind an ambulance with the rear doors yawning menacingly open. If anything, the house looked more careworn and shrunken in on itself. Empty.

Not waiting for Egorova, Kazakov climbed out into a puddle of slushy snow and started up the walk just as the front door opened. Two ambulance attendants and a black-swathed gurney carried Margarete Krupin's body outside. Kazakov stepped off the walkway into the sodden snow to let them pass. Egorova stood by the car, her body at silent attention.

The gurney wheels squealed in the freezing water as they rolled down through the gate. At the ambulance, the attendants lifted the body inside. Then one of them returned with a clipboard for Krupin to sign before returning to the ambulance and leaving.

They left behind a ruined old man. Kasimir Krupin clung to the open doorframe until Kazakov leapt up the stairs and caught him as his old man's knees gave. He looked up at Kazakov without recognition as Kazakov helped him inside. Egorova came up the stairs behind him.

"I'll make tea," she said quietly as she tugged off her boots.

"And find something stronger, if there is anything." Kazakov toed his boots off, too.

With a nod, Egorova headed back past the library-cum-sickroom where Margarete had lain and into the darkness at the rear of the house. Kazakov supported Krupin into the parlor at the front of the house and helped him into a seat by the fireplace.

Krupin was shivering and the hearth held only ashes. Kazakov went in search of firewood. He found Egorova in a cheery kitchen of bight white walls and cupboards with yellow window casings and curtains. A large antique woodstove sat against the wall radiating heat into the room. She clattered dishes and a kettle around in the kitchen as she searched the cupboards.

"Perhaps I'll bring him here. It's warmer."

She nodded as he retraced his steps. Krupin wasn't there.

Kazakov peered into the dining room that was now Krupin's study, but there was nothing but books weighting down every flat surface. He went to Margarete's sickroom, but there was only the empty bed and the lingering iron-scent of the sick. He looked up the stairs, but he hadn't heard the old man's footsteps. He yanked open the front door and found Krupin on his knees in the sodden snow, tears flooding down his cheeks.

Kazakov tried to help him up, but Krupin didn't seem aware. Kazakov scooped him up and was surprised at how light the old man was. Not much more than skin and bones it seemed.

He carried Krupin back inside and down to the kitchen. The old man was shuddering. His clothes were soaked, his hands red and chilled. Kazakov ran back to the parlor and claimed the blankets that he suspected had been for Margarete. The floral scent that came off of them confirmed it and he took them back to the kitchen to wrap Krupin's shoulders.

Krupin stared vacantly around the room.

"He weighs nothing. I don't think he's been eating."

Egorova shook her head. "There's almost nothing in the cupboards."

They both glanced at Krupin, still shivering in his swaddling of blankets.

"Everything went into her medical bills. I'll bet she's the only one who's gotten anything."

On the stove, the kettle boiled. Egorova pointed at the teapot and cups. "I'll run for groceries. There's no milk, but there's sugar. Get him to drink small amounts and that might help. I'll be back with food in a bit."

Efficiently, as she did everything else, she wiped the counter and disappeared up the hallway. He heard the sedan leave and busied himself in the silence making the tea.

When the tea was steeped, he poured the liquid and mixed three spoons of sugar into each cup. They'd make do with no milk. The important thing was getting something into Krupin. The sugar would give him energy and the hot tea would warm him up.

He sat down with Krupin and set a cup before Krupin. "Drink up. It's good for you."

Krupin didn't move, his gaze a horrible blank stare.

Sighing, Kazakov slid his chair around beside Krupin and gently held the cup up to Krupin's lips.

Krupin turned his face away.

"You have to have something. You've been starving yourself, old friend." He held the cup insistently to Krupin's lips and finally the old man sipped. He sipped again. And again.

Finally, two gnarled hands snaked up from inside the blankets and accepted the cup from Kazakov. His gaze met Kazakov's and the vacancy was gone.

"Margarete was my life." He sipped his tea and shook his head. "I—I wanted to die with her." A peek of color appeared in his cheeks, whether of health or embarrassment, Kazakov wasn't sure.

"From my brief knowledge of her, she was an amazing woman. I wish I'd known her when she was younger."

Krupin smiled. "She was—amazing. A beauty, but an unconventional one. Everyone noticed the beauty; it shone through her like a flame. That might have caught my attention like it did so many other men, but it was the other Margarete—the thinking, breathing, caring woman—who I could not get enough of. It was her grace and wit that got me where I was in the corporate world. And when things fell apart for me and I took the blame for the missing company funds, she could have left me. I swear most New Moscow wives would. But she stood by me with the same grace and charm as we had to sell our home and move here. Somehow, who and what she was kept her still in high esteem within her social circles. It was only the cancer..."

Krupin's voice faded and a tear streamed down his lined face. In self-defense, he sipped his tea until her regained himself.

"That was when she had to withdraw from social life?"

Krupin's gaze was far away and Kazakov feared he'd lost the old man again. His shivers had subsided, but he suddenly jerked and glanced at Kazakov again.

"Not at first. At first we denied that it would kill her. She kept up her charity work as we searched for the cure. Radiation. Chemotherapy. None of them worked and the cancer was progressing quickly. When she had to withdraw from overseeing her charity work, I swear it was like a giant tree fell in the forest. The silence from the world was deafening. No one came here. But I was here. I saw what it cost her. I think that hurt her more than the cancer."

From the front of the house came Egorova's footsteps. She reentered the kitchen carrying two web bags of groceries. From one she unloaded a bottle of milk, which she handed to Kazakov for the tea.

"Are you feeling better?" she asked Krupin.

"Like a scooped out melon," he said and managed a weak smile.

"Let's see what we can do to fill you up." She turned back to the kitchen and efficiently pulled out a frying pan, bowl, and whisk from the cupboards. She stirred the fire in the old stove and added wood, then pulled out sausage from her bag and set it frying. The room filled with sizzling and the delicious scent. She chopped up vegetables that she set aside in a bowl and set another frying pan on the stove. Butter went into the second frying pan, followed by the vegetables. The fragrance of onions and peppers and mushrooms joined the already delicious scents.

Kazakov's stomach growled.

How was it that most women had this skill? Set them in a kitchen and with a few ingredients they could create a feast. Except for Annuschka, his ex-wife, of course.

"Margarete moved like that," Krupin said. "Graceful and confident always. She was like that right to the end." His voice caught. "And smart. Always seeking a solution to problems, never wringing her hands if a problem existed."

"A very good way to live your life, I think," Kazakov said.

"And practical," Egorova added over her shoulder. "No use crying over spoiled milk, my mother used to say. Just make something that requires buttermilk."

"Women are such practical creatures," Krupin said. "I was never as good at it as Margarete. She used to say that I was her dreamer. That I dreamed big dreams. What she didn't realize was that my biggest dreams were always of her. I—I don't know what I'm going to do…" He scrubbed his face and wild gray hair with his fingers. "It isn't fair that she died before me. She would have been so much better at dealing with things."

Egorova turned from the stove and knelt beside him. "But you'll do what needs to be done because you're a smart man and you'll have Kazakov and me to help you. Now how do you like your scrambled eggs? Runny or firm?"

His expression turned from dazed to ready. "Firm, please."

"There. You see. Your first decision."

She turned back to the stove, quickly whipped eggs, and poured them into the vegetable frying pan. Steam rose up around her face as she stirred.

Krupin watched her, admiration in his face. "I truly don't know how they do it. The media makes women look like simpering fools, but really…"

"We do it because someone has to," Egorova said.

It was as if her words shot Krupin through the heart. He shrank back into his blanket, the teacup in his hand forgotten, so that Kazakov had to rescue it before Krupin dropped it.

"Kasimir? What is it?"

Egorova filled three plates with food and set them on the table. Cutlery found its way onto the table, but Kazakov ignored the feast to catch the old man's shoulders.

"Kasimir? Tell me."

Faded blue eyes looked up at him, all hope leached out of them.

"We knew the end was close. She couldn't move from her bed, and her breathing had become so hard. She would take a breath and then exhale and I would hold my breath, willing her to breathe in again. To live and be with me. I thought she was sleeping, but then her eyes opened and she looked at me. "I'm dying," she said and she smiled at me, "but that's part of life. Did you know that I always loved you from the first time we met? When we met, falling for you was the most natural thing in the world."

Tears streamed down his face. "Then she caught my hand, when I didn't think she could move. Her fingers were strong. Stronger than I'd ever felt them, and she pulled herself up off the bed. "I want to vote," she said. "I have to vote. Bure. He is not natural. He'll turn Fergana into a charnel field. You must do something, Kasimir. Don't let it happen."

Krupin went silent and buried his face in his hands.

"What happened?" Egorova asked softly from her side of the table. She reached over gently to touch his shoulder.

Krupin's hands fell to his lap.

"She died," he said, his face empty.

———

It was long after dark when Kazakov and Egorova left Krupin's home. The night air was cold but didn't carry the same breath of winter it had a few weeks earlier. The clouds continued to stream overhead, but beyond them were the stars, watered down by the streetlights of New Moscow. The streetlights spilled light in a pool at either end of the block. Around them, the small, neat houses glowed with light through curtains, masking the small lives of New Moscow's denizens. All of these neighbors and not one of them had come to check on Krupin. Had they not seen, or did they simply not care? How small lives had become, as if those curtains not only kept the world out, they held the people inside prisoner. It all depended on how you looked at things. He would bet that there were people in those houses who saw their four walls as prisons, not safe harbors.

Then again, he was likely being too negative. Perhaps they didn't come because they saw the vehicle parked outside Krupin's home.

Kazakov stood on the slowly freezing slush at the curb and inhaled the air. It tasted of soot from New Moscow's factories. A cigarette would taste particularly good at this moment.

"What are you thinking?" Egorova asked.

"Oh." Kazakov came back to himself. "Nothing important. You?"

"I'm worried about him. It doesn't look like he has anyone to help him with funeral arrangements and the like."

Kazakov shrugged. "He has us."

He glanced back at the house and the single light on upstairs. They'd made sure Krupin was headed to bed before they left. He'd seemed to revive after they finally got him to eat—not that anyone had really felt like eating. Krupin's story of Margarete's last words had been particularly disturbing. It was a horrible thing for Margarete to lay at the feet of her husband. What the hell had she been thinking?

"How could you do that to someone you loved?" Kazakov asked. He glanced from the lit bedroom window back at Egorova. "What is an old man like that to do?"

"Grieve," Egorova said. "He needs time to deal with the fact that he's alone. I'm sure it's a shock even though they knew it was coming." She shook her head, her blonde ponytail bobbing. "I can't imagine losing someone after being married for so many years. It must feel like half of your soul has been lost."

Kazakov shook his head. "And we wonder how spiritualists can find customers. Loss like we've just seen—it's fodder. People are so desperate to believe they can still communicate with their loved ones. That somehow the dead are still with us. Those people are easy pickings, I suppose."

"Haven't you ever wished you could communicate with someone you've lost?"

Feeling punched in the gut, Kazakov swung around to face her. There was no animosity in her gaze and no sign that she knew of his frequent trips to a certain graveyard and grave. He'd begun to think that when you lost someone, a little part of you died, too. It was as if when you met someone and cared about them, you gifted them with a little part of you that connected you. That was how they could hurt you. As long as they lived, they had that power, but it was in death that the real pain hit, for they ripped the connecting end right out of your heart.

He'd known hurt when Annuschka left him. It had hurt far worse when Maria had died, and he had known her only a few short days.

Under Egorova's regard, he shook his head. "Not in my makeup, I guess."

A glimmer in her gaze said she knew he lied. It was a chink in their partnership.

Sighing, he shook his head. "Listen. It's late. Why don't I drop you at the office? I'm going to the old city to ask some questions. Follow orders and all that. I'll see you in the office in the morning."

"You sure? It's not that late. I could come with you."

"It's better if I visit alone. It's questionable what my welcome will be, given what happened with Khan. And if he's alive—well, that makes it even more questionable. Having an unknown with me will just make them less likely to talk to me."

She finally agreed and he drove her back to the station and changed vehicles to his trusty Perseus. From the old city he could go directly home. The drive would let him sort out what he was feeling about Kasimir and the Konstantinova case.

The New Moscow streets were emptying out as he left the station behind and headed to the old city. The sky was dark, the haze of clouds too high to reflect the city lights but thick enough to erase all but the brightest stars. The cold air had frozen the moisture on the streets so it crunched under his tires as he aimed toward the bulk of Yekaterina Mountain, the spotlit statue of Yekaterina shining like a beacon from her perch just below the peak. A beacon of what, he wasn't sure.

The old city spread from the base of Yekaterina Mountain and was separated from modern New Moscow by Chelomeyev's gentrified warehouse area. Still, in the darker side streets, darker business occurred. Drugs. Prostitution. New Moscow might not be Constantinople, but it still had its problems.

The old city was the antithesis of the spreading pox of New Moscow suburbs. Confined by its terra cotta walls, the old city was a monument to what had stood on this place for a thousand years. Yes, the old city might have been razed by invaders a time or six, but the Kyrgyz and Uzbek people had always returned and always rebuilt.

The result was a clay- and stucco-walled community of two- and three-story, flat-roofed buildings that seemed to merge one into the other through their connecting walls. Along the streets there were broad doors at street level—some large enough to allow a vehicle to enter if the stout wooden doors were opened—but the walls were almost devoid of windows to the outer world. Instead, beyond those doors in the best homes waited courtyards with broad balconies to provide shade from the harsh summer sunlight. All of the rooms gave onto the balconies and the central courtyard often held fruit trees and flowers. They were like mini Gardens of Eden. At least that was in the better homes where a single family owned the home. These days, many of the old places had been broken up into apartments so that five or six families might share the space.

Kazakov drove the Perseus down deserted streets. Interesting, given it wasn't that late or that cold. But then, the riot had likely convinced people to stay home and safe. When the streets became too narrow, he parked, blocking the road, and climbed out. Only the wind rattled a bit of paper as it rolled down the curb. No voices, no stray strands of music through the thick wood and iron doors.

He set off on foot down what would be a dusty street in summer. In winter it was uneven with snow packed by the tread of many feet. He passed small shops locked up tight with shutters closed and the print shop whose owner had been so helpful in previous cases. He checked his watch. Too late to rouse the owner if Kazakov wanted to stay in his good graces. Instead, he struck out to a tea shop he knew.

It sat at a strange confluence where five narrow streets converged. A small fountain that was, surprisingly, still running in the cold, across from a narrow, wedge-shaped building between two streets. A blue door was all that would fit into the end of the building, thus the place was known as the Blue Corner Tea House. The window in the narrow door was shuttered, but Kazakov wiped his feet on the single step and pushed the door open into—warmth and light.

Small, rough-wood tables and stools were scattered around the narrow room that held a counter and large tea maker at the back. Around the outer edge of the building, a low ledge held worn hand-woven cushions for customers to sit on. The owner, a large bear of a Kyrgyz, glanced at the door and stopped filling a cup. The people in the room— all older tribal men who looked, from their worn attire, like they were returning home from work—followed his glance and the room went silent.

Kazakov stepped inside and closed the door behind him. He ignored the men around the room and nodded at the owner as he crossed to him.

"A fine night, Abdulin," Kazakov said, leaning on the counter.

The owner, Adilet Abdulin, had a thick black beard and piercing black eyes that currently glared unwelcomingly at Kazakov. Well, when all else failed, he had his official capacity, though that would likely get him nowhere.

"You're not welcome here, Russian," Abdulin said.

Kazakov smiled. "A cup of tea, please. It's cold outside."

Abdulin didn't move. "I thought you said the night was fine."

Kazakov lifted one shoulder in a half-hearted shrug. "It is what it is. Why don't you step outside with me and see?" Because there was no way the man would speak to him in the presence of his customers, if he would speak to Kazakov at all.

Abdulin snorted and turned back to his tea. He poured a cup and took it to a table. Kazakov didn't move.

"You're wasting your time. We don't serve Russians here. They have their own cafes," Abdulin said on his return.

"Aah, but what they call tea is not the same, nor is the conversation. Tonight, I prefer a Kyrgyz tea for a change."

From behind him came murmurs. He overheard the word spy.

He sighed and shook his head at Abdulin. "Can we try this again? I have been your friend and ally. I helped rescue Khan and his family. I solved the murder of your nephew. Surely that counts for something."

"You Russians—you shot Khalil Khan," said a voice behind him.

Another sigh and Kazakov turned to face those who accused him. "Yes. We did. A police officer did because Khan killed a man in cold blood and injured another. If there is anything that haunts me it is that fact. Khalil Khan was my friend. I would have given my life for him."

The room of unfriendly gazes barely wavered. Finally, one of the older men, a tribal with a tall fur hat and long coat, stood up and slammed out the door. Others followed until there was only Adilet Abdulin and Kazakov.

Kazakov turned back to the proprietor. "I ruin your business. Again. I am sorry."

Abdulin shook his head as he wiped his counter. "No, you aren't. You want something and you hope that I'll give it to you now that the others are gone. I should just toss you out on your ear. It would look better for me and probably increase my business."

"Give me five minutes and then I'll let you do it."

Abdulin cocked a brow at him. "You think five minutes will get you your answers?"

Kazakov smiled. Five minutes might give him a chance to prove himself. And he had to start somewhere, though where he'd go from here, he wasn't sure. Regardless of Rostoff's sense that Kazakov knew these people, Kazakov was still a foreigner in this part of the city.

"I will start by telling you what we are hearing: That there is a plot to assassinate Boris Bure."

Abdulin's bearded face betrayed nothing, though a slight twitch by his left eye might mean something—or just that the man was holding back his anger.

"So you come to me? You think I am involved in such a plot?" The

Kyrgyz man came around his counter. "There is the door. You can leave anytime. Five minutes, I said. No more."

Kazakov held up his hands. "You misunderstand. I think you are a smart man and you love your people. This is well known. In a business like this, you talk to many people. If such a plot was afoot, you would know—or you would know who would know."

A snort and then Abdulin shook his head. "If there was anything—you ask me to betray confidences. People would know if suddenly they were arrested."

So he knew—something.

Kazakov sighed. "I don't wish to cause you trouble." He thought a moment. "You have to know that killing Boris Bure would just lead to reprisals against your people. It would feed right into his rhetoric—rhetoric others may be willing to take up given his success in the polls. It could lead to a worse situation for your people."

Abdulin looked heavenward. "You think I don't know? So do all the elders among us. We council caution but, like you Russians, we have young hotheads." He looked away. "I am ashamed at what is happening to my people, my country."

"If it's any consolation, so am I," Kazakov said softly. "My people are so trapped in past glories that they cannot see what they have today. I mourn the great work our people could do together, but it seems neither side is prepared to try."

Turning back to his great kettle, Abdulin ran the spigot to fill a cup. He placed it on the counter and slid it down to Kazakov.

"We aren't so different, you and I."

"Just two citizens trying to do our jobs. You give people a safe place to talk. I try to give people a safe place to live."

Kazakov checked his watch. Five minutes were gone. He took a long sip of tea spiced with cardamom, closed his eyes, and sighed. "Ambrosia. If I lived in the city, I think I would be here every night."

Setting the cup down, he nodded and opened his eyes. "Thank you. Please spread the word that the authorities are watching and that killing Bure will only make things worse. There are ruthless forces at work here. They will stop at nothing to get what they want and there have been too many people killed already." Like entire villages wiped out to keep a secret.

Feeling tired and old, he headed for the blue door and paused. "Do you want to do this? It will make it easier for you."

Grimly, Abdulin crossed the room.

Kazakov held up a hand to stop him. "Before I go. Khalil Khan. I know he's alive. Tell him…" What? That Kazakov missed him? That he forgave him or that he never would? "Tell him to be careful."

Abdulin was stone-faced, but that twitch ran by his eye again. He slammed Kazakov's shoulders so that he crashed into the door. Kazakov hit the latch and stumbled out into the cold. "And stay out," Abdulin shouted. Then he looked Kazakov in the eyes. "Be careful yourself," he whispered.

Considering what he'd learned, Kazakov trudged back through the silent streets and found the Perseus with a cracked windshield and epithets carved in the engine hood. Not everyone in the old city shared Abdulin's openmindedness.

With an oath, he climbed inside and tried the key. Thankfully, the engine turned over. He sat waiting for the engine to warm, thinking of Abdulin's confirmation. Khan was alive.

Khan was alive! He didn't know whether to be furious or relieved. There was no proof other than Khan's admission that Khan had killed a man. There were, however, eyewitnesses to Khan's final attack on police officers. That, the man would have to stand trial for.

Asking himself why he'd left the message he had for Khan, he backed cautiously through the narrow streets until he reached a place where he could turn a corner and continue out of the old city. In the warehouse district, he turned away from downtown and toward the mountains. His headlights were yellow-white through the night and gleamed back off of the crusty snow as he wound through the suburbs and then up onto the open steppe lands up toward the forest in the lower reaches of the mountains.

Not everyone in the old city was involved or even agreed with the plot to kill Bure. That was clear. In fact it was, in Abdulin's words, young hotheads who were the problem.

If what he said was true.

Abdulin could have simply played along with Kazakov to get him to leave the Blue Corner without an altercation. Shopkeepers knew the troubles that police could cause them.

But that cup of tea on the counter had said it was more than that—that Abdulin truly was troubled by what was happening. The question was how could Kazakov use the information to find the culprits?

His brother detectives would come into the old city and simply round up all the men, but given what he had learned in Biysk, that would only anger the community and still leave quite capable women to carry out any plot. What he wanted to do was stop the plot at its heart.

How could one man do that? In this political environment with the threat that hung over the tribal communities, the removal of one threat would be more likely to breed another, like the heads of a hydra—cut one off and two others would grow in its place.

It was all about belief. As long as the tribal people believed they were threatened, there was the potential for something like this plot to arise.

It was the same kind of belief that Bure was capitalizing on amongst Fergana's Russian citizens. Turn the Russians into a tribe and erase Fergana as a nation, for a nation was home to many people. The Chinese Empire included many people. So did the Ottoman Empire, though in both cases those other people were second-class citizens. Was that how people had to live—subjugating those who were different so that the subjugator could feel good? Wasn't that not much more than the slavery of the Americans, or the white slavery that led to prostitution?

And Bure was bringing it to Fergana. So much for the Eden the country had once been. Not only had the Russians polluted the land and air, they had polluted their own souls.

He slowed as he drove past Agafya, his elderly neighbor's house, but decided it was too late to stop in. When he turned into his driveway, the Perseus's headlights cut through the trees, but the dacha was simply a greater darkness in the dark clearing. He swung around the place to park in the shelter of the building and climbed out, inhaling the colder, cleaner air of the mountains. Overhead, the clouds were thickening. The spring reprieve was over. There would be more snow tomorrow and, judging by the clouds, quite a lot of it.

11

———————

The next morning dawned cold and white, though Kazakov was snug enough inside the dacha once he'd stoked the fire. Koshka threaded around his feet and then munched on her kibble while he dressed in his suit and made himself breakfast. Standing over the kitchen sink, he ate bread toasted on the top of the woodstove and sipped black tea—he'd forgotten to purchase milk. He really should do another grocery run and this time ensure that Agafya received it. The world beyond his kitchen window was pale and indistinct from frost and snow as if the day did not know what to become.

Perhaps that was determined by what people believed it would be.

Leonid Nikolaev probably believed it would be another day of firefighting in the run-up to the election. Egorova believed it would be another day of investigation. Kasimir Krupin would expect another day of grief and pain. Bure would believe another day of triumph after triumph was his.

And Khan? Would he expect another day of hiding? Would he expect Kazakov's message? How would it change his way of seeing the world around him?

Or would it?

Kazakov doubted it. Each of them was trapped into seeing the world the way they expected, just as the tsarevich's brothers had been trapped in their own need for riches and rule. And the tsarevich? He had been trapped too—by the need to appear righteous and pure while taking what he wanted wherever he went. So the wolf was created to do the dirty work.

Something about that jangled in Kazakov's mind. There was something there, but he could not put his finger on what it was. His own expectations were blinding him.

His tea drunk, his toast consumed, he donned his gun, his boots, and his great coat and, after tamping down the fire, closing the flue, and giving Koshka a pat goodbye, he headed out the door.

This high in the foothills, six inches of snow had fallen, dampening sound and coalescing the spruce trees into huddled forms. The sound of a limb cracking shot through the forest as one of the endemic walnuts, poplars, or apple trees cracked under the snow's weight. An eagle cry lifted his gaze to the cloudy sky. Above the trees, downslope from him, a thin trail of smoke against the clear air said that his elderly neighbor was alive and well enough to make her morning fire. He would pick up the groceries today. He glanced back at the clouds. More snow would come before the end of the day.

Later, after the long drive into New Moscow across the snowy steppes, he pulled into the police station underground parking and climbed out. The place was busy with uniformed constables heading out on the road. He nodded at a few he recognized and their eyes widened as if surprised.

Inside, the squad room was busy as he pushed in the door. As usual, desks were littered with the coats and gloves of senior detectives. The detectives in question were crowded around the break room entrance, most with a mug of the office tea to hand. Laughter and camaraderie filled the room. Except for Chelomeyev and Egorova, huddled together at Chelomeyev's desk as if their discussion was too sensitive for other ears.

At Kazakov's entrance, the breakroom detectives turned to the door. There was a murmur from somewhere among them. Egorova and Chelomeyev looked up.

"Hey, Kazakov. I hear Rostoff's got you chasing rumors now. Must be nice not to have to worry about evidence anymore," Pogolin called.

Kazakov nodded at Egorova and Chelomeyev. "Artyom, I need to speak with you about one of your cases." He called Pogolin by his first name.

"Ooh. Pogolin's in trouble with the great Kazakov," Razin said.

Kazakov rolled his eyes, but Pogolin, laughing, pushed through his comrades.

"What can I help you with?" His blunt, lined features were actually serious—or he was doing a creditable job of the act.

"The explosives investigation. The one that took out Our Lady Yekaterina." He motioned in the direction of the city square where the massive statue of the great tsarina had been toppled.

"What of it?" Caution had come into Pogolin's gaze.

"I'm wondering whether there has been more evidence that points to the tribals."

Pogolin's gaze widened. "Now there's a surprise. I thought you were a proponent of the theory that the poor tribals were being framed."

Kazakov shook his head. "I'm a proponent of following the evidence."

"So what's changed? From what Rostoff told me, you had hints that the owner of Mountain Construction was complicit in the theft of the explosives from the company."

Kazakov sighed and shook his head again. "I know. I feel like I'm watching a chess game under an eiderdown blanket and I can't tell who's where."

Pogolin, all business-minded now, sat down at his desk and pulled out a file. "You want to take a look?"

When Kazakov nodded, Pogolin turned the file toward him.

"Thanks." Kazakov flipped the file open. "Any hints of some young firebrands coming up from amongst the tribals?"

"Not that I can think of."

"You mind if I take this to my desk?"

Pogolin shrugged, and like that the old, lackadaisical Pogolin was back. Kazakov nodded his thanks and carried the file to his desk, took of his coat, and sat down.

"Did you go see Krupin this morning?" Egorova asked.

"Not yet. I plan to later. Hopefully he'll have slept in."

She nodded. "Sleep is healing."

Or it could hold nightmares. Kazakov hoped that wasn't the case for the old man.

He went through the file. It dealt not only with the explosion in Yekaterina Square, but also an explosion by the New Moscow bus station and the theft of additional explosives that remained missing. There was enough missing explosive to bring down one of New Moscow's large buildings, and all of the major government installations had been warned to increase their security.

Pogolin and others had done good work. There were numerous interviews with young radicals as well as serious interrogation of the Mountain Construction Company owner, a man named Vladimir Bogomolov. Kazakov stopped. There was something about that name, but he couldn't put his finger on what it was. That was the trouble with getting old—you weren't as sharp as you used to be.

Bogomolov had been adamant that he had nothing to do with the theft, even though forensics was able to match his boot print—an expensive foreign brand—to the prints found in the explosive's storage building the morning after the latest theft. Unfortunately, without further evidence, what they had was circumstantial and definitely not enough to convict.

Kazakov looked up at Chelomeyev. The young detective probably held evidence in his head that was important enough for two attempts on his life. Unfortunately, injuries had left his memory with gaps that included what he knew about the explosion.

There were rumors of major plots, but nothing concrete. Some spoke of taking down the statue of the tsarina on Yekaterina Mountain—an obvious target, and security now blocked the trail up the mountains—but others suggested something else. There was no hint of what that something else was.

Overall, Pogolin had covered all the right bases and asked all the right questions. He closed the file and stood, returning the file to Pogolin.

"Thanks. Good detective work."

Pogolin nodded. "Thanks. Some of the rest of us do our jobs, too."

Kazakov took the chastening. Sometimes he forgot that they did, because too often they didn't "do their jobs" in Kazakov's opinion.

"Did it help?" Pogolin asked.

Sighing, Kazakov shook his head. "Just left me feeling I'm missing something and that I'm looking at a spider's web. I can't say why."

"Listen," Pogolin said. "There's something not in the file. An interview I was just getting typed up with a little tribal guy who says he knows you. He got picked up the other night for suspicious activities and in the interview he let something slip."

Kazakov tilted a brow at him.

Pogolin nodded. "Name is Semir Kadet—or something like that. He's still in cells. He said that he'd heard something was being planned. He used the words 'maximum casualties.'"

Kazakov froze. Kadet uulu Semir—Semir, son of Kadet—was a tribal businessman who owned a small print shop in the old city. He'd been instrumental in helping Kazakov save Khan when his family had been attacked.

Kazakov thought a moment. "How solid is the case against him?"

"Not too. I was going to let him sweat a little longer and see what I can learn before deciding whether to release him."

"Do you mind if I interview him?"

Resentment, fatigue, and frustration clouded Pogolin's face, but then cleared. "Go ahead. Everyone says you've got a way with the tribals. Maybe this time it will be of some use." He shoved another file at Kazakov.

Carrying the file, Kazakov headed for his desk. He called down to have Kadet uulu Semir brought up to an interview room and scanned through the file. Semir had been arrested on the grounds that he was found in the maintenance yard of the train station when he had no reason to be there. His excuse was that he had an interest in the trains and wanted to see the area. In his possession had been a camera that had carried a variety of photos of the area and the trains.

Soon, a uniformed officer arrived on the elevator with Kadet uulu Semir. He was placed in an interview room and Kazakov, with the file, entered the room.

It was the same interview room Kazakov had been in when he had been on Semir's side of the single table bolted to the floor. This time it smelled of Semir's sweat and fear. Semir huddled in the wooden chair across from Kazakov and the door.

The copy shop owner was a small man, diminished by age and perhaps by malnutrition when he was a child. His graying hair was wild, though his snow-white *ak kalpak* cap hid the worst of it. His narrow face was a little more lined and the cheeks more sunken than the last time Kazakov had seen him. He wore his usual long-sleeved shirt with ink stains at the cuff, and too-long trousers that currently covered his sock feet. His gaze widened when he saw Kazakov.

"You," he said. "I thought you were my people's friend." He looked away and shook his head. "If you think I'm telling you anything, you're wrong."

Kazakov slapped the file on the desk and sat down. "I am your friend. That's why I'm here. You're in a lot of trouble, Semir."

Semir shook his head. "I told the other detective that you have it all wrong. I love trains. I was taking their pictures to help me remember them. I thought that I might make a little picture book for children in my language."

Kazakov listened to the excuse and then shook his head. "But that's not quite true, is it? We know about the plot, Semir. You and the young firebrands…"

He held the old man's gaze and waited. Semir's clenched jaw said he wasn't saying anything.

"And Khan. We know about him, too," Kazakov said softly. "Killing Bure won't do anything to help your people—in fact, it will inflame the country against you."

Semir's old eyes watered in the dry interview room air. "It is our country. The mountains. The steppes. The forests of apple trees. Those are Kyrgyz lands. Not Russian. Perhaps it is the Russians who should leave."

"And let the Ottoman and Chinese Empires roll in unchecked? Who do you think funds our military? It's Russian taxpayers."

Semir slapped his hands on the table. "And who said we want your protection? We have brothers in Islam to the west. Could their Empire be any worse than this?" He waved his hands at the room.

Kazakov eyed him, deciding how to proceed. Semir was talking and he was talking himself right into jail as a traitor. The question was how deep the traitorous nature went and how broadly did it reach.

"So Enver Pasha helps you," he said and caught the telltale catch of breath in the print shop owner.

Kazakov nodded. "Yes. We know of his involvement in these things. He is an agent of the Ottoman government." He eyed Semir. "Tell me how the explosives will be used at the train station."

Semir turned stone-faced. He shook his head. "I will not say anything more." He looked away, half turning himself on his chair so that he did not have to face his accuser. Small shudders ran through his thin frame and Kazakov bowed his head. There were times that his job pained him, for he liked this little man.

He pushed up to standing. "Thank you, Semir. I would have preferred to see you at another time and place."

Semir shook his head. "It is what it is. It is Allah who chooses the times and places."

Kazakov left the interview room with the file and returned to Pogolin. "I wouldn't release him if I were you. There's something bigger going on and he's involved. I just haven't figured out how all the pieces fit together yet, but there's a good chance he's involved in whatever is planned for those explosives."

Pogolin's graying eyebrows rose. "That's not good news."

"Nothing is these days." Kazakov left him for his desk, but then turned back. "Another thought: we release him and see where it leads. If you want to go in that direction, I'd like to be involved."

Pogolin's eyes narrowed. Then he shook his head. "What is the world coming to? The great lone wolf wants to work together."

Kazakov frowned, thinking of the great wolf in Chelomeyev's story and how he had made the young tsarevich's misbehavior possible. Then he shook his head. "Not a lone wolf. Just someone who's choosy about who he works with."

Leaving Pogolin to puzzle out whether he'd been complimented or disrespected, Kazakov turned back to his desk and Egorova and Chelomeyev. He slumped at his desk and the two young detectives glanced up at him.

"We were just going over Chelomeyev's mapping work," Egorova said, brushing a strand of blonde hair back from her mouth.

"We think there's a pattern," Chelomeyev said.

Kazakov sat up. "What did you find?"

"See here?" Chelomeyev got up and brought the map to Kazakov's desk to spread it in front of him. Egorova came up on Kazakov's other side. "Those green dots are the places Madam Sobol told us Anna had visited on her errands. After we re-interviewed the people, we got a sense of the direction she left in, in about fifty percent of the cases." His long elegant fingers dipped down to touch the map where small arrows had been applied.

"These yellow dots represent the places where Anna's big-name clients received their readings when they weren't held at the Royal Caravanserai," Egorova said. "And these arrows represent the direction Anna headed when she left."

"It looks pretty scattershot," Kazakov said trying to determine what the other two detectives saw in the mass of information.

"That's what I said," Egorova said. She leaned in and unrolled a transparent plastic sheaf over the map. "Then Chelomeyev got his brainwave."

The young detective colored slightly at Kazakov's regard.

"Tell me," Kazakov said, eyeing the plastic sheet.

"It was something we found in Anna's room. Remember—we pulled it out from under her mattress and I couldn't figure why she'd hide it."

"The flyer for Bure's rally." Kazakov looked at the plastic overlay that showed a blue dot in direct proximity of Anna's path. "Are you telling me…"

"Every one of these blue dots represents a Bure town meeting, presentation, or rally," Chelomeyev said. "So I checked further. I went back to Madam Sobol and asked her for dates of the errands." He nodded. "I know. I was supposed to be resting, but these mostly match."

Mostly.

He decided to play devil's advocate. "It could be simple coincidence. Bure has got to be having a lot of sessions with the election so close."

"Eight times?" Egorova asked.

Kazakov thought of the blonde young woman Anna Konstantinova had been. She was exactly Bure's type, even if she wasn't sixteen. Could Bure have been her liaison and the father of her child?

No, that didn't work. If Kazakov's suspicions were true, Bure's genes weren't Caucasian and the child Kazakov had seen had looked Ottoman, not Chinese.

"But what would be her reason for going?" Kazakov asked.

Chelomeyev and Egorova glanced at each other.

"It's your theory," Egorova said.

Chelomeyev still hesitated.

"Whatever it is, spit it out," Kazakov growled.

Chelomeyev scanned the room as if checking the proximity of the other detectives. "What if she was sent? What if Anna was keeping an eye on Bure?"

It was an interesting theory, not one that had crossed Kazakov's mind. He nodded slowly. "Go on. A lot of people have their eye on Bure. Who are you suggesting? Was Madam Sobol trying to drum up business? Had she been sending Anna with messages like she did her other clients?" Kazakov looked at Egorova and Chelomeyev. "Did you ask her?"

They shook their heads.

But something wasn't right with that theory. Kazakov could feel it in his bones. Given what he knew of Bure, the man presented as a cold pragmatist. He wouldn't be seeking out a spiritualist's help.

"Here's another wild theory for you. Maybe Anna Konstantinova was a spotter for someone. Maybe she was sizing up Bure's security for someone else. I'm looking into allegations of a plot against Bure's life. Maybe the two cases are connected."

"Are you suggesting Bure had her killed?" Chelomeyev asked.

"People have killed to protect him before," Kazakov said. He checked his watch. "Derr'mo, it's almost 10:30 and I haven't checked in on Kasimir."

Shoving to his feet, he looked down at the map. "It's a good piece of work. We need to check this out."

Egorova and Chelomeyev nodded. "We'll head back to Madam Sobol's."

Feeling troubled that he was missing something, Kazakov headed down to the Perseus and out to the Krupin residence. If anything, the Krupin house looked older and almost abandoned. With its still curtains and dark windows, it gave the sense that it had sunk in on itself. A thin trail of smoke from the rear chimney suggested that the kitchen stove was lit, so that was something. A conspicuously shiny black vehicle sat in front.

Kazakov sat in the Perseus a moment as the vehicle cooled around him. The wind had picked up, swirling stray flakes that fell from the leaden spring sky. The parked vehicle had the look of an undertaker's vehicle—probably here to discuss Margarete's funeral arrangements. He didn't want to interrupt, but he wanted to make certain that Krupin was all right. Finally, he shoved out of the Perseus and stood there, letting the cleansing wind blow around him. It was warmer than it looked. True spring weather. He trudged through a light skiff of snow up the walk and knocked on the front door, scanning the street as he waited.

An old blue truck idled in the next block down the street, the lone driver a dark blip in the cab.

The rattle of the door lock turned Kazakov around.

Kasimir Krupin peered up at him. His shoulders were rounded, his back bent, so he appeared more Dedushka's age than Krupin's sixty-odd years. His hair was disheveled as if it hadn't been combed. He wore the same clothes that he'd worn the day before. Where always there'd been astute intelligence in his gaze, this time there was a vacant stare. Then the vacancy cleared.

"Oh. It's you." Krupin blocked entrance to the house with his body.

"I came to check on you, Kasimir. Are you all right? Egorova wanted me to make sure that you've eaten this morning."

Krupin nodded up at him. "That's very kind, but it's not necessary. I'm fine." He began to close the door.

Kazakov hesitated. This brush-off wasn't like Krupin. Was it really an undertaker with him?

"Kasimir, I hate to even ask a question at a time like this, but does the name Bogomolov mean anything to you?" Bogomolov was the name of the construction company owner from where the explosives had been stolen.

"Bogomolov? Construction? Well-connected fellow. Married to an artist. Talented one, too, if I recall. What about him?"

The man was sharp, there was no question of that, and the question seemed to have brought the old Kasimir back. The man needed a challenge.

"What are his allegiances?"

Krupin blinked. "That is a large question and not one that I can answer like this." He motioned at the door. "I'm sorry. I'm indisposed at the moment, planning Margarete's funeral. Can you come back later?"

Feeling like a fool for not only intruding, but also doubting Krupin, Kazakov agreed and left the porch for the Perseus. In the driver's seat he looked back at the house. The curtain in the dining room, Krupin's makeshift study, twitched. Checking on Kazakov?

Derr'mo, he was becoming as paranoid as people thought him.

He started the Perseus and left Krupin's house, winding through the neighborhood thinking. Eight times Anna Konstantinova had potentially been at a Bure meeting or rally; it had to be more than coincidence. Chelomeyev was on to something, but what did it mean? And Bogomolov. Why did the name keep niggling at his brain? He knew he'd heard it before, just not involved with this case. So where?

He needed the chance to think about it, but the cases kept pulling him in different directions. He needed to do something mindless that would let his subconscious work on the problem.

He went to the grocery store and pulled into the parking lot. A truck sped past him. Older. Blue. Lone occupant.

Climbing out of the Perseus, he watched the truck down the street. It almost looked like the damn thing pulled in a block up the street. Was someone watching him? Eric Clinton, again? The American spy wasn't exactly good at being forthright with his presence.

Leaving the Perseus behind, Kazakov set off down the street to confirm his suspicions. Sure enough, the blue truck was at the curb a block up. Not exactly a good position to keep an eye on whoever he was following. Clinton would surely do better than that and Clinton would certainly see Kazakov headed in his direction. If he didn't want to see Kazakov, he would have driven away by now.

Kazakov kept going until he was even with the rear of the truck. Lone occupant. Dark hair. He reached under his coat and loosed his weapon in its holster before approaching the passenger side of the truck cab. Hand on the door handle, he snuck a quick look at the driver and froze.

Not Eric Clinton.

Khalil Khan looked back at him.

12

———

Sunlight seemed to catch in Khalil Khan's dark gaze. Light through the driver's side window placed a halo around his face. He was dressed in simple workman's brown clothing, a heavy oilskin jacket pulled tight around his stubbled chin. And he looked thin and terribly, terribly tired.

Not the tidy M.E. Kazakov had known at all.

Kazakov pulled open the door, weapon still to hand, but there was no sign that Khan was armed.

"Get in," Khan said, his crisp medical voice gone to softer tones.

Kazakov shoved crumpled papers and food wrappers aside and slid onto the passenger seat. Khan pulled away from the curb.

"I'm hoping this isn't an abduction," Kazakov said as he eyed Khan. Alive. Here. The combination of anger and relief stuck in his chest. He didn't know how he felt. The damn man had tried to kill him! Had betrayed him and everything they jointly believed.

"It is a way for us to speak together."

Kazakov settled on anger. "I thought you said the time for conversation was over. That all of my suggestions—my options were over."

Nodding, Khan glanced at him. "I am sorry."

"You shot my partner."

"I was aiming at you," Khan said with a grim smile. "I suppose I couldn't do it. There is still too much unfinished business between us."

"Oh?" Kazakov glanced from the road to Khan. They had left the grocery store behind and were headed into the warehouse district. "What would that be?"

Khan frowned as he drove. "How to stop this?"

"I thought you wanted a war. Your people would survive it, you said."

"Do you remember when we talked that last night in the hospital—all the people intent on manipulating Fergana—from Clinton's Americans to the Chinese, to the Ottomans, to you Russians?"

"Everyone with his own agenda and no one really giving a damn about the tribal people hurt in the process. Not even me, if I remember correctly," Kazakov said, nodding cautiously but feeling the bite of bitterness in his throat.

Khan swallowed and turned to him. "Perhaps I was wrong."

The apology probably hadn't come easily.

He pulled the truck into the curb. To either side were the crumbling remains of steel and concrete warehouses, the concrete pitted from pollution and sand blown in summer, the steel red with rust from winter snows. The alleys between the buildings were overgrown with tall grass that poked through the rotten snow. Sporadic flakes swirled through the air as ephemeral as Kazakov's thoughts. Why was Khan here? Was someone coming? An attack? His gun felt cold and bulky against his side and he knew his reactions were too slow.

"I should arrest you. You're a wanted man."

Khan turned in his seat and half smiled. "But you won't. You don't have the evidence to prove anything about Zholdosh. Damned Ottoman agent. Perhaps you do, of the assault on Chelomeyev and the shooting of Egorova. Three eye witnesses would probably stand up in trial."

"What do you want, Khan?" Kazakov said. It would be so easy to slip into the familiar, friendly patter that he had always enjoyed with this man, but Khan had crossed a line. He was an enemy of Ferganese peace. He had tried to harm Chelomeyev.

"I hear you are asking questions. Investigating."

Kazakov watched the empty street, not sure what he was expecting. He nodded. "We know there's a plot to harm Bure. Word is, the tribals are behind it. After seeing you in the riot video, I figured it might be you."

He caught the widening of Khan's gaze. Then the ex M.E. had the grace to look embarrassed. "You saw that, did you? I hadn't planned to be there. In fact, the reason I was there was to get my people out."

"I don't give a damn why you were there. You're avoiding my question."

Khan cocked a brow at him.

"All right. Are you behind a plot to assassinate Bure?"

Khan closed his eyes and sighed. "Hypothetically, if I told you I was, you would arrest me and you would keep me in cells in the belief that by doing so you are lessening the risk—just as Kadet uulu Semir is being held." Turning, he held up a hand at Kazakov's shock. "Yes, I have my spies. I know you spoke to him. What if I told you that Semir and I keep things in check—or try to."

Kazakov shook his head. "That would fly in the face of what you said on Yekaterina Mountain. Before you died... You said we were out of options, that no matter what happened, Bure would win the election and Fergana would be torn apart by forces from within and without. You were prepared to take action—enough so that you would murder a man."

Khan studied Kazakov with the same intensity he used on a crime scene and that was with some of the sharpest intelligence that Kazakov had ever known. He wanted to squirm under that regard. Instead he met Khan's steady gaze and waited. What was the man trying to tell him?

Finally, Khan dropped his gaze to his hands clenched on the steering wheel. "That is true; and when I did what I did, I truly thought so. I wanted to lead the resistance of my people. I had the reputation, the respect of many. I thought I could make a difference and that the young men and women would listen to me." He shook his head and laughed sadly. "I thought. But the farther I sank inside this thing, the more it became clear that it was not me leading. There were other forces at work."

"What do you mean?" Kazakov could have kicked himself for interrupting Khan's disclosure, but Khan only glanced at him and carried on.

"It began with the simplest of things—youngsters announcing completed ventures that the inner circle of planners had not sanctioned. At first, they were relatively minor things, like a theft or distributing pamphlets, but then that damned riot in the market occurred. No one—I repeat, not one of the Council—admits ever suggesting such a thing. We were holding our forces inside the old city. We didn't want to show strength until it was necessary to protect our people. But then another bright light decides to lead a protest and the Russians responded and you know the rest. I was there after it started, trying to pull key people out of the melee. I've spoken to all of them. They tell me that word came down to them that they were to participate, but none of the Council sent such directions."

Khan looked a plea in Kazakov's direction. "There are other things as well, like Semir's arrest and detention. He wasn't supposed to be in the railway station. He told another associate that he received a message to go there with a camera. That the message was from me."

A weight seemed to pull down Khan's shoulders and exhaustion settled on him. "There are now whispers about me—that perhaps I have lost my edge. Perhaps I thought Semir challenged me and I wanted to get him out of the way. There are whispers that if I could betray you after the years we have worked together, then perhaps I could betray our people, too."

And suddenly Kazakov understood. Khan had been isolated, his authority undermined. A war was coming and he was afraid of what would become of his people. He wanted Kazakov's help to save them.

The question was what to do with the information. Could he trust it? How could he use this to get more from Khan? Or was he being too much like the tsarevich's older brothers even thinking that way about Khan?

He looked back and found Khan looking at him, half-masked hope in his dark eyes.

"I know that it cannot undo what has been done, but I am truly sorry. I treated my friend poorly and a friend is a precious thing—a family by choice, not blood."

A part of him wanted to trust Khan, to go back to the ways things were. But Khan had not only broken that trust, he had tried to kill Kazakov, putting his peoples' welfare first. Was this some kind of subterfuge? But working with Khan would give Kazakov a better chance to uncover just what was going on amongst the tribals. To work with Khan, though—it was the kind of decision that Rostoff would want to be involved in. It was also the kind of decision that Kazakov was known to make on his own. His "damnable lone-wolf decisions," Rostoff would yell. But then, could Kazakov even trust Rostoff? The man's sudden change of heart toward Kazakov was suspect, too.

Kazakov blew out a breath of frustration. "You ask a lot, Khan. I keep seeing you with that pistol aimed in my direction. The man who did that isn't someone I can trust. You're going to need to do a lot better to convince me to trust you." He looked at Khan sharply. "Tell me what the plot is against Bure."

Silence ached in the truck cab for a moment, but then Khan nodded. "All right. Giving you this information compromises many people who trust me." He sighed. "There had been discussions, but no decisions. The explosives—we were holding them in reserve. Some wished to erase that idol off of Sulieman's Mountain as a cleansing statement." He nodded in the direction of Yekaterina Mountain with its huge lit figure of the dead tsarina. "Others suggested using it at a Bure rally. Placed under the stage, how could he escape? But there would be too many others injured, too. And we would rightfully be blamed, our cause harmed. Cooler heads had prevailed, so though we wished to be rid of Bure, there were, as yet, no firm plans."

The considered assessment made sense, given what Kazakov knew of Khan and the tribal elders. But then, Khan hadn't really placed anyone specific at risk through his revelation.

"Where are the explosives now?" he asked, intent on seeing how far he could push.

Khan shook his head. "I can't tell you that. It pulls our stinger before we've made our point."

"That's not very trusting on your part," Kazakov said. "Especially when you say someone else is making your point for you."

Khan's face colored slightly and he looked away. "You're expecting me to leave my people defenseless. I'm sorry, old friend. Perhaps this was a bad idea. Perhaps there is no going back to friendship or even a little trust."

That was closer to Kazakov's assessment, and yet—something had brought Khan to him and Khan seemed genuinely shaken by what was happening amongst his people. "You suggested someone else was aiming your weapons…"

"I am not alone in that assessment," Khan said, shaking his head. "We cannot be stripped of our only playing card. Those explosives are closely guarded just so that they cannot fall into the wrong hands."

"Tribal elders' assessment of low risk will not mean much in Rostoff's eyes."

Khan's unflinching gaze gave Kazakov pause.

"So, not the elders. Clinton?" Was the American spy still in the country? Kazakov hadn't seen him since the investigation in the mountains.

Khan nodded slowly. "His whereabouts is not mine to give. He keeps a low profile."

That was worth a chuckle. "He never wants to be found unless he does. The last time someone followed me, it was him." As a spy, Clinton had often been a source of trouble, but he also often had information Kazakov lacked. "If you see him, tell him I'd like to talk. Now you'd best take me back to the Perseus before it gets towed, and I'll consider whether we are on the same side."

Khan nodded and started the truck.

They drove in silence through the late morning, thinning clouds allowing sunbeams to spotlight a derelict building, a mother and child walking, an empty park bench, a car parked next to a snowdrift. Each a fleeting impression, a fleeting thought.

At the Perseus, Kazakov climbed out and turned back to Khan. "How do I get in touch?"

"You have my number. This time I'll pick up," Khan said, his smile almost wistful. "It would be good to work together, old friend."

Kazakov just nodded and shut the door behind him, still unsure whether he felt the same.

After buying much-needed groceries for himself and his elderly neighbor and a bag of treats for Krupin, Kazakov headed back to Krupin's house. The house looked the same, the same thin runnel of smoke torn from the chimney by the wind, though the shiny black vehicle was no longer there.

Parking in front of the gate, Kazakov climbed out and went to the door. Knocking, he waited until finally he heard the shuffle of footfall. Again, the curtain beside the door twitched and then Krupin pulled the door open, releasing a scent Kazakov couldn't quite place.

"You came back," Krupin said, his gaze catching a beam of sunlight. If anything, Krupin looked even more thin and spindly, not much more than a scarecrow with his wild graying hair and oversized cardigan hanging off his shoulders. But there was a difference from the last time Kazakov had been here. Now Krupin's gaze was bright—almost unnaturally so.

"I said I would. I was concerned for you, Kasimir. Margarete was important. I can't imagine how you feel."

Krupin sighed and ran his hand back through his hair. Where usually Krupin's hands were the pristine white of the academic office worker, now there was a shine to the skin and black around the cuticles.

Krupin followed his glance. "I've been cleaning up Margarete's room. Amazing how much she accumulated in there."

"Perhaps it is time for a break. We could have a cup of tea…" Kazakov said, lifting the bag of sweet treats he'd bought at the store. The scent of sugar and cinnamon came off the bag.

Krupin glanced at the bag, briefly met his gaze, and looked away just as quickly. "I'm sorry. Not today. The meeting this morning with the undertaker… It took everything out of me. I need time alone." He gave a weak smile. "But I appreciate you checking on me. Let me reassure you, it's not necessary. I am fine."

Feeling a little foolish for bothering the old reporter, Kazakov gave Krupin the treats, apologized for bothering him, and retreated back to the Perseus. He climbed in and sat there.

Regardless of Krupin's reassurances, something didn't feel right. The usually friendly old man was far from that today. And Krupin had recovered far more quickly than Kazakov would have expected from the devastated human being he had been yesterday. Some people could pull themselves together that quickly, but not many. Krupin could be one of them, but…

Margarete had been everything to him. Could anyone recover so quickly from such a huge loss?

He looked back at the house. A swaying lace curtain in the dining room/study suggested Krupin hid there, watching. As if he wanted to make sure Kazakov left?

But then Kazakov didn't know Krupin that well. It was only Kazakov's investigations that had brought them together. Krupin had made it clear that he didn't want to be interrupted in whatever he was doing—at least not by Kazakov. He had to honor that.

With a sigh, he started the Perseus and headed back to meet Egorova and Chelomeyev at the station. He still had to decide how much he would tell them about Khan. As for Rostoff, he couldn't provide assurances that the plot was dealt with, but he could say he was making progress. Rostoff didn't need to know the details.

It was just before lunch when he came back to the office. Rostoff wasn't in, so he was spared the progress report. When he came back to the squad room, Pogolin was just leaving. Kazakov pulled him aside.

"We may have a problem," he said. "I've been in touch with sources and while it seems the tribals may have had control of the explosives, that might not be the case any longer."

Pogolin's gaze narrowed. "What are you saying?"

Kazakov shook his head. "I'm not sure. It sounds like there's a wild card out there. Things are happening that weren't sanctioned by the tribal power structure. The elders are struggling to regain control."

"You mean some young bastard's out to blow Fergana up?"

Kazakov shook his head. "That's not what I'm saying. Sure, some young hothead might pull the trigger, but something tells me there's someone else taking aim." He held up his hand. "Before you ask, I don't know who, but I'm asking questions. I might want to interview Kadet uulu Semir again. That all right by you?"

Pogolin shrugged. "You can try. The man's refusing to answer any questions now."

"Thanks for the heads-up. I'll give it a shot."

He watched Pogolin into the elevator and then turned back to the squad room. The place was empty except for Egorova and Chelomeyev, who were taking their coats off. A brown bag that leaked delicious odors of sausage and spicy pickle sat on the desk between them.

"We picked up German food. A place opened around the corner," Chelomeyev said and pulled out newspaper-wrapped buns stuffed with steaming German sausage, sauerkraut, and pickles. He waited until Kazakov had his coat off and handed him one, while Egorova settled at her desk.

"Did you see Kasimir," she asked.

Kazakov nodded. "Briefly. He didn't want company."

She frowned. "How did he seem?"

"That's what I can't put my finger on. He said he's all right. He certainly seems to be functioning better than last night. I think he's busy with arrangements for Margarete's funeral, but he seemed determined not to let me into the house and he watched the Perseus until I drove away."

Her frown deepened into furrows between her eyes. "Grief... it can make people behave strangely. They can do things that they normally wouldn't. It's like the loss sort of cuts them loose from the world. At least for a little while."

"Well, he seemed real-world enough for the moment. Just unsocial; and I'm probably letting my paranoid streak build mountains out of mole hills."

"You don't think he'll harm himself, do you? Sometimes seniors commit suicide when they lose their partner."

Kazakov thought about what he'd seen in Krupin. He shook his head. "I don't think so."

Thoughtfully, he bit into the sausage and crusty bun and was rewarded with the burst of hot greasy flavor and spice. "Mm. Good choice," he said, nodding to Chelomeyev.

"Don't look at me. It was Egorova who spotted the place."

Kazakov cocked a brow at her. "How come the newcomer knows the new places?"

"Dabria and I caught dinner there a few nights ago." She colored slightly.

"Thanks for pointing it out," He said around the sausage. "What'd you get from Madam Sobol?"

The two young detectives looked at each other.

"She wasn't exactly forthcoming," Chelomeyev said. "Why keep bothering her when the killer is out there somewhere, were her words. When she did share anything, it was mostly contradicted a few sentences later. We pointed it out to her and she was on about the spirits having conflicting messages for us. That's one woman I wouldn't want to put on the stand. None of her stories stick together."

Egorova pulled out her notebook. "She gave us the last dates that she sent Anna on various errands—to the best of her recollection. We need to check the dates against Bure's commitments. She said she didn't know about Anna's little side venture and, frankly, the anger of her reaction makes me tend to believe her."

"So we have an unreliable spiritualist whose business was being undermined by her assistant." Kazakov mused. "Sounds like motive."

Chelomeyev and Egorova nodded in unison. "We're checking her story that she was out of town."

"We've got Sobol's clients, or those she was trying to get as clients, who were apparently getting contacted about matters that they would rather remain private—so she was getting her information from somewhere—and don't bother telling me it was from the great beyond." Kazakov pulled out a sheet of paper and made a note of what Chelomeyev had said.

"We've got Anna, who started out on her own and apparently was trying to influence her clients to back Bure." He noted that down, too.

"We've got the OTO—using spiritualism to influence people, too, but not of one mind about who they're backing." Another note on Kazakov's paper.

"All this and an election in a few days." Chelomeyev shook his head.

"Could almost make you think this an important election," Egorova said around her sandwich. She got up and went to the break room. "Anyone for tea?"

Kazakov held up his hand. "Given Bure's involvement, this *is* an important election. Is that what this murder was about?"

Egorova came back to her seat. Kazakov set his bun down, half-finished, and Chelomeyev finished wolfing his down.

Kazakov looked from one to the other. "I keep getting this sense that there is another player—someone moving the chess pieces around. I thought I was being paranoid, but then I had a conversation. With Khan."

Egorova's eyes widened. Chelomeyev's mouth opened as if to protest, but both proved they were good detectives when they waited for him to keep talking.

"When Krupin wouldn't see me, I went for groceries. Someone was following me rather openly. When I went to confront the driver, it was Khan." He told them what Khan had said. "Someone is undermining the tribal elders and seems to be pushing for confrontation—or something more. Khan's admission that they have, or had, the explosives makes it more of a concern."

Chelomeyev closed his eyes and rubbed his forehead.

"What is it?" Kazakov asked.

Chelomeyev shook his head. "I'm not sure. Lately I keep having these dreams. At least I think they're dreams. Mura—you remember Mura Stepanova—she's whispering in my ear, telling me things."

Mura Stepanova had been a young prostitute who had come to Chelomeyev for help when she had witnessed something that Kazakov believed related to the theft of explosives and the subsequent explosions. Those explosions had destroyed the statue of Yekaterina and had injured a number of people at the train station.

"What is she saying?" Kazakov asked, almost holding his breath, for this was the memory that attempts on Chelomeyev's life had tried to erase.

"It's stupid. It's probably all this talk of spiritualists communicating with the dead," Chelomeyev said.

"Perhaps you should allow us to judge," Egorova said gently.

"That's the trouble," Chelomeyev said, glancing at Kazakov. "There's nothing to judge. It's all garbled, but while she's talking, a fog around us lifts and there is a group of three men talking. I don't recognize any of them, but just looking at them leaves me afraid." He shook his head. "Sorry. It's probably nothing, but when you mentioned the explosives, I thought I'd mention it."

Kazakov made a note of three men on his notepad and looked back at Chelomeyev. "You didn't recognize these men. Can you describe them?"

Chelomeyev squeezed his eyes shut and inhaled. "They go in and out of focus. One's smaller—tribal. He's older, too, clad in worn brown pants and an old shirt rolled up at the cuff. The second man is different. Russian, I think. Tall, blond, and wearing a suit under a great coat. I never saw his face. The third man, I didn't see his face either, but he's taller than the first man, but not so tall as the Russian. I think he may be tribal, but something is different about him. He has dark hair with gray at the temples—oh, and he's wearing heavy boots and I can see a pristine white collar poking out of his heavy winter jacket."

Chelomeyev shuddered and opened his eyes. "I don't know." He turned a troubled gaze on Kazakov. "I'm sorry I can't remember."

Kazakov shook his head, troubled by the descriptions. There was something there. "Maybe that's how Mura described them to you. Maybe this is your brain's way of returning memories to you."

He thought about the descriptions. "The Russian could almost be Bure."

Chelomeyev shook his head. "I thought of that when I first had the dream, but I can't imagine even Mura not knowing who he was. She would have called him Bure."

"Another tall blond Russian. Not too helpful." Egorova tipped her head at Chelomeyev, who fit the description. "It's not like there's only a few of them."

"True," Kazakov said. "But how many of them are involved in the explosives theft case? We need to involve Pogolin. Maybe this whole case comes back to that one."

He caught Egorova and Chelomeyev's glance.

"Yes, I will involve the investigating officer. Contrary to popular belief, I am not a total lone wolf."

No, the lone wolf was a creature of fairy tales. The creature that helped the tsarevich obtain his stolen treasures and helped him overcome the rightful heirs to the throne. Why did that image keep coming back to him?

"And the third man? Any ideas?" he asked no one in particular.

"A tribal man dressed for snow conditions and wearing a pristine white shirt—that could be anyone," Chelomeyev said.

Kazakov froze. He glanced at Chelomeyev and Egorova. "Derr'mo," he whispered. "Zholdosh."

The Ottoman agent had been found dead in Biysk after he had been arming and training the tribals. He had always worn a pristine white shirt —and that was the word Chelomeyev had just used to describe him. And Zholdosh had had dramatic gray at the temples.

He shoved up from his desk and tossed his half-finished sandwich in the trash. The room reeked of the sausage. He needed to clear his head. He needed to move so that all the thoughts crowding his mind could reshuffle and provide some kind of order.

"I need to interview Pogolin's prisoner. You two need to find our Russian." He headed for the door, had a thought, and turned back to them. "Try Bogomolov."

Chelomeyev sat up. "The owner of Mountain Construction? Of course! I only spoke to his manager when I ran the investigation…" His voice trailed off. His investigation had been handed to Pogolin after Chelomeyev had been beaten and left for dead. He'd spent a prolonged time in coma in the hospital.

Egorova was clearing their desks of lunch debris as Kazakov headed for the elevator. His mind was full of questions for Kadet uulu Semir, but in truth he almost had it. Patterns were rising from the swirling fog that seemed to have filled his brain from the beginning of this investigation. It was almost as if the fog was man-made, a device to obscure the hands of the conjuror.

Or the spiritualist.

In the basement cells he asked to see the elderly print shop owner. There was a small interview room off the booking area and Kazakov waited impatiently until finally the door opened and Kadet uulu Semir stepped inside, his skin gray from his time in cells. His watery gaze widened slightly.

"Have a seat," Kazakov said, trying to be friendly when he wanted to grab the smaller man by the scruff of the neck and wring the information from him.

Semir edged past Kazakov to the table and settled in the chair.

Kazakov eyed him. "You weren't quite forthcoming with me last time we spoke. I had to go out and dig up the information. You realize that's going to make it harder on you."

"I told you the truth," Semir said. He tugged at the sleeves of his shirt —sleeves he had rolled up from his wrists, presumably to save the cotton from the ink of his business.

Kazakov shook his head. "You made a nice show of it. You gave up enough that you thought we'd believe you and leave it at that. Poor man, trapped by another's actions. But it wasn't another man. You're the one who's betrayed the tribal elders." He leaned back in his chair.

"Never! I am Kyrgyz. I am for my people."

"And I'll bet you keep telling yourself that. As you betray them, you keep telling yourself that you know the right way forward for your people. You know the right allies."

What little color he had faded from his cheeks. "Always I am loyal to my people."

"Unless the elders have determined another way forward. I've spoken to another of those elders. They want to hold their people in reserve, keep them safe until the time comes that they must move. That didn't sit right with you—or with some others. Tell me, how long had Zholdosh been meeting with you and telling you what to do?"

Semir blinked. His throat worked as his gaze left Kazakov and scurried to the door.

"You're not going anywhere, Semir. Answer the question. You were seen, weren't you? A young prostitute named Mura Stepanova saw the three of you together. One of you had her killed for that and a young detective beaten. You even managed to lie your way through it with the elders so that an honorable man gave up his career trying to protect you. Khalil Khan did that for you. But the depth of your betrayal of your people goes even farther, doesn't it. Zholdosh—he wasn't just an agent. He was your handler, bringing you orders from higher up."

Semir sat frozen, but his gaze skittered around the room.

Kazakov slumped back in his seat, still trying to understand the breadth of the conspiracy. If Zholdosh was involved, then so was Enver Pasha. The Ottoman ex-general was a master of manipulation and subterfuge, but just how deep did that subterfuge go?

"What did Enver Pasha offer you?" Kazakov asked softly, taking a shot in the dark.

A twitch quirked Semir's left eye, but he said nothing.

"I can't believe that your loyalties are Ottoman and not Kyrgyz," Kazakov said. "I think whatever hold Enver has on you, it must be very painful for you to do what you've been doing."

Tension, rippled through Semir's face. He nodded slightly.

"It's dangerous for you to speak with me. Almost as dangerous as turning your back on your people."

A small sob escaped Semir's throat.

"Please," he whispered. "Don't make me do this. My daughter—she is studying in Tashkent. She is young. She goes to rallies that she would be better to leave alone. They have her under surveillance…"

"And if you don't do what Enver wants, he will have her arrested."

Semir nodded and covered his face with his hands.

"What is going on, Semir? What is the life of your daughter worth?"

"I don't know," he whispered. "I just do as they ask. I passed information to Zholdosh and then to the girl. I send instructions to our youngsters if there are things that need to be done."

"The girl?" Kazakov prompted.

Nodding, Semir took a deep breath. "Zholdosh was elsewhere. A girl started coming. Young blonde." He shook his head. "I wish I'd never seen her or Zholdosh or Enver Pasha." He spit out the last name.

"Is this the girl?" Kazakov fished Anna's photo from his pocket and slid it across the table to Semir.

He glanced at it and nodded and Kazakov felt a tremor of excitement. He was on the right trail. He knew it. He just needed to understand what it meant.

"How did you meet Enver Pasha?" Kazakov asked.

"My daughter was an art student. I met him at a show of her teacher's work. Khadija Bogomolov. He came up to me and started a conversation about art and how it mirrors a civilization. He made some comments about the art of students like my daughter feeling trapped and confined within Russian ideals." Semir shook his head, looking very old. "He told me my daughter was talented and that she should have a chance to grow at art school. Of course, no worthwhile art school in Fergana would take her because she was tribal."

Kazakov stayed silent, knowing the story wasn't finished.

"A few days later, Khadija Bogomolov told my daughter that she had a full scholarship to the Tashkent Art Academy. It is the premier Art Academy in the Ottoman Empire. She was so excited. How could I say no? It was her dream." He scrubbed his face with his hands. "How could I know that her dream was to become my nightmare? Once my daughter left for school, Enver Pasha had her and me—I found myself doing what he asked of me. At first it was little things like starting rumors. Then it became more. I—I sold my soul for my daughter."

Semir's breath turned ragged. His shoulders slumped and he began to cry silent, earnest tears that followed the channels of his face and dripped off his chin. He did nothing to stop them. Kadet uulu Semir was a beaten man, damned by his own actions.

Kazakov looked away to afford the older man what dignity he could retain. When Semir's breath calmed, Kazakov leaned forward. "Thank you. Thank you for telling me, because I think that your information will help stop a disaster for our country. Now I am going to have you brought paper and pen. I want you to write down what you have told me. Can you do that?"

Semir nodded, but would not meet Kazakov's gaze.

"Good man," Kazakov said and rose.

"How long?" Semir asked, finally looking up at him.

"Pardon?"

"How long will I be sentenced for?" Semir asked.

Kazakov sighed. "That is hardly mine to say. Treason is a serious crime. However, I think that the fact that your daughter was held hostage to force you to act—that will be in your favor. I'll ensure that your cooperation is noted in the file."

"And my daughter?" Semir asked.

Kazakov paused. "Perhaps news of your predicament will bring her home. I will see what I can do."

Leaving the copy shop owner to write out his statement, Kazakov thoughtfully returned up the elevator. Everything seemed to come back to Enver Pasha. He'd been there in every case—as an absent neighbor in the death of a Chinese spy whose body had been left just outside Enver's house. If Chelomeyev's dream was correct, and it seemed that it could be, then Enver's man, Zholdosh, had been part of the plot to blow up Yekaterina's statue at the same time as other Enver associates were involved in a murder. And Enver Pasha had been in the mountains when all the killing took place. It was as if his specter was everywhere in every case Kazakov was involved in, like a spider in a web.

Or a wolf that aided and abetted a tsarevich.

The wolf in the story had helped the tsarevich at every turn, allowing him to achieve riches and delights he failed to achieve on his own, all because the wolf had killed the tsarevich's horse. It made no sense that a wolf would shackle itself to a man for so long, even bringing him back to life, for such a thin reason. There had to be something more—perhaps the wolf wanted the tsarevich to ascend the throne because he was malleable, having already proven his own judgement was questionable. So what happened afterward in the ancient tale? Did wolves overrun the tsarevich's kingdom?

He went into the squad room and sat at his desk, his mind wandering into wilder and wilder theories. The elevator dinged and the door slid open. Egorova stepped out, carrying a plastic bag of strips of white paper, and marched stiffly into the squad room. She was followed by a blond man who, by his furious expression, must be Bogomolov, followed closely by Chelomeyev, who looked stern-faced and official.

Egorova led across the room to the squad's interview room and ushered Bogomolov inside, closing the door behind him. She turned back to Chelomeyev and grinned and then looked at Kazakov.

"That was fun," she said flexing her neck and stretching.

"His secretary held us in her office too long. We pushed inside his office and found him shredding papers, a small pack of clothing ready for him to pull a runner," Chelomeyev explained. "Sort of satisfying arresting him."

"Has he told you anything?"

"Not much," Egorova said, shaking her head. "Just that he's an influential man with friends in high places."

"He's threatened to have things fixed, has he?"

"You could say that." Chelomeyev said. "But he's worried."

Kazakov cocked a brow at the younger detective.

"He kept muttering and ringing his hands."

Leaning back in his chair and staring at the ceiling, Kazakov smiled. "I believe Enver Pasha's illusions might be unraveling, just like Madam Sobol's stories." He thought a moment. "All along, Enver Pasha has influenced us, through his words and actions and innuendos. Up to now, I've tended to believe him, because most of what he's said has turned out to be true. Or true enough."

He swung back to upright and looked at Chelomeyev and Egorova. "What if all of it was a ruse? What if all of it was to get us—me—to trust him? What if he planted seeds and let us believe what grew out of them?"

Yes. That felt right. It felt like he was on the right trail without the wolf beside him.

"When we were in Biysk, Enver told me there was an installation in the mountains. I was the one who filled in that it was Chinese..." The implications were staggering.

"All right. You need to interview Bogomolov. Interview him about Anna and see what you get, and then drop the bomb of the explosives on him. See what happens. In the meantime, I'm heading back out to Basil to visit Anna's workplace. Hopefully, I'll find someone willing to talk to me. And I want to visit the American Embassy—see if they can help me."

He checked his watch. He might just be able to pack all that in, but it was going to be late by the time he got home. He printed off photos of Enver and Zholdosh before he left, pulling on his coat on the elevator ride down to the parking garage.

Eschewing a police vehicle, he retrieved the Perseus and headed out through the weak early afternoon sunshine. New Moscow melted away behind him and he drove through the mostly open country of fields and farm houses. He passed the turn to Charlotte Newcomb's riding stable and carried on to the borderlands of the southwest. Basil grew up out of the snow-fields like a litter of soot-mired stones, the dirty warehouses sending oily fingers out into the landscape. Before he reached the main town he turned off into the massive Transcontinental Shipping compound and pulled into the parking lot just before two thirty.

To the rear of the function-built cinder-block central building, three huge, articulated transport trucks idled, spraying gray exhaust fumes into the air.

Kazakov climbed out of the Perseus, inhaling the tang of soot and old snow. He waded through the sloppy snow into the front office. It was a closet-sized room, barely big enough for a single guest chair and a single desk manned by an attractive young brunette who wore a brown sweater set buttoned up to her throat. Under the desk, trim ankles poked out of brown checkered trousers. Were the trousers for warmth, or to fend off too many appreciative looks? Two closed doors filled the wall behind the desk. One was marked staff only.

He pulled out his identification. "I'd like to see the manager. Please?"

The girl eyed his identification, wide-eyed. Then she gulped and nodded. "C-can I tell him what this is about?"

Kazakov just looked at her and let his presence do the work.

She hurriedly nodded and picked up her phone. From beyond the unmarked door came the sound of a phone. The sound stopped.

"Sir." The girl cupped the phone receiver with her hand. "There, there's a police officer here. He says he needs to speak with you."

She uh-huhed a few times and hung up. "He says he can give you five minutes in about thirty minutes."

"He did." Kazakov glanced at the door and turned as if to leave, then strode around her desk and opened the unmarked wooden door.

"Good afternoon," he said to the startled man behind an overflowing desk. "I'm terribly sorry to interrupt, but I have a murder investigation to conclude."

The office and the man were reflections of each other—the man's flesh threatening to overflow his wrinkled white dress shirt. Flesh bulged above his collar. The buttons down the front strained. The office walls were covered with documents pinned to the wallboard. One side of the room had a sign at the ceiling that said Outgoing Ottoman. The sign on the other side of the room said Fergana Receiving, so shipments coming into the country. The wall behind the man was filled with shelves heavy with worn binders. The one difference between the man and his office were the man's eyes. They were brown, large, clear, and lustrous with long lashes, perhaps the most beautiful eyes Kazakov had seen on a man.

Kazakov stepped up to the desk and introduced himself. "I will need more than five minutes of your time."

The man frowned up at him. His fingers ran through his thick black hair. "You expect me to leave off what I'm doing? I have a crisis here—a shipment of melons is caught at the border. It seems someone misplaced their paperwork. A few days sitting in this cold and the damn things'll freeze and be ruined."

Kazakov removed Anna's photo from his pocket and placed it on the stack of papers. "I believe this woman worked for you."

Glancing down at it, the man's eyes widened and a cloud seemed to pass over them. "Anna. Yes. She worked for us out front."

And you replaced her with the pretty brunette. Kazakov pulled out his notebook. "Your name, please?"

"Matvel Emin. Why do you need my name? What is the matter? What has Anna done?" The man's jowls shook. So did his belly, and fear filled his gaze.

For a moment Kazakov was struck by the notion that Emin was one of those hybrid creatures—half man–half desk, in his case.

"She was found dead four days ago at her employer's home in New Moscow."

Relief flooded Emin's face. "If she died there, it can have nothing to do with me. I am a happily married man. I have no time for young girls."

Interesting. Those eyes seemed to betray everything Emin was feeling.

"How long have you worked for Transcontinental?" Kazakov asked.

Emin's gaze once more flared with alarm. "Why ask about me? I told you. I haven't seen Anna since she left our employment."

"Please answer the question."

Emin slumped back in his chair. A leather belt cinched in his voluminous waist. Plain brown trousers belied Kazakov's fantasy. "I've been here eight years. The company brought me in from Tashkent because the last fellow made a mess of things."

An Ottoman, then. Interesting.

Nodding, Kazakov made a note of it. "And when did Anna Konstantinova come into your employment?"

"About three years ago. Our last girl had retired. Anna was competent enough. Interested, but too pretty by half. The loaders tried to take their breaks in the office until I put a stop to it. Nothing was getting done and trucks were delayed loading. Shipments were arriving late."

"Tell me about her," Kazakov said, eyeing Andreev over the notebook.

"What is there to tell? I told you. She did her job."

"Who were her friends? I understand that she began to attend social events with your other employees."

"At first, she was proper as a girl her age should be, but then, after all the attention she received, it began to go to her head. She began going out with the workers after work." He shook his head. "A woman should not do that. She should be home with her father and brothers."

Kazakov cocked a brow at him. "And if she has neither?"

Emin shook his head and looked away in distaste. "Then she can expect nothing good will become of her."

"And what happened with Anna?" Kazakov asked softly.

"She showed what kind of girl she was. No moral fiber. She became involved with—a man—in that way men and women will." Disgust filled his gaze as he looked back at Kazakov. "A woman should be married or she is no more than a whore. When I found out Anna was pregnant, of course I let her go."

"And the man?"

"How can a man be expected to say no when such sweetness is offered to him?"

"Aah," Kazakov said. "And who was this man who could not say no to such sweetness?"

Those expressive eyes showed fear again, but Emin quickly looked away. He shook his head. "I cannot recall his name. Some worker. We sometime get itinerant workers through here."

"Truly?" Kazakov closed his notebook and turned his focus on Emin. He watched the man squirm.

Kazakov pulled the photos of Enver and Zholdosh from his pocket and placed them on either side of Anna's photo on top of Emin's precarious pile of papers.

The man's alarm turned to cold fear when his gaze lit on Enver's photo, but relaxed slightly when he turned to Zholdosh. Sweat beaded his upper lip as his gaze swung like a metronome between the two faces. Then he sighed.

"Enver may have had her, for he could have any woman he wanted, but it was this one who kept her like a pet, giving her things. Treating her to meals and taking her away from her desk when she should have been working and making her feel too important."

"I thought you said she fell in with one of your workers. Surely a worker could not do such things. Who is he?" Kazakov asked.

Emin shook his head. "How am I to know? I simply arrange shipping in and out of the country. He is an agent for the company—at least that is how he was introduced. He came here regularly to take control of shipments across the border."

"Why would he do that?"

"Well… there were times Transcontinental trucks were too busy, so shipments would come over the border by other companies and then would be reloaded into our trucks here."

"And what were these other trucking firms?" Kazakov asked, not certain why he was interested.

Emin shrugged, setting off another roll of flesh. "Usually small independent truckers. I remember they'd be bringing in some kind of exclusive cigarette and have to reload those boxes after our items were unloaded."

Kazakov nodded. "Are such shipments still coming?"

Emin frowned. "As a matter of fact, no. This fellow," he picked up Zholdosh's photo, "stopped coming, but a woman came in his place. At first it was a tall blonde, but now it's some dark-haired woman that looks like a warrior."

Women who matched his description had been, or were, employees of Enver Pasha.

"And this man's name?" Kazakov asked, leaning forward to tap on Zholdosh's photo.

"Around here the men called him Mr. Z. Enver Pasha introduced him as Zholdosh, you see, but once I had a friend visiting from Constantinople and he recognized Zholdosh. He said his full name was Rustam Niyaz. Not that it matters. He doesn't come here anymore."

Because he was killed at a hotel in the Fergana mountains.

Considering what he'd learned, Kazakov thanked Emin and took his leave. He had a long drive home and he still wanted to drop by the American Embassy. Eric Clinton was Fergana's resident American spy and had been helpful in the past in putting evidence in a larger context. At the moment, the evidence in this case led to some conclusions that seemed absolutely absurd. He wanted a second set of eyes.

If the spy was still around. The last time they'd spoken, Clinton had indicated that he was being shipped home due to injuries he had sustained here in Fergana.

The drive back to New Moscow felt shorter than the trip out, his mind consumed with making too many connections to too many cases, and yet the murder of Anna Konstantinova still wasn't solved.

The long, straight highway guided him from the pristine white of the snowfields into the gray lands of warehouses around the city and then the sloppy gray snow of the city proper. He wound his way past the gaudy domes of New Moscow's sad replica of Saint Basil's Cathedral, the original long ago burned down after being converted to a mosque when the Ottomans took the original Moscow. Finally he reached a garden area of the city that now held embassies from around the globe. The two behemoths were the massive Chinese and Ottoman enclosures that faced off against each other across a broad boulevard. The Ottoman property unsubtly shot minarets skyward, while the Chinese raised tiered rooflines above the embassy's stout walls. A little farther down the street, the Anglo-German embassy was a utilitarian block growing out of a broad front garden that grew over the walls. Kazakov turned down a side street away from the edifices to a more modest brownstone brick building set back from the road by a small yard with a single tree. He pulled in to the curb.

The American Embassy sat in a row with a number of embassies from less significant countries around the world. Most of them were in the Americas because the Anglo-German's and Ottomans had overrun most of Africa and the Chinese had conquered all of Southeast Asia and had colonized Australia. The Anglo-Germans had taken a smattering of smaller enclaves around the world and most of North America except for the American stronghold on the eastern seaboard and as far west as the Mississippi Valley. The Americans and others of the smaller nations were trying to band together to protect themselves against the depredations of the larger empires. In particular, they were concerned about the potential of Fergana being overrun and setting off a war between the Ottoman and Chinese Empires. The winner of such a battle would be likely to then take on the Anglo-Germans and after consuming that major bite, proceed to feed one-by-one on the smaller countries until there was a global empire.

Eric Clinton had tried to stop it happening through his work in Fergana. Or at least he'd tried to keep an eye on what was happening, like a distant early warning signal.

Kazakov just prayed he was still around.

He climbed out of the Perseus and walked through late afternoon shadows spread by the sun through bare branches. He'd been here before on other cases, and had never felt particularly welcome. He pushed open the small iron gate and strode up to the front door, knocked once, and the door opened. He was faced by a brawny soldier in a pristine gray uniform with white belt. He held a rifle in his white-gloved hands, though in such close quarters a rifle would not be good for much. Still, it was a show of security and strength.

"Yes?" the soldier said.

"I'm here to speak to Eric Clinton," Kazakov said. He had been through this before. The embassy probably wouldn't even admit Clinton worked there. "I am Detektiv Alexander Kazakov. I am with New Moscow police. I need to get a message to him."

"Remain here a moment," the soldier said. He closed the embassy door in Kazakov's face. Kazakov scanned the yard and street and looked up into the narrow eye of a camera aimed down at him from halfway up the side of the building. Undoubtedly along with the Americans, observers from the Ottoman and Chinese Embassies would have noticed his presence. There wasn't much he could do about it. He turned back to the street ignoring the surveillance, and turned when the door opened again.

The young soldier stepped aside and motioned Kazakov to enter. He found himself back in the carpeted foyer of the converted old house. A lone man waited for him, gray-haired, a pair of pince-nez glasses balanced on a narrow, hooked nose.

"What can we do for you, Detektiv Kazakov? I'm Bradley Coombs. I've taken Clinton's place as attaché."

"You can get me Clinton. I need to speak to him."

Coombs shook his head. "Well, I'm afraid Eric is no longer in our employ…"

The last time Kazakov had been here they had said much the same. He held up his hand. "Only Clinton will do. He has the background. Do you have a way that I might get in touch with him?"

"I really can't say," Coombs said with a shake of the head.

Kazakov sighed. "Well, you'd better figure it out. Clinton and I—we worked on a few cases together that were of—let's just say mutual interest. I understand that your government is nervous about the Fergana election. Suppose I've uncovered something that should make us all very nervous, but the only person I'll talk to is Clinton." He nodded at Coombs. "Welcome to Fergana."

He turned and pushed past the soldier and out the door to the Perseus. The afternoon was bluing as the light faded. Clinton was either available or he wasn't. If he wasn't, then Kazakov, Egorova, and Chelomeyev were on their own. How the hell they were going to deal with this was, at the moment, beyond him.

No, not quite alone. There was Pogolin, too. A case like this demanded all hands on deck.

Kazakov pulled out his phone and called the police switchboard to be connected to Pogolin. The connection clicked and rang.

"Pogolin," the detective's gravelly voice came through the phone.

"It's Kazakov. Things are developing. We need to talk."

There was a moment of silence.

"I was on my way home."

Kazakov gritted his teeth. "Then turn around. This is bigger than we thought and we need to strategize. Meet me at the station. I should be there in ten."

He headed back to the station through end of day traffic. It was after five and he was late by the time he pulled into the parking garage. Everything had taken longer than he'd planned.

At the station, he took the elevator up to the squad room, but when the door opened, he found himself facing Detektiv Chief Inspektor Rostoff, his coat in his hand as if he was planning on leaving. Rostoff stepped aside to allow Kazakov to exit.

"Well? What is your report?" Rostoff demanded.

Kazakov glanced at the secretaries pulling on their gloves as they came down the hallway to the elevator to leave. "Perhaps this is not the place…"

Rostoff raised his gaze heavenward. "Would you just tell me? Is it truth or not?"

Kazakov swallowed. This wasn't what Rostoff wanted to hear. "Truth. And from speaking to the elders, it seems it is beyond their control. There are other forces at work."

Counting one-two-three, he watched his words sink in. Then Rostoff hooked his arm and dragged Kazakov down the hall to Rostoff's office.

Dabria had gone home, so the reception area was empty. Rostoff swung around. "What the hell are you telling me?"

Kazakov sighed. "I'm telling you that we have a worst-case scenario. There are explosives missing and there are hothead young Kyrgyz just itching for payback for years of systematic discrimination. They take out Bure and we'll have a bloodbath on our hands. The Russians will mob them and hunt them down."

"Derr'mo," Rostoff swore and settled on the edge of Dabria's pristine desk. The wood paneled walls seemed dull and lifeless, as hopeless as their situation. Rostoff looked back at Kazakov. "Are you certain?"

"As certain as I can be. A third party—at least I believe a third party—has set things in motion. I'm not sure what to do."

"Stop it, of course. Stop them." Rostoff stood up. "You're a New Moscow detective. Use your authority."

The advice was almost humorous. "Unfortunately, there are people who are a little more rarified than a detective, Detektiv Chief Inspektor."

"Who? Who is so important and yet undermines our election?"

Tell him about Enver? Kazakov chose his words. "Let us just say he is a foreign national with great prestige both here and in his home country. The matter must be dealt with quietly and effectively and with the utmost tact to avoid an international incident."

"Shit." Rostoff sank down on the desk again.

"Sir. May I go? I want to meet with the team before end of the day."

A distracted Rostoff waved him away. Kazakov took it as permission and left for the squad room.

The detective desks were mostly empty, but the air was still stained with the stink of old, cold tea and musty woolens that came from too many men using too small a space. Egorova and Chelomeyev were waiting. So was Pogolin, and a fourth figure swathed in a greatcoat. The data machine hummed in the corner as if waiting. At Kazakov's entry, the four people swung around. Egorova and Chelomeyev both looked tired. Pogolin looked impatient to leave.

The fourth man was Eric Clinton, his normal broadbrim hat replaced by a typical Russian fur hat, his handsome face hollowed out and cadaverous.

"You got my message," Kazakov said, focusing on Clinton.

"Apparently, no longer employed doesn't mean the same thing in America as it does here."

Clinton gave a shuffling shrug, but it looked like the effort took all the energy he had. "Roles change. They were sending me home. I was at the airport. Apparently, your visit stopped them."

"You mind telling me what this is all about?" Pogolin broke in.

Kazakov nodded. "It seems that your explosives theft is connected to bigger things than the previous two explosions."

Pogolin's gaze widened. He glanced at Egorova and Chelomeyev. "They've been dropping hints that your investigation and theirs and mine might all be connected. How? And what's an American doing here?" He gave Clinton the evil eye.

"Clinton, I take it you've met Detektiv Pogolin. He's our resident doubter. Clinton, here, happens to have insights far above all our paygrades. I'm hoping he can help us make sense of what evidence we've collected. I figured you might want to stay and see how your investigation fits into a greater whole. Or you can go home. Your choice."

Pogolin looked around the ring of four faces. Then his shoulders slumped and he sighed. "Fine. Who knows. Maybe I'll finally understand what makes you tick, Kazakov."

Egorova snorted. "Like that'll happen. No one understands how his mind works."

They all took seats amongst the otherwise empty desks, Kazakov leaning back to put his feet up. It felt good, his bed too long ago vacated and still hours away yet.

"Before we talk further, Clinton, can you tell me everything your government has got on Enver Pasha?"

Egorova's gaze widened. Pogolin and Chelomeyev looked puzzled, but Clinton's gaze grew veiled. He nodded.

"A very good question. Something I've had my government looking into since our last little adventure. There was something there…"

"Something that didn't fit," Kazakov agreed.

"Who brings men with assault rifles on a skiing trip?" Egorova said thoughtfully. She looked up at Kazakov. "You did say he was there to enjoy the skiing."

"Apparently Enver Pasha brings such men," Kazakov said.

"I suppose we were lucky that he did, considering what we found at the installation," Egorova said. "We'd have walked into live ammo fire."

Kazakov looked at Clinton. "I'm not so sure. Tell us about Enver."

"At heart, he's a soldier. He comes from a low-level functionary family in the Northwest of the Empire. Two hundred years or so ago, it was all independent countries. Enver's great-great-grandfather apparently saw the chance to advance by going into the then-independent Balkan states. Then the Ottomans swept in and took over. The family did well—born and bred Ottomans in an occupied country. Enver was a bright enough kid that he was sent to university and then he joined the military while he was still a teenager. Our sources tell us that Enver had determined that the military was the best way to advance. He did well, rising in the ranks, and attained general's rank early after quelling the Egyptian uprising. He was in his early thirties, though the Enver Pasha legend says he was younger." Clinton air-quoted the word legend. "Enver *was* the youngest ever to reach such a rank. It wasn't pretty what he did—basically wiped out the entire population in the Dakhla Oasis as the source of the infection. As a result he gained the title, Pasha.

"During his career he was able to meet and woo the sultan's granddaughter. It would seem that his star was on an unlimited rise and he was a young and handsome man, but ten years later in his midforties things began to unravel. First there was an incident in the Arabian Peninsula. There'd been problems there for years with the tribes resisting their Ottoman masters. Enver had been elevated to governor of the state. He tried the same thing with the Arabs that he'd done to the Egyptian tribes—he'd invited them for a peace meeting and ambushed a number of tribe leaders. But the Arabs weren't stupid. They'd seen what happened in Egypt. They came fully armed and instead of wiping out the Arab resistance, Enver lost a significant number of men in the initial battles. But then the Arabs began to attack in other places. They were purchasing arms from other sources."

"Like America, perhaps?" Kazakov asked.

Clinton only smiled and continued his story. "The trouble in the Arab Peninsula resulted in Enver being called back to Constantinople. It did not go well. Not only was the Sultan not interested in his excuses or his plans to quell the uprising, it seems word had reached home of his sexual exploits in the capital of the Arab state, Damascus. The sultan wasn't pleased with his grandson-in-law—not that he'd had a mistress or two, but that he hadn't been discreet. Enver was threatened with demotion. By age forty-seven he'd quit the military and started his company, Transcontinental. That was twenty-some-odd years ago."

Kazakov nodded. "I knew the larger outline of the story, but not all the details…"

Clinton's gaze was watchful as he nodded.

"There's more, isn't there?" said Kazakov. "I can see it in your face."

"Damn." Clinton shook his head. "I seem to be getting too easy to read."

"Your country's been watching him a long time. What aren't you saying?"

Sighing, Clinton closed his eyes a moment and sagged back in his chair. "The man comes from extremely loyal roots. He's shown himself again and again to put Ottoman interests before all else. And then suddenly he is in disgrace, more or less separated from his wife, and living here in Fergana. For a man who fought his way up to become the Sultan's grandson-in-law, it's hard to believe that he didn't fight for his reputation."

"What are you suggesting?" Chelomeyev asked. He sat perched on the edge of his seat at the side of his desk, his young face eager, regardless of fatigue.

"I think he's suggesting perhaps Enver Pasha was sent," Kazakov said.

Clinton shook his head. "Could be, but there's another possibility as well. He could be here to regain the favor of the current sultan, his brother-in-law. Just think, Fergana sits here like a stopper in a bottle that holds in the war between Chinese and Ottoman Empires. This sultan is relatively young and has long expressed frustration that he is a caretaker sultan, unlike the Ottoman leaders of old who led their people into glorious battle victory after battle victory. Think of the favor Enver Pasha would enjoy if he could give his sultan that opportunity."

Kazakov pulled his feet off his desk.

Chelomeyev whistled. "Are you saying that he's behind an effort to undermine our government?"

Egorova shoved a stray blonde hair behind her ear. "That's exactly what he's saying. But it's impossible. The installation in the mountains was Chinese. Boris Bure is linked to the Chinese, not the Ottomans. Why would Enver support that? Besides, he's not old enough to have instigated the replacement of Bure."

"Hold on a minute. Just hold up!" Pogolin leapt up. "What the hell is she talking about? There's no way in hell one man can orchestrate the end of Fergana. What's he going to do? Line us all up and shoot us? I thought you were going to bring up some evidence that's relevant to my explosives investigation, not waste my time on American conspiracy theories. If you don't have the evidence, then I have a wife and kids to go home to."

Chelomeyev and Egorova looked away from the fuming detective. Clinton stayed silent. Kazakov stood and faced Pogolin. "I know it sounds farfetched. I would feel the same as you if I hadn't lived through the past nine months of investigations. It seems every case I was assigned—and some not—kept leaving me with the sense that something was amiss. Not quite right. And each case had a common thread."

"Enver Pasha," Egorova and Chelomeyev said in unison.

Shaking his head, Pogolin scanned each of them. "You believe this?"

They both nodded.

"Where's the evidence? How did some Ottoman get involved in my case?"

Kazakov shook his head. "As you know, your case was initially Chelomeyev's until he was beaten and left for dead. He was beaten and there were attempts on his life because of information he had— information that linked the explosives theft not just to the tribals, but to the construction company owner and a third man—a man named Zholdosh who worked for Enver Pasha."

"You know this?" Pogolin asked of Chelomeyev. "Why the hell haven't you said anything before now?" Anger made Pogolin's ruddy features deepen in color.

"Because I can't be sure of my memory," Chelomeyev said.

"Because he was drugged with a memory-erasing drug," Kazakov explained.

"Now you're going to tell me Enver Pasha did that, too." Pogolin shook his head, but he sat back down in his chair. "All right. Say I believe you. So what? He got explosives into tribal hands."

"There's more," Clinton said.

Kazakov waited.

"To answer Egorova's question, Enver is presently sixty-nine years old —I know he doesn't look it, but he is. There are questions about that mountain installation, however. After Biysk, our people went way back over old records. Over the years there have been many adventurers in those mountains. My people pulled old diaries of mountaineers and compared them to what we know now about the installation's location. They got the Anglo-Germans to cough up historical data, too. After all, they have an interest in maintaining the status quo, too, even if the Anglo-Germans and my people aren't exactly friends in North America. About thirty years ago there were reports of roads being built in the mountains, first with the widening of trails through the mountains and then stories of meeting construction crews. At the time no one pursued it because the people who reported the activity were convinced the activity was Ferganese. The whole thing would have been easy to miss if you didn't know what we know now. What was interesting was that the first roads weren't reported near China. They came from South Asia."

"Ottoman territory?" Egorova asked.

"I expect that the Chinese were far more interested in the mountain passes to the north where they had to guard their frontier against direct confrontation of the Ottomans," Clinton said. "If I recall my history, thirty years ago there was a tense period between the two Empires. There were skirmishes in many spots along their border. It could even have been a ruse to draw Chinese attention away from what was happening elsewhere."

"Damn," Pogolin said.

"And less likely to be noticed by Ferganese forces given our attention was probably turned northward as well," Kazakov said. He looked at Clinton and Egorova and shook his head. "It was all a setup—a very elaborate one. That installation was Ottoman but they set it up to for us to think it was Chinese. It was the Ottomans who used it for their research and experimental operations. It wasn't the Chinese who killed those villagers. It wasn't the Chinese who transformed Bure. We had the mastermind of their deaths with us in the mountains."

"But that means that Bure isn't Chinese," Egorova said.

"What?" Pogolin said. "Bure, Chinese? He's tall and white-blond, like Chelomeyev, here. What shit is this?"

"I suspect Bure really is of East Asian descent, but I don't believe he came from China," Kazakov said. "There are populations of Chinese in many countries."

"Hold it right there," Pogolin said, standing. "Since when do Chinese look like Bure? Like I said: he's blond and tall and his eyes are round!" Pogolin's face reddened as he spoke.

"Cosmetic surgery," Egorova said quietly. "We found evidence at the mountain installation that they had been surgically altering people."

"And before that we found evidence of surgical alteration in a dead spy here in Fergana," Kazakov added.

Pogolin sat down hard in his chair.

"I think this is another of Enver's setups. At first glance, with Bure's rhetoric, it looks like he's trying to sever relations with the Ottoman Empire and enhance the relationship with China. His anti-tribal rants fit in with this. Questioning their loyalty and tying them to the Ottomans has been a political hot button and is pushing these confrontations like the riot the other day."

Kazakov thought a moment, choosing his words. "But the other thing Bure's rhetoric has done is foster anger and resentment amongst our tribal citizens. It's also increased their fear until they needed to protect themselves. As a result, explosives were stolen and I've recently found evidence that suggests weapons are being smuggled across the border and then distributed in Fergana by Transcontinental..." He looked down at his hands, feeling stupid that he hadn't seen it sooner. Clinton's information made all the pieces fit together—and make sense.

"He's playing both sides," Egorova said. "He's stirring Russian sentiment through Bure and arming the tribals. It's as if he wants the country to come apart."

"That's exactly what he wants," Clinton said softly. "Fergana's ethnic Russians attack the Moslem minority and the Ottomans will be able to say they took over to stop genocide."

"But that presumes that Russians attack the tribals..." Pogolin said, now perched on the edge of a desk and interested. "We're not barbarians. Why would we do that?"

"It would take something to incite the Russians," Egorova said.

"Bure," Kazakov said at the same time as Clinton and Chelomeyev.

"If a tribal kills Bure it would set off a bloodbath," Kazakov said.

Clinton nodded. "And after the dust settles and they examine Bure's body, imagine the outrage when they discover Bure is actually Chinese. The world will rise up against the Chinese. The Ottomans and their newfound allies will win and the Ottoman subterfuge will begin again—on their next targeted victim."

The room went silent. It was too horrible to imagine.

But at the same time it raised a question: how did the end of the world relate to Anna Konstantinova's death?

13

—————

The sun had set and darkness had long fallen by the time Kazakov left the office for home. The New Moscow streetlights glared and the city buildings were garish against the clear night. Here and there a few pedestrian stragglers struggled through the icy streets. On the outskirts of the city, as the land rose toward the mountains, house windows glowed warm and welcoming, and as the Perseus went higher still, the lights of New Moscow spread like a carpet of jewels in his rearview mirror. Four months from now, would they still be there or would they have been bombed out of existence?

Kazakov turned his focus back to the road. The headlights lit up the hardpacked snow and the huge plow drifts along the side of the road. All were stained with signs of melting. It had been a hard winter with more snow than came most years. It would be good for the runoff and the lowland farmers, not to mention the forests.

But thinking about farmers and forests was avoiding thinking about the foreboding conversation at the station. Surprisingly, Pogolin had stayed. The detective's countenance had grayed considerably by the time the discussion was over.

Egorova and Chelomeyev had reported that the construction company owner, Bogomolov, had admitted that he might have taken some of the explosives from his storage. With Pogolin present, they had Bogomolov returned to the interview room and had presented him with the police photographs of Kadet uulu Semir and Zholdosh. The businessman had cracked. He had been cheating on his second wife. He was sure no one had known—until a spiritualist named Anna Konstantinova had provided him with a reading. She had told him that his dead first wife wanted him to know that he would be fine as long as he worked with a dark man with white-winged hair who would contact him. If he did not work with the man, then ruin would be his. He had cried into his hands as he described meeting Zholdosh when the man came to his office. Someone knew of his indiscretions and would release them to the world. His wife would take half his fortune. So he had done what he was told.

The news of Anna's involvement in providing the reading only confirmed Kazakov's theory that she knew far more about Enver Pasha's business than perhaps the Ottoman had liked. While Zholdosh was alive, Anna was cooperative, probably because Zholdosh was her lover. When Zholdosh died, all bets were off.

Pogolin was ecstatic that they had solved the case. The problem was that there were still explosives unaccounted for. And Bogomolov's admission did nothing to solve the case of Anna Konstantinova's murder —it just gave them another suspect.

Chelomeyev hadn't been able to discover anything helpful about the OTO, other than confirming the schism within the group, with his father leading a faction that had not yet been convinced to support Bure. Bogomolov, unsurprisingly, was a strong Bure supporter. Otherwise there were no links to the murder that Kazakov could find, but the extent of the spiritual influence on Fergana's elite was troubling.

And then there was the question of Bure. Did the man know that he was likely doomed? The man made Kazakov's skin crawl, both for what he was and the ideas he represented to the world, but did he deserve the fate that seemed ordained for him? They had to stop the tribals from killing him.

And here he was, making predictions like Madam Sobol or Anna Konstantinova. But he was no charlatan.

Ahead, his headlights illuminated the dark spruce, naked walnut, and aspen as they parted at a snowed-in driveway. Kazakov pulled in close to the drift left by the last plow and climbed out to retrieve a bag of groceries from the Perseus's back seat. Then he set out, up and over the drift and on a snowy path along the driveway into the trees. There were small saplings pushed up through the snow. Agafya had given up on the driveway after her Russian husband died. It was as if the old woman was gradually trying to pull the forest up over her head and hide. Perhaps she would become a Baba Yaga.

The driveway led to a clearing with a low house of logs, stone, and sod built as if it was part of the earth. Only a thin stream of chimney smoke said the place was inhabited. Not even the narrow windows by the door gave off any light. He stopped. Perhaps the old woman had gone to bed.

But if she had, her chimney would be tamped down and not give so much smoke. She was a thrifty woman, like most older Kyrgyz. You did not waste firewood. It was too precious when many mountain areas had no trees.

He climbed the stairs to the rough wooden door her husband had shaped with his own hands, and knocked sharply.

From inside came the muffled shuffle of footfall and then a chain rattling. The door pulled open a few inches to reveal a single suspicious eye and release a thin stream of light across Kazakov's feet.

"Who is it? Go away," she said and started to close the door in his face.

"Madam Ryabkov. Good evening," he said and smiled, hoping the half-blind old woman would recognize him or his voice.

She hesitated.

"It's me, Kazakov. Your neighbor? We had Christmas dinner together. I brought *kutia,* remember?" He named the traditional Russian honeyed porridge. "I stop in regularly and left groceries for you a few days ago. I was hoping you could help me," he ended lamely.

Her single eye frowned as if it was hard to remember. Then her gaze cleared a moment and she pulled the door farther open.

Agafya Ryabkov was a tiny Kyrgyz woman who had done the unthinkable and fallen in love with a Russian. They had married and, when neither Russian nor Kyrgyz society would accept them, her husband had built their home here. Kazakov had befriended them as a child and had often met Agafya when she visited with Kyrgyz tribesmen who used to come down from the mountains to the streams that ran above Agafya's and Kazakov's dachas.

She wore her usual calf-length, black, felted skirt and thick stockings under an old sweater that had probably been her husband's. The sweater hung on Agafya. Her skin did, too, and she had deep hollows around her eyes. She had lost weight. A lot of it. So she may not have been eating the food he had been leaving.

Kazakov mentally kicked himself for not coming more often this winter and not forcing her to let him in the door.

"What do you want?" she said, her voice rasping.

Sighing, he went into his well-used patter. "Actually, I was hoping you could help me. I bought groceries and now I realize that I bought too much. I was hoping you could take some off my hands."

He eased himself past her into the house. The cabin's old stone walls reflected the heat of the woodstove chugging in the corner. A lone candle on the wooden table lit the room, leaving the rafters, their cobwebs, and ranks of dusty, dried herbs half-seen in the shadows. A narrow cot covered in a bright quilt sat against the back wall. Above the woodstove, a mantel held an old wedding photo of her handsome, blond-haired husband and a lovely young Agafya, as well as a radio that murmured in the background.

Kazakov set the bag on the table and glanced at a pot beside the sink. A thin gruel filled the bottom that almost looked like the fruit-filled kutia he had left her, but thinned innumerable times. Had she frozen the pot he'd left her and doled it out over time?

Guilt pulsing through him, he turned back to the table. Agafya was eying the bag. He pulled out a sausage, two loaves of crusty bread, and her lips trembled. A big bag of potatoes and another of beets and she started to blink. A block of cheese and she closed her eyes. Her throat worked as she shook her head.

"No. I cannot accept this. I have no money to pay you."

He knew it was the truth but shook his head. "Truly you would help me. I don't know what happens when I get into the store. I buy too much when I know that the bread will go moldy before I eat it all. Please take it. Better you eat it than it go to waste." He pulled a small sack of flour out of the bag, hoping she wouldn't think about how the flour might store, and followed it by a pound of butter and a bottle of vodka.

Her gaze locked on the vodka. "Here," she said. "Let me give you what I have."

She went to a small cupboard and pulled out a jar, poured its contents into her palm, and brought it to him. "It is not enough, I know, but I can pay something for the groceries. The vodka I cannot afford."

Her gaze was clear. She knew exactly what he was doing. She caught his hand with her withered one. Her papery skin was frigid against his. Then she turned his palm up and dropped the coins in his palm. He almost smiled, certain that they were the ones he had salted her snow with during one of his last few visits. It was little enough, but it left her with dignity that she could contribute something.

"The bottle is a gift," he said. "A gift for a wonderful neighbor. Who else would watch Koshka for me when I am gone?" Because he knew the little cat escaped out through a small cat door under his sink and came here when he wasn't around. Agafya took the little cat into her home when it was cold.

The radio squawked from the mantle and Agafya cringed. Her bird-bright eyes looked up at him. "That thing. That thing spouts hate all the time. That hateful man—saying my people cause Fergana ruin. It is the other way around." She shook her head.

"You mean Bure?" he asked.

"Bure. Whatever his name is. Someone should kill him." She eyed him. "You are police. You have a gun."

Horrified, he looked at her. "I *am* a police officer. A detective. I do not kill people—not even those I don't like. I stop people from killing."

But her eyes glittered at him. Then she looked at the food. "I've paid you. You should go now."

Kazakov nodded. All of his visits with Agafya ended more or less like this. She could not abide someone invading her home for long.

He paused at the door. "Take care, Agafya. If you need anything, please come and ask me."

He stepped outside and she immediately closed the door. He heard the rattle of the lock. If anything happened to her, it would be difficult to get in to help her. He would have to come back soon to make sure she still had food.

The sky was awash with stars. The white peaks of the mountains to the southeast glistened in their light. Feeling numb, he left the cabin and stumbled out to the Perseus, then drove the short distance up the road to his driveway. He parked behind the dacha and climbed out. Overhead the sky was clear, but the air was crisp and biting. He was glad when he stomped the snow off his boots and stepped inside. The world was smaller here. There were no threats against Fergana, no plots to end the world.

A mew and a small black form wound around his ankles before he could get his lantern lit.

And here, Koshka was waiting.

———

The mountain peaks rimmed the walled parking lot of the Royal Yekaterina Resort. Sunlight from cloudless blue sky bore down on the crowd of spectators that crowded Kazakov's elbows. He was dressed in his great coat and suit, which was odd because he didn't remember packing them for his trip to the high mountain valley town of Biysk. In fact, he didn't remember packing at all. Nor the drive to the mountains. He remembered going there before, for the murder investigation. But not this time.

From Biysk's main road came the sound of car engines. An entourage. Sure enough, a convoy of three dark Ziln sedans turned into the parking lot. The crowd surged forward in welcome. From the first vehicle, four burly men climbed out and held the crowd back from the second vehicle. Its driver climbed out and came around the side to open the rear passenger door. Blond hair almost steely in the sun and his black suit seemingly absorbing the light, broad-shouldered Boris Bure climbed out and smiled and waved at the crowd.

Kazakov moved forward with the crowd. Closer. Closer to the man with the overlarge teeth and the unconvincing grin. Bure waved once more and then stepped between his security men as they cut a path through the crowd to the stage Kazakov hadn't noticed. It filled a corner of the parking lot, lifting Bure high above the crowd and suddenly the crowd shifted and Kazakov was standing right in front of the stage.

Bure welcomed the crowd. He raised his hands high, and around Kazakov was cheering.

"He's got a gun!" someone shouted right into his ear.

Kazakov whirled around, seeking, and then realized he held his service revolver as he was cheering. Held it as he turned back to the stage. Around him, people were screaming. People were running. Bure stood frozen as Kazakov aimed and fired.

Bure crumpled in slow motion toward him.

Kazakov jerked awake into darkness. Sweat soaked the bedding and he gasped for breath. His heart raced and he lay there, staring up at the ceiling and trying to calm himself.

It was a dream. Only a dream.

But what a dream.

He could still feel the grip of his weapon in his hands, still feel the recoil as he shot Bure down. Derr'mo, he could still smell the cordite of the shot.

Shakily, he pushed himself up in bed and got an annoyed mew from Koshka, who had bedded down between his legs. He hiked his legs up and around her and sat head down at the side of the bed. Scrubbed his face and hair, but that didn't help by half. His head felt muzzy, as if he was still half in that dream. Nightmare more like. He'd killed a man—not a righteous kill in the line of duty, but an assassination.

He stumbled up and across to his corner kitchen and found the bottle of vodka he'd left under the sink. Hauled it out and thunked it on the counter, then fumbled it open and took a long, throat-burning pull. It burned all the way down. Another pull on the bottle and his hands gradually stopped shaking. His mind cleared and he recapped the bottle, but took it with him to the table. By his watch, it was only an hour until he had to get up. He might as well do some thinking and get a start on the day.

He looked at his hands, still feeling the weight of his pistol. The sweat was drying on his skin, but that left him cold and shivering. He hadn't had this physical sensation before. Not even after he had killed a man. So why now, for a nightmare? And why such a dream?

It had to be because of Agafya Ryabkov's statement last night. Why the old woman's words had struck him so deeply, he wasn't sure. Maybe it was because Agafya's words came on top of the discussion of Bure with Egorova and the others. If Bure was killed, it would deal with the threat he posed. If he was killed by Kazakov, it wouldn't lead to the bloodbath of the tribals. Fergana might regain itself. Perhaps it would even right some wrongs that had been perpetrated against the tribal people.

Perhaps.

It was disturbing, but something to think about.

He busied himself stirring the fire into life and adding more wood. Soon heat radiated off the heater. He filled the kettle and placed it on top, but took another pull of the vodka for good measure. Fortified, he washed himself and shaved in the kitchen sink, then pulled on clean underwear and his suit. The kettle boiled and he made milk tea and remembered his groceries, forgotten in the Perseus.

He pulled on his boots and ran out into cold and frost and frigid air to reclaim them. Everything was frozen solid. Still, he hacked off part of a sausage and tossed it in a skillet with a chunk of bread. Soon the dacha smelled of toast and rich grease. He fed Koshka, who got up at the scents, including a piece of the sausage as a treat on her kibble. Then together they filled their bellies. When he was done, though it was still incredibly early, he pulled on his weapon and great coat and aimed the Perseus toward the city.

The streets of New Moscow were almost empty at this hour, save for a few delivery vehicles trundling surreptitiously into and out of back alleys. He cruised the streets past Enver Pasha's house and the Red Veil brothel that was Enver's next door neighbor. If his discussions with Clinton and the others yesterday had been correct, was everything that happened at the Red Veil, including Maria's death, also Enver's doing?

Kazakov's hands tightened on the Perseus's steering wheel. If that was the case, then he had a score to settle. The image of Bure on the stage came back to him. Maybe it should be Enver Pasha at the wrong end of Kazakov's weapon.

Derr'mo! What was he thinking? His hands were shaking when he pulled over. He fisted them on the tops of his thighs.

He was not a killer!

But a person who would order the killing of an entire village. That wasn't a man—that was a monster.

He looked up at the lace curtains of Enver's house and thought he saw them shiver. Was Enver Pasha watching him watch the house?

He eased the Perseus away from the curb and headed to the office. At least there was nothing there that would reinforce the haunted feeling he had from the dream.

The underground parking at the police station was busy with shift change; officers inspected their vehicles before leaving the garage, and others headed home after nightshift. He nodded at a few and then rode the elevator upstairs. When the door dinged open, he was surprised to see Egorova and Chelomeyev already at their desks.

They looked up when he entered the glass-sided room.

"I see you decided on an early start," Kazakov said.

"Let's just say I didn't have the best sleep," Egorova said.

Chelomeyev nodded in agreement. "That was a disturbing discussion yesterday. I dreamt of New Moscow in ruins and more bombs falling on what remained. I was trying to take people to safety, but there was none." He shook his head, but by his pallor, it was easy to see that the dream still disturbed him.

"We need to find a way to stop the Bure assassination. Stop it, and we stop the bloodbath of the tribals."

"I don't think so," Egorova said. "Need I remind you that if Bure lives, they'll feel the same effect but slower. Death by a thousand cuts. Driven out of their city and probably the country. The Ottomans can still use that as an excuse to start a war."

"So what do we do?" Chelomeyev asked into the silence.

Kazakov took off his greatcoat and slumped down into his chair. It squealed in protest as he turned to his desk and scrubbed his face in his hands. "I have no idea." He looked up, feeling the two younger detectives' regard. "Sorry. Bad dreams like Chelomeyev. Maybe focus on our murder. Bure is a bit above our pay grade."

Swinging his chair around to face them, he rubbed his hands. "Any brilliant ideas?"

Egorova and Chelomeyev glanced at each other and then pulled their chairs around their desks to face him.

"Not a lot," Egorova said. "Like I told you. We interviewed Anna's customers. Most really thought she had some sort of connection to the afterlife. It was surreal to hear them talking about their dead loved ones as if they'd had a conversation with them. They didn't even question the advice they received—not even when apparently it set them in a different direction than they'd planned."

Chelomeyev nodded. "Belief is a powerful thing."

"Belief is all about what we want," said Kazakov. "Religion is like that. It fulfills a need to believe we're not alone and that there's a greater reason for being. A purpose. Something more than a chance meeting of cells that brought about consciousness." But he was thinking of the story of the wolf and the tsarevich and how the readers' beliefs were what were played with. By even calling the character a tsarevich, he was given honorability, so people wanted to believe in him, even though he was no better than a common thief. Perhaps that was what the Russian people expected in their leaders. Certainly, they elected such people.

He sighed. "Okay. Let's start at the beginning. Let's go over the evidence and see what we're missing."

All three of them pulled out their notes.

They started with the body. Found in the kitchen naked, drugged, and six weeks pregnant.

Kazakov frowned. "If her first child was really Zholdosh's son, then was she pregnant by him again? We need to check whether Zholdosh was in New Moscow six weeks ago. If not, then who's the father?" He thought a moment. "Damn. If only we had Zholdosh's DNA." Too bad he dared not request Gordiev do a comparison to Bure's DNA.

He looked from Egorova to Chelomeyev. "Madam Sobol's statement is that she was not around that weekend. She was visiting a client in her village in the north. Did you confirm it?"

Chelomeyev nodded. "It was one of the first calls I made. Apparently, Madam Sobol comes from there originally—a no-name village near Osaka. She still has old clients there she serves."

"So she has a solid alibi." Kazakov thought. "What about the neighbors? What did they see? I don't think you told me."

Chelomeyev shrugged and Kazakov suppressed a shudder.

"Not much," the young detective said. "I questioned the neighbors on both sides and across the street for the length of the block. No one saw anything except the usual postman at his usual time."

"They didn't see anything or there was nothing to see? Be precise, please," Kazakov said because often people said they saw nothing when they actually saw something that they thought was unremarkable.

Chelomeyev colored slightly, but flipped back through his notes. "They spoke about seeing people on the street like they normally do— children playing. Women herding children or shopping. The occasional delivery van that I've since checked out. A few workmen going to work."

"That's it? No one going to the Sobol house?"

Chelomeyev shook his head.

"Did you speak to the postal worker?" Kazakov asked.

"And there's the children. Often people ignore them and they see far more than adults give them credit for. They notice things—at least I did as a child." Egorova added and stood up. "Come on, Pavel. We've work to do."

Kazakov stood with them and pulled on his coat.

"Where are you headed?" Egorova asked.

"To speak with someone about the Bure assassination attempt." He couldn't quite bring himself to speak of Khan as a friend.

She met his gaze, her own turned dark and unhappy. "You should arrest him."

"He's the best hope we have of stopping this thing before it happens."

"Really?" She cocked a brow at him. "Maybe you should be thinking about how to rid the country of the likes of Enver Pasha. That might do more good."

With Chelomeyev, she turned on her heel and left the squad room, her anger clearly simmering.

She was right—again, but how else was he to gain access to the plots amongst the tribals? Sometimes you had to look away to do the right thing.

Or at least what he believed was the right thing.

He groaned and scrubbed at his face, feeling rough patches on his cheeks that he'd missing when he shaved. The disturbing thing was, even in the dry heat of the office, he could feel the cold mountain air and feel the weight of his nightmare's weapon. He scrubbed his palms on his trousers and then used his mobile phone to call Khan's number. It rang once before there was a click, but no answer.

"We need to meet," he said. "Yekaterina's Park. You know the scene."

He hung up and headed for the elevator and the quick drive to the eastern end of Potemkin Park, named after Tsarina Yekaterina's favorite lover and general. Through most of the city the park followed the river, but here it curved away from the ice-blocked water to a run-down, backwater copse of trees set amongst aging three-story walk-ups that were one-by-one being eaten up by the expansion of New Moscow's city core. Soon the low-income apartments would be replaced by office buildings and apartments for the more affluent. Where the current residents would go, he didn't know.

Kazakov pulled in at the edge of the park. The last time he had come here was last fall when the geese were flying and the air only hinted at snow. It had fallen soon after and kept falling like few winters before. He climbed out of the Perseus and stood in the cold. The mountains were white with snow, ringing in Fergana as if they afforded protection. But while he and everyone else had been feeling safe, danger had crept into their country and nested among them.

Setting off through the knee-deep snow, he eventually came to a small knoll surrounded by trees. Here the original murder victim had been found —Yekaterina Bure, naked on the ground, her clothing neatly piled nearby. Though Bure hadn't killed her, she was still the man's victim. She'd died because of it. And now here he was trying to find a way to save the bastard's life.

His throat burned with sour bile.

The crunch of snow behind him turned him around. Khan stood there, not in the dark Russian coat he had always sported while working as a New Moscow M.E., and not in the bright ski jacket he had worn in Biysk.

Now he wore a simple brown workman's jacket with the collar pulled up around his face and a peaked flat cap pulled low over his ears. His usually smooth cheeks and chin were covered in graying stubble and the circles under his eyes made him look haggard.

He nodded at Kazakov. "I hope you weren't waiting long. I came as quickly as I could."

"For a change, it's you who looks like hell, my friend. I'm sorry to meet here, but I've become paranoid about someone watching. I knew you would catch my reference and not go to Yekaterina Park."

Khan's lips quirked slightly. "I look like a man on the run. A detective should be arresting such a man."

"Thank you for coming," Kazakov said. "I saw Clinton yesterday. I won't bore you with the details but we have a bigger problem than we thought." He thought a moment about how to begin and decided to address this head on. "How closely do your people work with Enver Pasha?"

Khan's tired gaze widened. He smiled this time. "You always were direct. To answer your question, fairly closely. I think. I haven't met with him directly outside of Biysk, but I believe he's been supplying weapons here just as he was in the mountains."

Kazakov nodded, a little surprised at Khan's admission. Perhaps the man really was wanting to work together.

"That's what the evidence is pointing at, too. He's had a sweet little deal running where the weapons are brought in amongst American cigarette shipments by independent truckers. I'm not even sure if the drivers knew what they were carrying. Zholdosh would meet the trucks and take the weapons off and shepherd them to their destination. He worked in New Moscow for a time."

Khan showed no reaction.

Kazakov nodded. "You knew."

"I knew."

"Did you know that Enver Pasha is behind the whole thing? The guns. The installation. Even, potentially, Boris Bure's physical transformation. I suppose the murder of Bure's family, too."

"What are you talking about?" Khan frowned. "The installation was Chinese. The papers were Chinese. Collin Archer was Chinese!"

"Plants. At least I believe the papers were and so were those poor souls who died in the firefight at the installation. As for Archer, he might have been Chinese or he could have been Ottoman of Chinese descent the way he was playing both sides of the spy game before he was killed. On the other hand, maybe he was a real Chinese spy and Enver just copied the technology with Bure."

He told Khan what Clinton had told him and what they suspected. Khan finally had to sit on a boulder at the edge of the clearing as he tried to take it all in.

"So you see why those young tribal firebrands are a problem. If they act on Bure, it's just a matter of months, maybe weeks, before the Ottomans move in, ostensibly to save your people. When Bure's genetics are discovered, there'll be a hue and cry all over the world. The Ottomans will have allies. From there it's only a matter of time before there's an all-out global war. We have to find a way to stop your youngsters."

Khan sat motionless. He even seemed to stop breathing. His gaze seemed set on the mountain horizon over Kazakov's shoulder until he finally shuddered and met Kazakov's gaze.

"It may already be too late."

Kazakov's heart sank. "What are you talking about?"

"There's a group of five youngsters who've been pushing hard to act. The elders had stomped on their plans and set them other things to do, but I got word last night that four of the five had failed to show up for their duties. They've disappeared."

He looked down at his hands. "There's more. Our weapons store was broken into. Military-grade rifles were taken as were a few grenades and all of the explosives."

"Derr'mo!" Kazakov whistled softly and wished for a place to sit down. "Can you find them?"

Khan looked bleakly up at him. "I could lie and say yes, but I won't bore you." He shook his head. "We're looking, but there's a lot of our people who sympathize with them, who are simply hoping for someone to act so that they can feel safe again."

"You have to stop them. *We* have to stop them." He thought again. "Worst case scenario, any idea what they would target?"

Khan's nod was slow, as if answering was difficult. As if Khan and his people had made tentative plans for such an attack? Kazakov didn't want to believe, and yet… it, too, made sense. Khan had said his people were desperate.

"Bure has a rally planned for tomorrow evening," Khan said and then hesitated. "It's one of his last before the election and certainly the biggest. It's planned for the New Moscow Concert Center. We were going to rig the stage and have armed men posted at all the entrances. He wouldn't be escaping."

Kazakov nodded. "I can work with that. We can exclude young tribals from the event and have security personnel posted everywhere. Can you give me the names of the young men?"

Khan just looked at him, but then finally shook his head no. "That goes too far, I am afraid."

And again proved the rift between them. Kazakov sighed.

"Then I suppose we'll have to exclude all tribals. Not the best fix, but better than nothing." He looked hard at Khan. "A general exclusion is only going to deepen the divide between tribal and Russian."

Khan shook his head and stood. He began to walk back the way he'd come, then stopped and turned back. "I would have it go back to the way things were."

"So would I," Kazakov said, though he doubted the wound he felt at Khan's betrayal would ever heal. He watched Khan disappear into the trees toward the walk-ups beyond and wondered whether he would see the M.E. again.

B ack at the police station, Kazakov headed up to the squad room, but then detoured for Rostoff's office. Constable Dabria Smirnova looked up from examining files on her desk. Distress placed lines on her pretty face.

"Detektiv! How are you?" She quickly pushed the files away, her expression smoothing.

"I'm fine, thanks. And you?"

Her blonde hair made a halo as she shook her head. "Busy as always. He dumped these on my desk this morning and told me to decide whether to close them or send them back for further investigation. It is wonderful that I have his trust to do so, but I have not done such things before. I worry that I'll close the wrong file…" She looked down at the pile and shook her head.

"You have good judgement, Constable. At least as good as his." He lifted his chin at the heavy wood door to Rostoff's inner sanctum. "And if you have a question, ask him."

She looked askance at him. "And you more than anyone would know the problem with that option."

Rostoff's first reaction was inevitably to get angry. It seemed his only style of management. That Dabria had lasted in her position as long as she had spoke volumes of her diplomacy, but she deserved better.

"Well, if you truly need a second opinion, I am at your disposal." He nodded at the door again. "He in?"

"Of course. Just be careful of his mood. He has been almost bearable this morning."

It was odd that Dabria was so forthcoming with her opinion of her superior. Usually she was much more circumspect. He nodded, left her desk, and knocked on Rostoff's door. A gruff "Enter," came from within and he pushed the door open.

Rostoff's inner sanctum wasn't overly large, but it had space for the desk and two guest chairs and space for a man to pace between the window and the desk. At the moment Rostoff was doing just that, his large head bowed, his hands behind his back.

Rostoff's desktop was empty except for a china cup and saucer patterned in blue flowers that released steam from the amber liquid that filled it to the brim. On a sideboard behind the desk, a newfangled samovar sat steaming.

Kazakov stopped just inside the door, knowing better than to disturb Rostoff's thinking processes.

Finally, the detektiv chief inspector stopped his march to the window. He faced Kazakov. "Well? I hope to hell you've brought me good news."

"Good news is relative," Kazakov said and stepped farther into the room.

"So? Have you found the culprits? Or have you disproved the rumors?"

"Neither."

His answer seemed to reverberate in the room. Rostoff stopped his pacing and rocked onto his heels.

"If you haven't any results, then why are you here?" Rostoff returned to his desk to slip into his chair. He swung it around to face Kazakov and motioned to a guest chair. "Well? Tell me. I know you well enough to know that you would not be here unless there was something important to tell me."

This was a new Rostoff. Kazakov glanced at the door. No wonder Dabria was out of sorts. The uncertainty of Rostoff's new-found reasonableness could kill you.

He sat and met Rostoff's gaze. The man looked troubled and Kazakov wasn't going to make things any better.

"There is a plot. I have confirmed it. It is not the whole tribal people, it is, apparently, four or five unidentified youngsters. The target is believed to be the Bure rally tomorrow night."

"Derr'mo," Rostoff swore. "And the risk?"

Kazakov shook his head. "High, I'm afraid. There is reliable information that the young men have military-grade weapons, grenades, and all remaining explosive from the theft at Mountain Construction."

Shaking his head in disbelief, Rostoff sagged back in his chair. "It can't be. You're sure?"

Kazakov sighed. "It comes from a reliable source. One I would bet my life on." And he had in the past. Would he in the future?

Rostoff's gaze narrowed. "What source?"

Kazakov simply looked at him. "Do you want the source or the information?"

"If I have the source, I will have the information," Rostoff said.

"No. You will not, for my source would never betray the tribal people. On the other hand, my source believes that the death of Bure at tribal hands will bring about reprisals and worse. It could bring an Ottoman attack, and eventually war."

Rostoff looked heavenward. "Not your conspiracy theories again..." He shook his head and then took a sip of his still steaming tea. "For the moment let us say that we let your source be in the wind, as it were. Say the information is true. Then what do we do? I can't see Bure canceling his rally. It would set a bad precedent."

"You want my opinion?" Kazakov asked, surprised. Rostoff had never valued anyone's opinion but his own. So what had changed?

Sighing, Kazakov leaned forward in his chair. "I think we make the request of Bure because that would eliminate the target, but we make contingency plans based on the rally going ahead. You'll have to tell him that we will have security checkpoints at all entrances and must conduct a search of the premises before the event can begin. If he does not agree to that, then you will need to find a way to shut him down. It is one thing for Bure to place himself at risk. It is another thing altogether to allow innocent citizens entry to such a risky place."

Rostoff considered a moment, sipped his tea, and half-smiled. "That is good. If he doesn't cooperate, we cordon off the streets around the venue. No one in or out." Another sip of tea. "I want you to see to it."

Kazakov froze in his chair. "Sir. I can't order the resources such a thing would require. That would require the chief inspektor..."

Rostoff waved his protests away. "All these years you've railed against my leadership. Now is your time to take the reins. No arguments. I will get the approvals for you to move forward."

Stifling a frown, Kazakov stood. Would Rostoff truly get the approvals or was this a ruse before throwing Kazakov to the wolves?

Rostoff looked up at him. "Good then. See to it."

Kazakov didn't move.

"Is there something else? Nothing?" Rostoff nodded at the door.

Dismissed and still wondering, Kazakov left and stopped just outside the office door. "What the hell is going on?"

Dabria shook her head. "He went to an appointment the other day at the Royal Caravanserai Hotel and he has been different ever since. I don't understand it."

"Do you know who he met with?"

"Not really. Some senior officers were there as well as businessmen, I think. They were there to hear someone speak. A woman, I think because Rostoff seemed quite shaken when he returned and he kept saying things like 'how could she know'."

Kazakov thanked her and headed thoughtfully back to the squad room. A reaction like that and he'd bet money that Rostoff had been admitted to an OTO meeting. Spiritualists and belief. Like wolves in sheep's clothing, just what had the spiritualist been spouting and was it Madam Sobol?

14

The detective squad room was as empty as Kazakov felt as he labored alone at his desk. Well, perhaps not alone: the faint reek of cold tea and old sweat permeated the room like a ghost. He sipped the cup of milk tea he'd made himself, but it had long gone cold. He put the cup down again—too hard—and slopped liquid onto the desk and his papers. Swearing, he grabbed a towel from the break room and sopped up the tea, then sat down at the desk again. He'd been at it for over two hours and the morning was almost over.

Planning security for a man he despised was not exactly the way he wanted to spend his morning. This was one of those times when he almost sympathized with the hitmen, except for the long-term implications for Fergana and the world. He'd hunkered down at his desk, trying to plan the security details and the number of police needed to provide Bure safety, as detectives filtered in and then out again. He'd ignored them. He was on hold with the venue for Bure's rally when Pogolin tried to strike up a follow-up discussion from the revelations of the night before. Kazakov waved him away. Only Egorova and Chelomeyev failed to return to the office. The interviews must be taking longer than expected.

"Hello?" The male voice at the end of the phone had changed from the youthful voice of an assistant to something more venerable.

"Yes. This is Detektiv Alexander Kazakov of New Moscow police. I need to speak with the manager of your facility."

"This is Nikolai Chaykovski. I am the manager of the New Moscow Concert Center. What can I do for you, Detektiv?"

Kazakov looked at the phone. "I am afraid this is not something that we can discuss over the phone. I would like to come over and speak to you now."

"Now?"

Kazakov heard the hesitation.

"It is urgent. A matter of national security."

There came a sigh. "We have a major event tomorrow. I can give you five minutes if you can come before eleven."

Kazakov checked his watch. He had twenty minutes to get there. Then all bets about five minutes were off.

Thanking Chaykovski, he hung up, gathered his coat, and headed out the door.

The New Moscow Concert Center sat on Suvarov Way. It was a grand building, not copied from some long-lost edifice of the original Moscow, instead being one of the few original designs the city was graced with. While its street face was a line of Grecian columns, the building itself rose in stacks like an erratic staircase up to five narrow peaks that, from street level, seemed to act as a reflection of the heights of Yekaterina Mountain at the edge of the city.

When there were no free parking spaces out front, Kazakov double-parked in front of the grand flight of stairs that led up to the rank of front doors. Banners strung from the roof over the columns held images of Bure's smiling face and an invitation to purchase tickets to the rally.

Head down and feeling the weight of Bure's shark grin, Kazakov climbed the stairs and pushed inside the building at exactly five minutes to eleven. The entry foyer was a vast area of black marble floor and plush red-and-blue oriental carpet. Wood paneled walls climbed two stories with balconies with iron railings allowing people to look upon those who entered. Ahead was a refreshment kiosk, currently closed, but to one side a small, elegant door was stenciled with "Administration."

He knocked once and entered, finding himself in a utilitarian reception space of dark wood floors and bright white walls. A single desk was occupied by a young man in a pristine blue suit with slicked-back black hair who looked up from typing. The young man had vivid blue eyes set in a narrow face with an overly strong jaw. A second door was set into the wall beyond the young man's desk, as if he was the guardian of entry. Perhaps he was.

The young man's lips set in a line. "You must be that detective."

Kazakov nodded. "Chaykovski? Is he in?"

"He has a meeting at eleven about the event tomorrow. He cannot miss it…"

"Well then, he cannot miss meeting with me, either." Kazakov headed for the door beyond the desk, knocked once again, and entered.

A man in a gray suit looked up from a wide ebony desk. A potent aftershave sweetness filled the office. The room was far larger than the reception area, with room for the desk and also for a conference table. A window beyond the conference table looked out over the theatre's concert hall where workmen were busily checking equipment and hanging a sickening array of Bure banners.

Kazakov glanced back at the man who was framed by numerous autographed photos of the world's famous performers. Unlike Rostoff's array of images, none of these included the man who stood up behind the desk.

He wore a perfectly fitted suit of muted gray that matched the perfectly parted gray hair that was swept back over his head like wings. A high, white collared shirt with black tie completed the conservative attire; however, wide white cuffs with glittering cufflinks provided an air of flamboyance as he checked his watch.

His brows rose. "I thought you weren't coming given how close to eleven it is."

"I got here as quickly as I could. We have a credible threat against the Bure event. I would like you to cancel it."

Chaykovski's almost-black eyes widened. He sank back into his chair. "We've had crank calls, but never the police telling us something is credible."

Kazakov nodded. "It is a very serious threat."

But Chaykovski was shaking his head. "I can't cancel. The organizers would never allow it. They would sue."

"I'll speak to Bure. Or my boss will, but if they insist on going ahead, we need to ramp up security. First of all, no tribal workmen can be allowed to work on this event."

"Hold on!" Chaykovski half rose out of his chair, sending a cloud of the sickening floral aftershave wafting into Kazakov's face. "Most of my workforce is tribal. They are exemplary workers—electricians, carpenters, etc."

Stifling a cough, Kazakov shook his head. "I'm sure they are, but we can't take a chance. As much as it pains me, there can be no more tribals involved with this event—if for no other reason than if something happens, they cannot be blamed."

Chaykovski met his gaze. Finally, he sighed and nodded. "I would protect my workers and their families against reprisals. All right. I'll see what I can do. What else?"

"Security. I will need to have explosive specialists inspect the premises. Explosives could have been placed at any time and left for the event."

Half-sagging in his chair, Chaykovski mouthed "explosives." All his crisp edges seemed to have crumpled. Even his pristine collar seemed askew. "Is that all?" he said softly.

Kazakov shook his head. "We will need police presence at every entrance—public and service, to ensure no tribal presence."

Chaykovski blinked and nodded. "What makes you so sure the threat comes from tribals?"

"That I can't say, except that it is credible and trusted."

Checking his watch again, Chaykovski shook his head. "I'm meeting with the event planners—in fact, I'm late for the meeting. What am I to tell them?"

"What I've told you. I will meet with Bure as soon as I can. Thank you for doing this. We cannot have the man injured—or worse."

Feeling sick to his stomach, Kazakov excused himself and left the administration offices. In the foyer he stopped and heaved in clean air. It didn't help much. The entire idea of working for Bure's safety didn't sit well. His palms itched for the feel of gunmetal until he scrubbed them on his greatcoat.

He might as well get this over with. He headed out to the Perseus and drove to Bure's election headquarters, praying that the man himself would be there.

It was an unassuming storefront down the block from a beauty parlor that Kazakov recalled being on the list of Anna Konstantinova's regular errands list. He found a parking spot half a block away and walked back to the storefront. It was a low, flat-roofed building, the kind that was becoming derelict in the gentrification of many areas of the city. Old buildings like this were being pulled down and replaced by more expensive business and apartment buildings. Why Bure would choose such an unassuming location for his headquarters was suggested by the ordinary Russians hurrying down slushy sidewalks. This was a lower-income neighborhood, belonging to the ethnic Russians probably in direct competition with Fergana's tribals for jobs. Bure's rhetoric would speak directly to these people.

The storefront's broad windows were awash in posters portraying Bure amongst the Russian people. Bure swathed in his greatcoat and Russian furred hat. Bure speaking, the glitter of a fine, gold-encrusted, antique Russian religious icon like a blessing just over his shoulder. The slogan of "Fergana for Russians" was brazenly displayed for all to see. No wonder the tribals were worried. No wonder they were taking action to protect themselves. Bure had made himself into a target.

Or been manipulated into becoming one by a master manipulator. Frankly, Enver had succeeded in something that deserved at least a modicum of awe at the complexity of what he had planned and what appeared to be almost completed.

Kazakov pushed the glass door open and stepped inside. There were at least twenty young men and women busy at desks and on telephones. Many glanced up at him but were too busy with their conversations. He headed for the nearest desk, but a bearded young man approached him.

"May I help you?" he asked. He was black-haired, his five o'clock shadow also dark, his skin so pale as to be almost translucent so blue veins pulsed up his neck from the open collar of his flannel shirt.

"Detektiv Alexander Kazakov," he said, producing his identification. "I need to speak to Boris Bure."

The young man shook his head. "I'm afraid that's not possible. Mr. Bure is at lunch with a benefactor."

Kazakov shook his head. "This is urgent. A security matter. Where is he having lunch?"

The young man hesitated and then sighed. "The Silk Road Room. Do you know it?"

Kazakov did. It was the most expensive dining room at the Royal Caravanserai Hotel. He left, swearing at Rostoff for saddling him with this, even if it was connected to the greater investigation.

The Silk Road Room sat on the second floor of the Royal Caravanserai Hotel though it wasn't the kind of place Kazakov had been before. It was decorated with red, gold, and blue silk tapestries and wooden windows carved to look like ancient temple scenes. Unobtrusive lighting gave the place a dim, sensual appeal. Well-dressed patrons sat at strategically placed tables that each seemed private amongst tropical plants.

Too rich for his blood. Too rich for the blood of most honest

Ferganese. His assessment was confirmed as he walked up to the desk inside the restaurant's entrance. Most of the patrons he could see were politicians, foreign media types here to cover Fergana's election, and foreign diplomats by the look of them.

The maître d' looked him up and down, clearly assessing Kazakov's middle-class clothing. "Sir. How may I help you…"

It was a surprise that the man didn't simply try to stop him. Kazakov nodded. "I'm here to see Boris Bure," he said, producing his identification.

The maître d' shook his head of smoothed back gray hair. "Mister Bure is having lunch in a private room. He does not like to be disturbed."

"Well, today you and I are going to disturb him." Kazakov slipped the identification into his pocket and stepped past the desk.

The maître'd hesitated.

"You can show me where, or I can interrupt the lunches of all these good customers."

One look past Kazakov at the full tables and the maître d' led him around the edge of the restaurant to an unassuming blue enameled door. He knocked once and pushed the door open the smallest amount.

"I am terribly sorry to interrupt gentlemen, but there is a police officer here who insists on seeing you." He gestured Kazakov forward and swung the door open to allow him entry.

Kazakov stepped inside and the door shut behind him again, leaving him with the uneasy feeling that he would never get out.

Before him at a round table sat three people: Boris Bure, white-blond hair slicked back and dressed in a charcoal gray suit, white shirt, and gray-and-red tie; a second man that Kazakov didn't know with a fleshless face, auburn hair, and a tidy navy-blue suit; and the stunning blonde Annuschka Yevseyev who also happened to be Kazakov's ex-wife.

For an instant he paused, whether because of the glare Bure turned on him or Annuschka's dismayed gaze he wasn't sure. She'd been crucial to solving other cases in the past, but had drawn the line at providing anything damaging about Boris Bure. Her expression smoothed to one of distaste, similar to those she'd turned on him at the end of their marriage. Once upon a time, as teenagers, Boris and Annuschka had meant something to each other. Though Annuschka might be on her second marriage, her presence here suggested she still felt loyalty to her first love.

"Kazakov! What are you doing here? What do you want?" She wiped her lips and shoved her meal away. "I should have known you couldn't leave things alone."

Kazakov kept his attention on Bure. "I am sorry to interrupt your lunch, Candidate Bure, but we have credible information that there will be an attempt on your life at your rally tomorrow. New Moscow Police would like to request that you cancel your appearance."

Still holding his fork as if he refused to be interrupted, Bure's ice-blue gaze bored into Kazakov. Bure frowned, but then his expression cleared and he pointed his fork at Kazakov.

"I know you. You're the investigator who was charged with finding my stepdaughter's killer. You were shot or something."

Kazakov nodded. "All healed now. Will you cancel your rally?"

The other man at the table shook his head. Bure looked back at Kazakov. "Are you certain? It's hard to believe someone would threaten me."

Kazakov sighed. He did not want to go into detail, because the details of this situation would only further fuel Bure's hateful rhetoric.

Bure still looked at him. "Surely the police force will protect me from any threat."

Shaking his head, Kazakov approached the table. "At best we can have guards at the door and we can search the place and anyone entering, but that doesn't mean that we can deal with the risk—with the conspiracy."

"Conspiracy, now. You see?" Bure triumphantly set his fork down and turned to his companions. "Finally, the authorities believe me. Even this one. Let me guess: tribals are at the center of it."

As if he already knew what was coming. Could Enver have told him? Was Bure prepared to die? Surely that couldn't be the case.

"We don't know who is behind it, but we know they have explosives and rifles and that you are the target. Surely that gives you reason enough to cancel."

"Is that true?" Annuschka asked.

"Of course, it's true. Contrary to what you might think, I don't make a habit of barging in where I'm not wanted. I have better things to do." He clamped down on his annoyance. "If you will not cancel the event, your security must cooperate with the police. We'll be sending in explosives experts to search the premises and we will have personnel present at the event."

Bure shoved back from the table and stood, frowning. "This is real, then, is it? A real threat?"

He worked his broad shoulders and looked at his male companion. "What do you think? Wouldn't canceling be a sign of weakness?"

"Perhaps you should consider rescheduling…" Annuschka said.

Bure flicked his hand at her and her mouth clicked shut.

"Well… the blue-suited man said and glanced at Kazakov. "It is a credible threat. We should cooperate. The police can keep tribals out of a place they're not wanted. Of course I am assuming tribals are behind the threat." He grinned and his face resembled a death's head.

Kazakov refused to respond to the man's conjecture about the source of the threat.

"Will that do, officer?" The man tilted a brow at Kazakov. "Far be it from us to hinder real police work."

As if that had ever been the case, but Kazakov held his temper and nodded.

"We will do our best to keep you alive," Kazakov said to Bure and hoped his dislike didn't show. "Thank you for your time."

He swallowed his revulsion and let himself out of the room, gasping for air in the hallway as if Bure's room had been a vacuum.

He was out of the restaurant when Annuschka caught up to him. "Kazakov." She caught his arm, almost breathless.

Turning to her, he remembered how he had been caught by her blonde loveliness as a young man. Now she just seemed—false. A made-up creature sustained by her job in communications, now supporting a candidate who was every bit as false. How she could get away with it given her job as the current government's communications manager, he didn't know.

"What do you want?" he asked.

"Is it really true? Is there any clue you can give us as to what to look for?"

He studied her face, the full lips and the perfect double arches of her brows.

"So you can use it in your communications or his speeches? If I used the word tribal you would shout it to the world, so why would I tell you anything?"

"Kazakov, no. I wouldn't do that. I'm better than that."

"Are you? Or do you just hope to make yourself believe it? And me, as well, I suppose. We all have our beliefs about ourselves, Annuschka. You like to think you're a good person. It doesn't mean everyone else believes the same."

He turned and left her there, heading for the stairs down to the lobby.

"Bastard." Her voice floated after him.

Given his lack of friends, perhaps she was right.

On the drive back to the office, he called Rostoff and updated him on how the meeting with Bure had gone. Rostoff agreed to arrange a briefing of officers who were to be assigned to the rally for the next morning and to get the searchers in to look for explosives overnight. Kazakov thanked him for the assistance and signed off, suddenly tired.

He would have liked to avoid the office and the case and to head home to a quiet evening with his books and Koshka but it was too early in the day, and if he was going to be prepared for the briefing, there was too much work for him to do. Checking his watch, he decided to check in on Krupin one more time. The old man's suddenly reclusive ways worried him. Grief was powerful and did strange things to people. His own recent grief had had him turn to the bottle until Khalil Khan had brought him back to himself. He could understand how a person experiencing grief truly needed friends. Unfortunately, though Margarete Krupin might have been a social doyenne, he didn't get the sense that Kasimir Krupin was a well-liked man.

The Krupin house looked unoccupied when Kazakov pulled up. No lights shone behind the drawn curtains. No vehicles were parked out front and any smoke from the chimney was invisible against the sky. When he climbed out of the Perseus, the ice on the sidewalk to the front door had melted and frozen again since he'd last been here and there was no sign that anyone had tried to do anything about it. In the past Krupin had been fastidious about such things.

Gingerly, Kazakov picked his way over the icy walk and went up the few stairs to the porch and the door. He knocked and waited and finally was rewarded with the sound of slippered feet from inside. A curtain beside the door twitched.

"What do you want?" Krupin's muffled voice came through the wood.

"It's me, Kazakov. I came to have tea as we discussed. Remember?" God, Krupin was worse than he'd thought.

There was silence a moment. "This isn't a good time. I'm sorry. You should just go away."

There was the sound of coughing from inside.

"Kasimir? Are you all right? Do you need anything? A doctor?"

"I'm fine. Just fine," Krupin's wheezy voice came through the door.

"Are you eating? Have you got food in the house? I can get groceries for you if you'd like. Just tell me what you need…"

Silence again.

"Please, just leave me alone, Kazakov. I don't need your help. Do you understand? Just go away. I need to be allowed to grieve in my own way."

The sound of shuffling came from inside and gradually faded away. Kazakov stood in the wind trying to decide what to do. He wanted to break in the door, but acknowledged that that was a poor option. Was Krupin trying to starve himself to death? Who was there to call in cases like this? He didn't know enough about Krupin. Perhaps he had friends amongst the people at the newspaper…

Worried, he made the call to the *New Moscow Now* from the Perseus as he sat outside Krupin's house. He was put through to the newsroom editor.

Kazakov explained that he was a friend of Kasimir Krupin and was concerned for the aging reporter's wellbeing.

A sigh came through the phone. "I'm not certain why you're calling me. Krupin resigned two months ago. He said his wife needed him at home. I was sorry to hear she passed away. We're planning a tribute article on her."

"Surely Krupin had friends at the newspaper…"

"Afraid not. He's one of those self-contained individuals. Never figured he really needed anyone as long as he had his wife, I guess."

Kazakov thanked the editor and signed off, feeling helpless and as if he'd broken a promise. Margarete had never asked him to watch over Kasimir, but surely he had a responsibility to the older man—just as all people should care for each other.

And now he was sounding like some kind of fool. When had such an attitude ever existed?

Kazakov pulled away from Krupin's house and headed back to the station. Maybe he could ask Egorova to try with Krupin. She had a woman's touch and the old man had seemed to like her.

It was almost four o'clock and a cold wind was blowing from the eastern mountains, ripping at the barren tree branches and tumbling garbage and small ice balls down the pavement. At least Kasimir had the warmth of his house. He thought of the working girls on the street that most people believed deserved their fate. Belief, it seemed, was a horrible thing—as horrible as grief.

It was odd, for truly it wasn't right to kill a man, and yet here he was, feeling like he trespassed against his beliefs by saving a man every part of his soul said was not worth saving. He had to keep telling himself he was stopping the killing for the good of the tribals. For the good of the country.

It didn't help. He still felt like he had when he was being asked by Rostoff to collect hush money from the brothels in New Moscow.

He parked on the street outside the station and went up to the squad room. Egorova and Chelomeyev still weren't there. Pogolin was, seated glumly at his desk. He nodded up at Kazakov.

"Hear you got a promotion. That we're all supposed to be at your beck and call this evening and tomorrow," Pogolin said. "The great Kazakov, finally honored."

Kazakov rolled his eyes and went to his desk. "It's not a duty I wanted. Rostoff dumped it on the first person available," he said, stripping off his coat. "There tea? Have you seen Chelomeyev or Egorova?" Because the two young detectives had been gone a very long while.

Pogolin shrugged at the question. "Not since this morning. What's so bad Rostoff won't handle it himself?"

Kazakov headed for the break area. "How about Bure's safety detail? We've got credible intelligence that there's going to be an attack on the rally tomorrow."

Pogolin sat up. "I was going to take the wife and my oldest kid to that —see history in the making and all that."

"Well, you'll be there, but on duty—and I'd suggest you keep your wife and kid away."

"But there are others going to be there. I heard some of the high schools are sending delegations."

Just what Kazakov needed.

The teapot was cold so Kazakov poured out the tepid liquid and set about making a new pot, filling the kettle and filling a tea bulb with fresh tea leaves. He'd have to ask Rostoff to call the school districts and cancel school attendance.

"Then we'd better do a damn good job of searching the place tonight and guarding it tomorrow."

He waited for the kettle to boil, filled the pot, and poured himself a cup, then doctored it with milk and his three spoons of sugar before returning to his desk. He brought out a pen to make lists to sort his thoughts but they kept bouncing between concern for Kasimir Krupin, concern over the Bure rally, and wondering where Chelomeyev and

Egorova had got to. The mass of evidence that related to the Anna Konstantinova killing swirled in his brain.

Kasimir he could do little about, other than to send Egorova and keep checking himself to let the man know someone cared. The Bure rally filled him with disquiet, but he wasn't certain whether it was the imminence of the attack or an overflow of the concern he felt about the Konstantinova murder investigation. If Bure died, Clinton's predictions would likely come to pass. If Bure lived, his rhetoric would surely lead to the same result.

Fergana and her people were doomed unless he could determine another way out.

The ding of the elevator brought his head up from the mess of doodle lines. Egorova and Chelomeyev pushed in the door, both red cheeked from the cold. They threaded through the desks to their own chairs. Egorova pulled off her coat and gloves and rubbed red hands together.

"Is there more?" she asked, nodding at his steaming cup of tea.

"I made it fresh when I came in a few minutes ago."

She nodded at Pogolin and went to the break area, returning with two cups of steaming tea. She gave one to Chelomeyev, who sipped appreciatively.

"Strong. Good," he said and settled into his desk chair while Egorova seemed to huddle over her teacup for warmth.

"How were the interviews?" Kazakov asked, putting aside the need to grill them over what had kept them so long. "Learn anything interesting?"

The two younger detectives glanced at each other. Then Egorova spoke.

"We had to get permission from parents in order to interview the children. We tried to do it at school, so the whole permission thing slowed down the process. Finding the postal deliveryman on his day off was also a problem." She shook her head.

"But we got it done," Chelomeyev said. "It just took a while." He looked pleased with himself.

"And?" Kazakov prompted.

"There was something," Chelomeyev said triumphantly.

"This afternoon we spoke to an eleven-year-old who remembered seeing someone on the street near the Sobol house," Egorova said. "She remembered seeing the postal worker and the other person pass near the gate. She was in the process of setting up a snowball war—the last of the season given the snow will be melting soon. She was making snowballs but stopped because she was concerned that they were mostly ice. She saw the people as she was drawing the ice to her friend's attention."

"The challenge was, she only saw the back of the person, but she was certain that it was a woman," Chelomeyev added.

"A woman. Did the postal worker have a description?"

In unison the two young detectives shook their heads.

"Best he could recall was that she was about his daughter's height and young," Egorova said with a disgusted shake of her head. "But our eleven-year-old witness suggested that we might want to talk to another child—one who was sick that day. This girl, Nika Isaev, was watching out the window to see the snow fight. She might have seen something. Chelomeyev and I tried to catch her at school, but her mother had already picked her up. They weren't at home, so we've been skulking around waiting for them to return."

"And they did, an hour ago," Chelomeyev said. "It was worth the wait. The child—Nika—is twelve and very observant. She remembered the afternoon readily and the snowball fight as well as the postman because he brought a parcel to her mother." He nodded. "Nika also remembered the woman."

Egorova had her notebook open. "She described the woman as beautiful with long, black hair, smooth skin, and high cheekbones. She was tall, too, according to the child—taller than the postman she passed—or she seemed to be. She was dressed in a dark great coat but the girl said that what made her remember the woman was the way she moved. She described the woman as moving like a cat that is ready to attack a mouse."

Kazakov leaned back in his chair. "That's an impressive memory for a twelve-year-old."

"Her mother says she's like that—remembers most things after seeing, reading, or being told once," Chelomeyev said.

"The description remind you of anyone?" Egorova asked. The bright blooms of her cheeks had calmed, but her fingertips on the cup were still vivid red. A barely contained cat that ate the canary look had overcome her face.

Kazakov thought a moment. The woman sounded striking physically, but it was the description of how she moved that stayed with him most. It bespoke a physicality and athleticism that most women could only hope to aspire to. There were few women he had ever met who moved like that.

But there was one.

"Marta," he said, naming Enver Pasha's housekeeper-cum-bodyguard-

or-mistress or perhaps all three. "Derr'mo, it's been sitting here right under our noses for the past few days if we'd just asked the right people! This could be what we need to shut Enver down!" He stood up and started pacing. Well, perhaps not shut him down, but do serious damage to his plots and organization. Hell, if they could get Marta to talk, it might give them everything.

"All right. We bring her in for questioning tonight. That should make Enver uncertain." Kazakov checked his watch. "We all have a briefing at seven p.m. That should just give us time to pick her up. Chelomeyev, maybe you can grab us some something quick for dinner because that's all we're going to have time for. Dumplings, maybe. Egorova, sorry to take you away from your tea. Pogolin, I'll see you at seven in the briefing room downstairs."

It felt surreal to be giving orders, but he pulled on his coat and headed for the elevator, Egorova at his heels.

"It feels like we've done this before," she said as the elevator dinged, depositing them down at the parking level.

"Last time we got you shot. Let's try not to do that again."

She nodded and climbed in the driver's side of the police sedan. Kazakov sat in the passenger seat and rested his head back. It had been a long day after a restless sleep.

"So Marta killed Anna Konstantinova," she said.

"Seems like. It makes sense, given the timing. I'm thinking Anna came to New Moscow to follow her lover, Zholdosh. During their time together in Basil, she must have picked up on a few things and she probably picked up more when she saw Zholdosh on his visits to the city. But then he was killed. I'm betting she wasn't happy about that. Especially when she was pregnant the second time. Given what we've learned about Anna, she was smart enough or foolish enough to start her own spiritualist business by undercutting Madam Sobol. That makes me think that she might have been smart enough or foolish enough to try to blackmail Enver. Maybe she even connected him somehow to Bure. That could explain why she was turning up near Bure."

Egorova glanced at him. "That's a pretty big leap. Maybe Zholdosh let something slip, or maybe she met Zholdosh at Bure's meetings. They'd be busy places with plenty of people about."

"Maybe." He shook his head, considering. "Enver's been importing weapons for years by subcontracting shipments with private haulers. He gets them into the country and then shifts the loads to his trucks. Zholdosh was in charge of the operation. I can't imagine that a smart girl like Anna didn't at least figure out something illicit was going on. Something big. She wouldn't have even had to know about the weapons per se, just that something was happening. She could have threatened to go to the authorities with that information. Maybe she wanted money because Zholdosh was gone, or maybe she just wanted revenge because Enver sent Zholdosh to Biysk where he died."

Egorova's face was lit by the streetlights as she drove. She nodded. "There's a certain sense in that. Enver wouldn't take the chance of Anna blowing his whole operation open. Not when he's so close to the prize."

"Exactly. He's played the long game for too many years. I don't know if he had the sultan's permission to use that installation or if he simply took it over, but he certainly made use of it to get Bure into place and to set us after Bure."

"Almost unbelievable," she said.

"Almost diabolical, but I was doing some figuring. Bure disappeared for those two weeks when he was seventeen. That's twenty-six years ago. That fits with when the installation was in operation and Enver was in Fergana. For some reason he chose that family. He chose Bure and set about recreating him."

She nodded as they turned onto the crescent street that ran along the edge of Yekaterina Park. In the failing light, a light dust of snow was falling, but the wind swirled it up and away as swiftly as it fell. They parked even with a copse of pine trees that had once half-hidden a dead body. Kazakov climbed out into the wind to join Egorova. The lights of the Red Door and the strains of music from the brothel said the establishment was doing a brisk business.

He looked back at Enver's house with its white colonnades and veiled windows. Compared to the Red Door and its gingerbread facades, Enver's home appeared a demure virgin of a structure. Another proof that beliefs and looks could be deceiving.

15

———————

"Shall we?" Kazakov said to Egorova, who stood beside him, eying Enver Pasha's home.

Nothing moved at any of the windows. No lights shone in the windows on this fading afternoon.

"It hardly looks like anyone's at home," Egorova said. She glanced at Kazakov. "He couldn't know, could he?"

"Not likely. We barely know ourselves," Kazakov said and started up the tall set of stairs.

The door portico sat between two white pillars as if he was a supplicant standing at a temple entrance. But then Enver Pasha probably planned for whoever was at his door to feel that way. It was becoming apparent that Enver was a master manipulator in every way. He probably even planted the idea of killing Bure in the minds of the tribals. It wouldn't be that hard to convince them. Actually, it was amazing that there hadn't been a strike at Bure earlier. That was probably the result of the cooler heads of the elders—something that Enver had apparently managed to undermine.

He gave a quick double rap and waited. Egorova stood on the step behind him, gusts of wind tearing her blonde hair around her face and pressing her coat around her slim form.

No one came to the door so he knocked again.

"You think they might have skipped the country?" Egorova asked.

"Enver could be at his office."

From within the house came crisp footfalls. The door pulled open and Marta stood there, but not the Marta Kazakov was familiar with. Instead of the cool, military façade and tidy suits the woman usually wore, Marta stood there, dripping sweat, her black hair pulled back, her olive skin glistening. She was clad in sweat pants and an old, gray t-shirt that clung to her shoulders and breasts.

She looked from Kazakov to Egorova, her expression impassive. "Enver Pasha is not here."

"And where would we find him?" Kazakov asked.

"He was called away to Constantinople. His wife needed him. She is ill."

Which was convenient for the Ottoman. Be far away when the worst happens and the country descends into anarchy.

"Interesting that he left you behind," Egorova said.

"He is safe enough in his home country." Marta's black gaze glittered out at them. She crossed her arms over her breasts. "Your concern for him is touching."

"Nonsense," Kazakov said. "But we know how important you are to him."

Her glance between Egorova and himself was uncertain. "If that is all, I should get back to my workout."

She went to close the door, but Kazakov blocked it with his palm. "Actually, it is you we've come to see."

Marta went still for an instant. Then slammed the door toward them. Kazakov was too quick and rammed the door with his shoulder. Marta staggered back and Kazakov stepped in after her, Egorova at his back.

"Marta, I am arresting you on suspicion of the murder of Anna Konstantinova."

She turned and ran back into the house.

Kazakov went after her speeding figure. She ran down the hall that went straight back from the door, past Enver's office and then farther. She burst through double doors ahead and disappeared. Kazakov shoved through and found a brightly lit kitchen. Egorova shoved him forward as a knife cut through the air where he had stood and impaled itself in the wall.

Kazakov took one look and spun back to see Marta disappearing through another door. It slammed shut behind her. Kazakov ran to the door and paused, listening to the silence a moment before shoving the door open. A set of narrow stairs ascended. Servant's stairs and a muffled sound from above said where Marta had gone.

"Egorova, call for backup and go back to the main stairs and head up that way. Block her escaping. We should have brought reinforcements for this one. I'll follow her this way."

He left her on her phone and headed as quietly as possible up the stairs. They were narrow and had no handrail. The walls were painted dark and Marta had closed the door above so that he climbed into a dark well, his blood thundering in his ears. Finally, he reached a small landing. The stairs continued on—probably to servant's quarters, but he was fairly certain that the movements he'd heard had come from this level.

Blindly, he felt along the landing wall until he found a latch. It clicked and a narrow door swung open, giving onto an alcove in a broad, wood-paneled hallway hung with artwork. Careful of attack, he stuck his head out for a second. The hallway was lit by amber wall sconces similar to those in the Red Veil, confirmation of Kazakov's suspicion that Enver financed the brothel. Interesting.

He stepped out of the stairwell but remained in the alcove, back pressed against the wall. Down the hall, a pool of light suggested where the house's central foyer waited. Egorova should be coming up those stairs.

But for now, the hallway was silent, the house ticking around him, the wind humming in the eaves. Where was Marta, the trained assassin?

Hugging the wall and with weapon in his hand, he stepped out of the alcove and eased down the hallway to the first door. He listened at the dark wood but heard nothing. He clicked the door open and performed a quick inspection. A bedroom, well appointed with a four-poster bed with green duvet and green floral wallpaper, but no sign of anyone living there.

He silently closed the door and stepped back into the hall, spotting Egorova as she reached the top of the front stairs. He motioned her to wait there and crossed the hall to the next door. Again, standing to the side of the door, he paused to listen, then slowly turned the doorknob.

The explosion of gunfire sent him reeling back into the hall for cover. The door disintegrated into flying splinters. He looked away, but movement turned him back. Marta was at the door, her weapon to hand, an ugly beast of a firearm whose make he didn't know.

Her weapon hand came up and so did his. At this range she couldn't miss.

He watched her trigger hand.

"I will not rot in a Ferganese prison," she said.

"Then help us. Tell us what you know and something can be arranged."

Her gaze was black and unreadable.

"You haven't been with Enver that long. You don't owe him anything."

She chuckled. "Then you don't know Enver. You don't know where I and my family come from."

Her weapon hand tensed and he raised his gun.

"Don't do this, Marta!"

But her trigger finger twitched. Twisting to fire, he threw himself sideways. Her weapon tracked him as he slid across the carpet to the wall. The hallway roared with gunfire.

His. Marta's. Egorova's.

Marta danced a jig in the crossfire of his and Egorova's weapons. Then she crumpled.

"Call an ambulance!" He leapt up and went to her. A bullet hole pumped blood below her breastbone. Another had caught her high in the shoulder. A third had caught her in the thigh. He looked down the hall to Egorova. Marta hadn't stood a chance, but still she'd drawn. Suicide by police?

Egorova ran down the hall to him.

"Grab towels. Sheets, anything. We need her alive."

He pressed his hand on the chest wound to try to stop the spray of blood. His palm filled with the thump of her heart, her fight to live. Her dark gaze was wide. Pain and wonder filled her eyes.

"Stay with me, Marta. An ambulance is coming."

She opened her mouth on a sea of blood. Closed her lips and shook her head. Closed her eyes and coughed. Her lips moved again.

Kazakov bent down to hear her as Egorova reappeared. She folded towels into a thick pad and placed it over Kazakov's bloody hands. He used the pad to block the wound as Egorova set to work on Marta's leg.

"Tell me," he said.

Her breath trembled on his cheek and gurgled in her throat.

"I'm… sorry. For my mother," she said in a strangled whisper that barely reached his ear. "Tell… her…"

He felt the strain go out of her. She sighed as if suddenly relieved. Perhaps she was. Sorry for killing? For dying? For her mother?

Kazakov sat up. He didn't even know the woman's last name. She was only Marta, Enver's right hand. Or left, as the case may be, for she had done the Ottoman's unsavory work.

He glanced at Egorova and shook his head. "Not what I wanted to happen."

"She had you dead. We couldn't let that happen."

He sighed, knowing it was true, but just the same. They were left with a dead suspect and no witnesses. Again. That was most likely what Enver had counted on.

"There's backup and a crime scene team on their way," Egorova said.

Kazakov checked his watch. It was six fifteen. So much for dinner this evening.

Feeling tired and empty, Kazakov staggered up to his feet. Behind where he'd been, a bullet hole had shattered the wood paneling. If Marta hadn't been hit and her shot deflected high, that would have been his chest. Or his head.

He stepped past Marta's body and glanced inside the room. Another four-poster bed, this one clearly used. Bedside tables held candles and a book left open facedown. Women's clothing hung in a closet with the door half open. Another door gave onto a bathroom, and under the scent of cordite was the feminine scents of almond oil and myrrh. At the foot of the bed, a large wooden trunk was open. From where he stood, a rifle barrel gleamed dully in the lamplight. Marta kept her weapons close to hand. He supposed that was part of her job description.

He stepped carefully into the room and did a circuitous route around the edge to the bed. The crime scene team would search more fully, but he would take a look. There were no photographs on the dresser or bedside table. Nothing to give clues to the dead woman in the hall. The artwork on the walls were of the same taste as those in the rest of the house. The book on the bedside table was a history of the Russian people. The fact Marta read history reminded him of another dead woman—one he might have loved. Why would Marta read such a thing? She was not Ferganese—that was clear by her olive skin. But on the other hand, she could have ancestors who were Russian. Perhaps a family that was left behind when the homeland was overrun by the Ottomans.

He left the book and went to the chair by the window. He could imagine Marta here, just as much a prisoner as Maria had been in the brothel. Perhaps Marta had been trying to save her family wherever they were.

Sighing, he turned back to the room. There would be nothing other than the weapons to find here, he was sure of it, but surely the attack and the weapons store gave the police enough reason to place the entire house behind police cordon. Perhaps Enver had done them a service, for now they could search the premises.

If Rostoff and the senior officers could see the reason for it. Hopefully he could make them understand.

The crime scene team arrived. He and Egorova had to relinquish their weapons, but then Kazakov excused himself. Egorova stayed behind to give her statement, while Kazakov headed back to the station to update Rostoff and hold the Bure briefing.

Feeling tired and hollow, and with his stomach grumbling, he headed up to the third floor and the squad room, then detoured to Rostoff's office. Neither he nor Dabria Smirnova were there. Rostoff would just have to wait to learn the results of the Anna Konstantinova murder investigation. That case, at least, was ready for closure except for Enver Pasha's role in the whole affair. Of course, Marta's death meant proving Enver's involvement was nigh on impossible. The wily man had won —again.

And he still had other servants out there. Bure to name one. Possibly the most insidious of them all.

Stymied and frustrated, he took the elevator back down to the large briefing room on the first floor. The room was brightly lit, with white walls and a scuffed linoleum floor. Memos, photos of officers receiving awards, and the requisite painting of the great Tsarina Yekaterina decorated the walls. Rows of narrow tables lined with chairs all faced toward the front of the room. All the chairs in the room were full. At the front, the floor was raised a foot and a lone table sat crosswise to the room with three empty chairs facing the audience. One chair was likely meant for him. Who would be with him, he didn't know. Beyond the raised platform beside the Yekaterina painting was a closed door that led to the watch commander's office.

The space had an expectant feel, but the air carried the scents of hurried meals—curry, bread, potato, onion, and beef sandwiches and garlic swirled together along with low murmurs and boot scuffling. At the rear of the room, Pogolin, Razin, and three younger detectives stood talking. More uniformed officers talked in groups or lounged against the wall, but their attention turned toward him at his entrance and the hum of conversation faded.

Kazakov stepped up on the raised floor. Spread on the table were blueprinted pages that must be the layout of Bure's venue. So Rostoff had at least come through on something.

Kazakov faced the officers gathered before him, drew in a breath, and nodded. "I'd say thank you for coming, but I suspect none of you are volunteers."

There was a small response of scattered chuckles, as Kazakov removed his greatcoat and draped it on a chair back.

"You're here tonight because we have credible information that an attack is planned for the Bure political rally scheduled for tomorrow. The alleged attackers have at their disposal a number of military-grade rifles, an unknown number of grenades, and the outstanding explosives stolen from Mountain Construction a few months ago. Pogolin, Razin?"

The two detectives jerked to attention in their chairs.

"Based on the explosives that destroyed the Yekaterina statue and that damaged the market, how much explosive are we talking about?" Kazakov asked.

Pogolin glanced at Razin and swallowed. "Best we can figure, enough to take out a city block."

"Derr'mo," someone swore from amongst the uniformed officers.

Kazakov felt the weight of their full attention. He nodded.

"Bure's rhetoric, while popular amongst Fergana's ethnic Russian population, has met with less favor among the tribal cultural groups. So far, the tribal elders have kept a lid on that community's anger, but something has set off a small group of youngsters. All we know is that the elders have been trying to locate them—to no avail. Someone has hidden them and someone has helped arm them so that they can do their worst."

"Fucking tribals. The lot of them. Maybe Bure has the right of it," someone amongst the uniforms mumbled.

"This is not about the tribal community," came Rostoff's voice from behind Kazakov.

Kazakov spun around. Rostoff stood in the watch commander's doorway. He nodded in Kazakov's direction and stepped up beside him.

"This is about a few young extremists who want to do our country harm." He glanced at Kazakov and nodded. "If I hear of anyone doing anything that increases problems between the tribal community and this police force, they'll have me to deal with."

Rostoff took a seat at the table as if he said such things every day. He nodded at Kazakov to continue.

Trying to understand how Rostoff had come around to Kazakov's point of view, he turned back to the room. "We have two challenges. The first is that Bure refuses to cancel the rally. That means that we have to inspect the entire venue for explosives. The Bure rally is scheduled for tomorrow afternoon. Between now and then, we have to inspect every inch of that venue to ensure it's safe.

"Our second issue is ensuring that no tribals enter the rally. While I hate to exclude people based on ethnicity, it is the only lead we have to go on. We'll need to have officers posted at every entrance to check identification. Any tribals are to be excluded. That could be from name or visual appearance. Do you understand? Ensuring that no tribal threat enters is critical to Bure's safety. We're also going to need people to deal with any tribals upset by the denial of entry."

He scanned the audience and read their determination. If only he felt the same. The cold steel of his dream once more filled his palm. If it wasn't a tribal who killed Bure, would the results be the same? Would the world still disintegrate into war?

Blinking back from the precipice of following that thought, he looked down at his brother officers. "Detektiv Chief Inspektor, how many entrances to the venue?"

"Dabria's count was thirteen."

Kazakov looked at the room. "And how many officers have we called in?"

"We have the detectives you see as well as fifty officers."

"All right. We need a minimum of two officers on each entrance, preferably three. That takes thirty-nine out of search duty. Pogolin, I want you and Razin on explosives detail. The other detectives we'll place at the main entrances to augment the identification check and to help deal with any tribals who are upset. That means we have thirteen officers for the explosives search. Myself, Egorova, and Chelomeyev will assist once we've got some food in us." He nodded at the room. "Those of you on explosives detail please come to the front of the room. The others, please be here tomorrow morning at eight a.m. for briefing. Understand?"

The officers nodded as one.

"Good. And one more thing. Not a word of this to anyone. If word gets out, we'll have a riot on our hands and Rostoff will make sure there's a demotion for every one of us in this room. Understand?"

"Yes, sir." Spoken as one.

He waited as the majority of officers vacated the room. The thirteen search officers came up to Kazakov's table where Rostoff had been joined by none other than Dabria.

The constable looked crisp as new currency as she stood at the table beside the venue blueprints. Eyes shining, she nodded at Kazakov. It was high time that the bright young officer had time to be more than a secretary. How she had managed to have Rostoff give her this role was beyond Kazakov's understanding.

"Sir. I've had the chance to review the details, if I may share them with you?" she said.

"This is Constable Smirnova," Kazakov introduced her to the assembled officers. "Please continue."

She walked them through three pages of diagrams representing the three floors of the building above ground. Then she pulled out a cardboard roll from under the table beside Rostoff and produced another two rolls of paper. "These are the two basements. The first contains the props and staging equipment for performances. There are also storage facilities. The final basement is for things like furnaces, electrical, air, etc. All the mechanicals. A bomb in either of these areas would focus the explosion upward and probably bring the whole structure down, while a bomb on one of the upper floors would cause great damage and loss of life, but probably not bring everything down—unless it was a huge amount of explosive." She nodded at Kazakov and stepped back from the table.

It was his turn now. He assigned his men, the majority going to inspect the basements first, after which he intended to restrict access to those areas. "Pogolin and Razin will explain what we are looking for. When you are searching, if you see anything that looks suspicious, you are to call one of these two detectives or myself. When you are done inspecting your assigned area, you're to come back to me in the foyer and obtain your next search assignment. I hope you all had a good night's sleep last night, because it's going to be a long one tonight." He made eye contact with his men and then nodded. "I'll see you at the venue. Good hunting."

———

The gray light of early morning filtered through the windows high up on the walls of the second and third floors of the concert hall's open foyer and highlighted the many scuff marks left from heavy police boots. Kazakov poured himself yet another cup of sweet milk tea from the huge urn set up courtesy of the venue manager at Kazakov's request. Also on the table were the decimated remains of what had once been mountains of beef sandwiches and bread and cheese. All that remained now were empty platters and smears of mustard and butter—that and the lingering homey scent of bread that made Kazakov's stomach growl again. He'd left the sandwiches for the searchers and it was a long time since the quick dinner of Chinese food that he had grabbed with Chelomeyev and Egorova. The three had met at the police station to obtain new weapons for Kazakov and Egorova while their own were kept as evidence. Then they had eaten and spent the night as part of the search force.

All for nothing.

Overhead, the sound of tired feet came on the broad stairs from the third floor. Egorova and Chelomeyev had taken the last section of the building to search when they'd seen how dead on their feet the remaining team of uniformed constables had been. Kazakov had sent the tired search team home, but they'd volunteered to come back to assist with the door control. It restored Kazakov's faith in the police force a little, though it remained to be seen whether they would actually show up.

He eased the shoulder where he'd been shot. It ached this morning and had all night—probably from when he'd thrown himself across the hall in the firefight in Enver Pasha's home. That was what they should be doing with Boris Bure—tell the man to duck and roll when the shots started. With any luck the shooter would still get him.

Derr'mo, he was sounding more like the other older detectives all the time. Well, Bure being shot wasn't going to happen. At least not on his watch and not by a tribal. Between him and Khan, they'd stop this from happening.

Egorova and Chelomeyev came around the last corner in the stairs and headed down toward him. Egorova was smiling. Chelomeyev just looked wan and tired.

"I was just telling Chelomeyev he's going to have to get back to the gym. He's moving like an old man." She raked Kazakov with an assessing grin. "Not much better than you."

"Thank you for the encouraging words. Anything?" He tipped his head at the upstairs.

"A lot of dust and cobwebs and enough ropes to hang all the lawyers and all the politicians," Chelomeyev said, picking a cobweb strand off of Egorova's shoulder. "We covered the public areas as well as the back of house storage. There's nothing there."

Kazakov shook his head and turned away. "It doesn't make sense if Bure's really the target. This is the time and place to get him."

"Could they be planning the attack for his transport here? You know, ram his car and then shoot him? There'd be less collateral damage if they were concerned about that."

"You think these youngsters would be concerned?" Kazakov asked. "If they were thinking, they wouldn't be doing this at all." But he nodded. "We'll arrange a police escort. One marked car in front and behind. That should do it."

He scrubbed his face and felt the thick stubble of beard and the grease of too long a day on his skin. His eyes felt like there was sand in them. He looked back at Egorova and Chelomeyev. Both had dark circles under their eyes.

"You two head out. Get some sleep and be back here by one p.m." He checked his watch. That would give them each almost six hours of shut-eye.

"You should follow your own suggestion," Egorova said. "You look beat."

He shook his head. "I think I'll check on Kasimir Krupin. The man has me worried."

Egorova shook her head. "From what I've heard about where you live, you've got a lot farther to go than me to get some sleep. I'll check on Kasimir later this morning. Who knows, maybe he won't be so abrupt with a woman. Maybe he'll let me in."

It was one less thing to be responsible for and at the moment his head was full. He finally nodded. "But let me know what happens, will you?"

"You will get a full report." She turned to leave, Chelomeyev with her. "And don't forget to go home and get some sleep," she said over her shoulder.

Kazakov waved her and her concerns away and watched the light gradually increase in the upper foyers. Where he stood was still in shadow. He went to report the result of the search to the concert hall manager, who had stayed on-site all night, and also planned to call on Rostoff with the report. When all that was done, he might still have time to find a quiet place to park the Perseus and catch a few hours of sleep.

The briefing of the manager took only a few minutes. Kazakov thanked him for his thoughtfulness in providing the tea and sandwiches and then advised that he'd back on-site at one. Then he climbed into the Perseus and headed back to the station. Traffic was gradually filling the streets. A bus full of passengers trundled by sending a spray of filthy slush onto his windscreen. All these people totally unaware of the clock ticking them toward Fergana's fate. How blissful it must be not to know that a war could break out in a matter of days, all because of the death of one man.

No, not because of Bure's death, because of who killed him. Enver Pasha had planned it out neatly. Through his agents he'd primed and then lit the fuse of the young tribal men and then vacated the country, leaving Kazakov, Khan, and others to try to undo what he had done.

All these months Kazakov had barely been able to look at an image of Bure and it was really Enver Pasha he should have been hunting. He should have shot the man during the firefight in the mountains. Things would be much simpler now, he had no doubt.

Instead Kazakov had gone running to Enver Pasha to inform him that there might be a plot to kill him. How rich was that? He turned the Perseus into the police garage, still feeling the heat on his face. Damn Enver. Damn his plans.

There had to be more Kazakov could do to stop them.

He left the Perseus and took the elevator up to the third floor, then, on the off-chance that Rostoff might be in, strode past the empty squad room and down the hall. He knocked once on the door to Rostoff's reception area office and stepped inside. Surprisingly, Dabria was there, her uniform crisp, her blonde hair twisted neatly back behind her head as she shifted boxes of files around the office. Her gaze was bright and alert—the total antithesis to how he felt.

His fingernails scratched through his nascent beard.

Dabria's eyes widened. "What are you doing here?"

"I should ask you the same. It's early for you, isn't it? We just finished the search. I just sent the last team home for some shut-eye." He unsuccessfully stifled a yawn.

"In fact, I'm always in early to have things in order before Rostoff arrives," she said primly. "And why are you here and not following your own advice?"

He cocked a brow at her. "You're the second person who has asked me precisely the same thing in almost exactly the same words."

Dabria turned back to her desk, but he caught a bit of color in her cheeks. "What are you doing here?" she asked again.

"I thought Rostoff would want to know the results. We found nothing." He shook his head and futility and weariness surged through him. "That bastard Enver is going to get away with this. He's going to bring a war down on us."

Dabria settled in her desk chair. She nodded at the closed inner office door. "Believe it or not, he's in. I think he's been waiting for you."

Kazakov knocked twice on the door and went in. He was too tired to wait for Rostoff's invitation.

Rostoff was at his desk, pen in hand, documents spread before him. His uniform looked freshly pressed, but his face was a pasty gray that suggested lack of sleep. Probably the same color as Kazakov's own.

He crossed the room without invitation and settled in Rostoff's guest chair, trying to come up with the best way to relay the bad news, but his brain was too tired. "The place is searched. We found nothing. They're using the explosives elsewhere."

———

K azakov jerked awake from an uncomfortable slumber in the driver's seat of the Perseus. The vehicle rocked in a wind gust. The windshield and other vehicle windows were fogged and the air felt unnaturally moist and warm. The afternoon light was a haze through the windows, the parking lot by Potemkin Park indistinct. His neck was cricked from his uncomfortable sleep, but he no longer felt he had just spent a lifetime in Baba Yaga's dungeon. Still, his shoulder ached and so did his side. Come to think of it, everything else did, too.

He was getting old. His next birthday was not that far away.

Working his shoulder and neck, he checked his watch. Quarter to one. He had just a few minutes to meet Egorova and Chelomeyev and the security detail at the venue. Just three hours until Bure's rally.

The Perseus started with the turn of a key and he drove out of the lot and turned toward Suvarov Way. The parking at the front of the concert hall was filled with news vehicles staking their territory. All the major international media stations were there. He pulled in behind them and turned the Perseus off.

The banners swathing the New Moscow Concert Hall were brightly lit as the sun ducked under the Ferganese cloud cover that swathed the city. He studied the brilliance illuminating Bure's face. It was almost symbolic, Bure ascendant. With the sunset, in the west the sky would turn red and bloody on the underside of the clouds. He sat in the vehicle for a moment, then climbed out and stretched. His shoulder holster didn't feel quite right, the weight different with the service revolver he'd been issued until his own weapon was released from evidence.

He felt better than he had that morning, but not one hundred percent. Not by a long shot. He was tired and his brain still reverberated with a dream that he'd had. He couldn't remember what it was, only that it had left him shaken and his palm still burned.

He flexed his offending hand, his gun hand, and looked up at Bure's oversized image, then looked away. Pulling his great coat collar up around his chin against the gusts of cold wind, he climbed the stairs to the concert hall's front entrance and went inside.

The foyer was hushed, but when he crossed the marble floor and pushed into the great hall where the rally would take place, the huge space was awash with movement. Theater-style seating winged upward on either side of him. The room's lower-floor seating had been removed to allow a "standing room only" space. Higher up the walls, more ranks of seating were accessible from the second and third level foyers. There would be perfect line of sight for a marksman from any of the higher seating. Even the lower level seating would be adequate, though the marksman would have to consider the downward trajectory of the bullets.

And the crowd on the floor? Depending on how crowded it was, there could be room for a marksman to ease his way to within shooting distance. Kazakov shook his head as a member of the technical crew pushed past him with a bundle of cables. On the floor, camera crews set up feeds for the hungry media.

The entire venue was an assassination waiting to happen and Bure seemed quite oblivious, as if danger to himself was incomprehensible. It would make him almost admirable if he didn't stand for so much that was wrong in Fergana.

Leaving the hall, Kazakov went to the administration office and advised them that he was in the building. Then he headed for the building's boardroom that had been agreed upon as the police staging room.

It was in a corner of the building's main level, next to Bure's venue, but set back in an area where it would be less intrusive to the event. He pushed inside the double, blond-wood doors and found Egorova and Chelomeyev waiting. They had the blueprints of the building spread before them on the long table and were deep in conversation. They both looked up together.

"You're both early," Kazakov said as he walked past them and sat down at the side of the table to review the roster of names he'd assigned to the various entrances.

"We wanted to give a couple of spots another going over. We were pretty tired last night," Chelomeyev said.

"And?" Kazakov asked. They were young. They were careful. They'd both already proved they deserved to be where they were.

Egorova shook her head. "Nothing. Absolutely nothing. Not even any sign that might indicate a plan of something. You're sure that your information is credible?"

Kazakov closed his eyes. That was the question Rostoff had asked him last night. The meeting with the detektiv chief inspektor had not gone well from his pronouncement that the explosives would likely be used elsewhere.

For all the public support Rostoff had shown before, in his office the man had seemed far less supportive of Kazakov and his information. He'd mused aloud the same question that Egorova asked.

"He has never lied to me," Kazakov said in response to Egorova.

"Except that his entire life has been a lie. He was never simply an M.E. He plotted against our country," she said.

The truth cut deep, but he nodded. "Unfortunately, I have to believe. Otherwise we have nothing."

"It could all be a ruse to pull our men away from something else," Egorova said.

"It could be, but I don't think so," Kazakov said. "No, something is going to happen here today. I feel it in my bones."

Or was it old age creeping closer? Maybe—after all this was over— maybe he would consider retiring. Get work that didn't require him to doubt the worth of humanity.

He found Egorova and Chelomeyev looking at him as if they didn't believe what he'd just said.

"Consider me one of Madam Sobol's spiritualists. You just wait. You'll see. Next I'll be joining the OTO."

Chelomeyev grinned. Egorova rolled her eyes.

"By the way, I went to see Krupin this morning," she said. "He let me in. We had a quick cup of tea and he told me about the plans for Margarete's funeral. It will be tomorrow. A small family affair followed by cremation. He seemed sad, but as if he'd made his peace and was moving on. He's still thin, though. I told him that I'd be back with groceries after my shift." She grinned.

It was a relief to hear, one less worry for Kazakov.

Gradually, uniformed officers filtered in to the boardroom, seating themselves around the room until the place was packed with officers awaiting the briefing and Kazakov's handing out of assignments. Pogolin and Razin pushed inside and found seats at the rear of the room, even though they'd searched last night and had to be almost as tired as Kazakov. Finally, he stood and thanked the male and female officers, reminding them of what they were looking for—individuals with tribal sounding names or looks. All such individuals were to be turned away. He then read out the entrance assignments and officers filtered out in teams, ready to do their jobs as the crowds began forming. Given many of the officers were Bure believers, it was fairly certain that they would do a good job.

Kazakov sat down and slumped in his chair. He wanted his bed and the quiet of the dacha, with Koshka slumbering at his side. He hoped he'd left enough food out for her, but then again, the round little cat had fended for herself before.

"Where can you use us?"

Kazakov looked up wearily at Pogolin and Razin. "You aren't scheduled here."

Pogolin nodded. "We're on days off, but we figured you could use the help. Besides, the explosives theft is our case." They glanced at Chelomeyev, who'd had the case before he was injured.

"All right. How about helping at the main entrance. That's where the biggest crowds are likely to be."

They left and the sound of voices came through the door. Egorova peeked out of the boardroom.

"Foyer's filling up," she said and looked back to Kazakov. "How about if Chelomeyev and I mingle with the crowd. If we see anything of concern, we'll call you." She hauled out her phone.

The two young officers left and Kazakov looked at his papers. Sitting here was going to be a lesson in waiting and he had never been particularly good at it. He went to the boardroom door to peer out.

Egorova was right. The foyer was awash in humanity, all interested in what Boris Bure had to say. The crowd was diverse, from well-dressed, older couples to youngsters in overlong hair and military jackets. There were families with young children and elderly couples. About the only thing there wasn't represented was Fergana's tribal population. Without a doubt, most of those attending were ethnic Russian.

He left the boardroom and stepped out among them, catching sight now and again of someone with darker skin who must have been searched at the entrance. He found himself drawn toward these individuals, circling around them until they became aware of him. Let them know they were being watched. He would not let this happen.

The crowd thickened as the appointed hour approached. He caught glimpses of people he knew, off-duty police officers, people he'd met through his investigations, even the unpleasant receptionist from the M.E.'s office. He even saw a wild-haired figure that, from the rear, could be Kasimir Krupin, though that was farfetched. He couldn't imagine Krupin being out in this crowd—not with Margarete's death so recent.

He heard the engines of Bure's motorcade outside and the resulting roar of the crowd. Thankfully the concert hall had the capacity to take Bure's limousine into a secure underground parking area. The uniformed escort would ensure it stayed that way and Bure would enter the center's waiting area until his rally began.

The flood of people in the foyer diminished as Bure's start time approached. Kazakov continued to mingle with the crowd and went to check inside the rally venue. The massive room hummed. The seats were full and too many people were crammed into what had been the open floor. God help them all if there was need to evacuate.

He eased back out of the room, just as the lights dimmed and flashed on and off. Three minutes until the rally began.

A few stragglers were coming in the main entrance doors when a flash of brilliance lit the darkening sky outside.

Kazakov frowned. Too bright and too red. The light faded, but was replaced by rumbling.

He ran for the entrance and shoved outside.

Police and citizens alike all stood frozen on the steps of the concert hall and in the street. The sunlight was failing in sullen clouds and the streetlights had come on. To the south, east, and north, the white peaks that ringed Fergana caught sunlight like fangs. But it was closer in, at the western edge of New Moscow that had caught everyone's attention.

High on the flank of Yekaterina Mountain, a bright flame burned within a dark cloud that had swallowed the huge statue of Tsarina Yekaterina. From the size of the cloud, it was doubtful that the statue that commemorated the great Russian leader would still be standing in the morning.

"Those bastards," someone in the crowd murmured.

Kazakov turned toward the speaker just as another explosion rocked the shocked city. This one came from southwest of town toward Basil. Across the city, street and building lights flickered, faltered, and went out. The city sprawled in darkness. Someone screamed.

Behind Kazakov the concert hall was in darkness, but a moment later a distant humming sounded from deep inside the structure. Lights inside flickered and went on, spilling wan light onto the sidewalk. In the distance, sirens wailed.

Kazakov spotted Pogolin. "Weapons ready. We could be in for an attack! Spread the word."

Pogolin nodded and headed down the broad platform that ran behind the columns at the front of the concert hall. Kazakov headed in the other direction, warning the uniformed officers at each entrance, urging people to leave for the safety of their homes or to take cover inside. Most dispersed into the street. The traffic increased.

He met Pogolin at the rear entrance to the building.

"Have you told Bure or his handlers?" Pogolin asked. "Someone should warn them."

Kazakov shook his head. "I will. Someone should give people the chance to disperse and go to their homes. The sooner we can clear people out to safety, the better. At least the explosions are well outside the city center."

"They took out Our Lady," Pogolin said, his expression stricken. "That statue has been a symbol of Fergana forever. My entire life, I've looked up to her."

"That mountain was another people's sacred site long before we came here. Suleiman's Mountain it was called. They just don't teach that in our schools," Kazakov said. "Maybe they want that changed."

From the street came the screeching of tires, people yelling, a scream. He closed his eyes a moment, too tired to consider how to deal with the crisis, then regrouped. He opened his eyes on Pogolin, whose expression had turned unfriendly.

"I'm sorry," Kazakov said. "I can't help the truth, even if we don't like it. Tonight, it seems, the tribal youth are having their revenge." And he knew where it would lead. "There's a reasonable chance they'll be coming here next. We need to get Bure out. Get Bure away and this place is no longer a target."

"Go," Pogolin said. "I'll keep circulating amongst the entrances."

Kazakov nodded and went inside. He was in a long tunnel of a hallway wide enough for shipments to be received. His phone went off as he rushed down the hall and he fished it out of his pocket.

"Kazakov," he answered.

"This is dispatch," a female voice said. "All officers are to report to headquarters. A state of emergency has been declared."

"Hold on a minute! I'm at the concert hall protecting Bure."

But he was speaking to an empty line. The dispatcher had rung off. He swore at the phone and started running down the hall to an elevator and stairwell at the end. He stabbed Rostoff's number into his phone and listened to it drill across the distant as he climbed the stairs two at a time.

The line clicked.

"Rostoff! You can't pull the men off. You're leaving Bure as a sitting duck if you do!"

"Kazakov. I bet on you and you were wrong. Accept it. The wild theories were wrong. The tribals have attacked our symbol and our power. There's a manhunt starting. I need you involved. You know the tribals."

Kazakov hung up and knew there'd be hell to pay. The police were doing exactly what he'd want them to do if Bure was his target. These tribal youth were working from a plan far subtler than anything he expected them to use. There was no direct attack when the police were prepared. No, these attacks were planned to draw the police away.

Which meant that the danger here was even more imminent and he had a concert hall of people to protect.

He plunged through a doorway and found himself in the warren of hallways to the rear of the stage. Bure's voice through hidden hallway speakers exhorted the crowd to take back Fergana and make it great again. Kazakov groaned. Damn it, the man had begun his rally. It was expected, but so not what the country needed. A cell phone brrred ahead and to his left. He followed the sound down a hallway and found Chelomeyev standing looking incredulously at his phone.

"They've ordered me back to headquarters," he said when he saw Kazakov.

"They're calling all of us back. There's a state of emergency. The explosives took out the statue on Yekaterina Mountain and the main power plant. We're working on generators here in the building."

"That's why the lights faltered."

Kazakov nodded.

"You're not going?" Chelomeyev asked.

"I think they'll be coming for Bure next and we all know what that will mean," Kazakov said and pushed past the young detective.

"Do you want me to stay with you?" Chelomeyev asked.

"You've got your orders. I can't ask you to do anything else."

Chelomeyev looked once more at his phone, then stuck it in his pocket. Then he struck out after Kazakov. "What do you need me to do?"

Kazakov stopped. "You're sure? You've been ordered back to headquarters."

Bure's voice ranted about the tribal menace.

"I know the danger is here."

"Good man." Kazakov clapped him on the shoulder. "Then what I'd like you to do is find Egorova and anyone else who agrees that we've got a risk here, and get them to start moving people out of this building. The building security types can help. Get these people leaving and pray we get them out of here before any attack."

"I'm on it." Chelomeyev headed back the way they'd come.

Kazakov continued down the corridor and came to the rear of the stage. Here Bure's voice was in stereo from the man's own voice and, a delayed second later, from the overhead speakers. In the wings stood Annuschka and Bure's handlers.

Kazakov grabbed Annuschka's arm and tugged her back from the curtain edge. "The city is under attack. They've taken out the power plant and the statue on Yekaterina Mountain. Police headquarters are pulling our men, but I think they're wrong. It leaves this building vulnerable, just the way the young tribals want it. We need to get Bure out of here before they come."

She was wearing one of her power suits. This one of cream with a pearl-colored sweater underneath. With her blonde hair swept up and her cool blue eyes, she was the ice queen as she arched a brow at him. "So now the great Kazakov knows better than anyone else in authority?"

"Annuschka, I don't like the man. From my perspective, we'd be better off without him; but if a tribal kills him, it's going to drag this country into a war that will be the end of everything. I'm trying to save his life, when everything about him tells me not to try. Do you understand?"

Her throat worked. She looked toward the stage where Bure's voice rose and fell in a seductive call to regain Russian greatness. Then she turned back to Kazakov. "What do you want me to do? He's in full flight with his speech right now. No one can stop him."

"We have to. We need his handlers and his security on-site. I've got people trying to get the crowd to leave, but that's not going to be easy. It would be best if we could get Bure to ask them to leave for their safety. Then we get him out of here. Alternatively, we get him out of here and then we explain."

Annuschka shook her head. "Try to take him out of here and you'll have a riot on your hands. These people—they love him. They've been looking for a great leader—one that speaks to their frightened hearts. He does that. They'll protect him."

"So we try for his help. How?"

"Leave it to me." She hurried back to the group of men in the stage wings. Kazakov came up behind her and peered out into the crowd. The stage footlights caught on Bure at his podium. The man *was* a great orator, eschewing notes and simply speaking to the crowd, apparently from his heart. In the footlight glow, the front rows of people peered raptly up at Bure. Beyond them, the crowd in the standing pit seemed a single beast that inhaled and exhaled together as Bure spoke. The ranks of seating around the sides of the theater and at the second and third floor levels were lost and indistinct in the darkness.

Please let Egorova and Chelomeyev get the people moving. But they were only two officers and there were far too many people.

He turned his attention on Annuschka, who was now arguing heatedly with her compatriots. Finally, she threw up her hands and came to Kazakov.

"They won't do it. I'm sorry. They say if the police don't believe there's a threat, then they don't either. They're staying and so is Bure."

"There has to be something we can do."

Annuschka's cool gaze searched his face. "You're really certain, aren't you?"

"As certain as I can be of anything. It makes sense. It's what I'd do if I was intent on killing Bure."

Chewing her lower lip, she thought a moment. Then she nodded. "Come with me."

She led him around a layer of curtains to a panel of switches. She gave him a look. "You realize we'll both probably lose our jobs for this?"

He nodded.

She grabbed two of the large switches that were in the off position and cranked them to on.

A shout came from beyond the curtains.

Kazakov left Annuschka and went back around the curtains to the stage wings.

Bure still stood on the stage, but he looked out onto a well-lit seething sea of people. Blinking at the sudden light, they looked uncertainly around them. Bure's voice faltered, but then picked up in volume and slowly the crowd's attention turned back to him.

But the crowd wasn't the single entity Kazakov had thought. Far back, at the edges, disturbances were rippling out. People faded back and were dispersing! Chelomeyev's work, surely. And it was happening in more than one place so he had found Egorova and perhaps others. There was that, at least.

But Bure was still here, still ranting his hatred in words veiled in loyalty and strength. Why couldn't people see through him? They acted like mesmerized creatures. But then, what he said only built upon the beliefs that Ferganese society drilled into their children from birth. It was a falsehood of Russian greatness that hid their fear of inferiority. Bure had tapped into the desperate need to propagate the myth, just as the spiritualists tapped into the omnipresent Russian wellspring of grief.

The crowd's voice roared in response. Ripples seethed through them as they pressed toward the stage.

A rough pop-pop-pop. Pop-pop-pop-pop sound ripped through the applause.

Kazakov stopped. It couldn't be. Not now. Not so soon.

He shoved Bure's handlers aside and plunged out onto the stage. Bure had frozen where he stood and the crowd froze with him, then slowly turned.

A scream came from the foyer, and across the crowd he saw Chelomeyev draw his weapon and shove through the uncertain crowd toward the room's exit. A disturbance by the other door suggested Egorova was there, doing something similar.

"Everyone stay calm!" Kazakov yelled from the stage. "There are police officers here to keep you safe."

He hoped. He prayed. But what good were service weapons against military-grade rifles?

More weapon fire came from outside. The crowd stirred and milled below the stage. Bure stood at the microphone but peered back at his handlers. If he left, he would have abandoned the people and would be shown to be a coward. If he stayed, it would make him out to be a hero. He glanced at Kazakov and leaned in to the microphone.

"Please stay calm. There's no reason to panic. We have New Moscow's finest right here."

Only Kazakov recognized the smirk on Bure's face.

But the crowd still churned below the stage. They were looking for a safe way out, but at the moment all the exits were suspect.

Among the milling people, Kazakov glimpsed a familiar face. Looking hollow and gray, his hair wild about his face, Kasimir Krupin stared intently up at Bure.

It *had* been Krupin who Kazakov glimpsed earlier. What the hell was the old man doing here?

There was something in how Krupin's gaze never wavered from Bure's face. Something predatory as a wolf fixed on a deer. He took advantage of the milling crowd to ease toward the stage, for the disturbance outside had shifted the people toward the exits.

Krupin was planning something unless Kazakov acted now. "Bure, get off the stage! Get him off the stage!"

Bure turned. His handlers stumbled over themselves as Kasimir Krupin reached the front of the crowd. From under his sweater he produced a weapon. A woman near him screamed.

Kazakov leapt for the edge of the stage. He threw himself at the old man, just as Krupin's weapon bucked and bucked again.

Bure staggered back and back, his chest exploding in a plume of blood.

Kazakov landed in the screaming crowd, came up on his knees as the crowd parted around him. He pulled his weapon and aimed at Krupin.

"Put the gun down!"

Krupin turned from Bure to face him. His face was mild—the thoughtful Krupin that Kazakov knew. On the stage, Bure's handlers were nowhere to be seen. Annuschka knelt beside the fallen man, her suit bloody as she tried to stop the bleeding.

Krupin pointed his gun at Kazakov and smiled.

"Damn it, Krupin! Drop the weapon. I don't want to shoot you!"

Krupin shook his head. "I'm afraid that's not possible." He glanced back at the stage. "We both know it's better this way."

"Krupin, think of Margarete. She wouldn't want this! Not for you to die."

"There's where you're wrong, Detektiv." Krupin smiled as he steadied his weapon. His trigger finger tightened.

Kazakov took his shot.

Krupin's weapon spiraled from his hand. He staggered and collapsed at the wound high in his shoulder.

Kicking the weapon aside, Kazakov knelt beside the old man.

Krupin blinked up at him. His breath was fast and wheezy, blood frothed his lips as he smiled up at Kazakov.

But it shouldn't be. He'd specifically aimed to stop the shooting, but not kill.

"Thank you," Krupin whispered through the blood. "It was for Margarete. But now I can tell her myself."

Kazakov closed his eyes. "You're not dying, you old fool."

He caught Krupin's hand and held on.

Krupin looked up at him, but his breath was crippled gasps. His lips worked feebly, as if struggling for words, but his grip tightened on Kazakov's hand and drew him down.

Kazakov leaned in close.

"You—you set me free," Krupin said. Then his hand went slack.

Kazakov sat up, suddenly aware of the crowd's silence. Of the approaching sound of sirens, of Annuschka's sobbing on the stage.

Looking rumpled and elated, Chelomeyev stood over him. Egorova's eyes were over-bright as she took in Krupin's body.

"We got them," Chelomeyev said. "The young tribals attacked the building. There weren't many of us to hold them off, but help comes from unexpected places."

Kazakov stood up. On the stage a team worked over Bure, probably medical people from the audience. Annuschka stood to one side, her cream suit bloody.

"Now we know what was wrong with Krupin, and why he was different today," Egorova said, coming up quietly beside Kazakov. She knelt down and gently closed Krupin's eyes, then handed Kazakov the weapon Krupin had used, now safely bagged as evidence.

The sirens stopped, and as one, he and Egorova turned to the rear of the room as the doors of the concert hall were flung open.

16

After a horrendous evening of paperwork and statements, Kazakov returned to the police station the next day barely refreshed. He might have slept in his own bed, but the ghost of Kasimir Krupin inhabited the dacha with him. At three in the morning, he sat at his bare wooden table with a half-full bottle of vodka, deciding whether to escape into a haze or toast Krupin's bravery.

He finally settled on the latter and, beside his woodstove, leaned back in his wooden chair with Koshka in his lap. He stroked the cat's midnight fur and nursed a single drink until first light. Then he fed Koshka and washed, shaved and dressed himself before driving into the city. Krupin was gone. Shooting him had been the hardest thing Kazakov had ever done. Hopefully it was the right thing.

It didn't feel like it. Derr'mo, he couldn't feel anything.

In the city he found that he was named a hero by *New Moscow Now*. The newspaper carried his photo on the front page under the fold. The headline read *Detective Brings Down Lone Gunman*. The above-the-fold headline read *Bure Assassinated*.

When he came into the squad room, he found the front page pinned to the wall and the others in the squad awaiting his reaction. He tore it down, crumpled it up and threw it in the garbage and took his leave of the office.

"Kazakov! Wait!" Egorova followed him out of the room.

He stabbed the elevator door button and managed to escape her and ride the elevator down.

He'd reached the parking garage when his phone started to ring.

He turned the ringer off and stuffed the phone in his pocket, then climbed in the Perseus and headed out of the garage.

It was a clear day in Fergana. At least the skies were clear blue, the light painfully bright as he steered aimlessly through the city. To the east, north, and south, the mountains rose, still virgin white like a wall built to keep Fergana's people safely slumbering in a false sense of peace. They were fools, all of them, if they believed it. For to the west lay open land all the way to Constantinople and clearly the Ottoman Empire's gaze was upon them.

He found himself suddenly driving past warehouses and mechanic shops, just outside the walls of the old city. He knew where he was, and knew where he was heading. It was like a nagging pull that was always with him.

There was a parking spot in front of the graveyard and he climbed out of the Perseus and stood there eyeing the iron graveyard gate and the slope of monuments beyond. Once this was the preferred graveyard of Fergana's Russians, but that had changed. Now the Russians buried their dead beyond New Moscow's city limits in graveyards stolen from the open steppes.

With a sigh he pushed through the rusty gate and climbed the hillside, following an icy path that his boots had created over the winter. The gravesite of Maria di Maria rested in a beam of warm sunlight, the gray headstone he had bought for her shimmering slightly as if from a light inside the stone. He ran his fingers over the arch of stone and tried to remember what her skin had felt like, but all he could feel was the cold iron of his gun. Was that all he would ever feel? It seemed burned into his flesh at the moment.

Unbuttoning his greatcoat against the spring warmth, he looked beyond the ranks of headstones and monuments out over the city gradually being released from its long winter of snow. The wind carried the sounds of vehicles and the clank and brr of work from the mechanic shops that surrounded the old city, but closer in was the trickle of water as the snow melted away. He breathed in. There was still the stink of cordite in the air and the slopes of Yekaterina Mountain were forever changed, Yekaterina's huge statue erased, the mountain now, in the opinion of some, once more pristine. What side he was on in that debate, he wasn't sure.

A lone figure approached the graveyard gate, looked up at him, and waved. Slim and wearing his customary long Russian coat, Khalil Khan climbed the hill but stopped short of Kazakov.

"You're here again," Khan said.

Kazakov eyed him and wished for a smoke.

"Afraid I'll see something I shouldn't?" Kazakov lifted his chin at the old city.

Khan's lips curved briefly and he turned and took in the view. "I told you before that you should not spend your life on the dead when the living need you."

"Says the man who let me think he was dead."

"And I am sorry about that, but I could not let you arrest me, not while I was trying to determine what and who was undermining my people."

As if that was a good enough explanation. "We could have worked together."

Khan shook his head. "You had to believe and so did everyone else. But we're on the same side. We always were."

Sighing, Kazakov looked at the ex-M.E. "So I hear. You and your men stopped your youngsters from coming into the concert hall after the police security force was recalled."

"When the explosions went off, we knew what was happening. It was a typical Enver Pasha subterfuge: force the authorities to rethink their tactics and pull their protection." Khan toed a patch of bare earth with his boot. "We didn't know about Krupin."

"No one did," Kazakov said bitterly. "But I should have. I should have seen it. Hell, after his wife died, he so much as told me, but I was too taken up with my investigation to give him the time." And now a good man was dead.

And a bad one.

"Perhaps he did us a favor."

Kazakov lifted his gaze to Khan and frowned. "Us? You killed a man, Khan. That will always be there. As for Bure, he didn't say anything that the Russians weren't already feeling—he just gave them permission to say it out loud."

"Hopefully, our help against the gunmen will undo that bias."

"That's your plan, then? Let things go back to the way they were and hope they'll improve?"

Khan smiled a little broader. "Did you hear? They've delayed the election due to Bure's death and the state of emergency." He licked his lips. "I was wondering… I want—I want my old life back. I want to turn myself in for what I've done. I was hoping you might go with me. Given the positive press coverage of the tribal militia stand against the attackers, I might even stand a chance in the courts."

The request was a surprise, but when Kazakov thought about it, perhaps predictable. It was the perfect time for Khan to throw himself on the mercy of the court of public opinion, given the newspaper articles celebrating the Kyrgyz militia that had stopped the attack on the New Moscow Concert Hall.

"Big changes, then," Kazakov said, not sure how he felt about Khan using the circumstances to his advantage.

"Yes. Big changes. Will you go with me?"

The sun beat down on Kazakov's shoulders and he looked up again at the injured flank of Yekaterina Mountain. No, not injured—it was cleansed of Russian interference. It was now the shining five peaks of Suleiman's Mountain.

Beyond, to the west, there were clouds hiding the breadth of the Ottoman Empire. They left Kazakov uneasy. Enver was there. Had they outsmarted the Ottoman or fallen into a trap? Either way, something was coming.

He met Khan's gaze and, hesitating, nodded.

If you enjoyed *Ivan's Wolf* you might enjoy *Through Dark Water,* the first book in the Phoebe Clay Mysteries. To try it out, turn the page.

THROUGH DARK WATER

It was dark out—black in the campground—the only light coming from the humming fluorescent fixture over the washroom outbuilding door. Phoebe Clay stood under the canopy of dripping, old growth cedar, hemlock and spruce and tried very hard to ignore that light. Fluorescents were too harsh, too stark. Too reminiscent of things in her past she would prefer not to remember. Nope, the almost total dark of the mostly uninhabited northeast coast of Vancouver Island was scary, but it was also a thick blanket that she could use to hide from so many things. Like Rick.

Around her in the chilly dark there were other campers stirring from the half-seen RVs and trailers scattered among the huge trees and the light brush of huckleberry bush, salal, and fern. Mostly the other campers were fishermen up early for a day chasing salmon in the northern Pacific waters. There were no other crazy fools like her in a tent.

She unlocked her Subaru that hunkered down beside the campsite and pulled a Coleman stove and breakfast supplies out onto the night-damp picnic table. A couple of matches later and she had a hissing propane burner going and water heating to brew coffee. Beyond the sounds of the campers stirring came the distant low rumble of ocean surf. The Inside Passage up the western coast of North America was ready and waiting just a stone's throw away—if she could get her niece, Alice, up out of her sleeping bag.

"Come on, kiddo," she said. "We've got to get moving if we want to get our pick of kayaks for the day."

It was an early July morning and Phoebe stuck her head into the blue, three-man, domed tent where Alice, her twelve-year-old niece, had performed another face plant onto her sleeping bag. The girl was still in her sleeping t-shirt and underwear, though she *had* managed to pull socks on. A little progress, then, but a groan was all Phoebe got in response, from somewhere under the mop of blonde hair that hid Alice's face. That and a snuffle that was suspiciously like a snore in counterpoint to the sound of the ocean.

"You make me come in there and you're not going to be happy," Phoebe sing-songed. To demonstrate, she reached in and tickled a sock-foot. In a sudden sign of life, the foot yanked away like a kid trying to hide a note in class, and then a single eye peered up at her through the matted curls, capturing what little light there was.

"But it's cold out there. And wet. And I hardly slept last night."

"Tell me about it. All your tossing and turning and complaining didn't make my sleep any easier either. But I want to see whales. I thought you did, too. So you've got five minutes to get yourself in gear and get out here for breakfast or I'm eating it all and leaving you here all day with rocky sleeping arrangements for company."

Alice groaned and dramatically covered her eyes with her arm. Phoebe turned her back on the tent and poured boiling water through filtered coffee and then poured a cup and sipped. Hot. Strong. Good. She clutched the steaming red mug between both hands to keep her fingers from freezing. This early in the morning it *was* flipping cold. A chill morning fog clung to the campground under the trees. Their thick branches tangled overhead with moss and ocean mist. It was morning, but dawn had yet to find the space under the trees. The darkness had lifted some, though. Instead of half-perceived points of movement, people were now sinister specters around the campground.

Most of the camp's fifty spaces were taken up with expensive RVs and trailers hauled by powerful pickups. Her little Subaru SUV looked like a pretender amongst all that metal and steel. The otherworldly glow of mist-diffused electric lights now came from inside those trailers and motorhomes as more people woke. The scents of bacon and eggs and omelets filled the air with enticements, along with the low drone of a morning news station reporting on the latest missing girl in the string of disappearances that had occurred along the Northern Vancouver Island highway. There'd been no bodies found yet. So much for happiness in the world.

She was glad she and Alice had run away for a little while. She turned back to the little Coleman stove, wondering why people would chose to bring the big bad world with them. It wasn't her idea of a holiday—nor of how she wanted to enjoy her first days of retirement. Not that freezing her butt off on a chilly morning was, either, but for the chance to see live killer whales close up and personal in the wild, she'd do it. After a career of placing order on the bedlam of her classrooms, it was time to put some adventure back into her life.

Sighing, she held her hands over the stove, then dug four eggs out of their supplies and a bowl and frying pan. Now if Alice would just get her butt in gear.

It was thanks to her habitual over-planning that she had breakfast makings at all. She'd brought the stove and groceries as a last minute decision to be prepared for the worst—something she'd learned to do in twenty-five years in the classroom. She'd mistakenly thought that Pirate Cove, the highly publicized and picturesque resort and jumping-off spot to salmon fishing, killer whale viewing, and the famous Robson Bight would provide some amenities. Instead, the place was in reality no more than a campground and string of three-hundred-dollar-a-night cottages that were set up for the fishing and whale watching tours that ran out of the harbor. The restaurants weren't open early enough to buy a hot breakfast for her and Alice before a day spent exploring and getting a feel for the water before the official whale watching kayak trip they would join tomorrow.

A rustling sound came from behind her and finally two socked and sandaled feet stuck out of the blue nylon tent followed by slim legs in black leggings and a grumbling girl in a blue Gore-Tex jacket.

"Geeze. It's still dark out."

"It's lighter than it was a few minutes ago. We get out from under these trees and it'll be daylight."

"What time is it?" Alice asked, fists grinding at the sleep still in her eyes. It was a movement she'd had ever since she was a baby and one that still stole Phoebe's heart. Sometimes she could still see that innocent toddler staring out at her from this moody preteen body—or the precious infant that her mother and Phoebe's sister, Becca, had brought home from the hospital.

Alice scowled up at her. "The time?"

Well, maybe make that *challenging young woman*. And stubborn. And demanding. All the things that had had Becca asking over and over whether Phoebe was *sure* she wanted to take Alice with her on her first après-retirement adventure.

Phoebe lifted her chin at the concrete washroom building fifty feet away. Its flickering white light glared through the hazy mist around the door. "It's six-thirty. Go get washed up. I'll have breakfast ready when you get back."

Still grumbling, Alice stood, zipped the tent behind her, and headed over to the amenities. Phoebe settled on the picnic table's damp bench, sipping coffee, and turned on the second Coleman burner; the scent of propane tanged the air. Butter melted in the battered frying pan on the blue-flamed burner while she broke and whipped the eggs into a bowl. When Alice emerged from the washroom, she poured the eggs into the sizzling butter and stirred. Pulling the coffeepot off the other burner, she fished a couple of slices of bread from a bag and set the bread on the flame to toast.

By the time Alice returned, scrub-faced and with her still-matted hair pushed behind her ears, Phoebe was stirring almost fully cooked eggs and had two pieces of only semi-charred toast. She grabbed two paper plates—all she had for dishes—and shared out the food. "Eat up. It'll warm you up. There's apple juice in a juice box if you want one."

"I want coffee. It's hot."

Not what she'd expect a twelve-year-old to drink. "Does your mother let you drink coffee?"

"Sometimes." Alice shrugged and Phoebe sighed. The kid was born into the Starbucks age where twelve-year-olds were sucking back peppermint lattes; she might not agree but she poured her a cup. Handed it to her. "This morning only. I will not have your mother saying I corrupted her daughter, you hear? And by the way, there's no milk. Or sugar."

She smiled to herself when Alice stared at the cup like it was from outer space.

Alice sipped, made a face, but the heat in the cup must have overcome her disgust. She tucked into the food and didn't even mention the charred toast—fresh air somehow burned away youthful fussiness even when coupled with lack of sleep. Or maybe it was the promise of whales. When they were done, the stove and supplies cleaned and packed away in the car, they headed out together. The light had increased and the mist had dissipated some—now it simply hovered in the branches overhead like a memory just out of reach. Around them the campground echoed with the sounds of voices—fishermen and women heading down to the pier and their waiting charter boats. The whale watching boats wouldn't be out until a more livable hour.

Thankfully, the food seemed to have revived the spirit of adventure in Alice. She hopped over the puddles like a kid, then remembered herself and fell back to Phoebe's more sedate pace. "This is going to be fun, right?"

"It is."

"And we'll see whales?" Alice's big blue eyes were even bigger than normal in her fine-boned face—if that were possible. She was still a sylph of a girl who had inherited her mother's slim build as opposed to Phoebe's more solid construction. It was always strange how children went through a transitional purgatory between childhood and teenagerhood, when they were neither fish nor fowl, instead threading through those years in the middle with a foot in each world.

"We should. Like the brochure said, there are resident whales here. That's why all the tourists come here. Even Jacques Cousteau said it was pretty amazing."

"Who?" Alice looked the question at her, and Phoebe felt even more her age: fifty-five and she had already lived over half of her life. Now she was just on the downhill slide.

She sighed. "A marine biologist and oceanographer. He did a whole series of TV shows on the wonders of the underwater world." God save her from the terminally young.

Alice grabbed her hands and burst out laughing. "I know who he is, Aunt Bee. Mom hauled his shows up off of YouTube and made me watch them along with a zillion other things before I left to come here." She giggled. "You should have seen your face—like you thought you were so incredibly out of touch or something."

Still chuckling, she settled beside Phoebe; at twelve, her stride was already almost as long as her aunt's even though she hadn't reached her full growth. Where Phoebe was a solid five feet eight, Alice was only about five feet six, but the kid was all leg and had all the signs that she was entering another growth spurt. Given her dad was six feet four, she was likely going to be taller than her aunt by a long shot.

The briny scent of seaweed and the sound of surf met them as they rounded the corner from the campground and reached the tiny enclave of Pirate Cove. It spread before them, its ice cream colored clapboard buildings clinging for dear life to the backdrop of mist-draped cedar. Low marine clouds covered the sky, but wind off the water was stripping the clouds away and hints of blue shone through.

The water of the little bay was mostly smooth, the wind sending lazy, black, one foot swells curving onto the gravel shore. A lot of the buildings weren't even built on land. Instead they sat precariously on boardwalks that strung out along the high bank shore on water-grayed pilings that were thick with mussels. At the far end of the boardwalk sat a warehouse-sized building painted rust red that glowered across the water. In the early 1900s, a prosperous salmon cannery and lumber mill had thrived in the town. Those businesses had been replaced by tourism and now a portion of the old cannery housed a Killer Whale Interpretive Center that Phoebe intended to visit before they were done.

They walked downslope toward the boat launch where they were supposed to pick up their kayaks and a packed lunch arranged through Pirate Cove Resort, but though the kayaks were there, their bright colors slashing the monochrome morning grey, no one else was. Instead a string of apparently abandoned trucks with fiberglass fishing boats on trailers stood in a line waiting to launch, while a silent crowd had formed halfway along the shoreline's narrow tidal flats underneath the boardwalk pilings. The wind curling around the bay ruffled Phoebe's short gray-blonde hair, but brought the stink of something…dead. She recognized the scent from her nightmares.

Long dead, by the eye-watering stench of it.

Alice covered her nose with her hand. "What *is* that?"

"Something unusual by the look of it." And judging by the crowd, something that drew attention despite the smell. "Shall we go see?"

Nose still wrinkled against the stink, Alice looked between the kayaks and the crowd. "There's no one here to give us our kayaks anyway." She shrugged and led off down the boat launch and around onto the narrow beach between the water and the steep bank of the cove. Her bright blue jacket was a happy counterpoint to the grey morning.

Water lapped through the treacherous stones under their feet as they slipped and slid across the seaweed-slimed stone and driftwood. Among the barnacle-embossed stones were small colonies of sea anemone and large purple sea stars. The boardwalk was ahead and if the tide was fully in, they'd be walking knee-deep in water. The crowd of about twenty people had gathered under the pilings, a mix of the drab working fishermen's colors of the locals with a few bright splashes of designer Gore-Tex that clearly marked visitors to the cove. But regardless of the rancid smell, the way they huddled together said something was seriously wrong.

Phoebe slowed and caught Alice's shoulder. "Stay back here a moment while I check it out."

Alice glanced up with teenaged resentment in her eyes—one of those moments.

"Just do it because I'm your favorite aunt, okay?"

"You're my only aunt."

"So that should make me extra special."

Alice sighed as only a teenager could.

Leaving Alice a few steps away from the crowd, Phoebe reached the gathered people in the shadow of the boardwalk. Water splatted her head in a sad, briny rain from the mussels and seaweed that covered the pilings.

The people were strangely quiet—almost funereal. Whispers hissed between those at the rear of the gathering and someone closer to the center was sobbing, but mostly the people were strangely respectful.

"What's happened?" Phoebe asked softly, coming up between a man who clearly was a local, wearing a gray-green mackinaw and jeans, and a rangy young man with freckles and a quick smile who looked like he could be the older man's son. The older man had a thatch of sun-and-salt-faded brown hair, weathered lines around clear blue eyes, and clearly looked uncomfortable at what was happening. The younger one didn't yet have his father's breadth of shoulders, but he shared the older man's blue eyes. He just looked interested.

"A death in the family, I guess you could say," the older man said. "One of the whales. Going to be a pall over the tour boats today." He shook his head.

The crunch of footfall over the stones behind her turned Phoebe around. Another man pushed past Alice. He was tall, official looking and wore a shockingly bright red jacket and pressed jeans.

"Bert." The newcomer nodded at the man Phoebe had been speaking to. "What've we got?"

"One of the whales," Bert said and tipped his head toward the center of the crowd.

"Dead?" asked the newcomer.

"O' course dead. Can't you smell it?" Bert said.

The newcomer pushed through the people and they parted like butter, revealing three people at the center of the crowd standing beside a huge black-and-white body that had rolled broadside onto shore. It lay half on its side, the massive black dorsal fin sagging against the steep bank of the cove. Killer whale. Orca.

In the gravel and seaweed, it was so unlike the majestic animals she'd come to see that it could have been a fake covered in white and black neoprene rubber. But it wasn't. A blond-haired man in a blue jacket almost the same color as Alice's knelt at the front of the body, examining the bottle-nosed head. Where its eyes should be were just red sockets, as if something had eaten out its eyes. Something was wrong with its mouth, though she couldn't figure out what. A woman with dark hair pulled back in a ponytail and wearing the same colored blue jacket stood beside the man. She was the source of the sobbing.

At the other end of the body stood a youngish man—eighteen or nineteen, maybe—still feeling the weight of new-come adulthood. His hands were stuffed in his pockets and he glared resentment at her so hard that she almost left right there and then. Didn't he like the fact that people were staring at the whale or was something else the problem?

The boy was tall, clearly Aboriginal, black hair worn long over the collar, with high cheekbones and narrow face that suggested a heritage that might harken back to great plains tribes rather than the coastal nations. When he looked away, his black gaze locked on the body of the whale as if he could not believe it was here.

"Jeezus," the red-clad newcomer said, stopping beside the man at the carcass's head. "Do something, Wilbur. That damn thing is going to stink up the entire village. You think people are going to want a meal with this blowing in their faces?"

The blond-haired man stood up from examining the whale's mouth, his face pale. He was tall—taller than the newcomer—and had none of the manicured look of the latter. He had a weathered face, and she pegged him at about forty years old, like the man next to her, but something about the thoughtfulness of his face suggested he was no fisherman.

"So just what would you like me to do, Sam? Blow her up like the fools did with that humpback down south?" said the man named Wilbur. "We could spread rotting whale meat all over this village if you like."

"Who are they?" she murmured to Bert, the fisherman.

"That's John Wilbur of the Whale Interpretive Center," Bert, volunteered. "He's a marine biologist who keeps track of the whale population or some such. The woman's his assistant, Ayisha Meredith. She's doing her PhD or something. Both of them whale crazy, you might say. The guy in the red jacket is Sam Rayburn, the resort owner. He basically owns everything in Pirate Cove, including the Whale Interpretive Center building. This is my son, Donnie. I'm Bert. Bert Clarke."

"Phoebe Clay." She nodded and waved Alice forward. "My niece, Alice. It's a dead orca, Ali. You sure you want to see?"

Of course she did. Kids were fascinated by death. Using her smaller size, she weaseled her way forward to the front of the crowd. Phoebe trailed after her until they stood at the inner circle of bystanders.

"Well, you can't leave it here. It has to be moved straightaway. Couldn't we just tie a rope to it and drag it out to sea?" said the manicured Sam.

John Wilbur's hands flexed as if he was restraining himself. "'Fraid not, Sam. This is A39, one of the resident females. She's clearly been dead for a few days judging by the damage done by other sea animals." He shook his head. "Damn shame. By the shape of her, we'd thought she was carrying a calf. Looks like she still is. It's a blow to the restoration of the population. We need to determine what killed her. Fisheries and Oceans will want to examine her."

"Well, the body can't stay here. It has to be moved out of the harbor. Now." Sam looked around as if for backing and his gaze seemed to lock on the fisherman she'd been standing beside. "Bert. Get the Zodiac. Back in here and tie a rope to this thing and haul it out to wherever John wants it. It just can't stay here."

"Not going to happen, Sam," John Wilbur said. "Can I have a word in private? Meredith, would you pull yourself together? I need you to call Fisheries and also the police." He dragged Sam aside and they spoke in low, angry voices.

It didn't look like a happy conversation. Sam's voice rose and he looked like he was going to lunge at Wilbur. "What the hell are you playing at, Wilbur?"

John Wilbur shook his head. "I'm not *playing* at anything. But something's not right with this carcass. The tide brought her into town last night, right? And young Alex here was first to spot her." He motioned to the young Aboriginal lad. "Then how come somebody's been able to remove every tooth from her mouth? That's a crime, Sam. Removing and selling the body parts of threatened and endangered species is a crime."

To read more of *Through Dark Water* go to www.karenlabrahamson.com/books/through-dark-water/ or ask for it at your favourite book seller.

TO MY READERS

1. Thank you for reading *Ivan's Wolf*. I hope you enjoyed it. If you did (and even if you didn't), it would be immensely helpful if you would leave a review. Reviews help other readers find this book.
2. Sign up for my Newsletter, and receive a free novel, a novella, and an award-nominated short story. To get your FREE eBOOKS, go to my website at www.karenlabrahamson.com.
3. While you're there, check out my website for information on my books, my adventures, and extra content.
4. For more links and offers, or to chat with me, check out Facebook at www.facebook.com/karenlabrahamson.

THE DETEKTIV KAZAKOV MYSTERIES

Set in an alternate history Russia, the series is introduces Detektiv Alexander Kazakov, a loner detective committed to finding the truth for the dead and murdered. The series takes place in a world where Catherine the Great's conquest of the Crimea woke the slumbering Ottoman Empire and brought the great Khans down upon Moscow. Two hundred years later the remains of the Russian population dream of Russia's past glories, while their new country of Fergana lays like the gristle in a joint between the rumblings of the Ottoman and Chinese Empires. The death of a young Russian girl sets Kazakov on a series of investigations that have implications for the entire world.

BOOKS IN THE SERIES:
After Yekaterina
Mareson's Arrow
The Tsarina's Mask
Ivan's Wolf

ABOUT THE AUTHOR

Karen L. Abrahamson writes fantasy, romance, and mysteries as Karen L. Abrahamson and K.L. Abrahamson. Her best known books are the unique Cartographer series in which secret agents of the American Geological Society use their powers to take on the purveyors of dark magic. Her romantic suspense and mysteries take readers on adventures to dangerous locations around the world.

Her short fiction has appeared in numerous magazines and anthologies; her short fantasy story "With One Shoe" was nominated for an Arthur Ellis Canadian Crime Fiction Award.

Karen's background includes time as a police officer, corrections officer, and probation/parole officer.

To find out more about her and her writing, visit www.karenlabrahamson.com

ALSO BY K.L. ABRAHAMSON

Aftermath

Afterimage

Terra Incognita

Terra Infirma

Terra Nueva

Other Fantasy

Emberstone

Mutable Things

The Crystal Courtesan

Ice Dragon

MYSTERY, FANTASY AND ROMANCE
FROM TWISTED ROOT PUBLISHING

If you enjoyed this book, you might enjoy other titles available from Karen L. Abrahamson in your local bookstore or wherever e-books are sold through

www.karenlabrahamson.com

THROUGH DARK WATER: Eagles, Orcas and a killer stalk the kayaking Mecca of Pirate's Cove, British Columbia. On a holiday with her niece, school teacher Phoebe Clay has to solve the case to protect herself and everything she loves. Find it at http://www. karenlabrahamson.com/books/through-dark-water/

AFTERBURN: Vallon Drake, agent of the American Geological Survey, the secret arm of Homeland Security that protects America from illicit changes to its landscapes, discovers her partner smothering in a wall. Now someone is rewriting the Seattle maps and killing AGS agents. Their actions threaten the safety of the entire Northwest and only rogue agent Vallon can stop it. Find it at http://www.karenlabrahamson.com/books/afterburn/

SHADOW PLAY: Star reporter Kaitlin Blackwood arrives in Cambodia and lands right in the case of her missing father. When men try to abduct her, the wrong man rescues her: B.J. McCallum, ex-man of her dreams, who comes with his own heap of trouble. The two must put aside their differences long enough to solve the case— and maybe save themselves in the process. Find it at http://www. karenlabrahamson.com/books/shadow-play/